THINK OF THE CHILDREN

Kerry Wilkinson is something of an accidental author. His debut, *Locked In*, the first title in the detective Jessica Daniel series, was written as a challenge to himself but, after self-publishing, it became a UK Number One bestseller within three months of release. Kerry then went on to have more success with the second and third titles in the series, *Vigilante* and *The Woman in Black*. The next book in the series, following *Think of the Children*, is *Playing with Fire*. This title will be published very soon and an extract is available at the end of this book.

Kerry has a degree in journalism and works for a national media company. He was born in Somerset but now lives in Lancashire.

For more information about Kerry and his books
visit his website: www.kerrywilkinson.com
or www.panmacmillan.com

By Kerry Wilkinson

LOCKED IN

VIGILANTE

THE WOMAN IN BLACK

THINK OF THE CHILDREN

KERRY WILKINSON

THINK OF THE CHILDREN

PAN BOOKS

First published 2013 by Pan Books
an imprint of Pan Macmillan, a division of Macmillan Publishers Limited
Pan Macmillan, 20 New Wharf Road, London N1 9RR
Basingstoke and Oxford
Associated companies throughout the world
www.panmacmillan.com

ISBN 978-1-4472-2340-5

1 3 5 7 9 8 6 4 2

A CIP catalogue record for this book is available from the British Library.

Typeset by Ellipsis Digital Limited, Glasgow
Printed and bound by CPI Group (UK) Ltd, Croydon, CR0 4YY

THINK OF THE CHILDREN

1

The windscreen wipers on Detective Sergeant Jessica Daniel's battered old car thundered from side to side in an attempt to clear the pouring rain. She leant forward for what seemed like the hundredth time since starting the journey, wiping a thin layer of condensation away from the inside of the front window.

Jessica steered with one hand while continuing to clear the windows, muttering curses under her breath that related partly to her car, partly to the daily commute, but mainly to the weather itself. She had lived in Manchester for over a decade and if there was one thing the natives were used to, it was rain. She shivered slightly as cool air poured out of the car's vents. It was almost five minutes since she'd set the fans to the hottest temperature possible but they still weren't producing anything other than a light but decidedly arctic-feeling breeze.

Glancing away from the road, Jessica looked at the man in the passenger seat. 'If you could stop breathing for a while it would make this a lot easier.'

Detective Constable David Rowlands gave a half-smile. 'Was that one of the selling points when you bought this thing? "Works perfectly as long as you don't breathe when it's raining".'

'You can walk if you'd prefer.'

Out of the corner of her eye, Jessica saw the constable take a half-glance out of the passenger window but it was clear he wasn't thinking about it seriously as the rain continued hammering on the roof of the vehicle. 'You're all right. I can't believe you make this journey every day.'

Jessica sighed, continuing to edge her car forward in the slow-moving traffic. She lived in the Didsbury area, south of the main city centre. In a region that offered everything from high-priced flats at Salford Quays and multi-million-pound footballers' mansions all the way down to some of the most deprived housing estates in the country, it wasn't a bad place to call home. The biggest problem where she lived was the traffic jams on the way to the Longsight police station where she worked. The tailbacks were bad enough at the best of times but with the weather the way it was, everyone was moving even more slowly than usual. She kept tight to the car in front, ignoring the person in the vehicle she knew was trying to cut into her lane.

'You didn't have to stay at mine last night, you know,' Jessica said.

'Yeah, but we had a good time, didn't we?'

Jessica paused and smiled, thinking about the night before. 'Don't say things like that around the station or you'll start rumours.'

'Ugh, yes. You're right.'

'You don't have to be so disgusted at the idea of being associated with me. Anyway, I'm amazed your girlfriend came for tea; I've spent the last four months thinking this "Chloe" was imaginary. At least I've met her now and verified she isn't clinically mental.'

Rowlands sighed. 'Is that an official medical term?'

'Yes.'

The temperature changed almost instantly from freezing cold to searing hot. Jessica's car's fans didn't differentiate between anything other than the two extremes. The shift meant the windscreen did at least begin to clear, although the only thing it revealed was rows of traffic seemingly not moving and a set of traffic lights in the distance, the red light beaming through the misty greyness of the morning.

Jessica shuffled uncomfortably in the driver's seat, trying to stop her legs from cramping, and sighed again. 'It wasn't that long ago I was on a beach for my only holiday in years reading crappy books, drinking cocktails and enjoying the sun.'

'How can I forget? They dumped all your paperwork on me. I can't picture you lying around not doing anything though. In all the time I've known you, you never stop.'

Jessica didn't want to admit it but he was right. She had spent the first morning on the beach with a book trying not to look at an overweight tourist wearing leopard-print Speedos and a sailor's hat. After getting bored and hiring a car, she spent much of the rest of her three-week break driving around the Greek island. She had intended for the holiday to be relaxing, a chance to get some space after a series of murders where the killer had sent her severed fingers from the victims through the post. After almost becoming the final casualty herself, Jessica had wondered what she wanted from her future. Given her state of mind and accrued unpaid overtime, she was given permission to take a longer holiday than most officers got.

She went away not knowing whether this was the job for her and returned none the wiser. So little had changed.

Jessica ignored Rowlands's assessment, slowly moving her car forward as the lights ahead turned green and the line of traffic inched along. The car that had been trying to cut into her lane edged in behind her and Jessica felt a small pang of utterly irrational elation at the minor victory.

Dave started to hum an upbeat tune Jessica didn't recognise, which only added to her irritation. The lights flicked back to red just before she could drive through and, although she thought about not stopping, she slowed before putting on the handbrake, coming to rest at the front of the queue.

'Can you stop doing that?' she asked irritably.

Rowlands turned to look at her. 'What?'

'The humming.'

'Sorry, I didn't even realise I was doing it.'

'You've been doing it a lot recently. This whole domestic bliss, moving in with your girlfriend thing has almost turned you into a normal member of the human race. Albeit one that hums.'

Rowlands laughed quietly to himself. 'It's Christmas in a few weeks. Aren't I allowed to be cheery?'

'No, it's unnerving.'

Jessica reached towards the fan controls and turned them off. She hoped the mixture of cold then hot air would even itself out and make the final five minutes of their journey bearable. To her relief, the thudding rain on the metal roof started to ease. She peered up at the still-red traffic lights, then looked to her left where cars continued to speed across the junction.

The screeching noise was the first thing she heard. It sounded as if it had started some distance away, but it was hard to tell because of the rest of the din going on around her. Jessica quickly looked to her right as a black car squealed across the junction, wheels locked, spinning on the drenched surface. Everything seemed to happen in slow motion, the vehicle twisting a full circle and smashing into a lamppost in the centre of the junction before being hit by a blue car coming from the opposite direction and completing another half-spin.

Jessica blinked, trying to take in what she had just witnessed. For a fraction of a second, it was as if everything had stopped, even the rain. Without thinking, she switched off her engine and got out of the car. She didn't say a word but Rowlands was moving too and together they dashed across to where the mangled car had come to a halt. Jessica headed for the black vehicle, Rowlands towards the blue one.

Jessica could feel her heart beating quickly as she arrived at the wreck. There was a huge crack in the windscreen, the deflating airbag pressed against it. Car horns blared around her and other people were approaching the car. Jessica took out her police identification and shouted for them to stay back, at the same time pointing at a man who had his phone out and telling him to dial 999.

Because of the way the car had spun, it hadn't entangled itself with the lamppost, instead bouncing after being hit by the other car. Jessica moved to the driver's-side door, trying to peer through the cracked glass. The mixture of rain and condensation made it hard to see through the other windows and she took a snap decision to open the door. As she did, a splash of dark red blood from the inside dribbled onto the ground; the cream material lining of the seat was also drenched.

Jessica knew instantly the driver was dead.

The blood-soaked airbag had begun to sag onto the driver's lap as Jessica finally allowed herself to look at the victim. She had seen plenty of dead bodies in her time but this one was a distorted mess. Jessica quickly realised why: the seatbelt clasp hung limply by the door, unfastened. She felt a shiver go through her as it started to rain again, droplets of water streaming down her face as she tried to put the pieces together. Despite the mess, the driver's greying hair made him look as if he was in his fifties. She didn't know for sure but it appeared that his neck had snapped. It could have been him hitting the windscreen or the force of the airbag colliding after the impact. Not that it mattered considering the way the pulped skin, blood and glass made his face look like a warped, dropped pizza. Jessica could not look for more than a second or two. Not wearing a seatbelt had cost him his life.

Jessica shut the door, knowing there was nothing she could do and not wanting to contaminate the scene either through her own presence or by letting rain in.

She again warned members of the public to stay back before walking the short distance to the blue car where Rowlands was crouched, talking to a young woman still sitting in the driver's seat. As Jessica came closer, it was clear the woman was crying hysterically, a seatbelt stretched across her. She reached the car and put a hand on Dave's shoulder, shaking her head slightly to let him know the fate of the other driver before crouching herself.

Rowlands spoke slowly and deliberately. 'This is Laura. She was on her way to work, weren't you, Laura?' The woman nodded, eyes wide with disbelief as tears continued to flow down her face. Jessica knew her colleague was doing his best to keep the woman calm, using her name frequently to keep her attention until help arrived. Outwardly, aside from long dark hair which was tousled across her face from the impact, the driver looked fine, but she was obviously suffering from shock.

'Are you okay, Laura?' Jessica asked. The woman nodded again but said nothing.

Jessica left Dave talking as cars swerved around the accident, sirens blaring in the distance.

She stopped to take a deep breath, swallowing a feeling of claustrophobia despite being in the open. The car horns and engines, the chatter of nearby pedestrians, the patter of the rain: it was becoming overpowering. Jessica felt a few drops of rain slide down her neck, struggling not to shiver as she made her way back towards the black car while tying her long hair into a ponytail.

The vehicle looked much more of a mess from the other side. It was a mid-size four-door model that Jessica thought of as always being advertised with a family sitting inside, as if the machine itself was the key to parenting bliss. A scrape ran the full length of the passenger side, the front headlight a concertina of mangled metal.

Jessica blinked the water away from her eyes as she saw the flashing lights of an ambulance a few hundred metres away, the noise from the siren blaring ever louder. Her eyes were attracted to the rear of the vehicle where the car's boot had popped open ever so slightly. She put a hand on the metal, at first thinking about pushing it shut, but curiosity got the better of her and she opened it instead.

If she'd had to, Jessica would have struggled to guess the contents of her own boot. There might well have been jump leads and possibly a petrol can but she wouldn't have put money on it. She definitely wasn't prepared for the sight that met her in the rear of the smashed-up black car. Thick plastic sheeting was wrapped tightly around an object with heavy-looking tape sealing it into a tight cocoon. Next to the object was a rusting spade with a muddied plastic handle. Jessica felt something in her stomach urging her forward as if she already knew what it was.

She pushed the boot down but didn't lock it in place. As the ambulance drew up, she ran to her own car, opening the driver's door and digging into the well before pulling out a pair of scissors.

Her father had always been good about keeping things in their old family car just in case but Jessica hadn't inherited his forward thinking. She had found the scissors not long after her dad bought her the car second-hand a decade or so ago, left by the previous owner. She dashed across the junction again, silently thanking whoever that previous owner was and feeling justified for never cleaning out her car.

As she arrived back at the black vehicle, paramedics stepped out of the ambulance. Jessica flashed her identification and told them the fate of the driver. One of them went to check on him anyway as another walked to where Rowlands was still comforting the woman from the blue car.

More sirens blared in the distance as Jessica returned to the black car's boot, opening it and moving the spade to the rear of the compartment out of her way. Layer upon layer of plastic sheeting was wrapped tightly around the object and Jessica struggled to force through the blunt blades of her scissors. As she pushed harder, it started to rain more heavily, huge drops bouncing off the tarmac road. Jessica could feel the force of the water smashing into the top of her head. She continued to cut and finally felt the scissors push through the top few layers of the plastic. Reaching in with her hands, she pulled hard to try to tear the material apart. Slowly, it began to give and, with a combination of her hands and the scissors, she opened up part of the wrapping.

With the plastic pulled back, all she could see was a piece of cloth that had a flowery pattern. It reminded Jessica of the curtains her parents used to have at their house when she was a child, a hideous mixture of yellow and brown. Still reaching into the boot, Jessica tugged at the fabric, finally freeing it with a gasp.

Jessica tried to force herself to look away but the pale skin and clamped eyelids held her hypnotically: the haunting lifeless face of a dead child.

2

By the time Jessica arrived at Longsight Police Station, various photographs of the crash had begun to show up on Internet news sites. Almost all of them had been taken by passers-by with their phones but luckily none seemed to feature what she had found in the car's boot. Instead, the news stories were focusing on the length of time the junction had been shut and the knock-on effect it had had on the flow of traffic into the city.

Weather and a traffic jam: people's two favourite talking points all wrapped up in one.

Jessica had no doubts about who the body in the boot was and wondered how long it would take for the real story to leak out. Isaac Hutchings was eleven years old and had gone missing almost three weeks ago. Jessica had never been able to figure out why some missing-children stories caught on, while others were barely reported. Sometimes a kid would disappear and there would be a national media storm that seemingly engulfed everyone. Other times, there would barely be a mention in the local papers, let alone anything wider. One of the other officers told her about an instance where a missing-child case had next to no attention until one of his friends, a blond, blue-eyed nine-year-old boy, gave a tearful appeal that had been partly stage-managed by the force. After that, the cameras came flooding in.

For whatever reason, the disappearance of Isaac Hutchings had barely registered anywhere other than on the local police's own website.

Jessica wasn't part of the specialist missing persons team and hadn't been involved in the case in any way other than the fact it had happened on her patch and she was aware of it. But, as she stared into the pale face of the body she had found in the boot, she knew his identity immediately.

There was a nervous hum of energy in the air as Jessica walked into the Longsight station. Early information would have begun to leak back through the various ranks during the morning about what had been found and, as when anything major occurred, it didn't take long for the news to spread.

Jessica headed straight for the stairs at the back of the reception area but was immediately put off by a string of tinsel wrapped around the bottom of the banister. She had noticed something similar the previous day in the canteen, where the frame around the door was decorated with bright Christmas streamers. Jessica shook her head in annoyance and then jogged up the stairs two at a time on her way to Detective Chief Inspector Jack Cole's office. After discovering the body, she had phoned in to the station to give the brief details she knew, giving her boss the opportunity to start the investigation from their end while she waited for the Scene of Crime team to show up.

As Jessica reached the office, she could see Detective

Inspector Jason Reynolds and the DCI waiting for her through the glass walls. Both turned to face her and she didn't have time to knock before being waved in.

DCI Cole had recently turned fifty. Since taking the chief inspector's job around eighteen months ago, he had really started to look his age. When Jessica first began working with him a few years before, they had both been in more junior positions. Back then he seemed to take everything in his stride and remained unfazed by more or less anything. After his promotion, he had begun to change. At first it had been subtle but in recent months, Jessica had found herself less confident around him. His hair was now fully grey and new wrinkles had appeared around his eyes. His cool approach had taken a hit and Jessica had seen him angry on a few occasions, something she couldn't have pictured beforehand. The pressure of the job, financial cutbacks and the anxiety to meet government targets were having an obvious effect.

Cole was sitting behind a large wooden desk with a selection of certificates on the wall above him and a couple of cardboard files on the table. Opposite him sat Reynolds, an imposing black officer who Jessica used to share an office with. As she entered the room, the DI shuffled his chair sideways, allowing her room.

Cole waited for a moment, eyeing her up and down, then spoke with a grin. 'Raining out, is it?'

Jessica felt puzzled for a moment, then saw her boss nodding towards the floor where she had left a trail of drips which no doubt ran the length of the corridor and all the way down the stairs. With everything that had happened during the morning, Jessica had forgotten how wet she was. Now she shivered slightly, almost in recognition of her boss's point. She could feel her wet hair plastered to her left ear and brushed it away with her hand.

'Sorry, Sir . . .'

The DCI waved his hand, realising his joke had fallen flat. 'No, it's fine. I don't know if anyone filled you in but the car with the body in the boot is stolen.' Cole typed on the keyboard in front of him before shaking his head. 'I've not got the information here but the owner reported the theft yesterday. The mother of the missing boy has been notified and we're hoping she can identify the body one way or the other at some point today. It's awkward for obvious reasons.' He leant back into his chair, running a hand through his hair.

'Do we know who's doing what yet?' Jessica asked.

Jason answered: 'It's all a bit of a mess because the missing persons team were involved but now it looks like a murder investigation. You know what the politics are like around here but I think we'll end up taking it once the body has been formally identified.'

It occurred to Jessica that she'd missed an obvious point. 'If the car was stolen, do we know who the driver is?'

The two men exchanged a glance and Jessica realised that was what they had been talking about before she arrived. It was again Reynolds who answered.

'We don't know yet. The Scene of Crime boys and the coroner will be involved. If we're really lucky he'll have a wallet in his pocket, if not we'll have to wait a few days but might get a match from his DNA to the national database. Other than that, we're going to be struggling. His face is in such a bad way, we might not be able to get a picture we can use. Did you see anything in the front of the vehicle?'

Jessica shook her head. 'It was a bit of a mess with the airbag and blood and everything. After I went to the boot, I didn't look anywhere else.'

DCI Cole picked up the phone from his desk. 'I'll check to see if anyone on site found a wallet or something to get us moving. Someone's going to have to take another statement from the person whose car was nicked but we can come back to that.'

He dialled some numbers and then leant back in his chair, the receiver to his ear. Jessica offered a thin smile to Reynolds after he caught her eye as they listened to one half of a conversation which seemed to consist largely of acknowledging grunts.

After a couple of minutes, Cole put the phone down and looked up at the other two detectives. He scratched his chin and grimaced slightly, accentuating the wrinkles around his eyes. 'They've not found much,' he said. 'No wallet or ID on the driver and it's going to take a little while for them to test the blood to see if they can get a match. For now we have no idea who he is.'

Reynolds hummed in response but Cole continued. 'They did find two things on the passenger seat. They might be nothing but . . .' He tailed off as Jessica felt the hairs on the back of her neck stand up. It could have been because of the dampness of her clothes but something in the tone of her boss's voice made it sound significant. It was almost as if he had paused for dramatic effect. The chief inspector started to shuffle papers on his desk again before picking up a pad and pen and beginning to write. 'They're going to have to check them for fingerprints and the like, but there was a key and a map. We'll get them handed over later today or early tomorrow when they're finished with them.'

'What type of key?' Jessica asked.

'I don't know. We'll have to wait.'

Jessica thought about the state of the vehicle when she had arrived on the scene. The passenger's side was far more damaged than the driver's and, because of the airbags and condensation, that was probably why she had missed the items. She was still annoyed with herself for not spotting them though. Cole looked up from his pad and held it up for them to see. He had written the number '61'.

'Does this number mean anything to you?'

Jessica stuck out her bottom lip and looked at Reynolds as they both shrugged their shoulders.

'In what context?' the inspector asked.

Cole put the pad back down. 'The keys were attached to some sort of fob with the number sixty-one on. It could be a key for someone's flat but it seems unlikely you'd have your own door number on it.'

'Maybe it's from a hotel room?' Jessica suggested.

The two men nodded before Cole spoke. 'Perhaps. We'll have to wait for it to be analysed and released back to us.'

'What about the map?' Jessica asked.

'They still need it but someone's going to email over digital photos. The guy reckons they're clear enough to use if we want to follow them up before we get the actual map.'

Jessica stood. 'Right, let's go follow the map.'

She knew it wasn't really her call to decide which cases she was allocated but, having found Isaac's body in the boot, she wasn't ready to stand aside and let someone else take it up. From their reactions – and considering how well they knew her – there were no objections from either of the other two.

Cole nodded. 'Jason's on this too. I don't know where the site is yet but you'll need a team with you. Start sorting that and I'll forward you the emails when they arrive.'

As Reynolds and Jessica exited the office and began to walk down the corridor, the DI put one hand on her shoulder. 'Are you all right, Jess?'

'Yeah, just wet.'

'I mean the body you found. I know what you're like, just breezing through everything. I found the body of a child once . . .' He tailed off but Jessica didn't give him an opportunity to continue.

'I'm okay. But I could do with a towel.' She knew that wasn't the question her colleague was asking but she didn't want to stop working. Reynolds knew her well enough not to push.

'All right, you sort yourself out and I'll get a few calls in.'

Jessica was glad to get away from the inspector. It wasn't that she didn't like or respect him but she never enjoyed it when anyone asked questions that might make her think about her own well-being too much. She went off to dry her clothes and hair as best she could before finding Dave in the large open-plan area which the constables shared on the station's main floor.

She couldn't help but smile as she followed a trail of water to find him towelling his own hair as he hunched over a desk.

'You look as if you've been dragged from the bottom of a lake,' she laughed.

'You look as if you've been swimming with your clothes on.'

Jessica grinned. 'How was Laura when you left her?'

'Shaken, but she'll be okay. When she got wind that the other guy was dead, she kept saying it was her fault. I don't know what she could have done about it.'

'Do you want to come back out? We found a map in the car with the bodies. No idea what it leads to but we don't know who the driver is yet and the body from the boot hasn't been identified formally so we don't have anything else for now. There was a spade in the boot so it might be where he was going to bury the body but I don't know why you'd need a map for that. Something doesn't add up.'

Rowlands rubbed the top of his head with his hand. 'Do you think there's a point you reach where you can't get any wetter?'

Jessica was confused. 'What?'

'When you're out in the rain, absolutely soaked, do you think there's a point where you're so wet, it doesn't matter if you stay out in it because you're already as wet as you can possibly be?'

Jessica screwed up her eyes, arching an eyebrow. 'When most people settle down with a girlfriend or boyfriend, it does absolute wonders for their personality. With you, it's just bloody weird. I preferred it when you spent half the day looking at those shite lads' mags, now you're offering philosophical opinions about rain.'

'I was just . . .'

'Whatever. Are you coming?'

Rowlands gave a small smile. 'Yeah, but I'm getting one of those big coats from storage that uniform use before we head out.'

Jessica shared a car with DI Reynolds and Dave Rowlands while two other vehicles carried teams of officers to the location marked on the map. The digital photographs were decent quality and someone in the administration department had made copies for the team to take with them. As Reynolds drove, Jessica looked intently at the printouts in her lap. She had never been great with directions but the images appeared to come from an Ordnance Survey map. A red cross marked an area just outside the M60 ring road not too far from the main road that would take them to Altrincham.

Jessica didn't know the district too well but the map showed some woods and a few large fields which backed onto an area that one of the other officers told them was an industrial park. The cross itself seemed to have been marked very deliberately, slightly into the woods in red pen. The photographs were a little out of focus but offered an accurate idea of what the original map would look like.

The entire team were now in heavy waterproof jackets and their bulging coats made the vehicle feel much more fuller than usual. At least the heater was working a lot better than the one in Jessica's car did.

Rain lashed the roof as DI Reynolds drove carefully towards their destination. There was little small talk as Jessica focused on the map and the inspector concentrated on the road. Only one of the officers knew the area to which they were headed and he drove in front, the other cars following. Jessica watched as the leading vehicle turned off the main road and began to follow a tight one-track lane with high hedges on either side. Luckily there was no other traffic as it would have been awkward to squeeze more than one car through.

Eventually the front car pulled onto a verge next to a wide metal gate which opened into a field. The three vehicles just about squeezed onto the same patch, allowing access to through traffic.

Jessica slid the printout of the map into a plastic wallet to shield it from the weather and stepped out of the car. The sound of the rain bouncing from the vehicle was almost deafening. Jessica and the team of officers started walking along a thin track that ran alongside the field, their heavy boots splashing through the pools of water that had built up on the muddied ground.

No one knew what to expect, with some of the officers carrying shovels, while another had a metal battering ram. The initial visit to the location was more to get a feel of the surroundings and see if there was anything obvious. If need be, excavation experts could be brought in to dig up entire areas.

Jessica was wearing an old pair of leather shoes and could feel water squelching through her socks. She tried not to show her discomfort as the group continued to follow the two men at the front. They soon reached a stile, which the men climbed over. Jessica took her time as the coat she had borrowed was far too big and, though she was usually quite fit, she was struggling to lift her legs because of it. Dave climbed the fence after her and though she expected a joke at her expense, he was also struggling in the sodden conditions.

Slowly they crossed a line of trees into a wooded area that was nowhere near as overgrown as Jessica might have guessed if she had looked at it from a distance. The tree trunks were thin but evenly spaced, the branches overhead stopping at least some of the rain from coming through. As her shoes slid along the ground, Jessica quickly realised the soil was still soft despite the cover. She hoped someone had thought to bring torches. Although it was daytime, the skies were grey and murky, the trees blocking out much of the natural light. Her eyes took a few moments to adjust and, although she could still see, visibility was far from good.

Reynolds waved everyone into a circle and took his copy of the map out of a pocket, shouting over the surrounding noise so that everyone could hear him.

'My colleague here assures me this is the right place,' he said. 'From what I can tell, we're looking at an area maybe a hundred yards square. Let's skim around and see if there's anything obvious. If not, we'll come back when it's stopped pissing down.'

Jessica had the urge to point out that could well mean they never returned but she held her tongue. The group spread out and began to mooch through the trees. It was clear no one really knew what they were doing and Jessica was beginning to feel her earlier enthusiasm about coming to the site was misplaced. She exchanged a glance with Rowlands as if to say 'sorry', and then looked back at her feet as she moved in as straight a line as she could manage without walking into any trees.

Aside from mounds of dirt and roots she did her best not to trip over, Jessica couldn't see anything of note. The only observation that seemed slightly out of the ordinary was that the entire area appeared untouched. Most woodland like this would either be overgrown and unkempt, or surrounded by signs letting people know where they could and couldn't walk.

As she continued, Jessica tried to keep her mind focused, looking for anything unusual. She edged further into the trees, which were becoming more densely packed, blocking even more of the light. Just as she was beginning to think they would have to come back another time, Jessica heard a shout from the far end of the line, turning to see the silhouettes of two people in thick jackets converging on a spot around thirty metres away. Her first instinct was to run but, after two steps, she realised that attempting to do so would leave her sliding along the ground.

Jessica moved as fast as she could without losing her footing and immediately saw why the officer had called them over. While most of the soil was damp on the surface, he had stopped by a patch of land that looked as if it had been dug up recently. It had been covered by stray branches which, if anything, drew more attention because the rest of the ground was clear of clutter.

Jason was the last person to reach the scene and looked straight at Jessica, not saying anything but asking the question with his eyes instead: 'What do you want to do?' Even though he was her supervisor and it was his call, Jessica knew he was deferring to her. She assumed it was because of her earlier insistence on being involved, or perhaps he was simply asking if she wanted to get out of the rain. Either way she reached out to take a spade from an officer standing next to her.

'Let's dig.'

Instead of handing over the shovel, the officer stepped past Jessica and slammed the spade into the ground himself. He was quickly followed by four others as another placed the metal battering ram on the floor and sat on it. Jessica stood silently next to Reynolds. The steel tips of the spades thudded into the ground as the rain continued falling around them. Gradually piles of mud began to build up before, finally, everyone saw what they had come for.

The five men stopped digging in unison, glancing towards the two detectives. Jessica stepped forward first, crouching next to the hole which was around a foot deep. She picked up a large see-through plastic bag that reminded her of the freezer bags with the white zips which her mum used for leftovers. She wiped away some soil with her bare hands, surprised at how neat the object was. Jessica didn't open the plastic; she didn't need to. Inside she could clearly see a tidily folded light blue football shirt and a pair of jeans.

Given the size there was no doubt they belonged to a child.

3

Jessica held the bag up for Reynolds to see but it was Dave who spoke. 'Is that a Man City shirt?'

Reynolds shook his head to say he didn't know but one of the other officers stepped forward, nodding. 'Yeah, it's a City shirt. Few years old though, they've not had that sponsor in years.'

With the light fading, Reynolds signalled for everyone to return to the cars. Two officers were left to make sure no one interfered with the area. DCI Cole or a superior would decide what they should do next.

Usually when they found something of note, the officers would be buzzing but it was more or less a silent journey back to the station for Jessica, Reynolds and Rowlands. She figured it was partly because no one understood the significance of what they had discovered, not to mention the fact that they were all soaking wet. Jessica thought about the body of the child she had found that morning and how it might be connected to the clothes. She still felt there was something not quite right about the fact the driver was using a map. It seemed obvious you only needed one if you didn't know where you were going. If the driver was heading either to bury Isaac Hutchings or, for whatever reason, dig up the clothes, wouldn't he already know the location?

Back at the station, many of the day-shift officers had already left. DCI Cole had waited for them to get back but, aside from handing the bagged clothes over to an already overworked forensics team, there wasn't much else any of them could do.

Jessica spent the whole of the next day feeling as if she was going through the motions. She hadn't been present but Isaac's mother had identified his body and their murder investigation had officially begun. The football shirt had been easily identified by other officers as being somewhere between twelve and fifteen years old because of the sponsor's name. Jessica's gut feeling was that there would be further excavation work required in case there was something they had missed but, aside from the map that had led them there, its significance was a mystery for now.

Their other lead was the key with the number 61 on the fob. It had been returned by the scientists who had determined there were no fingerprints or anything else of note on it. Jessica left Rowlands and a small group of officers with the task of trying to find out its use as she went to visit the owner of the stolen black car.

Partly to make up for leaving her at the station the whole of the previous day but also because she liked working with her, Jessica took DC Izzy Diamond with her for the interview. Izzy, who had long bright-red hair, had become a good friend to Jessica in recent times.

The relentless rain from the previous day had gone, replaced by a light drizzle that seemed to define the area.

Jessica drove one of the marked police cars while Izzy gave directions.

'Have you told anyone yet?' Jessica asked as they waited at a set of traffic lights.

'Why? I'm not starting to show yet, am I?'

Jessica giggled gently. 'You're paranoid about getting fat. Of course you're not showing, I'm just terrified of accidentally telling someone you're pregnant before it's officially out.'

The constable didn't sound too fussed. 'I'm sure I'll blab it soon enough. I think Mal's told his mum anyway. We said we wouldn't but she dropped some hint about me not being allowed to drink the other day. Still, I guess I've told you so we're even.'

'I don't know what I'm going to do when you go off on maternity. I'm going to be left talking to Dave all the time and he's so obsessed with Chloe he'll probably be spending his lunch breaks writing sonnets in the canteen by then.'

Izzy laughed. 'I've got a few months before I disappear. Anyway, what's she like?' DC Diamond had not met the woman, with Jessica the only person other than Dave able to confirm her existence.

'Chloe?' Jessica asked.

'Yeah, I would've put a tenner on either "imaginary" or "blow-up".'

Jessica put the car in first gear and gently pulled away from the junction. 'Me too but she's all too real. She's sort of normal as well. You know, two arms, two legs, one head, not mentally impaired. Normal. Christ knows what she sees in Dave.' The two women exchanged a glance. 'What does it feel like?' Jessica added.

'What?'

'I don't know . . . having something inside of you.'

DC Diamond cackled. 'I didn't realise you were that shy.'

Jessica snorted, realising what she'd said. 'Not like that. I mean the baby. What does it feel like?'

Out of the corner of her eye, Jessica saw her colleague put a hand on her stomach.

'I don't know. It just feels . . . right. Like it's meant to be there. Did I show you the first scan photo we got?'

'Yeah, it sort of looked like a pean . . .' Jessica tailed off before finishing the sentence.

Izzy sounded part-amused, part-offended. 'Were you going to say "peanut"?'

'No.'

'Penis?'

Jessica laughed again. 'Definitely not.'

'You know, out of you and Dave, I think it's getting to the point where he's the mature one.'

'Sod off, is he.'

'Okay, enough about my unborn child that apparently looks like a peanut. What's going on with you?'

'How do you mean?'

'Dave reckoned you were seeing his friend, that magician guy.'

Jessica wasn't too pleased at people gossiping about her but tried to hide it. 'Hugo? No, we're just mates. He comes round and cooks for me every week or two.'

'"Cooks"? Is that what you're calling it nowadays?'

'Get out, he's just a mate. Anyway, where's this house we're going to?'

'Ooh, changing the subject, very suspicious.'

Jessica was glad she had taken Izzy with her. She wouldn't have admitted it if anyone had asked but the image of Isaac Hutchings had stayed with her and she had struggled to sleep the previous night. She tried not to think too much about her own health but couldn't avoid the fact that her ability to sleep deteriorated significantly each time she was involved with a serious case. Trying to have normal conversations with people like Izzy was something that allowed her to feel as if her life wasn't being overtaken by the job.

After a little more teasing, they reached the address where the black car had been stolen from. Jessica had read the report and knew the car had been taken from a driveway but it seemed sensible to go back over the details now the vehicle was part of a murder investigation.

She parked on the road outside the property, climbing out to feel yet more drizzle. As Jessica scanned the surroundings, she could almost still feel the clingy dampness from the day before when she had been soaked.

When Jessica had started in the force and worked in uniform, car crime had been fairly common. That had been around a decade ago when stereos were easier to steal and provided a quick chunk of money for addicts needing a fix. With improved security devices, cars had not only become harder to break into and pull apart – but also tougher to actually steal. Vehicle theft had significantly decreased and most instances these days meant an owner had left the car unlocked. The area they were in wasn't a high-crime district at all. It wasn't quite an idyllic paradise but most of the houses were well kept with neatly trimmed lawns and Jessica knew a car being stolen from a driveway would be a rarity.

She didn't need to check to remember the name of the person whose car had been taken because she had been so taken with 'Daisy Peters' on the front of the report. Without meeting her, Jessica thought the name conjured thoughts of summer meadows and sunshine which perhaps wasn't quite an accurate picture given the weather.

The woman's driveway was clear, backing onto a closed bright white garage door. A narrow pathway ran along the tarmac, separating it from a small patch of grass. Every property on the estate looked the same.

Izzy made her way around the car and Jessica resisted the urge to ask if she was all right. She herself had no particular wish for a baby or even a husband, but she figured the last thing she would want if she were pregnant was someone asking her every five minutes if she was okay.

They cut across the drive and reached a white double-glazed door next to a bay window that jutted out into the front garden. Jessica went to ring the doorbell but, before she could, the door swung open and a woman with short blonde hair stood in front of them. 'I saw you through the window,' she said. 'Come on in, the kettle's already on. I'm Daisy.'

Jessica made sure she wiped her feet as, even from the doorway, it was clear the interior of the house was incredibly neat. The woman led them along a short hallway into a living room completely free of clutter. There was a computer desk at one end, with a sofa and two armchairs at the other facing a television. Daisy asked if they wanted tea and, after receiving two positive replies, left the room.

Izzy blew out through her teeth. 'If she does her own cleaning, she can come round mine any time.'

Jessica nodded in agreement. 'Clean people always creep me out.'

'Why?'

'I don't know, I guess I just think it's weird.'

'What, tidying up?' Izzy again seemed part-puzzled, part-bemused.

'Maybe, I don't know.'

Jessica used the time to take in the room. It wasn't that Daisy was a suspect but she had found over the years that a lot could be learned simply by watching, or looking at family photos of graduations or weddings. The walls of this house were completely free from decoration, except for an analogue clock hung above the flat television that was sitting on a pine cabinet.

'What do you reckon?' Jessica asked in a loud whisper. She was fairly confident of her own conclusions but wanted to know what her colleague thought.

Diamond was as driven as anyone Jessica had met and she knew the constable wanted to be as good at her job as she could be. For now it was a guessing game but the red-haired woman played along. 'Single?' Jessica nodded to indicate she agreed. 'Clean freak, obviously.'

'Why, though?'

The constable screwed up her face slightly. 'I don't know. Parents?'

'I reckon it's rented. No photos, no real furniture.' Jessica pointed towards the computer desk. 'I think she works from here too. Maybe she's a rep or something?'

Izzy shrugged. 'Does that matter?'

'Maybe. We don't know who the driver of her stolen car is – or even if he was the one who took it. If whoever it was knew the area, or lived locally themselves, they might have noticed a single woman on her own moving into a house. The report said the car was taken from her driveway.'

Daisy interrupted as she returned carrying three mugs, which she put on the coffee table before sitting in an armchair opposite the sofa both detectives were on. She smiled but seemed a little nervous.

'I know my car was in an accident yesterday because someone called,' she said. 'I saw the photos on the Internet and I've been talking to the insurance company. They're sorting me out with a courtesy car but I'm not really sure what I can help you with . . .'

News about what they had found in the car's boot had been kept quiet and Jessica wasn't about to give anything away.

'We'd like to go back over the details you've already given,' Jessica said. 'I know you've already told someone about it but we might have a few different questions.'

Daisy cradled her mug, shrugging as if to say it wasn't a problem so Jessica continued: 'Can you tell us what exactly happened?'

Daisy took a drink of her tea then put it down on the table. She looked slightly embarrassed as she started to talk. 'I know it sounds stupid now but, at the time, I didn't think anything of it. Basically, I used to lose my keys all the time. They'd show up everywhere: in the fridge, under chairs, in my shoes, all over. So I got this key-rack thing and hung it in the hallway. It meant that I couldn't walk through the front door without seeing it. Every time I got home, I'd see the rack and hang my keys up.'

Jessica had a similar problem with losing her keys and phone and knew exactly where the story was going as Daisy took another drink before tucking a strand of her short hair behind her ear and continuing.

'The insurance company are being arsey about it because they say they haven't yet determined if I'm to blame. Either way, I'd hung my keys up as usual a few nights ago after going to the supermarket. I work from home, so I'd done some stuff on the computer, watched a bit of TV, and then gone to bed. I came down the next morning and had been working but then I had to meet a client. I went to the rack but the car keys were missing. It was after lunch and I'd not even noticed. I checked everywhere because at first I thought I'd forgotten to hang them up. Then, after about half an hour, I looked outside and realised the bloody car was gone.'

Daisy was speaking more and more quickly, as if she couldn't get the words out fast enough. She had also begun to play with her hair, pulling strands out from behind her ear and curling them with her fingers before tucking them away again.

'I didn't know what to think,' she added. 'I called you, of course, and the guy on the phone said he thought someone might have hooked my keys out through the letterbox. I went and had a look but there was no sign, although I'm not sure that there would be. The investigators came round and said they were looking for footprints or fingerprints but didn't seem to find anything. They didn't sound confident but left me with a number to give to the insurance company. Then I got the call yesterday saying my car had been in an accident. That's about it really.'

Izzy had been taking notes, although Jessica knew Daisy hadn't revealed anything they didn't already know. She let her colleague finish writing before moving on. 'How long have you lived here, Daisy?'

'Not long, a few months. I work as a rep for this electronics company. They're based in London but trying to break into the north. They pay half the rent because it counts as an office and I pay the rest. The money's good, which is one thing, I guess. I've still got a flat down south, which is where most of my stuff is. I don't know if this is going to be a long-term thing yet.'

Jessica resisted the urge to smile at having her suspicions confirmed and took a sip of her own tea. She asked some follow-up questions about whether Daisy had seen anyone suspicious, or if she knew anyone locally who was familiar with her domestic situation. The lack of a clear photo of the driver didn't give them much else to work with. It seemed pretty clear Daisy was simply waiting for the call so she could move back south and hadn't made much effort to integrate into the area.

As they were getting ready to leave, Jessica's phone rang. She apologised to Daisy and stepped quickly into the hallway.

Rowlands's mobile number flashed onto the screen. 'What's up?' Jessica asked.

'Are you on your way back?'

She knew her colleague well enough to know from his tone that he was excited about something. 'Not quite, we're just leaving. What's going on?'

Rowlands paused as if for dramatic effect. 'We know where the key comes from.'

4

Jessica felt a small surge in her chest as she always did when something important happened. She resisted the temptation to say anything nice. 'Took you long enough. Where's it from?'

Rowlands laughed. 'I knew you'd be appreciative. We're pretty sure it comes from an allotment shed. We'd been going around in circles talking to hotels and the like, and then one of the uniform boys came in and reckoned his dad had a key just like it. We spoke to the council who were as useful as ever but they put us on to some allotment society secretary guy who knew what he was talking about. We emailed him a photo of the key and he knew straight away where it was from. He said something about it being colour-coded by the fob. Anyway, we're heading out there now. The DCI was going to phone you to say to meet there but then he got called away along with Jason.'

'Have we got anything back from the clothes we found?'

'I don't think so.'

'Right, where am I meeting you?'

'You know the reservoir out Gorton way? There's a big plot near there. Just call if you can't find it but we'll wait for you.'

Jessica hung up and quickly said her goodbyes to Daisy

before heading off in the car with Izzy. The rain had finally stopped and she could feel the beginnings of that buzz that could herald finding something horrific or something else that could help break a case.

'You were right about the woman,' Izzy said after Jessica had found her way off the estate back onto the main road.

'When I'm not comparing people's unborn children to salted snacks I'm not too bad.'

Izzy laughed. 'I don't know how you get to a point where you just see things.'

Jessica shrugged with one shoulder as she continued to drive. 'Practice. When I first got out of uniform there was this old DI guy called Harry who let me tag along. He seemed to know everyone and everything. We were around this bloke's house once for an interview. He asked if I wanted tea. I wasn't fussed and said "no" but then Harry asked for one anyway. I was annoyed because I thought he was wasting time but then, while the guy was in the kitchen, Harry was poking around and sizing the place up. He reckoned you should never turn down a drink whether you want one or not because, while the owner's away from the room, it gives you a chance to look at the walls, the furniture and the carpets, things like that, and assess what you might be up against.'

'Clever.'

'I know. Sometimes you'll be talking to actual suspects, but most of the time it'll just be a witness. Either way, you never know what might happen or whether someone might slip up, so you learn to look for things.'

'Like what?'

'I don't know, maybe stray shoes in a hallway? What size are they? Could they be male, female or a child's? That kind of thing. It gives you a feel of the type of circumstance someone might be living in. Daisy seems pretty straight-up but it does sound as if whoever took her car knew about her living arrangements. Who knows, maybe they'd knocked on her door once and saw the keys hanging?'

'Like a postman?'

'Or a neighbour or someone else that knew she was an outsider living on her own. She said she didn't recognise the photo of the driver but perhaps that just means someone else took the vehicle? Something about him needing a map still doesn't sit right. Ultimately, you get used to picking up on these things.'

Izzy paused for a few moments, taking in Jessica's words. 'So what's this Harry guy's last name? Does he work in a different district?'

'It's Harry Thomas. He's . . . retired.' Jessica felt uneasy talking about the man. He had been stabbed in a bar fight a few years previously and, after spiralling down into alcoholism, had had to quit the force while the person who attacked him was acquitted by a jury. It then emerged he could have been involved in inadvertently protecting Randall Anderson, the serial killer who tried to murder Jessica and was currently in a high-security hospital. Only Jessica knew about his possible connection to Harry but she had never looked into it properly for fear of finding out it was true. At least by not knowing she still had some good memories of the person who had mentored her but if those were taken away, she'd have nothing but bitterness.

Perhaps it was Jessica's tone but Izzy didn't pursue the question. Instead they drove in relative silence, even when they were held up in unexpected traffic at Ardwick Green. Suited and booted crowds were streaming out of the theatre, even though it was the afternoon, leading Jessica to assume there was a corporate event going on. If she had been driving a marked car, she would have flicked on the lights but instead she waited with as much patience as she could muster.

Jessica didn't know exactly where they were going but the allotments were signposted and two marked police cars were already parked in front of a wide metal gate which separated the plots from the road. As Jessica pulled in behind the vehicles, Rowlands got out of the one at the front and came towards her.

'Do we know who runs plot sixty-one then?' she asked, pulling on a jacket.

'Sort of. We found out that the council owns the land but the running of it is handed over to individual allotment societies. Each society has a secretary. The one from here is the guy that identified the key for us. Anyway, he says number sixty-one has been registered to a "Glenn Harrison" for the best part of twenty years.'

'I don't recognise the name.'

Rowlands shook his head. 'No, and we don't have anyone in our files that would fit it either. The secretary read us the guy's address but . . .'

'. . . it doesn't exist.' Jessica finished the constable's sentence with a slight wince as he nodded to confirm she was right. Izzy had walked around the vehicle and heard the final part of the conversation.

'So who pays for the land, then? Isn't it like fifty quid a year or something?' she asked.

'Er, yeah. How do you know that?' Rowlands replied.

'My dad used to keep a plot. I think he just went there to get some peace to be honest.'

Rowlands gave her a 'don't blame him' look, adding, 'The secretary says it's forty-eight quid a year. He checked his files and said Harrison paid in cash. He reckons the society are trying to get people to switch to direct debits and the like but a lot of their members are older and will only deal in cash.'

Jessica spoke next. 'So does he know who this Harrison guy is?'

'Apparently not. He says some people pay direct to the council, others post him cheques and so on. He's looking into it now but I think we'll have to visit him.'

Jessica was wary of what they might find at plot sixty-one. She was only too familiar with the horrors people could commit when their identity was known, so the thought of what someone could have been up to when it wouldn't be traced back to them was something she didn't want to anticipate.

With little else to say, Rowlands and Jessica led their small party through the gate. The patches were numbered sensibly in rows of ten, becoming larger as the land widened. Some of the plots proudly displayed their numbers either on a shed or attached to a piece of wood hammered into the ground. The patches became bigger still as they moved deeper into the site, a few gardeners tending their plants nearby. The presence of men and women in suits and police coats was undoubtedly out of the ordinary and the few who were around watched them edge through the site.

Jessica tried her best not to step on anyone's plants as Rowlands led them along a path that cut through a selection of plots. She saw a large '5' painted onto the side of a shed and looked up ahead to see where they were going. Plot sixty-one seemed to be unmarked, the land itself relatively untended, while the wooden shed was somewhat larger than the ones close to it. Someone had fitted guttering to the roof, which allowed water to run onto the pathway as opposed to falling on the soil.

Taking the key from Rowlands, Jessica pressed the side of the shed. It felt thick and unmoving. She looked to see if there were any windows but there seemed to be no way in other than the door, which was secured with a heavy metal padlock. She slid the key into the lock with ease, turning it until it made a solid click, then opened the latch, taking a deep breath before pulling the door open.

The hinges creaked as Jessica stepped around the swinging door and crossed the threshold. For the second day running no one had thought about the light situation. Jessica asked Rowlands if he'd brought a torch but he pulled a face and held his hands up open-palmed. Jessica waved him and Izzy into the hut then asked everyone to clear away from the entrance in order to let as much light in as possible.

Her footsteps echoing off the creaking wooden floor,

Jessica surveyed the gloomy interior, noticing a metal desk pushed up against the wall opposite the door with a swivel chair underneath. Despite the poor light, she could see yellow foam spilling out of the backrest. A gas canister and small portable stove were in another corner. From what she could see, there wasn't anything pinned to the walls and, apart from flecks of dried soil, very little else of note.

'See anything?' Jessica asked. The other two officers answered 'no' at the same time. Jessica wheeled the chair out from under the desk and sat on it. 'Something's not right about this place,' she commented. Rowlands was tapping the walls with his knuckles for some reason. It was the kind of thing people did on property programmes but Jessica figured they knew what they were doing while she wasn't convinced the constable had any real idea.

'It doesn't *feel* like an allotment shed, does it?' Izzy said.

'Go on,' Jessica answered.

'Where are the tools, spades, rakes, sweeping-up brushes and so on you'd expect in a shed like this? I know some people might use it as somewhere to go for a bit of peace and quiet but you'd still have something, wouldn't you? Even just a radio?'

Jessica nodded. 'Exactly and it doesn't look like there's much in the way of plants outside. Whoever's been using this place hasn't been doing much gardening. So what have they been doing?'

She spun the chair around so she was facing the desk again. The entire unit looked thick and solid, a huge job for just one person to move. The right side had three drawers and she pulled the first one, hearing the rattle of a ballpoint pen sliding to the front. Jessica went to pick it up but then stopped herself, taking an evidence bag from her pocket and sealing it inside. She doubted there would be any fingerprints or DNA on it but it would be careless to touch it herself.

The second drawer was empty but the bottom one was stuck tighter than the compartments above it. Jessica pulled hard until it sprung forward. At first she didn't see anything but, as Izzy stepped to the side allowing in fractionally more light, Jessica noticed a pad of paper pushed towards the back. She took another evidence bag from Rowlands and put her hand inside, pulling the notebook out before placing it on top of the desk.

She took her phone out of her pocket and tapped the screen making it light up, hovering the device over the paper so she could read the words. It was a list written in blue biro and there was no doubt about the name at the top. Izzy gasped as she leant in and read it for herself.

'Isaac Hutchings' was written in neat block capital letters next to an address.

5

The mood was dark in DCI Cole's office. Only occasionally did they find something so out of the ordinary that no one knew how to react. The pad and pen from the desk had been sent off to the labs, which were always creaking under the sheer amount they had to do.

The three detectives each had a photocopied version of the front page of the pad. Jessica had endured another sleepless night, aware of the implications of the list.

She could hear Reynolds tutting as Cole began to speak. 'I think we can all agree this list of names is pretty disturbing. The good news is that, aside from Isaac Hutchings, the other eight children mentioned have all been accounted for and are safe. We've been discreet when talking to their parents – the last thing we need is a panic. But we have asked them to be vigilant.'

'Who the hell is making lists of children?' Reynolds asked, sounding as angry as Jessica had ever heard him.

'The only connection we know of is the dead driver of the stolen car,' Jessica replied. 'We're still waiting on results to come back but as it stands we have no idea who he is. I spoke to someone this morning and they said we might get something this afternoon – but that's only if DNA from the body matches someone already in their database. They haven't been able to remove enough of the glass from his face, which means the only photo we have is so horrendous there's no way we can release it to the media.'

She looked across to Cole, who added: 'It's doubtful we will get anything better but they're trying to find a digital artist who can create a likeness of what he might look like without all the glass. The guy talked me through a list of the injuries earlier and said there's serious damage to the driver's bone structure too. They've said it's going to take a while, which is code for "we don't have enough money to pay this guy unless we really have to".'

'Great,' Jessica replied. 'The cause of death is a broken neck from not wearing the seatbelt. The airbag itself possibly killed him but there is so much damage, it could have been one of many things.'

Cole nodded, picking up the conversation. 'I've been onto the labs about the clothes found in the woods. There's not much to report. We already know the football shirt is around thirteen years old and the trousers the same age too. They're both children's sizes. We asked his mother and know they aren't Isaac Hutchings's but beyond that, nothing. We're going to ask the parents of the other eight listed if the clothes belong to their children but it's a bit of a long shot. As for their age, we don't know what to make of it. They could have come from a charity shop or one of those vintage places and the labs say they appear to have been washed relatively recently. Christ knows why you'd bury them.'

'What about Isaac?' Jessica asked, changing the subject slightly.

The chief inspector looked pained. His own children were barely older than the boy she had found in the car boot. 'Our people who were looking after his mother before the body was found are still with her. We've all got the reports about how he went missing. All we know so far is that there was no apparent sexual assault on him. That's one thing, I guess, but it does leave us without a motive for whoever took him. We've got officers looking into the usual suspects, family members and the like, but a lot of that had already been examined when it was a missing person's case. There's nothing new to report.'

There was a silence as the three detectives looked at each other, hoping for inspiration. 'We should get someone looking into unsolved cases from ten to fifteen years ago,' Jessica said. 'I know it's a lot of work but maybe there'll be something that could link to the clothes? If not that then I guess it's the media?'

Cole nodded his approval. 'We have people walking back through the woods to see if we missed anything but there's nothing yet. Another team are heading off to the allotment later to see if there's anything more there. We contacted the people who run the plots on either side of number sixty-one last night but none of them say they've ever seen anyone around that land. We don't know if the driver is the person who used that shed and, even if he is, we don't know *who* he is. We're still looking into Glenn Harrison as the plot is in his name but we definitely know the address listed with the allotment secretary doesn't exist.'

The DCI paused for a moment, peering at Jessica. 'Do you think Isaac could have been kept at the shed?'

Jessica shrugged. 'Maybe but there was nothing there to suggest that. Unless he was drugged or subdued or something, anyone nearby could have heard him shouting. I don't know how it all connects together. Given the direction the stolen car was going when it crashed, it's possible the driver could have been heading away from the allotments but we didn't see any food or anything that would give the game away. It just looked abandoned.'

Reynolds had been quiet for a few minutes but leant forward and spoke forcefully. 'What I don't get is how this list of children was put together.' He held up the photocopy to show them what he meant. 'We've all read through this but how would you know their names and addresses? A couple go to the same school, some of the others live close to each other but there's nothing apparent to link them, aside from the fact they're all boys between the ages of ten and twelve. So how would you know who they were and where they lived?'

It was something Jessica had briefly considered but not had time to think about properly. 'I can't see how it would be a teacher but maybe someone who has access to school admittance records? It'd still leave a lot of questions about why those nine specifically. It could be someone who worked in a doctor's surgery, or one of the local cub or scout leaders – even the coach of a football team. It's a mystery but I don't know where we'd start.'

There was another silence but this time no one had anything else of note to add. They were all struggling to understand quite how all of the elements linked together.

Jessica eventually broke the silence. 'If you're both

happy to take the briefing downstairs, I'll go visit the secretary guy from the allotments. I doubt he'll have anything but you never know.' The two men nodded; clearly relieved it was one job they weren't going to have to do. 'I'll go downstairs and set someone looking into unsolved cases first of all,' Jessica added.

She stood but Cole called her back before she got to the door. 'Oh yeah, sorry, I forgot. I know it's a pain but we're all supposed to be having new photos taken for the website tomorrow. You'd think the press office would have better things to be working on but there's some relaunch happening. I've got the paperwork somewhere . . .'

Jessica exchanged a look with Jason, who seemed as nonplussed as she felt.

She responded with an 'All right, I'll be here', then left the office and made her way downstairs, striding through to the main floor, which seemed to be a hub of confusion, the various officers waiting to find out what they were supposed to be doing. Jessica had no problems spotting Izzy, her flash of red hair standing out against the rest of the bodies. She moved across the room and sat on the corner of the desk the constable was working from.

'All right?' Jessica asked.

Izzy glanced up. 'Oh no, you've got that look.'

'What look?'

Diamond widened her eyes. 'That look that says you've got a shitty job you want me to do.'

'I'm really going to have to work on that poker face.'

Izzy smiled. 'Let's have it then.'

Jessica did her best to look sorry as she spoke. 'Obviously

47

you know everything's a bit of a mess at the moment and no one knows how it all fits together . . . well, I want you to grab a couple of people and start looking through the cold cases. Those clothes we found in the woods are around thirteen years old. They were washed fairly recently but could still relate to something that happened back then. They're children's clothes so start with anything that seems relevant: missing kids, dead kids, kids who were in accidents, that kind of thing. You might not find anything and it's not as if there's a shortage of children wearing football shirts but we don't have much else at present.'

Although it would be a long-winded job, Jessica knew Izzy was ruthlessly efficient and would be the best person to coordinate something from the station.

As she had been speaking, the constable had begun to take notes. 'All right, I'll get on it,' Izzy said, starting to add something before stopping herself.

'Are you sure you're all right?' Jessica asked. The constable put a hand on her stomach. Again it seemed as if she had done so unconsciously.

'It just . . . makes you think, doesn't it?' She paused for a moment but Jessica waited. 'You're bringing kids into this world where someone is cataloguing their details, kidnapping and killing them. I don't even know what to say about it.'

Jessica wasn't sure what to add. If she was pregnant, the same thoughts would surely be weighing on her mind too. As it was, Izzy shunted her chair backwards, standing to indicate she was ready to get to work. Jessica put a hand on her shoulder, smiling in as reassuring a manner as she could. It felt a little silly but Izzy seemed to appreciate the sentiment.

'I'll call in later,' Jessica said. 'I'm off to meet the allotment society secretary.'

She had volunteered to go because she wanted to feel as if she was doing something. The briefings were necessary because of the number of people who had to be organised and assigned to various roles. It was that type of work which made Jessica feel glad she hadn't been promoted any further. At least as a sergeant she could get out and investigate things. She could see first-hand how Cole and Reynolds often had their hands tied because they were the ones supposed to be sorting out everyone else. It also helped that they trusted her enough to get on with the job.

Keith Nunns was exactly how Jessica would have pictured someone who ran an allotment society. She knew it would be a deeply insulting thing to say out loud but sometimes, knowing what someone's job was before seeing them, she found that the person ended up living up to every prejudice and stereotype she felt bad about having. He was somewhere in his late fifties, short and slightly overweight with narrow strands of hair combed across his head.

And he could talk.

He lived with his wife in a semi-detached house not far from the allotment and, after inviting Jessica in, proceeded to give her his life story. Usually she would have taken control and made sure he addressed the questions she needed answering – but listening to him tell her about his forty-year career in the engineering industry seemed reassuringly normal after everything that had gone on in the past few days.

When it seemed as if he was finally running out of steam, Jessica steered the conversation towards the things she needed to know. 'I was wondering if you could talk me through the process people go through when they pay their annual fees, Mr Nunns?' she asked.

He enthusiastically leapt up from his armchair and started digging in a cupboard underneath the TV, pulling out a large folder and sitting next to Jessica on the sofa. 'I know I should really do it all on a computer but I had enough of that at work before retiring. Between you and me, I don't really know what I'm doing on them beyond what I had to do with my job.'

He opened the folder and flicked through the pages. Each one had a number at the top to indicate the plot, followed by a name and address, then a list of payments. Some numbers had multiple pages assigned to them.

'You'll notice that I keep the pages for people who gave up their land,' he added. 'When someone else takes it on they get a new page but I also hang on to the old one. I've been doing this on and off for twenty-five years now.' Jessica feared he was about to give her another chunk of his life story but instead he skimmed through to number sixty-one. 'There's only one page here,' he added. 'The guy who had the records before me has died now and I inherited his information. I copied a lot of it from his notes into my own files but it has only ever had one owner.'

Keith tapped his finger on the page and Jessica's eyes were drawn to the name inked in tidy joined-up handwriting: 'Glenn Harrison'.

Jessica scanned down the page and could see the annual deposits written in the same neat writing. The amounts had grown each year as the price increased but everything else seemed straightforward. 'I know it sounds like an obvious question,' Jessica began. 'But did you ever meet Glenn Harrison?'

He instantly shook his head. 'I know it might seem odd but I probably only know around half the people who have plots. Some apply through the council and they've been trying to get people to pay via direct debit. Others are long-term people who pay with cheques or cash. Some of the ones I know personally will give me their money when it's due.'

'How did Glenn Harrison pay you?'

'I would get an envelope through the door with cash in. It's not that unusual but admittedly most people see me in person. After I'd taken over the job, it took me a while to sort out all the separate accounts. A few people used to put cash through my door back then and one or two never stopped.'

'Would you have kept any of the envelopes or anything the money was posted in?'

Keith shook his head again. 'No, I bin all that stuff. I'd have no need to keep it.'

Jessica had been pretty sure that was what he would say but it was worth asking. 'What about the address details? Someone's told you it's not real, haven't they?'

Keith sounded defensive. 'Yes but . . . I'd have no way of knowing that, would I?'

'Oh no, it's completely understandable. I'm just asking how you would have been given that address.'

'I suppose it was one of those things I inherited. I would have copied it over from the scraps I was given.'

Jessica knew he wouldn't take it well but had to ask anyway. 'Is there any chance you could have copied it incorrectly?'

'Definitely not.' Keith was as firm as he could be and didn't elaborate.

'Can you explain to me about the keys?' she persisted.

He nodded, still willing to engage. 'I'm sure you noticed that around three-quarters of the plots have sheds but not all of them. It's partly due to how boundaries have been redrawn over the years. The key itself is actually nothing to us because people have their own padlocks. A few years ago there was a bit of money left over and the society agreed to pay for these key fobs. It was so everything looked neat.'

'How would Mr Harrison have got one if his address wasn't correct?'

'We never sent them out because of the expense. The shed for plot one is left unlocked during the day specifically so people can either borrow the odd supply or, in this case, pick up their key fobs. We've done it with other things in the past too. Sometimes we get promotional bags of seeds and the like and they're always left in that shed.'

Jessica knew she was heading into another dead end but showed him the photograph of the anonymous driver from the car crash, apologising for the glass shards in the dead man's hideously deformed features. Keith reeled in shock, shaking his head and saying he didn't know the person. Not that there was much to recognise. Jessica felt bad for making him look at it and knew there was little point in trying to show it to anyone else; it was a stupid thing to do in the first place.

She stood ready to leave and Keith followed before nervously asking the question he had clearly spent the last forty-five minutes holding on to. 'I was wondering if you could tell me what's going on?'

Jessica didn't think it was a good idea to tell him much else. 'I can't, I'm afraid,' she said.

'You've roped off the whole of sixty-one; do you know when things might be back to normal?'

Jessica again shook her head. 'I'm sorry, I don't know that myself.'

Back at her car, Jessica sat in the driver's seat and took out her phone. She dialled Izzy, who answered on the second ring.

'Are you okay?' the constable asked.

'I didn't get much here from the allotment guy,' Jessica said. 'Have you come up with anything?'

'You're hopeful; it's only been an hour.'

'I know but no one seems to have a bloody clue what's going on.'

Izzy laughed. 'You can add me to that list if you want. I do have some news though.'

'Good news?'

'Just news. The lab results are back from the dead

driver. His DNA doesn't match anyone in the national database. They also tested it against Isaac's and know they're not related. Basically they have no idea who he is.'

Jessica ended the call, sighing. She stared at herself in the rear-view mirror before turning the key and pulling away, no idea of what to do next.

6

Rachel Corless kept her eyes on the roundabout as one of her two sons helped spin the other around with a little too much relish. 'Marcus,' she shouted but the boy either didn't hear or, more likely, didn't want to. 'Marcus,' she tried again before a final, *'Marcus!'*

Finally the boy stopped pushing on the metal bars, turning to face his mother. 'What?' he called back.

'Stop pushing your brother so hard.'

Marcus turned around and gave the roundabout another shove which his mother had to admit was at least slightly gentler than the previous ones had been.

Rachel turned to the woman sitting on the bench next to her. 'How come your two just play happily on the swings while mine seem intent on spinning each other around until they're sick?'

Diane Briggs laughed. 'You should see them when they're back at home. Last night they were doing wrestling moves on each other. I was in the living room and heard a massive bump on the floor. I rushed upstairs and it turned out one of them was leaping off the top of the bunk beds onto the other.'

Rachel grinned. 'I'd settle for that. Two weeks ago, I heard them shouting in their bedroom. I went up and

Lloyd was in the process of taking a run-up to punch his brother in the shoulder.'

'My two are always fighting.'

'No, they weren't fighting. Marcus was standing there sideways waiting for it. I asked them what was going on and they were having a competition to see who could give the other the biggest bruise.'

'I once caught Andrew hanging over the end of his bed with his head drooping down and Matthew flicking his ears. They said they'd heard that you lost all feeling if you hang upside down. He couldn't understand why he could still feel the pain in his ears.'

'Surely it's the other way around? If you hold your arm up and the blood flows down, then you lose feeling?'

'I didn't tell them that. I guessed they'd figure it out sooner or later. Either that or one of them would lose an ear.'

The two women laughed together. '*Boys*.'

Diane took out a flask from a canvas bag and held it up. 'Do you want some tea?'

'No, I'm all right, it's not that cold actually. Maybe we'll have another mild winter?'

The other woman unscrewed the cup, pouring the steaming liquid into it before reattaching the stopper to the flask. 'I'd take less rain and more cold. And it's dark by four.'

Rachel looked up to the sky, which had barely changed from a light murky grey all day. 'What have you got them for Christmas?' she asked.

'Andrew wants some computer games which we've

half-sorted, although one of them apparently isn't out yet. His dad knows what's going on with those. Matthew wants a new bike.'

'What happened to his old one?'

'Don't ask.'

Rachel smiled, knowing from experience that the answer could be anything.

'What about yours?' Diane added.

'Marcus has decided he's too old for toys and bikes now he's a teenager. He only turned thirteen last month. He said he wanted cash but I told him I'd give him vouchers instead.'

Diane laughed, cradling the plastic cup from the flask. 'You know what that means, don't you?'

'What?'

'*Girls.*'

Rachel grinned. 'I think he'd run a mile if a girl even tried to speak to him.'

She was still keeping an eye on her two sons playing on the roundabout. They had swapped positions and Lloyd was now pushing Marcus. She wondered how much longer they would play together openly before one or both of them started to barricade themselves in their bedroom in between temper tantrums. It couldn't be longer than a few months at most and, from what some of her friends talked about, she was privileged her thirteen-year-old son even acknowledged her existence. She quite liked the fact he was a bit immature and could still be amused by a trip to the park.

Diane finished drinking her tea and screwed the cup back onto the flask. 'What have you got for Lloyd?'

'Oh, he's definitely still into toys, he's only eleven. I've got him some robot thing, which he'll probably break within an hour, then some football stuff.'

'Are they staying with you or their dad on Christmas Day?'

'Me for Christmas Eve and Day, then they're off with Adrian for three days.'

The four boys were now passing a football around as a street light slowly started to flicker above the bench where the two women were sitting, as if considering whether it was dark enough to come on.

Rachel looked at her watch. 'We should probably head back but it's been good catching up. It's just a shame we're both so busy all the time plus, give it a week, and it'll be dark at this time so no more park after school.'

Although it was time to leave, neither of the women moved as they watched their children contently kicking the ball around. Aside from some older teenagers standing around smoking at the far end of the grass, the park was deserted, the boys' laughs echoing around.

'Right, it really is time to go,' Rachel said, getting up. She shouted to the boys: 'Marcus, Lloyd, come on now.' The younger son turned but, as he did, his brother was in the process of kicking the ball to him. It skimmed through the air, smashing into Lloyd's face as he spun back, sending him falling.

Rachel saw the incident unfold in slow motion and dashed towards her youngest. He was sitting on the muddy grass holding his nose, his eyes wide, his face a mixture of blood and soil. Marcus dashed across. 'I'm sorry,' he said. 'I didn't mean to.' Rachel felt a little in shock herself as the other boys and Diane joined them.

'Are you all right?' she asked. For a moment it looked as if Lloyd was about to cry but then he took his hands away from his face and smiled widely, blood dripping from his top lip to the bottom.

'Quick, get a photo on your phone,' he said to his mother. 'This is well cool.'

Rachel looked back at him with a mixture of puzzlement and sympathy. 'Doesn't it hurt?'

'Yeah, but get a picture first, I want to show everyone at school. David Baker reckons he fell off a rollercoaster once and landed on his head. He reckoned there was blood everywhere but I think he's making it up. I bet this looks well good.'

As the boy's mother reluctantly took her phone out of her bag she failed to notice the silhouetted figure standing close to the park gates.

The person squinted into the distance wondering what exactly had happened to Lloyd Corless to make everyone run over to him. Whatever it was, it wouldn't be long before he and his mother were parted.

7

Jessica tilted her head to a slightly downward angle and tried not to launch into a volley of swear words. She had recently become a lot better at holding her tongue and was making a conscious effort not to lose her temper as often. As she tried to smile, she thought that if there was one person who deserved to be greeted by a string of bad language, it was the photographer standing in front of her who wouldn't stop saying 'smile'.

Jessica knew that anything to do with making the force look good was taken very seriously by people working for the police who weren't actually officers. As such it shouldn't really have been a surprise that the press office had hired a professional photographer to take new pictures for the website relaunch. But it would have been a surprise to the photographer and on-looking chief press officer if Jessica had picked up the man's tripod and found a creative way to shut him up. A few potential methods had certainly occurred to her.

The photographer was tall and lanky with spiky black hair and was possibly the most enthusiastic person Jessica had ever had the misfortune of meeting. She was on her way out of the station when Cole told her to have her picture taken before she left. The man had set himself up with his camera in the ridiculously named Longsight Press

Pad, which was the room where the force held media briefings. He seemed utterly oblivious to the fact Jessica had work to do and had no pretensions of wanting to be a model. She thought it would be a quick glance at the camera and then she would be on her way. Instead, the photographer had perched her on the edge of a desk and was trying to get her to twist her head to the side and smile. Jessica thought she *was* smiling but, apparently, whatever look she was giving wasn't good enough.

'That's brilliant,' the photographer said as his camera flash went off again. 'Right, a couple more. Look down a bit, please.' Jessica tilted her head once more. 'No, further down,' the photographer added.

'I *am* looking down.'

'No, tilt your head down then look up.'

'I thought you wanted me to look down?'

'No, angle down, eyes up.'

Part of Jessica's job involved trying to get into the minds of criminals and finding out why they did what they did. As she tried to force another smile, she thought the unrelenting cheerfulness in the photographer's voice went some way to helping her understand what could make a person turn to violence. If anyone was unfortunate enough to share a house with this man and ended up smacking him in his gormless, grinning face, she thought a plea of temporary insanity would be a very easy sell for a solicitor.

'Right, that's brilliant,' the photographer announced, finally lowering the camera. Jessica didn't give him an opportunity to add a 'Let's just try this . . .' before standing and storming past him out of the room.

Jessica was well aware she had always been short-tempered. She could remember being a child and her mother telling her to 'count to ten'. The problem was she would get to two, occasionally three, and be too frustrated to get anywhere near ten. She knew there was undoubtedly a psychologist, psychiatrist, psychoanalyst, or some other person who stuck the letter 'p' randomly at the beginning of their title who was waiting to pick her apart one day. She figured the more time she spent around joyful photographers, the sooner that day would come.

Jessica stomped through reception and headed out of the station towards her car, her mood not improving as yet again it had begun to drizzle and she had again forgotten to bring a jacket. She dashed across the car park and struggled to unlock her car before finally hurling herself onto the driver's seat and slamming the door. She took a deep breath – another piece of advice from her mother about keeping cool – and realised that a lot of her annoyance was down to the fact she hadn't been looking forward to the day anyway.

Cole had called her the previous evening to say that Isaac Hutchings's mother had asked if she could speak to the person who found her son's body. In policing terms there was no particular need for Jessica to visit her because other officers had been dealing with the initial missing child aspect of the case, and a support officer would also be assigned. The woman had given several statements and certainly wasn't a suspect. Despite all of that – and even after the chief inspector said it was her call – there was no way Jessica was going to deny a grieving mother such a simple request.

That didn't mean she was looking forward to it.

Everyone in the force had experience of breaking bad news or dealing with people coping with extreme situations but there was no textbook to predict how a mother who had just lost a child would react.

Izzy was still in the process of looking through unsolved cases. The task was complicated because a computer system upgrade a few years previously had copied some files but not others. Everything was a mix of digital information and actual paper trails. After Cole's call the previous evening, Jessica thought about taking Izzy with her to see Isaac's mother but figured it would be pretty insensitive given her friend was pregnant. Not to mention it would be for Jessica's own indulgence when the officer would be better employed going over the old files.

Jessica drove through the rain to the address she had printed off. The Hutchingses' house was pretty similar to the one Daisy Peters was renting a few miles away. Isaac's mother was obviously expecting Jessica and invited her straight into their living room before introducing herself as Kayla and offering the obligatory cup of tea.

Jessica had read the Isaac Hutchings file thoroughly and knew his mother was only thirty-four, the same age as she was. As well as Isaac, she had a daughter, Jenny, who was thirteen. As Kayla brought in two mugs of tea and placed them on a coffee table, Jessica thought she would have struggled to guess the woman's age if she hadn't known. The greasy unwashed black hair and sallow skin colouring, coupled with dark bags under her eyes, made her look comfortably into her forties. Jessica was well aware it was almost impossible for someone childless, as she was, to understand what the woman in front of her had gone through.

Kayla sat on the brown sofa next to Jessica and offered a weary smile. 'Thanks for coming,' she said. 'The person I spoke with said they didn't know if they would be able to arrange it . . .'

Jessica shuffled in her seat, uncomfortable at meeting the woman's stare. 'It's not a problem. What would you like to know?'

Kayla stumbled over her words. 'I . . . I don't know really. They've not let us have the body back yet so we can't even plan the funeral. My husband, Mike, went back to work yesterday. I didn't want him to but I think he just felt trapped in here . . .'

She indicated towards a selection of photographs pinned on the wall. Jessica had noticed them as soon as she entered the living room. They showed various shots of Isaac and his sister playing, as well as group pictures of the parents with their children. Kayla tailed off before beginning to speak again. 'I think I just wanted to hear what he was like when you found him.'

It was the question Jessica had expected but was dreading. She tried to choose her words carefully. 'Mrs Hutchings, I . . .'

'Kayla.'

'Sorry, Kayla, I'm not really sure what I can tell you. You identified the body . . .'

'I know but what was he like when you found him? I know he was in a car.'

Jessica had a tough decision to make. There were no

rules she had to follow regarding disclosure of information, so she was free to tell the woman from that point of view – but it was always a balancing act of whether the information would cause too much emotional distress. Jessica glanced up and caught the woman's pleading eyes, which made her mind up for her.

'He was wrapped up in some sort of sheeting in the car boot when I found him. I didn't really look at him too much after that.'

'Did he look . . . okay?'

Sometimes people would only give a quick glance when identifying a body, not wishing to prolong their agony. She would have been told there was no sexual element to the disappearance but that would likely offer only a tiny amount of comfort. It was a hard question to answer. Jessica genuinely hadn't seen that much of the boy after cutting him free.

'He looked peaceful. His eyes were closed.'

It was about as much reassurance as Jessica could manage.

Kayla nodded, wiping around her eyes, although she wasn't obviously crying. 'Thanks.' She sniffed, then continued. 'Do you know how he disappeared?'

'I read the file.'

Kayla nodded again but seemed keen to tell her story. 'Everyone keeps saying, "It's not your fault", but it's shit. They're just words. I know it's down to me. Mike blames me and he's right.'

'I don't think it's your fault, Kayla.'

The woman offered a small shrug of her shoulders. 'The

other officers talked me through everything and I saw the CCTV footage. He was walking home from school the same way he always did. I would pick him up if it was raining and I keep thinking, what if it *was* raining? I mean it rains up here all the bloody time, doesn't it? It's always pissing down but, on the one day it would actually have helped, it was dry.'

Isaac had disappeared on his way back from school. Camera footage was limited but they had images of him on a device placed outside a newsagent's on his route home. The next time he would have been spotted was four hundred metres away on a traffic camera but by then he was gone. Cars going into and out of the area had been checked with no clues and there were apparently no witnesses to anything. It was as if he had simply vanished.

Jessica was struggling to know what to say and beginning to wish she had brought someone else with her but Kayla broke the awkward silence.

'I've still got his Christmas present upstairs,' she said. 'He wanted that new games console thing. Mike went to the city centre and waited in a queue at midnight when it first came out because everyone was saying they'd sell out straight away. It's wrapped up under our bed. I guess when he first disappeared I just thought he'd be back in time to have it.'

Jessica was becoming more and more uncomfortable. She tried to say something reassuring but Kayla spoke again, this time in a slightly harsher tone. 'No one's told me anything. I had someone asking me questions about a football kit, then something about a car. All everyone ever says is that they'll keep me up to date with developments. I've had to keep Jenny off school because of the other kids. She's only thirteen . . .'

Kayla tailed off again and this time there were definitely tears. She reached forward and took a tissue from the coffee table, blowing her nose loudly.

Jessica was trying to see both sides. The woman would obviously want to know who had taken her son and why but, if she had too much information which she then revealed either to the media or her relatives, it could end up harming the investigation. Although the press had reported on the car crash, some of the most important details had been kept back, largely because they didn't really know what the dead driver looked like. They hadn't had anything back from the woodland dig, the clothes they had found or the allotment connection either.

At some point the media would be brought in but it wouldn't do any good if they released all of the information in one go because they didn't yet know if it all linked together. Jessica had seen the media used in a bad way a few years previously when one murder completely unconnected to a serial killer was assumed to have been done by him. The resulting coverage had created big problems for both investigations and she was glad people had learned their lessons.

Almost as if on cue following Kayla's outburst, Jessica heard a voice coming from somewhere just outside the room. 'Mum?'

A girl with straight blonde hair down to her shoulders walked in. She was wearing a pair of jeans and a tight wool jumper. She eyed Jessica suspiciously but barely got into the room before Kayla turned around and spoke sternly. 'Jen, I told you to wait upstairs.'

'I know but I'm hungry.'

Jessica stood, knowing it was a good time to go. Kayla rose too and peered from Jessica to her daughter then back again. 'Are you leaving?' she asked.

'I'm not sure there's anything else I can help with,' Jessica said.

The woman blew her nose again, pocketing the tissue. She gave a small, entirely unconvincing smile. Jessica returned it, then took out a business card and left it on the coffee table before saying her goodbyes and walking back to her car. She knew the meeting hadn't gone well but had no idea how she could have made it any better.

As Jessica arrived back at her vehicle, she took out her mobile phone. There was a single text message from Izzy: 'Know uve got big morning & dint wanna interrupt. Call when u can.'

Jessica phoned her colleague. 'Did you want me?'

'We found something in the old case files,' Diamond said. 'It's not been transferred to the computers and the whole thing's a bloody shambles but we think we know where those clothes in the woods come from.'

'You're joking?'

'Nope but it's going to sound horribly familiar. Fourteen years ago an eleven-year-old boy went missing from around here. He was never found but, when he disappeared, he was wearing a light blue Manchester City shirt and a pair of jeans.'

8

Jessica struggled with what to say before finally managing to get the words out. 'Why didn't anyone remember this? There must be people around now who were working back then?'

'I have no idea, I'm just pulling everything together. Are you on your way back?'

'Yeah, I won't be long.'

Lunchtime traffic was as infuriating as ever but Jessica avoided the main roads and managed to arrive at the station without too much swearing. She walked purposefully through to the main floor but Izzy was nowhere to be seen. Rowlands told Jessica their colleague was in Reynolds's office, which was down the hallway from her own. While Jessica's half of her office was a complete mess, the inspector was definitely one of the tidier colleagues she knew. An outsider would never have guessed after Jessica knocked and entered his room. His desk had been shunted off to the side, while he and Izzy were sitting on the floor with a mass of papers spread across the surface. As Jessica opened the door, a gust of air sent half-a-dozen sheets of paper blowing across the room to disapproving looks from both of them.

'Sorry,' Jessica said.

Reynolds waved her in properly, pointing at a spot on the floor next to them. 'Take a seat.'

'Why are you working from the floor?' Jessica asked but was met by pitying looks from her colleagues as if she had asked the stupidest of stupid questions.

Izzy leant across and picked up the papers that had been dislodged, then answered. 'There's more room down here.'

Jessica still wasn't convinced. 'We do have tables. Upstairs, in the incident room, in the Press Pad.' It was clear her colleagues weren't interested in her complaining so she crouched and sat cross-legged next to Izzy. Reynolds winked at her to acknowledge her objections but she could see there was a serious look in his eyes.

'We've already been upstairs to see the DCI if you were wondering,' he said. 'He's busy trying to get an excavation team in to go through the woods properly while we go over this. Some of the other officers have got photocopies of these documents too and are looking into things.'

Jessica said what it seemed they were all thinking. 'Are we assuming there's a body buried in those woods?' The other detectives said nothing but Jessica knew that was exactly the reasoning. She leant back against the door. 'What have we got?'

Izzy handed Jessica a photograph of a boy with sandy-coloured short hair. He was grinning at the camera, wearing a school uniform. Izzy was clearly already familiar with the file as she spoke quickly and confidently. 'That's Toby Whittaker. Fourteen years ago he was playing on a disused industrial park with some of his friends. It was just wasteland and, from what his mates said at the time, was somewhere lots of young people would hang around playing football and so on.'

Jessica knew the 'so on' probably referred to smoking and drinking if not a few other things as the constable continued.

'Toby was only eleven at the time,' Izzy went on. 'But it looks like most of the people who hung around there were a bit older: fifteen- or sixteen-year-olds.'

Izzy briefly paused, adjusting the position she was sitting in before pointing towards the papers on the floor. 'There are all sorts of witness statements, not many of them that useful. Toby went there with his friends to kick a football around but one by one they went home. There doesn't seem to be anything fishy about their statements and none of them were suspects at the time. It seems as if Toby was left on his own and then, at some point, he just disappeared.'

'Did anyone see anything?' Jessica asked.

Izzy picked up a page from the floor and skimmed it, looking for a certain detail. 'Apparently not. Have you ever been with your mates on a night out and, before you know it, there's only one or two of you left standing? It sounds like that. He'd gone to play, it started to get dark and he was left by himself. A couple of the witnesses, people who weren't his friends but were hanging around the site, say they saw him on his own, while one of his mates say they went their own ways when it was just the two of them left. It sounds a bit odd but I remember things like that happening when I was a kid.'

'Eleven's a bit young, isn't it? How close was the land to his house?'

Izzy put down the paper and reached for another.

'Not that far, maybe half a mile? I don't really know the area.'

'And how close is this site to the woods where we found the clothes?'

Izzy returned the set of papers to the floor and shuffled her position. 'Pretty close, a few hundred yards maybe?'

Jessica said nothing for a moment but there was something concerning her. 'Why do you think we found the clothes now? We know they were washed relatively recently and presumably buried at more or less the same time? Someone must have been keeping them ever since Toby was taken. Not only that but the driver who had Isaac Hutchings in the back of his car had a map directly to the spot.'

It was more a statement than a question. The similarities between the two abductions were obvious and Jessica wondered if their unknown driver was the person who had kidnapped Toby all those years ago. If that was true, why would he need a map to the boy's clothes? It seemed that every time they found an answer, it opened up another set of questions.

There was another short silence before Jessica spoke again. 'So what happened with the investigation?'

Reynolds and Izzy exchanged a look before the inspector answered. 'From what we can tell, not a lot because there weren't any leads. Parents, uncles, aunts, all the relatives were accounted for and no one seemed to have a motive. Apart from the witnesses who said they saw him walking away from the site, there were no suspicious car sightings, no signs of a struggle, nothing. There weren't as many CCTV cameras back then, so there's nothing from that. One of the parents said something about having a falling out with one of their neighbours because of an incident involving Toby riding a bike across the person's front garden but it sounds very petty and it looks as if it was discounted.'

'So it was just unsolved and he was never found?' Jessica asked.

Izzy nodded. 'Exactly. When I was going through things I was surprised by how many unsolved missing children cases there are. It's not just our district, obviously, but over the years there are hundreds of kids unaccounted for. You never hear about them.'

Jessica knew the statement had extra meaning for the constable because of her own pregnancy. 'Does anyone here remember the case?'

'We've asked around but no one knows anything specifically,' Reynolds said. 'I wasn't here but the DCI says the boundary of who investigated what was much more blurred back then – although he wasn't here either. I'm sure someone will remember but we've not really had time to properly ask yet.'

Jessica knew what he was talking about. She worked for the Metropolitan branch of Greater Manchester CID, while there were separate divisions for the north, south, east and west areas of the city. Everything had been broken up not long after she joined as a uniformed officer around a decade ago. She knew that fourteen years back there was just one CID branch covering the entire area. Because of that, it was no wonder the paperwork was so disorganised as detectives and officers would have been moved to new departments and things would have been lost along the way.

'Do we at least have the name of whoever was leading the investigation?' Jessica asked. She saw Izzy and Reynolds swap a nervous glance and felt something sink in her stomach. She knew the name of the person involved before the inspector spoke the words: 'It was DI Harry Thomas.'

Jessica stared at the row of six intercom buzzers and took another deep breath, her third in less than a minute. Each time she hovered her finger over the button, before withdrawing it. She was standing at the top of a small flight of concrete steps outside the block of flats where Harry lived. She hadn't seen him in over three years and hadn't thought she would ever do so again. At the station both Cole and Reynolds had offered to visit Harry instead of, or with, her but Jessica insisted she wanted to do it on her own. Both officers knew how close Jessica had been to him at one point as they were both already detectives when she started in CID and Harry was their colleague too. As with a lot of things, probably too many, they trusted her judgement and, on this occasion, Jessica wanted to go on her own.

In most cases where a former officer needed to be spoken to, he or she would be invited to the station formally if it was something serious, or it could be a lunchtime chat in the pub if it wasn't. Harry had deliberately cut all ties to his former workplace so Jessica talked her fellow detectives into letting her doorstep him. No one was confident he would be helpful if they gave him much notice. As far as they knew he hadn't moved to another property but there was only one way they would find out for sure.

Jessica again raised her finger to the doorbell without putting any pressure on it but her mind was made up as a pitter-patter of raindrops began to fall behind her. She hunched her shoulders and pulled the top of her jacket over her head. It was almost as if a higher power was telling her to get on with it and Jessica finally relented, pushing the button and hearing a buzzing noise from the intercom. The noise of the rain increased and she tried to shelter her body under a small roof that overhung the front door. If anything, it was only making her wetter as water dripped from where she could see the eroded sealant above her.

Jessica stabbed the intercom again and, just as she was beginning to eye her car parked on the road as the only available dry spot nearby, the device finally crackled into life. 'Who is it?' said a voice from the other end.

'Harry? It's Jessica Daniel. Can you let me in? It's shitting it down out here.'

The intercom hissed and went silent. For a moment, she thought nothing was going to happen before a click indicated the door had opened. Jessica quickly pushed her way into the deserted hallway and pulled her jacket back down from over her head. The rain reminded her of what Kayla Hutchings said that morning about how she would have picked her son up if it had been a wet day. Jessica thought about how entire lives could change because of something as random as whether or not it rained.

Jessica had visited Harry at his flat in the past and started to walk up the hard, echoing concrete steps at the back of the porch. The place where he lived was in a row of old civil-service buildings not far from the city centre. Each property had been converted into six flats around twenty years ago, and then sold off to private investors. At some point they would have been attractive places to live but Jessica could see paint flaking from the once-cream walls as she walked up the stairs.

Harry lived on the third floor and Jessica was dripping water up the steps as she moved. She wondered if the man she once thought she knew so well might be waiting for her but the landing on the top floor was as deserted as the rest of the building seemed to be.

The falling rain echoed on the roof as Jessica walked along the corridor to Harry's flat. She knocked but the door swung inwards as it had been left on the latch. Jessica stepped over the threshold and closed it behind her, unclipping the button which allowed it to lock.

'Hello?' she called. 'Harry?'

No one replied and she couldn't hear any noise. Jessica could only vaguely remember the layout. She was standing in a hallway with two doors on her left, one directly in front of her and another on her right. All of them were closed but she knew the one at the far end led into the living room and dining area. She opened the door, immediately spotting Harry in an armchair watching a portable television in the corner of the room.

The smell was the first thing that struck Jessica. It wasn't exactly bad but it was as if she had walked through an invisible wall where everything on the other side had a stale odour. It made her remember being fourteen. She had left her PE kit in a bag over the summer holidays and only found it as she was sorting out her belongings for the new term. Her polo shirt and skirt were still caked in soil and grass and it was that exact smell which met her as she walked into Harry's living room. The place hadn't been cleaned in a very long time.

He didn't acknowledge the door opening or even Jessica repeating 'Harry?' as he continued watching the screen. It dawned on Jessica that the television was muted but she walked around his chair so she was facing him.

'Harry, are you okay?'

The man was wearing what would have been smart suit trousers at some point but the black material was grubby and fading. Harry was in his mid-fifties but looked older. He'd been overweight when she worked with him but he had put on at least another stone and a half since then and his belly was bulging against a blue-and-white checked shirt that was only half-buttoned, allowing grey chest hairs to poke out from the top. He used to sweep his hair across his head but had clearly given up and now had a large bald streak. The skin on his face was blotched and red.

Harry finally glanced up at her but wouldn't meet her eyes, staring off to Jessica's right. He started as if to speak but began coughing before clearing his throat loudly, then finally found his voice. 'Detective Sergeant.'

It was an acknowledgement of sorts but his words had no real warmth to them. His north-east accent sounded heavier than Jessica remembered.

'Are you all right, Harry?'

He nodded but didn't speak. Jessica saw a bottle of whisky wedged in between his thigh and the chair's arm-rest. Perhaps it was because she had seen the bottle but all of a sudden she could smell the alcohol. It was more of an undercurrent to the stale odour she was becoming used to but the sharp scent was distinctive. Harry must have noticed her eyes because he pushed the bottle towards the rear of the seat. When it was clear he wasn't going to answer, Jessica spoke again. 'I'm here because I was hoping you could help.'

Harry shifted his gaze back to the television and mumbled quietly, 'I'm retired.'

'I know but it's about a case you worked on fourteen years ago. It's important.'

He shuffled in his seat and Jessica didn't think he was going to say anything. Not for the first time that day she was struggling to know how to handle a situation when Harry finally replied. 'What's the name?'

Jessica had deliberately left the file in her car because she didn't want to involve Harry too heavily and didn't have a photo of the dead driver anyway if he was their link from the old case to the new one. She remembered the name of the missing boy, having read everything available before leaving the station. She guessed they would be two words she wouldn't be forgetting in a while. 'Toby Whittaker.'

Harry answered immediately but still didn't look away from the television. 'The missing boy.'

It wasn't a question.

'Yes.'

'Did you find him?'

'No, we . . . think we found his clothes.'

'A Man City shirt.' Again it wasn't a question; Harry knew what he was talking about.

'Yes, buried in some woods along with a pair of jeans.'

'Did you find a body yet?'

'No, a team's going to excavate around the trees where we found the clothes. It's a bit strange because the clothes were washed recently and bagged up before being buried. Someone's kept them all this time.'

Harry nodded, picking up a remote control from a small wooden table next to his chair and switching the television off. He finally looked at Jessica, who was still standing, meeting her eyes. She could see a small twinkle in his that reminded her of working with him and, if you could look past the state of his skin, made him look younger. 'I knew there was something not quite right but I couldn't figure it out,' he said.

'We've been reading back through the files but it doesn't look as if you ever had a suspect.'

Harry shrugged, sitting up straighter. It was almost as if he was a new person as he spoke with enthusiasm. 'Are you re-opening the case?'

'We don't know. It's too early to say and it's not up to me but I would think so.'

'How did you find the clothes?'

Jessica winced a little, not wanting to go into too many details. 'We were led there.'

'There was another body, wasn't there?'

Jessica didn't want to shut down Harry's enthusiasm as she still needed answers. 'Yes, another child's.'

'Isaac Hutchings?' Jessica was puzzled for a moment but remembered the missing boy had received some low-level media attention. As if reading her thoughts, Harry continued. 'I still keep up with everything.'

When they had worked together, Harry had always spent time each morning reading the newspapers. His knowledge was borderline encyclopaedic. It didn't surprise Jessica that he was still keeping up to date. She spoke slowly, weighing up how much she should give away. 'Yes, Isaac.'

Harry pointed towards a dining table in the far corner of the room. It was made of white plastic and looked as if it belonged outside. Two fold-up stools were leaning against it.

'Grab a chair,' he said. Jessica did just that, carrying it across so she was sitting in front of him. Harry was angling forward in his seat and the smell of alcohol was much stronger because of his proximity to her. 'What do you want to know?' he asked.

'Who were your suspects?'

Harry smiled but it was more as if he was enjoying feeling a part of something again than any fond memories of the case. 'You always look at the parents first. They were right characters and always bickering. I saw them have two blazing rows with each other and I only went to their house three times. I never thought it was either of them though. You get a feeling and they both had alibis. We looked into other family members but there was nothing I remember. There was this neighbour . . .'

Jessica was about to give him the name but Harry waved his hand to stop her. He made an 'um' noise for a few moments before clicking his fingers.

'Someone "Hill". "Simon Hill", that's the guy. He used to live a few doors down from the Whittakers. There was some sort of dispute and I spoke to him. There wasn't enough to say he was involved but there was something not quite right about him.'

'How do you mean?'

Harry breathed in deeply, scratching his head. 'I don't know. I couldn't figure it out but he didn't like being investigated.'

'Do you think he was involved?'

'Maybe, his only alibi was his wife but I couldn't find anything specifically to say he was lying. Some people just stick in your head as not being right.' Harry stabbed his index finger into his temple as if to emphasise the point.

Jessica couldn't believe the turnaround in him over just a few minutes. He had gone from being sullen and withdrawn to being upbeat and interested. His memory was astonishing too. She knew from experience it had always been good and he could comfortably recall events and people from years previously but, given the state he appeared to be in, the attention to detail was remarkable.

'Was there anyone else?' Jessica asked but Harry was already nodding before she finished the question.

'There was a teacher. One of Toby's friends said something about the two of them having a close relationship. We spoke to him but you know what it's like with teachers and so on, you have to be careful what you accuse them of. There was no evidence of anything untoward and maybe it was just a bloke who wanted to help. You know what I'm like – suspicious.'

Harry gave a small laugh but Jessica felt a chill go down her back. She wondered if she did know what he was like but tried to forget everything that happened three years ago, at least for now. Her priority was getting the information she needed.

'Can you remember the teacher's name?' she asked. She had read it in the file but wondered if Harry's memory stretched that far.

'Ian someone.' Harry shook his head as if trying to jog his memory before finally admitting defeat. 'Sorry, I can't remember the last name.'

Jessica got to her feet. 'Have you still got my phone number?' Harry had an initial look of disappointment but quickly stood.

'Yes.' His response sounded like an apology for not contacting her; he didn't know that, until now, Jessica hadn't wanted anything to do with him. There was a moment where he looked at her and Jessica thought about asking him the question that had been in her mind for three years: 'Did you help Nigel Collins become Randall Anderson?' Would he even know the significance of those names? Did she want to know the answer? It was as if the man she would have once called a friend was reading her mind again as Harry looked at her expectantly.

'I've got to go,' Jessica said. She didn't trust herself to stay quiet and walked past Harry towards the front door. She was about to open it when she heard him shouting behind her.

'"Sturgess".' Jessica turned around and saw Harry entering the hallway. '"Sturgess", that was the teacher's name. "Ian Sturgess".' Jessica faced him and nodded to indicate she knew he was right.

'Call me if you think of anything else,' she said before opening the door and making her way quickly back to her car.

Rain continued to fall as Jessica sat in her vehicle. Everything Harry had told her was already in Toby Whittaker's file, but it had helped to hear it from someone involved and she knew there were now two names to concentrate on – Simon Hill, the neighbour, and Ian Sturgess, the teacher.

She phoned the station where DI Reynolds said the dig at the woods would be beginning the following day. Jessica told him what she had found out and they agreed to meet again in the morning. Someone would be assigned to find out what Hill and Sturgess were up to nowadays, which would hopefully be straightforward.

Jessica drove home but thoughts of Harry swirled in her mind to such a degree that she wasn't even annoyed by the queuing traffic and falling rain. Something made her wonder if she would ever see him again.

As she pulled into the parking space outside her block of flats and switched off the engine, it took her a few moments to get her bearings. It felt as if she had completed the journey without any conscious thought of where she was heading. Picking up the photocopy of Toby Whittaker's file from the passenger seat, she held it under her armpit so her jacket would shield it from the rain. Hopping out, she locked the car and bolted down the pathway to her front door, her head down as she ran. As she neared the porch Jessica felt her foot connect with something and found herself falling forwards. Her first thought was to hold onto the file, which she managed to do at the expense of her forehead which crashed head-first into the doorframe.

Jessica's head felt fuzzy as she tried to turn to see exactly what had happened. Before she could swivel completely she heard the person's voice.

'Oh God, Jess, I'm so sorry.'

9

Caroline Bateman was Jessica's oldest friend and they had known each other for over fifteen years. They had travelled together, moved to Manchester at the same time and shared a flat before drifting apart and finally reconciling shortly before Caroline's wedding almost a year and a half ago.

Jessica stood, still feeling a little groggy from the fall, and turned to see Caroline also getting to her feet. She could see two large rucksacks on the ground, one of which she had fallen over. 'What are you . . . ?' Jessica started to ask but her friend's tear-streaked face stopped her.

'It's over . . .' Caroline was crying uncontrollably, a combination of the rain and her own sobs drenching her face. Jessica put down the file on the floor underneath the overhang of the porch and pulled the other woman into a hug.

'What's over?'

'Between me and Tom, I've left him.' Jessica had been a mixture of chief bridesmaid and 'father' of the bride at her friend's wedding to Thomas Bateman. She didn't know him that well but had met him on plenty of occasions. This was the first she had heard of any problems between them.

Jessica released her. 'Let's go inside, you're soaking.'

She picked up both of her friend's bags, wedged the file under her arm, and then led Caroline upstairs to her flat. The other woman seemed in a daze and followed without saying anything. After getting inside, Jessica took her friend into the kitchen and gave her a towel while putting the kettle on. Jessica rarely made hot drinks for herself but she knew Caroline was an avid tea-drinker. They sat opposite each other at the table, her friend half-heartedly drying her hair.

'Do you want to talk about it?' Jessica asked.

Caroline had stopped sobbing and put the towel on the table. 'You were right,' she said, not looking up.

'About what?'

'Do you remember when I got married and I asked if you thought I was on the rebound from Randall? I wanted you to say "no" but you just said you didn't know. The problem was that I knew, but I didn't want to admit it.'

Jessica could feel the burden of Randall and therefore Harry hanging over her even more heavily than before.

Caroline stared at a spot on the table. 'We've been arguing on and off for ages. He's always at work but it's not even that. I just don't love him. It's taken me all this time to admit it. We had a massive row this morning and I ended up telling him I hated him.'

'Oh, Caz . . .'

'It's okay. The thing is it feels awful but, at the same time, it feels like everything has been lifted too. I've known since before the wedding it wasn't going to work out but it's taken until now to say anything.'

Caroline made a noise that was somewhere between a

laugh and another sob before they were interrupted by the sound of the kettle boiling and clicking off. Jessica made two cups of tea, even though she wasn't that bothered, and put one down in front of her friend, hanging onto the other one to warm her hands.

'What are you going to do?' she asked.

Caroline picked up her own cup then looked at Jessica. 'I was hoping I could stay here for a while until I've figured it all out. I don't know yet.'

'That's fine but isn't it your flat you were sharing?'

'It was. I took out the mortgage but then added Tom onto it. It's both of ours but he doesn't have anywhere to go. I just want somewhere to stay for a bit until we've decided what to do.'

'Have you told him it's over?'

Caroline looked away again and moved the cup in front of her face, as if trying to hide behind it. 'Sort of.'

'You have to say something; it's not fair to him otherwise.'

'I wrote him a letter and left. I said I was coming here and asked him to leave me for a few days.'

Jessica offered a thin smile. 'I guess that's better than a text message.'

Caroline laughed a little. 'I feel like a right bitch.'

Jessica wanted to say something comforting but, after a short pause, the best she could manage was, 'Come on; let's find you some dry clothes.'

The rest of the evening was spent watching television and not saying much. Caroline clearly didn't want to talk any further, while Jessica still had the case on her mind.

She read through Toby Whittaker's file a couple of times, looking to see if there was anything she might have missed. As she read, she could only come up with more questions about how Toby and Isaac could be connected and whether the anonymous driver was the person who had taken both boys. She hadn't had a useable photograph to show to Harry, Kayla Hutchings or Daisy Peters. They would look back into Simon Hill and Ian Sturgess in the absence of any other leads, while also trying to identify the driver.

Managing the situation and not causing a panic was still the main priority but they were hoping someone who matched the driver's description would be reported missing by a concerned relative who didn't know what he was up to.

The two women shared Jessica's double bed and Caroline was up early the following day to get to work. She worked for an advertising agency in the city centre and was determined to keep some semblance of a normal life. Jessica hugged her as her friend left in the morning, before giving Toby Whittaker's file one last read.

Cole and Reynolds were going to see the start of the dig for a body at the site where they had found the clothes. Even though they didn't necessarily expect to find anything straight away, it was a significant symbolic act. Jessica was going to visit Toby's mother, Lucy. Someone had already told her they believed they had found clothes belonging to her son but, with the case on the brink of being reopened, someone had to formally speak to her – even if her memory was likely to be hazy fourteen years after the event.

Reynolds had organised things the previous evening and the plan was for Jessica to meet DS Louise Cornish at Lucy's house that morning. The two sergeants shared an office and, after a rocky start to their relationship, just about got on. It wasn't that they disliked each other; they just had nothing in common. While Jessica still lived day to day, Cornish was efficient and committed to her job, as well as being married with two children at school. The sergeant was currently involved with a case in which a string of burglaries seemed to be linked and would likely be given more involvement in the combined Hutchings and Whittaker case that so many officers were now being assigned to. Usually Jessica and Cornish would work separately but it was felt it would look better if two detectives more senior than constables visited Toby's mother, given the time that had passed.

Jessica drove to the estate where Lucy lived and saw Cornish's car parked around a hundred metres away from the house. She pulled in behind her colleague and saw the other sergeant getting out of her vehicle. Cornish was approaching fifty and had short dark hair which she swept away from her face. Despite being in her thirties and having equal rank, Jessica saw Louise as a grown-up compared to herself. The other woman was as smartly dressed as usual, with a crisp blouse and trouser suit. She greeted Jessica with a formal, 'Are you ready?' before leading the way towards Lucy's house.

The estate was a complete contrast to the areas where Daisy Peters and Kayla Hutchings lived. While those were filled with identically well-kept houses, Lucy lived in a place in which council houses alternated with housing association properties and a mixture of the two that had been sold off. It was a combination of bungalows, flats and semi-detached houses in various states of repair. Some buildings looked well-maintained but others had over-grown gardens and one house they passed was boarded up and covered with graffiti. In the distance Jessica could see two boys who should probably be at school playing foot-ball in the road. The two sergeants exchanged a knowing look as they approached the front door and DS Cornish rang the doorbell.

After a few moments a man answered. He was tall and well-built, large shoulders filling a rugby shirt. He intro-duced himself as Neil Martin and invited them into a cluttered hallway, apologising for the mess. Jessica noticed sets of children's shoes thrown to one side. There were also school photographs, which seemed recent, of two girls who were maybe five or six years old hanging in the living room. He offered them the sofa and said Lucy wouldn't be long before disappearing to make them a cup of tea. The two detectives were alone but Jessica couldn't think of anything to say. She scanned the walls, which were rela-tively clear aside from the photos.

She couldn't see anything of Toby.

Neither officer broke the uncomfortable silence before a woman walked into the room. She was thin with long black hair that was still wet and wearing tight jeans with a baggy jumper. Jessica and Cornish both stood but the woman Jessica assumed was Lucy waved her arm, then sat in an armchair opposite them. She didn't say anything but glared at the two officers and Jessica felt bound to start the conversation. 'Lucy Whittaker?'

'Not Whittaker, it's Martin now, I got remarried six months ago.'

That change wasn't in the information Jessica had but should have been checked by someone. Lucy sounded annoyed but Jessica didn't think it was because she had called her by the wrong name.

'Sorry,' Jessica said. 'I know someone spoke to you yesterday about what we found.'

'Toby's clothes?'

'Yes.'

'It took you long enough. I've been waiting for you to find him for fourteen years.'

Jessica knew she had to be careful about how she chose her words. 'Because of everything that's happened, we wanted to run through a couple of details with you,' she said.

The woman shrugged, shaking her head slightly. 'Is there anything you expect me to know now that I didn't then?'

Before anyone could respond, Neil returned with four mugs of tea on a tray. Jessica thought her consumption of hot liquids was beginning to hit ridiculous levels. Prior to becoming a detective, she didn't drink anything during the day other than water or lemonade. Now, if she was placed on a drip feeding Earl Grey directly into her system, it would probably provide only slightly more tea than she ended up drinking anyway.

After handing out the mugs, Neil sat on the armrest

next to his wife, resting a hand on her shoulder. Jessica glanced at the pictures of the school girls on the wall and wondered if they were Neil's or Lucy's from a previous relationship – or if the couple were in a long-term relationship but had only recently got married. Lucy didn't seem to be in a receptive enough mood to ask and Jessica was feeling under-prepared as Toby's mother continued to eye her suspiciously.

The two detectives ran through some of the basic details they already knew. Lucy and her former partner Dean moved from one side of the city to the other around a year after Toby disappeared. That created problems for their daughter Annabel, because she had to leave her friends. Lucy told them Annabel now lived and worked in London with her boyfriend and had minimal contact with them. Lucy's own relationship with Dean had broken down and they had gone their separate ways within three years of Toby disappearing.

Because of Lucy's hostility it took the two sergeants quite a while to get to the specifics. Cornish eventually established the two girls on the wall were called Olivia, who was six, and Natasha, who was a year younger. Neil and Lucy were natural parents to both of them and it sounded as if they had been in a relationship over some years.

Neil was still sitting on the armrest of his wife's chair, stroking her hair. Perhaps it was his presence but Lucy slowly began to open up. It was clear her memories from fourteen years ago were still vivid.

'Can you tell me about the football shirt Toby was wearing?' Jessica asked.

Lucy took a deep breath. 'His dad was a big City supporter. They used to go to games together. I would have to stop him wearing it when it was dirty because he'd keep it on all the time otherwise.'

'What about the area where he went missing? Did he play there often?'

'I guess. He used to pick up his football then go out with his friends. He'd usually be back by the time it got dark but . . .' Lucy didn't finish her sentence and Jessica didn't push it.

Neither Neil nor Lucy recognised Daisy Peters, although it was definitely a long shot that they would have done.

After forty minutes, Lucy stood. 'I'm going upstairs for a lie-down,' she said.

The two detectives had asked more or less everything they needed and the woman seemed sleepy. At some point she would likely be asked to look at the clothes to confirm they were from her son – although there were no real doubts they belonged to Toby because the football shirt sponsor, style and size matched what had been reported at the time and it was more a formality than anything.

Neil escorted his wife out of the room, then returned and sat fully in the seat himself. 'Don't worry about her; it's always hard at this time of year.'

Jessica nodded. 'I guess it would be coming up to Christmas and all.'

'It's not just that. It was the first week of December when Toby went missing. It always brings it back, especially when it gets dark so early.'

Jessica paused for a moment. She had read the file

through at least three times and the significance of the date of Toby's and now Isaac's disappearance had somehow passed her by. It was likely because the file was in such a jumbled mess but, now she thought about it, they would have gone missing on more or less the same date fourteen years apart. Neil didn't seem to notice Jessica's confusion and continued talking in a quieter voice. 'It's actually one of her good days today.'

'How do you mean?' Cornish asked.

Neil lowered his voice further, leaning forward. 'She drinks quite a bit. I've got used to it now we've been together for a few years. We used to have arguments about it but I kind of let it go now. I try to shield Olivia and Tasha from it.'

'What happened to Toby's father?' Jessica asked.

'Dean? He's living somewhere in Wales, just outside of Cardiff, I think.'

'Did he get remarried?'

'No but he does have a girlfriend and kids. He's a decent guy actually. I've met him a few times. I think that losing Toby pushed them apart and there was no going back. I guess it worked out all right for me.' Neil must have realised how this could be interpreted because he quickly corrected himself. 'Sorry, I don't mean I'm glad he was taken or anything like that . . .' He reached across to pick up the empty mugs. 'Can I get anything else for you?'

It was clearly a cue for them to leave.

Jessica and Cornish stood up together. 'No, but I'll leave you my card,' Jessica said. 'If anything comes up, just call me.'

Neil lowered his voice until it was almost a whisper. 'Do you think you'll find a body?'

Jessica looked into his eyes but couldn't figure out why he was asking. He had no way of knowing they were digging in the woods. She chose her words carefully. 'I'm not sure.'

Neil nodded. 'After all these years it would be nice for Lucy to get some closure.'

10

The two sergeants didn't exchange much more than small talk after leaving the house but Jessica could hear Neil Martin's words bouncing around her mind on her drive back to the station. Some people did things for revenge but, for others, it was because of the reward waiting for them at the end. Jessica felt uncomfortable sharing her thoughts with anyone else as she had next to no basis for them but Lucy's new husband had certainly gained from everything that had happened.

Back at the station, Jessica typed his name into their computer system to see if there was something from his past. Aside from a few driving offences, there was nothing but she used the Internet to search his name as well, although that didn't reveal much. She knew it was probably nothing but felt it was worth keeping Neil's name in mind.

After that she re-read the file relating to Toby's disappearance and checked in with Izzy, who was working with Rowlands on paperwork for a few other cases, while also trying to find time to track down Ian Sturgess and Simon Hill. What they knew was that neither man lived in the same house he had fourteen years ago. Jessica left them to it but asked them to call if they came up with anything.

She drove out to the woods where the dig had begun.

A row of cars and vans was parked close to the pathway she had walked along a few days earlier but the entire area looked different now it wasn't pouring with rain. The day hadn't really brightened up and the overcast skies were threatening but so far it had stayed dry. Jessica weaved her way along the trail, trying to avoid puddles that didn't seem as if they were going to disappear any time soon. She could hear noises in the distance and caught sight of activity just across the threshold of the woods as she crossed the stile.

As well as actual police officers, forensic archaeologists were used when there was a chance they could discover a buried body. Because some parts of the soil might need to be forensically examined, the whole process was incredibly slow-moving. Jessica could see Reynolds and Cole standing at the edge of the trees talking. Jason noticed her first. 'Are you all right?' he asked as Jessica approached.

'I want to feel like I'm doing something,' Jessica said.

Cole was wearing a heavy coat and pulled it tighter as a gust of wind blew across them. 'There's not much to do around here. We've spent most of the day watching.'

Jessica was wearing her suit and felt a chill breeze through it. She tried not to shiver. 'I know, I was wondering if either or both of you wanted to come for a drive?'

'Where to?' Cole asked.

'I wanted to drive the route – go to the land where Toby Whittaker was taken from. I brought the maps from the station, it's not far.'

Reynolds looked at their boss and stepped forward. 'I'll come, it's bloody freezing here.'

Cole smiled at the two of them. 'Aye, aye, leave the old man out in the cold.'

'You've got the big coat,' the inspector replied with a grin of his own.

'Maybe I'll just pull rank?' He looked back to Jessica. 'How was Toby Whittaker's mother?'

'She's remarried, it's Lucy Martin now. She was under-standably annoyed and upset. It helped clear things in my mind seeing her though.'

The other two detectives nodded as Jessica chose to keep quiet about Neil Martin's possibly ambiguous remarks. She wondered if Louise had the same opinion about him.

Jessica and Reynolds made their way back to her car after another light-hearted crack from their supervisor about leaving him at the mercy of the elements. She had printed some maps off the Internet which Jason picked up from the passenger seat as they got in.

'Do you know where we're going?' he asked.

'Sort of, have a look yourself. I read through the files and checked the location. I was trying to match the old descriptions with how it is now but it's hard to figure it all out online.'

Reynolds was scratching his chin, looking through the papers. 'It looks like there are buildings on this site now,' he said.

'That's exactly what I thought and why I wanted to look it over.'

Because of the intensity of the investigation, no one had actually had time to revisit the scenes from the old case. It was highly unlikely they would be able to find anything significant that had been missed so many years ago but, having read the file to the point of almost memorising it, there was something concerning Jessica.

With Reynolds navigating, they made their way through a series of lanes back towards the main road. It soon became clear that the wasteland where Toby Whittaker had last been seen was now anything but. An industrial park had been erected on the site, with a dozen enormous warehouses spread out on their own plots and various interconnecting roads that had been built recently. Jessica parked her car half on the pavement and the two officers got out before examining the map together.

Reynolds pointed at a dark green building that had a large empty yard at the front. A sign bore the name of an electronics manufacturer. 'I think he was taken from somewhere around there,' he said, before indicating towards the way they had already come. 'The main road would have always been there but this bit we've parked on is new.'

'Where are the woods in relation to here?' Jessica asked. The two of them looked at the map again and turned around so they were facing in the opposite direction. Reynolds held his arm out towards a second warehouse behind them but they both figured it out.

'We've had to drive the long way around but it's only going to be a few hundred yards over the back of there. Maybe half a mile at most?' Jessica suggested.

Reynolds nodded in agreement. 'What is the significance, do you think?' he asked. Jessica's tone had clearly indicated something was on her mind. She walked the few paces back to her car and leant on it facing where the woods would be. Reynolds joined her.

'Something has bugged me about that map ever since we found it,' she said. 'I think we can both agree that you'd only need a map if you didn't know where you were going, right?'

'Yes.'

'We don't know if our driver was looking to bury Isaac's body, collect the clothes or do something else – but it's logical to think that, whatever he was doing, he hadn't been to the site before.'

'Either that or he hadn't been in a while.'

Jessica nodded, turning to face her colleague. 'That might be true but I think this place is key. Say whoever took Toby all those years ago is our driver; maybe he was looking to bury Isaac in the same place he'd left the first boy? The problem is that all these buildings have now appeared. Because of that, he was going to bury Isaac in the closest place to where we're standing. Somewhere it was unlikely to be found. We never would have found the spot in the woods if he hadn't had that car crash.'

'So do you think Toby is buried somewhere around here?'

Jessica shrugged. 'I don't know. Perhaps. Maybe he is in the woods where we're digging? I just think it's a bit of a coincidence that we found one dead kidnapped child in a car with a map leading us to a place so close to where Toby went missing from.'

'Why would that person bury the clothes?'

'I don't know. Maybe it was some weird way of return-ing the clothes to Toby if that is where he was buried? Or

100

perhaps he's buried here like I said? It could explain the map. Let's say Toby was killed, and his body was buried somewhere around here before the warehouses went up. Whoever did it kept the clothes for whatever reason and then, fourteen years later, kidnapped Isaac. At some point those clothes were buried in the closest spot to where Toby was, maybe as a sick goodbye? When Isaac was killed too, that person was going to bury his body in the same place. It could explain why our guy needed the map because he made it when leaving the clothes after finding out all these warehouses had been built.'

Reynolds seemed slightly confused and not entirely convinced. He replied quietly. 'I'm not sure . . . you know we'll never be able to dig the whole area up around that warehouse just in case there's something there. We'd need proper evidence.'

Jessica agreed. 'I know. I'm just thinking out loud. We need to find out who the driver is but we're nowhere near getting that digital impression.'

'I've asked, so has Jack. They say they're having to guess the bone structure because there was so much damage done to the skull. It doesn't sound like it's very simple. They have other things on the go too. We've been checking missing persons reports every day with no luck. It's hard without a photo we can realistically use.'

Jessica knew he was right. She and Reynolds climbed into the car but instead of starting the engine, Jessica took out her phone and put it on loud-speaker mode before calling Izzy's desk phone. The constable answered on the second ring.

'Hello.'

'Hey, it's Jess. I'm with Jason. Have you got anything yet?'

'Bits, it's been Dave mainly to be honest. Hang on.' The line sounded muffled for a few moments as Jessica could hear someone moving around and then Rowlands's voice.

'Jess?'

'Yep, it's me. Have you got anything yet on those men from the Whittaker files?'

Rowlands cleared his throat before answering. 'Yes, first off, the teacher Ian Sturgess. Basically, we don't have a clue. He moved house within about six months of Toby going missing, then left the school he was working at around ten years ago. As far as we can tell he no longer teaches plus he moved from that other house he was living in. There doesn't seem to be anyone locally who matches the age and name, although we're still trying to check nationally.'

'What about the neighbour?'

'We're not sure, we might have something. We know Simon Hill moved quite a few years ago but his name is fairly common. We've had a few age matches and called around. We managed to eliminate all but one. We've got a phone number which no one is answering but we have an address too. We've been waiting for someone senior to get back.'

Jessica asked him for the address and Reynolds noted it down, along with the name of Simon's wife.

Traffic was heavy as they made their way out to Bury to the north of the city. By the time they arrived, the sun had almost set and street lights were beginning to flicker on. Any rain that might have been around had cleared, along with the clouds, but that created a larger problem with dew already beginning to set and an overnight frost an inevitability. Jessica didn't know exactly where she was going but Reynolds directed her to the road where they believed Simon Hill had lived and they eventually found the correct house. The lights were on inside the property.

The temperature had dropped significantly in the last hour. Jessica shivered as she got out of the vehicle and Reynolds asked her if she was okay. She waved away his concerns, wondering how the digging crew would fare the next day if the soil froze overnight.

She rang the doorbell of the house and instantly knew there was someone in, as she could hear what sounded like a vacuum cleaner switch off moments after the chime. The detectives waited as the door was opened by a short woman somewhere in her late forties. She had long grey hair and was wearing a knee-length skirt and blouse, as if she had been working in an office.

'Hello,' she said, a puzzled look on her face.

'Are you Paula Hill?' Jessica asked.

'Yes, who's asking?'

'I'm Detective Sergeant Jessica Daniel and this is my colleague, DI Reynolds.' Jessica glanced down at a pad of paper and read out the address of where Simon Hill lived fourteen years previously. 'Can I ask if you've ever lived at that house?' she added.

'Why do you need to know?'

'It's complicated at the moment.'

The woman shrugged. 'Yes, Simon and myself lived there for a few years but we moved ages ago. What's the problem?'

'We wanted to speak to Simon if that's all right?'

'He's not here.' Paula was beginning to sound annoyed.

'Where is he?' Jessica asked.

She was still looking down at the pad but almost dropped it as the woman replied. 'I don't know, I've not seen him in nearly a week.'

11

'You've not seen him?' It was a pretty pathetic response but Jessica blurted it out without thinking. If Simon Hill hadn't been seen in around a week, that would correspond with the time it had been since their nameless driver had crashed.

'Yeah. What's it got to do with you?' Paula, one hand on the front door, was now sounding defensive.

DI Reynolds spoke before Jessica could. 'Your husband's been missing for a week and you're not concerned?'

The woman seemed bemused. 'Who said he's missing?' The three people looked at each other wondering where the confusion had come from. Paula clocked that something had gone over her head, continuing: 'Why do you think he's missing?'

'Where is he if you haven't seen him in a week?' Jessica asked with a little more aggression than she intended.

'He works as a lorry driver . . . he's often away for a week or two at a time, then he's home. What's going on?'

With a little persuading the two detectives managed to get invited in. Jessica insisted the woman had nothing to worry about, they were simply looking into new leads for old cases. Paula didn't seem entirely convinced but answered all of their questions.

She and Simon had moved into a smaller house

because, at the time, they were struggling to pay the mortgage on the property they owned. Paula then got a job working as a clerk for a legal firm and they moved to the place they were now in. Everything from that point of view seemed perfectly fine but Jessica still wondered about the woman's husband. Paula reluctantly gave them the details of the haulage firm employing Simon and they left.

Before they got back to the station, Jessica tried calling the company but they were closed for the evening. They could have followed things through by trying to find the owner, then contacting him, but Simon Hill was still not a suspect in either case, and his wife's explanation for his whereabouts seemed legitimate.

It was an annoying end to an equally frustrating day as Jessica dropped Reynolds at Longsight. He put a hand on her shoulder and told her to get some sleep as he said goodbye. She thought she must look bad if someone she considered a friend was saying she needed to rest, even though it was barely early evening.

As she opened the door to her flat, it took Jessica a few moments to remember Caroline was staying. A delicious smell was drifting from the kitchen, something which had barely happened the entire time Jessica had lived there. Her usual diet consisted of either microwaved food or takeaways and the only thing she trusted herself to cook was toast and occasionally either a fried egg or some baked beans. Her friend Hugo had cooked for her a few times but, aside from that, her kitchen was mostly unused.

It was probably because Jason had implied she looked exhausted but Jessica spent large parts of the evening yawning and telling Caroline she wasn't tired. While she was doing that, she could clearly see her friend trying to act as if everything was normal. She told Jessica she had spoken to Thomas and told him she wanted to separate – and that she meant it. She didn't want to elaborate and Jessica thought there was probably more to the situation, although she wasn't going to push the point.

She made up her mind that evening to not bother calling Simon Hill's employers the following day; instead she would go there unannounced. She checked the address on the Internet and realised it was less than five minutes away from Rowlands's house. After clearing it with Reynolds, Jessica sent a text message to Rowlands to tell him she would pick him up in the morning because they had somewhere to go.

After another night's sleep broken by a nagging feeling she had missed something, as well as not being used to sharing a bed with anyone – even if it was her best friend – Jessica was already in a bad mood by the time the morning came. It didn't get any better when she left the flat only to find her car frozen under a thin coating of ice. She didn't fancy another trip upstairs to boil a kettle, so spent ten minutes hacking at the ice to clear the windscreen.

The icy roads made what Jessica thought would be a routine half-hour journey across the city a frustrating series of start-stop manoeuvres punctuated by an increasingly irate string of swear words. She even turned off the radio because every station seemed to be playing festive music, something else she couldn't stand. It wasn't that

Jessica disliked Christmas but she never decorated her house largely because she knew that it would still be up in the summer.

By the time she reached Rowlands's house, she definitely wasn't in the mood for his 'What took you so long?' greeting as he got into the car.

'Sod off. Why are you so cheery anyway?

'Am I?' Rowlands put his seatbelt on as Jessica pulled away.

'Were you out with Chloe last night?' she asked.

'I was actually.'

His upbeat tone of voice was infuriating. 'Oh, for f . . . Can you please stop being so nice?'

'What?'

'Just take the piss out of my car or something. All these pleasantries are weird.'

Dave smiled. 'Are you jealous?'

'No, I just preferred it when you were unhappy.' Jessica spoke with a laugh but realised there was a little truth in the statement too. Everyone seemed to be moving on, while she was stuck doing the same thing. In many ways she felt better about her own life when her close friends were stuck in the same rut as she was.

Before Rowlands could answer, Jessica tried to gloss over what she had said. 'What did you get up to last night then? And spare me the graphic details.'

'After I left the station, I picked Chloe up from judo . . .'

Jessica interrupted before Rowlands could finish his sentence. 'She does judo?'

'Yeah, she's a blue belt.'

Wondering if she had misheard, Jessica queried: 'A black belt?'

'No, blue, it's a few levels down.'

Jessica didn't have a clue what he was talking about. 'So she's a bit shit then?'

'Well, put it this way, she could kick my arse.'

'*I* could kick your arse.'

Rowlands sounded outraged but Jessica suspected he agreed with her. 'Whatever. Anyway, she could kick both of our arses, probably together.'

'So why isn't she a black belt?'

'Because you work your way up. You start at white, then there's yellow and a few others. Anyway, red's the highest.'

Jessica had no idea what she was talking about but didn't want to concede the point. 'What about black?'

'I don't know, I just know red's the highest.'

'So, hang on, if she's not even black – and that's not the highest – how hard can she be?'

'Why are we even talking about this? Do you want to fight her or something?'

'I don't know, maybe. Blue belt sounds a bit crap.'

Rowlands was laughing. 'Okay, well, I'll tell her that. Anyway, after I picked her up, we went to the Palace Theatre.'

Jessica indicated to pull around a stationary car and flashed her lights at a driver on the opposite side of the road who didn't give way. 'Oh, piss right off. *You* went to the theatre? This time last year you'd spend your evenings drinking cans of Carling and playing PlayStation games.'

'This time last year you kept taking the piss *because* I spent my evenings drinking cans of Carling and playing PlayStation games.'

'Exactly, that was way better. Right, what did you do after that?'

'I thought you didn't want to know that bit.'

Even more annoyed than she had been when she set off, Jessica ignored him and continued driving. Deep down she was pleased he was doing all right. The problem was deeper than that, she *was* a little jealous he seemed to be settling down. With everything that was going on in the case – as well as having Caroline staying at her flat – Jessica could feel an invisible burden upon her.

The haulage firm was based in an industrial area similar to the one Jessica had visited with Reynolds the day before. Tall metal gates surrounded the structure, with the company's name printed across a large blue sign at the front. Jessica parked the car and they steadily made their way across the icy pavement into the large courtyard. The tarmac was covered with a layer of frost, only broken by long patches of clear ground where lorries would have been waiting overnight. Slowly, Jessica and Rowlands walked across to a small structure not far from the main gate. It was barely bigger than a caravan but Jessica could see the grey brick building had wire mesh across each of its windows.

She knocked on the door and heard a gruff 'come in' from inside. As they entered, there was a man with his feet on a desk leaning back in a comfy-looking office chair. He peered around a newspaper with a curious look on his face, clearly not used to dealing with people who wore suits. Jessica would have guessed he was somewhere in his fifties. He had closely cropped grey hair with the same shade of stubble on his chin. Putting his feet on the floor, he dropped the paper on the desk but didn't stand. Behind him on the wall was a large map of the UK, along with four foil Santa faces. Loose strands of tinsel lined the front of the desk. In the corner was a small fake Christmas tree on a table with a string of fairy lights wrapped around it, blinking. As far as decorations went, Jessica thought it was about as half-hearted an effort as she would make.

'Who are you?' he asked in a broad local accent. Both detectives took out their identification and the man rolled his eyes. He spoke before either of them could say anything. 'Christ alive, haven't you got proper crimes to be solving? There are old ladies out there being attacked and you keep coming around here.'

Jessica had no idea what he was talking about but didn't want to let him know that. 'Why do you think we're here?'

He tutted, rolling his eyes again and pointing outside as if to emphasise his point. 'Look, I've checked all the tyres and they're fine. The log books are in order, the paperwork is all filed away. If you want to be pricks, then go ahead but you won't find anything.'

It was Jessica's turn to roll her eyes. 'Blimey, you're a smooth talker. I bet you're a massive hit with the ladies,' she said sarcastically.

The man leant forward in his chair. 'This is harassment. I know my rights.'

'Do you really?'

'Yeah, I know you can't keep coming around here.'

'I didn't know you were so up to date with all the various laws and legal rulings. Are you a part-time lawyer on the side? You know, lorry firm by day, legal advice by night?'

He was clearly confused, undermining his claim to knowing the law. 'What?'

Jessica couldn't be bothered winding him up any further so sat in the seat across the table from him. There was a plastic-looking plaque on the desk with the man's name and 'President' engraved underneath it. If it were made of an expensive metal, it would have been the type of thing found in a boardroom. Jessica pulled a face as she read the words. 'Right then, Mr President, believe it or not we're not here to check your vehicles' tyres, go over your paperwork or look at any of the log books. We simply want to ask about one of your employees.'

He clearly didn't believe her but acted as if he would play along. 'Who?'

'Simon Hill.'

'Si?'

'If that's what you call him.'

The man looked as if he was trying to figure out what the officers were really up to. 'What about him?'

'How long has he worked here?'

Jessica kept a steady gaze as he shook his head. 'I don't know, ages. Ten years? Probably longer.'

'What does he do?'

'He's just one of the drivers.'

Jessica nodded and could hear the gentle scratches of Rowlands making notes behind her. It wasn't that they wouldn't remember anything but it helped add to the pressure and Jessica was glad he had almost read her mind by taking his pad out.

'Where do you send him that means he needs to be away for weeks at a time?' she asked.

The man shunted his chair back a little, scrunching up his face. 'What are you on about?'

'It's a simple question – where does he drive for you?'

'What do you mean? I told you all the log books are in order.' He clearly thought the detectives were trying to pull some sort of trick.

Jessica sighed and leant forward. 'Just answer the question. Where does he drive for you?'

'I don't know, a few places, mainly up north. He goes to Scotland for some bits and usually goes via the northeast on the way up. Newcastle or Middlesbrough, places like that.'

'So he doesn't go on long journeys abroad or anywhere?'

'No, he's only part-time. I've only got one or two guys who go to Europe. Why, what's the problem?'

There was a short pause, where even Rowlands's pen had stopped writing. Jessica felt she had to check the information. 'So Simon Hill works for you but only part-time and he never does jobs that take longer than a day or two?'

'So what? I've got the paperwork to prove it.' He was being overly aggressive and Jessica took photocopies of the documents just to confirm it.

The owner may have had issues with the police over various things but everything he handed over seemed to be in order. The two detectives left the office and walked slowly back to Jessica's car.

Rowlands spoke first when they were far enough away from the office so there was no danger of being overheard. 'What was that?'

'I don't know but something's not right.'

'You think he was lying?'

'No, and I don't think Simon's wife was either. For whatever reason she thinks her husband spends weeks at a time on driving jobs.'

Rowlands said what they were both thinking. 'But if he's not working then where is he?' Jessica didn't reply but, given Hill's possible connection to Toby Whittaker fourteen years ago, finding out was their new priority. That was until her phone begun to ring, with DI Reynolds's name flashing up.

Jessica answered, wanting to tell him what they had found but not getting a chance before he started speaking. 'Jess, you remember that list of children you found at that allotment?'

She felt a shiver go down her spine unrelated to the weather. It was something she would never forget. 'Of course.'

'One of the other kids has gone missing.'

12

Lloyd Corless looked at the duvet cover but couldn't bring himself to smile.

'Come on Lloyd, it's football, I know you like football.'

Lloyd did enjoy football and he liked the players on the duvet cover – but he didn't understand why he couldn't go home. He had been told that his mum was hurt, and got in the car. He had expected to be taken to the hospital but instead they had come here. Lloyd asked why they couldn't go to the hospital but he was told that visiting hours were over. It didn't sound very convincing.

After the person had left, the boy lay on the bed, peering around the rest of the room. There were so many things that in normal circumstances he would have enjoyed. On the wall were posters of more footballers and of a few cartoons and films Lloyd liked. There was a PlayStation connected to a television in the corner and a satellite box underneath so he could watch whatever channel he wanted. There was even a brand-new computer game among the stack in the drawers. He had wanted to play for ages but his mum kept saying he was too young. Lloyd had thought things would be more fun without his mum around to nag at him, but was now feeling pretty worried about her.

One thing which did annoy him was that his phone

had been taken away. Lloyd had only been given it a few months ago and, even then, his mum told him to use it only for emergencies as he was too young to be using it for anything else. One of his friends had sent him some jokes he didn't really understand and he played a few games on it but, other than that, he had done as she had asked. If he still had it on him, he would use it to call his mum. She had said to only use it if he absolutely had to but surely, if she was in hospital, that would be allowed?

Lloyd got off the bed again and walked around the room. The carpet was soft on his bare feet and it did at least feel warm. He had never been in an attic before. When he had been told to head up the ladder into the roof, he hadn't known what to think. To find a whole room up here was astonishing – something he had never seen anywhere else. It was strange that he was tall enough to stretch up and touch the ceiling in some areas. It sloped up to a steep point where he definitely couldn't reach, which was where the window was, but it was all a new experience.

Before being left on his own he was told not to worry about his mum but something didn't seem quite right. He asked where his brother Marcus was but got no response.

The boy completed another lap of the room, running his hand around the wall and touching the low parts of the ceiling where he could reach. He wondered if he would be back with his mum in time for Christmas. He knew she was getting him the big robot which changed into a lorry from his favourite movie but didn't know what else he might end up with. He wondered if he would still get the robot if he had to stay in the attic.

As Lloyd continued to examine the room, he began to feel tired. It was still early, at least a few hours until his usual bedtime, but his eyes were feeling heavy. It was strange because he rarely felt sleepy. His mum would tell him it was bedtime but he would often spend a while playing games on his phone without her realising.

As his legs grew sluggish, Lloyd lay on the bed again. He had enjoyed his most-recent meal – sausage and chips was his favourite. His food had already been covered with a generous helping of tomato ketchup but he didn't really mind.

The boy stared at the window high above, trying to keep his eyes open. He could see the stars through the glass and thought about the PlayStation games in the drawer, wondering what he might get up to the next day. Earlier he had been told that he didn't have to go to school any longer. At first it sounded good but then he realised he wouldn't see his friends. He kept thinking about his mum, hoping his brother Marcus was looking after her.

As Lloyd's eyelids flickered and closed, he drifted into a sleep consumed with dreams of his mother lying in a hospital bed somewhere.

13

Jessica scowled at DCI Cole, making sure both DI Reynolds and DS Cornish were well aware of her displeasure. Just in case there were any doubts about her opinion, she clarified it as emphatically as she could.

'This is complete bollocks,' she said.

After speaking to Reynolds, Jessica had driven back to the station with Dave before joining a meeting with the inspector, the chief inspector and Cornish in the DCI's office.

Cole leant back in his office chair, exchanging a look with Reynolds across the desk. The two of them had worked with Jessica for long enough to know that tact wasn't one of her strong points. Louise would have no doubt figured that out for herself in the past eighteen months too.

The DCI looked back at Jessica. 'Whatever you might think, this is what's happening. The Serious Crime Division has a specialist kidnap unit and they have to deal with it.'

'But we're dealing with Isaac Hutchings's murder and skirting around Toby Whittaker's too. We found Lloyd Corless's name on a list that connects both those cases and now you're saying we can't be involved with investigating his disappearance?'

Cole spoke firmly. 'No, I'm saying it's not up to us to lead anything. If you and Jason want to talk to the victim's mother, we can have you work with the kidnap squad, but it's that or nothing.'

Jessica considered telling them again what she thought of the Serious Crime Division but instead said nothing. The chief inspector raised his eyebrows. 'What's going on with this lorry driver guy?'

Jessica took a deep breath. 'Simon Hill was a possible suspect in the disappearance of Toby Whittaker fourteen years ago. He was a neighbour at the time and the connection was tenuous. On the day Isaac Hutchings's body was found, Mr Hill went missing. His wife is under the impression he goes away for days, if not weeks, at a time on business, but his employer says that isn't true. Now that we have another kid missing, he's someone we need to find.'

Reynolds was nodding. 'Do we think he might be some sort of accomplice to whoever the driver is?'

Jessica wasn't sure. 'Maybe. The wife didn't recognise the driver's photo and we don't think Simon Hill has any connection to the allotments. That said, we know plot sixty-one was kept by someone calling themselves Glenn Harrison. We've been presuming that was an assumed name of the driver but if Simon Hill was an accomplice, it could be him.'

Cole spoke next. 'I've set the wheels in motion to see if we can get a warrant to check his bank records. You know what it's like, things will take a day or so – especially as we've not really got anything to connect him to Toby,

Isaac or Lloyd. We're trying the same with his mobile phone to see if he's made any recent calls. The superintendent says he'll get it done one way or the other but it's going to take time. Meanwhile, I've spent all morning talking to various people about Lloyd Corless. The SCD have been talking with our press department and there are all sorts of people involved.'

He looked at Jessica as if attempting to tell her that he was trying his best, despite her displeasure. 'The upshot is that this has to be a joint venture between us and the kidnap team. Lloyd's photo is already out with the media as there's a separate team taking calls on that. So far we've not told them about Lloyd's name being found on the same list as Isaac Hutchings's. The fact two boys have gone missing within a shortish period of time is going to cause panic enough.'

Cornish had been working on other cases but, with the latest disappearance, had been brought into the senior team briefings. 'What do you want me on?' she asked.

Cole checked the notes in front of him. 'I'm going to spend most of the day liaising with the super and the SCD. Jason will be going back over the Toby Whittaker case as well as working with the team at the dig site.' It was clear they had already spoken about it but the chief inspector looked at Reynolds. 'Things aren't going well today because the ground's frozen.' He looked at Cornish. 'Louise, I'd like you to take on the information relating to Isaac Hutchings and the car theft. I know we've hit a few dead ends but maybe a new set of eyes will give us something fresh?'

Louise was making notes, nodding.

The DCI raised his eyebrows and focused on the final member of the trio. 'Jess, the SCD have agreed we can work alongside them. You can visit Lloyd Corless's mother along with one of their officers. Leave me to sort out the warrants for Simon Hill's mobile phone and bank records but we don't have anything specific to link him to any of the disappearances yet, so let's find out as much as we can about Lloyd first.'

He leant forward and gave Jessica a Post-it note bearing the name and details of the SCD officer she would be working with.

The three detectives stood almost in unison. Jessica knew she was being given possibly the most trusted job because she would be looking into an active part of the case. She felt a little silly for her earlier outburst.

After getting Lloyd Corless's address, Jessica called Esther Warren, her contact from the kidnap squad, who told her that a support officer was with Lloyd's mother, who had already been interviewed once. The situation was unusual because a missing child wouldn't necessarily mean the kidnap squad had to be involved. Because Lloyd's name had been found on the same list as Isaac Hutchings's, usual procedure had been bypassed. The truth was no one actually knew if the boy *had* been taken.

The two women met a couple of hundred metres away from the Corless house, much as Jessica had done with Cornish a few days ago when they had visited Lucy Martin.

Esther was around Jessica's age, with long brown hair

and a smart grey suit. She got out of a large saloon car and shook Jessica's hand as they stood on the pavement. The frost from the morning had cleared but the cloudless skies meant it wasn't very warm. Esther invited Jessica into her car and they sat to exchange notes.

Jessica wouldn't have admitted it but she actually liked Esther, even from a first impression. There was something about the gentle, knowing smile on her face; the look of 'I know we have to work together, I hate it, you hate it, let's just be mates', that endeared her immediately.

'Have you read the case notes?' Esther asked when they were both settled.

Jessica nodded. 'I read through the initial interview notes. Lloyd went missing last night, yes?'

'Right. I think we're best going over all the details again with his mother. Have you ever spoken to a parent in a situation like this?'

'Not exactly . . .'

Esther was flicking through a file but looked up to catch Jessica's eye. 'All right, I'm sure you'll be fine. She'll be keen for people to be out there looking for her son. It's always the thing – everyone assumes that if there are two people talking, then that's two people who should be on the streets. No one ever realises that most people are found away from any of that. We'll have to keep her calm, let her know there are lots of officers on the case and that we're simply trying to get as much information as possible to help the police who are already searching.'

'Do you know who's already with her?' Jessica asked.

'One of her friends and a support officer.'

'Husband or boyfriend?'

Esther looked down at the papers. 'I don't know. There's definitely a father in the notes but I don't think they live together.'

Jessica was used to being the person in the know who took the lead but was happy to take instructions from the other woman. Her outburst from earlier felt even more misplaced.

'All right, let's go,' Jessica said.

The estate wasn't as new and clean as the one Isaac Hutchings had lived on – but was a step up from where Lucy Martin was living. Some of the homes were well looked after, with tidy front lawns and cars parked on driveways but Jessica saw an old washing machine dumped in the front of another. One of the first things she looked for when she was assessing an area was the number plates of the various cars. It was a fair indication that the estate encompassed all types of people, given that the vehicles varied from being less than a year old, to one or two that had been on the road for fifteen years or more. A few of the windows had tinsel pinned around them, others had fairy lights. Two properties side by side looked as if they were in a competition to see who could have the most elaborate Christmas decorations. One had a giant inflatable Santa fluttering in the breeze on the front driveway, the other had a tree almost as tall as the house decorated with any number of lights and hanging decorations. Esther noticed the houses too, muttering a 'tacky shite' under her breath that made Jessica like her even more.

The Corless house fell into the 'tidy' category. The front lawn had been paved over and had a small car parked on it that was a few years old. In the front window was a foil 'Happy Christmas' sign with a string of fairy lights ran around the inside frame.

Esther rang the bell and the door was opened by the support officer, who had been expecting them. The officer introduced both women to Rachel Corless, her friend Diane Briggs and Marcus Corless, Lloyd's older brother. Rachel was sitting next to her friend on a battered leather sofa with a hole in one of the arms. She didn't stand to welcome the officers but did tell Marcus he had to leave the room. The support officer took him upstairs, Jessica and Esther each sitting in an armchair facing the sofa. In the corner was a Christmas tree nearly as high as the room. It was decorated with more lights and various shiny objects.

Jessica watched Rachel closely but she didn't offer much emotion. She had short brown hair and was wearing a pair of jeans with a loose jumper. Perhaps unsurprisingly, she looked as if she hadn't had much sleep and, much like Kayla Hutchings, had dark bags under her eyes. Her expression was blank.

As they had entered the house, Jessica felt as if she was walking into a wall of heat, which only got worse as she entered the living room. The central heating seemed to be fully on and she could feel herself beginning to sweat. Everyone else seemed oblivious and Rachel was hugging her knees into her chest, as if she felt cold.

Diane did much of the initial talking but, after plenty

of reassurance from both detectives that officers were out looking for Lloyd, Rachel was finally persuaded to talk about what had happened the previous evening.

She spoke quietly, not looking up from the floor. 'Lloyd started at the comprehensive this year. It's the same school his brother Marcus goes to.'

She tailed off quickly and Diane picked up the conversation. 'I gave them a lift to school, along with my two. We both work at a factory a few miles away. Usually we try to arrange it so one of us is off, which lets us pick them up. Sometimes we're both off and we go to the park or something but, once a week or so, it just doesn't work out. Yesterday we were both down for late shifts. It's not really late but it means we don't finish until six o'clock.'

Esther was taking notes and looked up from her pad. 'Do they walk home when they can't be picked up?'

Rachel didn't look as if she was going to answer and it was Diane who spoke. 'Yes, it's only a mile or so away.'

Jessica had already read the initial report so knew the rest of the story. The officer who had taken the statements had spoken to Marcus Corless as well but there was no need to go over his details a second time. Other officers were visiting the school to take more statements.

Esther asked the next question. 'We know Lloyd left his final lesson with classmates and there is CCTV of him leaving the school,' she said. 'Do you know if he regularly walks home with his brother or other friends?'

Diane answered. 'I asked my two. They said they didn't see Lloyd after I'd dropped everyone off in the morning. They're all in different classes.'

She looked at her friend. For a few moments it didn't seem as if Rachel was going to speak but wearily the words came out. 'Marcus *knows* he is supposed to walk home with his brother when we aren't able to pick them up. Lloyd is on the small side for an eleven-year-old and Marcus has always been a protective older brother. He says he didn't see him after school. Someone said last night there was camera footage of Lloyd leaving school but I don't think the boys had a specific meeting place.'

That was exactly what Jessica had read. She had not seen the camera footage but knew Lloyd had been seen walking off-site around two minutes before his brother was seen waiting by the very same gates. No one knew why Lloyd had left without waiting, but talking to the number of students who might have seen him by those gates – or witnessed him leaving with someone – was going to take a while.

Jessica was feeling increasingly uncomfortable because of how hot the room was. As she was thinking about undoing a button on her shirt, Rachel put her feet down and sat up slightly straighter. 'I know who's got him.'

Jessica and Esther exchanged a confused look. 'Who?' Jessica asked.

'It's his dad, Adrian. I told the police last night and this morning they should be round his house to find him.'

Jessica had also read that in the report. Someone had visited Adrian Corless to let him know his son was missing but he insisted he hadn't seen the boy.

'What makes you say that?' Jessica added.

'We separated last year and have been arguing over custody ever since. The court ruled in my favour a month or so ago and he said then he wasn't going to leave it there.'

Jessica was surprised by how calm the woman was. It was clear she was in some sort of shock but Jessica would have expected her to be showing more emotion. As Rachel finished speaking, the Christmas-tree lights switched themselves on and began to blink. The woman barely acknowledged them, simply saying, 'They're on a timer.'

Esther finished writing and looked up. 'Can you think of anyone else, aside from your former husband, who could be involved?'

Rachel shook her head. 'Why did someone contact me last week making sure Lloyd was okay?'

Jessica knew it was because Lloyd's name had been on the list she had found at the allotment. So far that information had been kept within the force. Revealing its existence to the parents of the children involved would almost certainly result in one of them talking to the media. That was the type of thing which could cause very unhelpful headlines or, even worse, a panic about how safe children were in general. The added problem now was that if the media did find out about the list, the force would face massive criticism for not being open about it in the first place. Jessica knew she would be better placed to answer but also realised she had to be careful what to say.

'That was a reaction because of Isaac Hutchings's disappearance,' she said. 'We were checking in with parents who had children of a similar age.'

It was a half-truth but Jessica felt uncomfortable uttering the words. There were lots of follow-up questions that

127

could have been asked – especially as there was no obvious link from Isaac to Lloyd – but Rachel said nothing.

With not much else they could get from Rachel directly, Esther and Jessica exchanged a look and stood together. They said their goodbyes, left a business card and slowly walked back to their cars.

The sky was still clear of clouds but the temperature had dropped by a degree or two, a total contrast to the heat from Rachel's living room. Jessica knew dusk was imminent, children walking along the street in ones and twos on their way home from school. Across the road, the large Santa sitting on the driveway was now lit up, rippling in the breeze.

'What do you reckon?' Jessica asked.

'I reckon that Santa needs a bloody kitchen knife taking to it,' Esther replied. Jessica laughed, appreciating her response. 'Honestly? I don't know,' Esther added. 'I'm going to have to phone in and see what's going on at our end. No one knows who's supposed to be leading the investigation. From what I gather, our lot have been at the school today trying to see if anyone saw anything, while your lot have been checking cameras in the local area. Someone's going to have to sort out who's supposed to be doing what.'

'I want to see the ex-husband,' Jessica said. 'What are you going to do now?'

Esther looked at her watch. 'Oh, sod it, I'll phone in later. Let's go see this Adrian guy.'

'What did you make of Rachel?' Jessica asked.

'She's in shock, you never know what you're going to

walk into with these situations. Everyone thinks a mother's going to be shouting and demanding results, either that or running through the streets trying to find their kid. Some are like that but a lot act like Rachel – they don't know what to do with themselves. They sit at home and wait for the phone to ring or the doorbell to go. It's the right thing to do really.'

As they reached their cars, the lights flickered to life on the giant Christmas tree at the front of the house next to the one with the oversized Santa. The illuminations alternated colours, blinking on and off. 'Imagine living opposite that,' Esther said. 'I'd be out there with a chain-saw in the middle of the night.'

Jessica was partly in agreement. 'Nah, that's too obvious. The best thing to do is pour a litre or so of petrol in the pot it's in. The whole thing will wilt in a few days.'

Esther looked at Jessica with a big grin. 'Ooh, that is naughty. Aren't you a dark horse?'

Jessica shrugged. 'I've had thirty-odd years of people pissing me off – I'm full of ideas.'

'Well, I'll remember not to get on your wrong side then.'

Jessica unlocked her car. 'Do you know where we're going?'

'I have the address somewhere. I know it's not in Manchester – I think it's up Preston way. Just follow me.'

As Esther got into her vehicle, Jessica watched her in the rear-view mirror, wondering why she had made such a fuss earlier.

14

Jessica rarely took her battered old car on the motorway, largely because she didn't trust it not to break down. Esther's powerful new vehicle could have comfortably sped away from her at any point as they travelled in convoy along the M61.

Unmoving traffic was backed up in the opposite direction as they drove and the sun had disappeared below the horizon by the time Esther parked outside a house on the outskirts of Chorley. Jessica pulled in behind her, only realising how cold it was when she got out of the vehicle. She could feel chills on her exposed hands as she opened the door to get into Esther's car.

'It's bloody freezing out there,' she said.

Esther reached across to the back seat and picked up a file before handing it over. 'I'm in a bit of trouble,' she said. 'I'm supposed to be staying with the victim. I'm heading back after this.'

'Why did you want to come here?'

Esther flicked her long brown hair behind her head and scratched her ear. 'I'm not in *trouble* trouble. It looks like I'll be spending a decent amount of time with Rachel until her son is found . . . or not.' She hesitated over the last two words before continuing. 'I just want to meet Adrian.

We've only heard one side of the story but it would be nice to have both before going back.'

'Do we know if he's got a girlfriend?' Jessica asked.

Esther shook her head. 'There was nothing in the file so, if he does, she doesn't live with him.'

'That's what I thought.' Jessica opened the car door and again felt the bitter cold. 'Right, let's go.'

Because it was almost dark, it was a lot harder for Jessica to judge the type of area where Adrian Corless lived. His house didn't appear to have a number, leaving Jessica and Esther to check the adjacent terraced properties to make sure they were at the right one. Rather than a plastic double-glazed door, the house had an old-fashioned wooden one, the type Jessica knew officers loved to kick in if the opportunity ever arose. She'd had a conversation with a member of the tactical entry team a few months ago in the station's canteen where he told her new-style doors had taken most of the fun out of the job. 'It's one thing to use a battering ram on those things,' he said, 'but nothing feels quite as good as sticking your boot right through one of those old wooden ones.'

In the apparent absence of a doorbell, Esther thumped loudly on the frame. A light flickered inside and the door was opened by a tall thin man with round-rimmed glasses. He had a shaven head and was wearing a pair of jeans with a slim-fitting T-shirt. He looked the exact opposite of what Jessica might have expected. Perhaps because Rachel was so insistent he was somehow involved in Lloyd's disappearance, Jessica had a picture in her head of him being large and menacing. Instead, after seeing the man, she had two letters in her mind: 'IT'.

Longsight shared a computer specialist with another police station in the area. He was on call at all times and, in theory, would fix their terminals whenever there was a problem. His advice usually consisted of turning the machine off and then on again. If that didn't work, he seemed as lost as anyone else.

He also looked very similar to Adrian Corless.

Adrian didn't appear particularly happy but forced a smile after the two officers had introduced themselves. He had a weary look on his face as he said, 'He's not here', then waved both women inside.

There were few niceties as he led them into a sparsely filled living room, offering them each a chair at the dining table. The house didn't seem as if it had been decorated in the previous twenty years or so, with faded brown wallpaper and a patchy, thin dark blue carpet. Aside from an armchair facing a television and a round dining table with three hard wooden chairs, there was no other furniture in the room – not that there would have been much space in any case.

The two officers sat at the chairs by the table but, before they could say anything, Adrian pointed to the room behind them. 'Do you really think I'd take my son and keep him here? I know it's a complete shithole and I have to live here.'

Esther nodded gently towards Jessica, who spoke. 'Why are you assuming that's why we're here?'

'You've not found him, have you?' Adrian was still standing but his tone was hopeful and sounded sincere.

Jessica replied. 'I'm sorry, we haven't.'

The man's face fell. 'So you are here because you think I've got Lloyd?'

Jessica figured a direct question was as good as any. 'Have you?'

Adrian pointed to the rest of the room again. 'No. I told your people that yesterday when they came round. Why aren't you out there looking for him?'

'We are looking for him but we have to examine all possibilities.'

Adrian sighed, running a hand across his head before sitting on the third chair at the dining table. 'I know . . .' He paused, leaning back into the seat and continuing. 'Look, I know you're only doing your jobs but he's not here. He's just not. Whenever it's my day for visits, I try to take the boys out so they only have to sleep here. I don't know why Rach is saying I took him. Maybe it's to get back at me or perhaps she's just hoping.'

The two women exchanged a glance. Jessica believed him and it was clear from the look in Esther's eyes that she did too.

'Can you think of anyone who might want to take Lloyd?' Esther asked. Adrian shook his head. 'Your ex-wife says there was some sort of issue between you regarding access?' she added.

Adrian stood and let out another large sigh. 'It was my idea to break up, did she tell you that? She's just . . . she's a pain in the arse, I can't think of a better way to put it. When we got together, we had a good time. My mum didn't want us to get married but we did anyway – but that was partly because Rach was already pregnant. First Marcus and then Lloyd came along, we just got into a routine.'

He had started to pace and it felt like he was talking to himself. He wasn't facing the officers and Jessica thought he was speaking to clear his own thoughts as much as anything else. 'For the first few years, I used to work with computers,' he continued. 'I was the main IT guy for this call-centre place up in Preston. It was good money and we saved loads for the wedding and had all sorts of plans to get a bigger house and so on. Then the company was bought out and I lost my job. I got bits and bobs from the job centre but that's where it started to go wrong.'

Jessica resisted an urge to smile at the revelation Adrian had worked fixing computers. Even though it wasn't necessarily relevant to the case, she was interested in where the story was heading. She knew from experience that sometimes the best way to get information was to stay quiet and let them speak.

Adrian didn't seem to know if he wanted to sit or stand but ended up resting his hands on the back of the chair, leaning forward. He made eye contact with both women, then stood and started pacing again. 'Look, I'm not perfect but I love my kids, I just couldn't get on with *her* any more. We both knew things were shit, I was just the one who admitted it first. She wanted the boys and so did I. My solicitor told me there was no point in going to court because the mother always wins. I did it anyway, even though I ended up paying him most of my wages and now I have to live here. The judge ruled for her and I get them every other weekend.'

'When was the last time you saw Lloyd?' Esther asked.

'Weekend before last. I took him and Marcus to the football on Saturday. We were going to do something on the Sunday but it rained all day.'

'You've not seen either of them since?'

'No. I didn't even find out Lloyd had gone missing until one of you contacted me. Rach hasn't bothered to call. The worst thing is that she's telling you I've got our son and, while you're here talking to me, he could be any-where. I went out last night, driving around in case I saw him anywhere. Then I had to come back here and answer questions. Now I'm doing it again.'

'Where were you yesterday afternoon between 3 p.m. and 5 p.m.?' Esther asked. Both officers had already read the answer in the file.

'I was here, on my own, watching TV.'

As alibis went, Jessica knew it was pretty terrible.

Adrian stepped away from the table and stopped pacing, holding his arms out wide. 'There's not much else I can say, just look around for yourself and then, when you're done, can you please get on with finding my son?'

The two women looked at each other and then stood in unison. Adrian turned around and sat on the armchair, switching on the television with a remote control. Esther left the living room, entering a small kitchen with Jessica just behind her. Together they walked into the hallway and up the stairs. Looking around someone's house wouldn't usually be so straightforward but, as the man had offered, there was no reason to turn him down.

'Seems fairly genuine, doesn't he?' Jessica asked when

they reached the top and were out of his possible earshot.

'Yeah, he's got a point too. If Rachel's busy telling everyone who'll listen that he's involved when he's not, it's just taking resources away from where we should be looking.' Esther clearly believed what he had said, as much as Jessica did.

'Maybe the break-up was so bitter she can't see past it?' Jessica suggested.

'Probably, but it's pretty stupid if that's the case. I'll see what I can get out of her when I go back.'

'It might be just blind hope that Lloyd's safe and that Adrian's got him somewhere? At least then he wouldn't be hurt.'

There were three closed doors at the top of the stairs. 'Which one do you want?' Esther asked.

Jessica pointed to the one on their left. 'I'm guessing that's the Presidential suite, so I'll have that.'

Esther stepped towards the opening on their right as Jessica opened the door she had chosen. It certainly wasn't anything approaching 'Presidential' on the inside. There was no carpet or wooden flooring, leaving the floorboards exposed. A single bed with a metal frame was pushed up against the back wall, the only other furniture a single chest of drawers that was almost as big as the bed. Despite its size, clothes were strewn across the floor and, because of the adult-sized shirts, T-shirts and jeans in the pile, it seemed a fair assumption this was Adrian's own room. Jessica looked around the door, checking the ceiling for an attic but she couldn't see anything of note and turned back around.

The room Esther had gone into was the only one that seemed to be decorated. There was a new carpet on the floor, the walls unmarked and recently painted. Two single beds were made up with matching bedding and a portable television was on a chest of drawers.

As Jessica entered, Esther was staring out of the window. 'Anything?' Jessica asked.

'Nope, not too bad in here though, is it?'

'Much better than the other room. This must be where Marcus and Lloyd sleep when they stay over.'

The rest of the house offered very little of note. There was a large cupboard downstairs but no sign of a basement, attic, shed or any other place someone could obviously be hidden. Jessica hadn't expected there to be, given Adrian's openness in letting them explore. His name would be checked against storage units and, in the wake of everything that had happened, other places that could be rented such as allotments. Jessica didn't think they'd find anything. If the example of 'Glenn Harrison' had shown them anything, it was that using a fake name was easier than it should be.

Adrian was talking to someone on his mobile phone when the detectives re-entered after looking around. He stood and ended the call. 'I'm going back out in the car,' he said. 'He's got to be somewhere. One of my mates is coming over and we're going around all the parks. I tried calling Rach but she's not answering.'

Jessica wasn't sure if the two parents contacting each other was for the best considering the allegations Rachel had made but, considering neither of them were suspects, Adrian wasn't breaking any laws.

The two officers left and Jessica followed Esther to her car and climbed in. The other woman started the engine and switched on the heater. Esther phoned someone from her department and, even from the one half of the conversation she could hear, Jessica knew there was very little happening. When she hung up, Esther confirmed just that. 'It doesn't sound like there's much going on at our end,' she said. 'No one's seen anything on the CCTV cameras. None of the kids at the school saw Lloyd going off with anyone or getting into a car. I think someone at your end is going over the traffic cams but that will take a while. It looks like he just vanished into thin air.'

Jessica sighed. Now she had spoken to both parents, the disappearance felt real. In some cases, she had to work with hardly any leads. This was the opposite; they had so much to go on but none of it made sense. Every time they found an answer to a question, it left them with more questions.

After saying goodbye to Esther, Jessica drove home. Gritting lorries were charging along the main roads, spraying salt across a surface that already felt a little skiddy.

She was feeling tired as she pushed open her front door. Part of it was because she was leaving for work when it was still dark each morning, then returning after the sun had set too.

As she closed the door behind her, she heard Caroline calling out from the living room. 'You're home.' Her friend sounded far more excited than she expected on a cold December evening.

Jessica turned around to see Caroline bounding into the hallway, a large grin on her face. 'I've got a surprise for you,' she said.

Jessica was only in the mood for putting her feet up on the sofa, drinking a few glasses of wine, and falling asleep in front of some rubbish television show. She tried to smile and offer some enthusiasm. 'Go on . . .'

Caroline pointed towards the door. 'It's in there. Close your eyes though.'

'If I close my eyes, I'll walk straight into the wall.'

'It's only a few feet, come on.'

Jessica couldn't be bothered arguing, although she didn't trust herself not to collide with an inanimate object, so closed her eyes and allowed her friend to lead her into the living room. When she heard Caroline's excited 'ta-da', Jessica opened her eyes.

It wasn't a surprise she would have expected or hoped for.

In the room was a large Christmas tree, stretching from the floor to the ceiling. It had been meticulously decorated with lights and many other hanging objects she couldn't even begin to describe. Across the ceiling were lines of metallic-looking streamers.

'Well, what do you think?' Caroline asked, an even bigger grin on her face.

Jessica tried to hide her true feelings. 'It's . . . bright,' she said, with as much joy as she could muster. Lights on the tree were flashing on and off to a silent tune as her friend, seemingly oblivious to the lack of enthusiasm, walked around the room pointing at things.

It wasn't that Jessica disliked Christmas decorations, she just preferred things plain and simple. She didn't want to have to come home and see all sorts of things stuck to her ceiling, she merely wanted to enter her flat, take her shoes off, and flop in front of the television. Or, better yet, her bed.

As much as she had enjoyed living with Caroline in the past, it was quickly becoming clear that, with all the time that had passed, she now preferred living alone. She had become used to being able to come and go as she chose and not having to worry about someone else. She was happy for her friend to stay while she sorted herself out but, with the effort Caroline had put into decorating the room, Jessica was wondering how short-term the stay would be.

After assuring Caroline she liked the new-look living room, even though she didn't, Jessica said she had some work to do and spent the rest of the evening in the bedroom doing very little. She was feeling uncomfortable in her own flat but knew there was no way she would ever say anything about it.

Watching the evening news on the portable television in the bedroom, Jessica saw Lloyd's photo. He was getting more media attention than Isaac had, although there was a mention of the first boy's disappearance too. Jessica used her phone to check her emails and swapped a few text messages with Dave, who told her the dig that day had barely started before being abandoned because of the frozen state of the ground. Despite all their leads – and the unanswered questions – it seemed as if things were stalling, certainly in relation to Isaac.

Even though she was exhausted, Jessica again struggled to sleep. She lay on the bed next to Caroline staring at the red LED lights on the front of her alarm clock. The time was almost taunting her and Jessica found herself trying to work out the maximum number of hours she would be able to sleep before having to get up.

Jessica drifted in and out of sleep and woke for the final time when there was still half an hour before her alarm would go off. She lay staring at the clock when her phone began to ring. At first the sound confused her, as she wasn't completely sure if she was awake or dreaming. It was only when Caroline began to move that Jessica snapped out of her dreamlike state and reached out to answer. Reynolds's name flashed on the screen. Jessica hauled herself into a sitting position and pressed the button to answer.

'Morning,' she said wearily.

'Jess? You sound as if you've died overnight.'

'Maybe I have.'

He sounded apologetic. 'Er, yeah, sorry. It's Simon Hill, we've traced his mobile and know where he is. I'm on my way to pick you up.'

15

Jessica was only two minutes into the car journey with Reynolds when she realised his claim to know the location of Simon Hill was only partially true. The man's mobile had been traced to a mast in the Sunderland area, a minimum of three hours away. That meant they knew the rough location of where he *had* been – but certainly not where he was. Local officers had been dispatched to the area in the hope of finding him but Jessica and the inspector were travelling there in the hope of either discovering his location themselves, or questioning him if he had already been picked up.

As she yawned and stretched in the passenger's seat of Jason's car, Jessica knew there was no way she would be lucky enough to get through a tiresome journey, then find the person they were looking for sitting in an interview room waiting for them to arrive.

The first hour was spent driving in the dark. Jessica had always got on with Jason Reynolds but they had little in common. While she could have got through a journey and probably had a degree of enjoyment with Dave, Izzy or even Esther, whom she had only just met, Jessica simply had nothing to talk about with the inspector. By the time they hit Leeds, rush-hour traffic was beginning to peak and conditions had become more hazardous. There had been overnight snow which had turned to slush. Cars weaved dangerously across lanes around them as Jason drove steadily.

Jessica didn't know what to do with herself. With conversation at a minimum and the radio firmly set to a station she didn't think she would start listening to regularly for at least thirty years, Jessica tried to content herself with fiddling around on her phone. The presenter was in the middle of some spiel in which he was dedicating a string of songs from husbands to wives and vice versa. If Jessica was married, or had a boyfriend, she would have been very suspicious if her other half went through the whole procedure of contacting a radio station to ask for a special song. She wondered if it was that natural mistrust which stopped her from getting too involved with anyone.

As it was approaching the point where she didn't think she could take any more, they finally passed the sign indicating they were within Sunderland's city limits. Reynolds pulled over to the side of the road and made a phone call to whoever his local contact was. Jessica often thought Manchester was bleak but the grey overcast skies and string of run-down houses on their route in meant she took an instant dislike to the city. She knew it was irrational and more than likely based on how tired she was but she was already desperate to get in, find their man, then get out again.

Reynolds drove to a police station which had clearly been recently renovated. The red-bricked outside was clean with the glass on the door leading into reception completely transparent. To anyone else, it would have seemed normal but, at Longsight, although it had been tidied up a few years ago, the constant battering by the elements meant the exterior always looked dirty. The doors leading into the station were translucent at best with a film of brown and grey dirt coating the surface. Jessica had visited plenty of other stations both in and out of her district over the years and whenever something else was better kept than theirs, she instinctively wondered why other areas had money to spend while theirs seemingly didn't.

Inside, they were quickly ushered through to a ground-floor office occupied by a woman who introduced herself as DCI Linda Dawson. She was somewhere in her early fifties, with long hair dyed brown, with grey roots coming through. Smartly dressed in a grey suit, she welcomed both officers, offering them a seat. Jessica took an odd pleasure from seeing the woman's office wasn't as nice as Cole's. It was as irrational as her dislike of the city based on the weather but Jessica was feeling strangely parochial.

When they were settled, Dawson began to skim through the notes on a pad in front of her. 'Obviously you know Mr Hill's SIM card was traced to a mobile phone mast,' she said. 'We've been in contact with the network operator but there haven't been any further hits so far. Has either of you ever been up here before?'

Jessica and Reynolds shook their heads.

'Okay, his signal was traced to somewhere in the Penny-well area, which is a mile or so away. I know your DCI spoke to someone at the phone company. I've been in contact with him all morning. By all accounts, they can trace the call to within a few hundred yards. There is a row of shops not far from there which seems like a good place to start. We've had officers going door-to-door with the man's photo. So far, nothing's come back but I figured I can take you out there and we can have a look around for ourselves.'

With little else they could do, it seemed as good a plan as any. Jessica and Reynolds followed DCI Dawson and a constable, who went in a separate vehicle. They stopped at the back of a supermarket car park where frost still sat on the ground in an area in shade. The sun had begun to appear through the clouds but that was making the day even colder. Jessica was glad she had remembered a coat that morning and picked it up from the back seat of the car. The two local officers removed heavy coats from the boot of their vehicle and put them on before the four of them walked towards the supermarket. Across the road, Jessica could see a row of red-brick semi-detached houses with black slate roofs. The supermarket was close to a row of shops and all of the local buildings were similar in appearance.

DCI Dawson stopped when they were a few feet away from the shops. As the other officers moved towards her, she spoke quietly to ensure it was just them who heard. 'It's a very densely populated area around here,' she said. 'There are literally thousands of houses all within a small radius and a few flats too. That means your man, assuming he wasn't just passing through, would find it very easy to hide – if that's what he's trying to do.'

Jessica took three copies of the same photo of Simon Hill out of her pocket. They had been printed on standard paper from the station and were grainy to start with. The quality looked even worse because of the creases from how she had folded them but Jessica flattened them against her stomach, handing a copy to each of the other officers. She had emailed the photo to her phone and was happy to use that herself.

From the headshot, Simon Hill had a shaven head and, judging by his double chin, was quite overweight. Jessica looked around at the handful of people walking past the shops and realised an instant problem that everyone was wrapped up in a mixture of jackets, hats, scarves and gloves. Everyone looked overweight when you took into account the large padded coats being worn, plus anyone who had a shaven head would most likely be wearing a hat, or a hood.

It was always going to be a long shot to go looking for the man based on the location of a phone call but the odds of finding him were now even lower.

Dawson walked them past the shops until they reached the supermarket's entrance. 'Has anyone been in the shops showing that photo around?' Jessica asked.

The chief inspector was clearly trying to hide how cold she felt but Jessica saw the other woman's face twitch as she suppressed a shiver. 'Yes,' Dawson answered. 'This was the first place we started. Without getting a bus into the centre, this is where most people who live around here would see each other.' She pointed towards the super-market. 'There are CCTV cameras inside and out, which we've requested images from but we haven't been given the okay yet. We could go for a warrant but everything's happened really quickly and, to be honest, we don't know if your man's been in. The mobile signal was just from somewhere around here.'

Jessica caught Reynolds's eye and gave him her best 'We're wasting our time' look. It wasn't quite as good as her 'Stop being such a dick' face, or her 'Sit down and shut up' expression, both of which she had perfected through working with Rowlands, but it did appear to be successful.

'I think we might go for a drive around the area,' the inspector said to Linda. 'While your team are out and about, I'm not sure there's much we can do. At least this way we'll get a feel for the place.' Jessica thought he could have added, 'And it's bloody freezing out here', but he didn't.

Dawson nodded, clearly thinking something similar. She assured them she would call if anything came up.

Back in the car, Reynolds rang Cole and told him there was little going on. It was a similar story in Manchester, with frozen ground again impeding the dig in the woods where Toby Whittaker's clothes had been found and no sign of Lloyd Corless. Jessica sent a text message to Esther asking how Rachel Corless was faring but the reply simply told her the boy's mother was still quiet and borderline uncooperative. It was becoming clear everything further south had stalled.

'What do you reckon?' Jessica asked.

Reynolds sounded resigned. 'Between you and me, officers are being moved back to other jobs or the districts they came from. Someone up top isn't happy with our progress.'

It was the first Jessica had heard of it. She stumbled over her words, trying to hide at least part of her annoyance. 'But we've got so many things going on. How are we going to get through it all with less people?'

'I think that's the problem. Jack told me he's been trying to hold things off for a day or two but it goes way above him and the super. There's the investigation into Isaac Hutchings's murder, everyone's expecting Toby Whittaker's body to be found in those woods at any moment, then there's the allotment, the list of kids, whoever Glenn Harrison is, the driver of the stolen crashed car and now Lloyd Corless. Plus everything in between, including Simon Hill. Jack's tried to keep it all to himself but I've heard whispers people upstairs are unhappy with a lack of focus and so on.'

'It's not his fault, is it?'

'I agree but there's not much we can do. I don't think anyone knew how big this would get. One minute it was a missing child, the next we're trying to run multiple cases. It was always going to be too big for a DCI.'

'So who's going to run things?'

'Chief super I guess.'

Jessica wasn't convinced. 'Why would he be taking people off the case?'

'Probably just to focus on finding Lloyd. I guess if we can find him, it might lead us on a trail back to everything else.'

'Or finding out what happened with Toby or Isaac could lead us to Lloyd?'

'Maybe, but it's not got us far yet, has it?'

'If we find Simon Hill with Lloyd it will have.'

Reynolds didn't reply but his silence said more than words. Jessica herself had thought about the trail that had brought them to a freezing supermarket car park in Sunderland. Aside from the fact Simon Hill had been involved in a petty dispute fourteen years previously – and that he had lied to his wife about what he was up to – there wasn't anything to link him to Lloyd or Isaac's disappearance.

'Let's find somewhere to eat,' Jessica said. 'Maybe we'll strike lucky and our man will come in for a fry-up with Lloyd in tow.'

The cafe they ate in was as greasy as Jessica could have hoped for. Reynolds munched his way through a bacon sandwich while she had a full English breakfast, although the lack of black pudding was a cause of concern.

'I don't know how you eat that,' the inspector said as Jessica wiped up an egg yolk with some fried bread.

'What?'

'All that fat. Even looking at your plate makes me feel like I'm putting on weight.' He held up the remains of his sandwich. 'My wife would be annoyed if she knew I'd eaten this.'

Jessica grinned as she finished off a hash brown. 'This is a bit of a treat. Usually I just eat pot noodles and toast.'

'Together?'

'Of course not . . . although that's not a bad idea. It's just fair to say that I definitely wasn't a gourmet chef in a previous life.'

'What do you reckon you were?'

'Oh, I don't know. You see all those dickheads on TV

and everyone reckons they were some Roman emperor or a Greek goddess or something. I was probably a chimney sweep or something else not very interesting.'

'Ever the dreamer, then?'

'You know me.'

Jessica finished off the last of her sausage and looked at the clock on the wall above her colleague's head. Because of the journey, the time spent in DCI Dawson's office, plus eating, Jessica had lost track of the day. As she thought about the fact it would be dark within an hour and a half or so, she had an idea, taking out her phone and checking for further directions.

'Are you ready?' she asked.

'I finished ten minutes ago.'

'I've got an idea.' Jason rolled his eyes and leant back in his seat. 'What?' Jessica added indignantly.

'I know what your ideas are like. Whenever you've come to me with an idea before it usually ends up with me doing something I don't particularly want to.'

'This one's simple. There's a school a few hundred yards away from that supermarket. All the kids will be leaving in a few minutes. Let's go and watch.'

Reynolds narrowed his eyes and, for a moment, Jessica thought he was going to say no but instead he started fumbling in his pockets before pulling out his car keys.

They parked around fifty metres from the school gates, just outside of some zigzag yellow lines where people were not supposed to stop. Reynolds had one of the pictures of Simon Hill on his lap, Jessica had the photo on her phone.

She knew it was desperation but then so was the journey. There was no particular reason to believe the man they were looking for might be around but, as it was the only school in the area and they thought he might have some connection to either Isaac Hutchings or Lloyd Corless, it was at least worth a go.

Jessica was trying to watch as many of the adults as she could, looking for someone who could possibly be Simon Hill. As they were observing, a black 4x4 skidded to a halt on the zigzag lines, blocking their view. Reynolds motioned as if he was going to move but Jessica opened the car door. 'I'll handle it.'

Jessica marched around the vehicle and hammered on the driver's side door. A woman with long blonde hair peered out of the window towards Jessica. She looked half-annoyed, half-perplexed. In case she was in any doubt about what the problem was, Jessica bashed the door with her fist a second time. The window slid down with an electric hum, any trace of confusion on the woman's face replaced by absolute fury. 'What the fuck do you think you're doing?' she said angrily in a sharp north-east accent.

'I'm telling you to move your car. Now.'

The driver screwed up her face even further. 'I'll have ya if you touch my car again.' The woman was clearly fuming but something about her pristine appearance told Jessica she'd never been in anything that could even loosely be described as a fight. For a few moments, Jessica thought about banging on the door again just to see what the woman would do. Instead, she reached into her pocket and took out her identification, holding it up for the woman to see.

Jessica smiled just to antagonise the woman even further. 'Tell you what, you take your shit hair extensions and stuck-on nails and piss off and I'll pretend you didn't just threaten a police officer.'

The driver stared at Jessica but re-started the engine and pulled away just as students began to spill out of the school gates in small groups. Jessica banged on the back of the vehicle as it moved, before turning to face Reynolds in his car. As she swivelled, her eyes were drawn to a small blue hatchback parked on the opposite side of the road a little behind the inspector's car. A man in a red coat was roughly hauling a boy onto the back seat before slamming the door. As he turned around, Jessica got a clear view of the person's face.

Simon Hill stared down the road before quickly stepping around the front of the vehicle and opening the driver's door.

16

For a moment Jessica felt fixed to the spot, focusing on Simon Hill's face. She didn't need to check the pictures on her phone to know he was the person they had come to look for. It was only when he turned away that she fully took in the fact she had just seen him force a child into the back seat and slam the door. Jessica sprinted across the road but had forgotten about the conditions. As she reached the kerb on the opposite side, she skidded across a patch of frost, cannoning onto the pavement with a painful crunch.

For a moment she could just hear ringing in her ears but it was soon replaced by people laughing.

Children laughing.

Jessica rolled over and could see a handful of kids in school uniform standing nearby. A few of them looked concerned but some of the older ones were giggling. Jessica stood awkwardly, wincing as a jolt of pain shot from her hip. The palms of her hands felt raw but she wasn't concerned as she looked frantically towards where the blue car had been.

It wasn't there.

Jessica glanced quickly from side to side. Everything had happened in a matter of seconds, so it couldn't have gone far. She stepped gingerly back off the kerb, still looking around before finally seeing a blue shape moving away from her in the opposite direction to which Reynolds's car was facing. Jessica shook her head to try to clear it.

'What happened to you?' a man's voice said.

Jessica hadn't realised it but Reynolds was standing next to her with a hand on her upper arm.

'It's Hill, he's in a blue car.' Jessica pointed to where she thought he had headed. The inspector started to say something but instead helped her hobble across the road into the passenger seat. He did a three-point turn and began to drive in the direction Jessica had indicated.

'Did you see him turn off anywhere?' he asked. Jessica mumbled a 'no' while trying to pull her phone out of her pocket. She was relieved to see she hadn't fallen on it and dialled DCI Dawson's phone number before passing on what had happened.

The entire time from her falling to Reynolds turning his car around was likely less than a minute, so Simon Hill couldn't have gone far. Jason reached the end of the road as Jessica was still talking and turned right, back towards the supermarket.

Now she was sitting, Jessica was beginning to feel the pain through her body. She tried to ignore it as she ended the call.

'Linda says the message will go out to all officers to look for a blue hatchback,' Jessica said. 'More cars will be on their way. She reckons the estate is so much of a maze, there's no way he'd be able to make the main road without being seen by one of the officers on duty.'

'He forced a kid onto the back seat?'

Jessica hadn't told the inspector that but he had overheard her half of the phone conversation.

'It looked like it, I only saw the end. There was some sort of struggle and he just pushed the kid in and slammed the door.'

'Did you see if it was a boy or girl?'

Jessica winced uncomfortably and wiped grit from her hands, letting it fall into the foot well. The skin on her hands had been scraped off and her palms were red and painful. 'Boy, I think. Maybe nine or ten?'

Reynolds took his eyes from the road for a moment, looking sideways at Jessica. 'Are you all right?'

'Yeah, I just slid on the frost and crashed over the kerb. If I wasn't so concerned about that blue car I probably would have abducted one of those little shits who were laughing at me.'

Despite the seriousness of the moment, Jason laughed. 'It was pretty funny. One minute you were standing there arguing, the next you'd taken off across the street. Then I saw you sprawling across the pavement. There's bound to be a CCTV camera somewhere . . .'

Jessica chose to ignore him. 'Are we heading back to the shops?'

'Yes, these are about the only roads I know around here and that's only because it's where we came from.'

Jessica clung onto her mobile phone willing it to ring with news the car they were after had been stopped. She looked from side to side, hoping to see something. As the inspector turned back onto the road that circled around the supermarket and shops, Jessica banged the dashboard without thinking.

'Stop.'

Reynolds screeched the car to a halt, much to the annoyance of the driver behind, who beeped his horn. Jessica opened the passenger door and dashed as quickly as she could given the pain in her knees and hip across someone's front garden. This time, she was careful to keep an eye on where she was going, hopping across a flower bed and skirting around another patch of frost. Wind whipped around her, blowing her hair into her face, but Jessica kept moving, sliding around a bollard which separated the main through-road from a cul-de-sac.

As she neared her target, she felt her knee almost give way. Jessica gritted her teeth and kept moving before almost collapsing onto the boot of the blue hatchback she had seen at the school. It was parked on a driveway. Using the car to pull herself back into a standing position, Jessica peered through the rear window but there was no one there.

'Oi, what do you think you're doing?' The voice was loud and angry, carrying on the wind in Jessica's direction. She leant back onto the vehicle, letting it take her weight as she turned to see Simon Hill charging down the driveway towards her. He was still wearing the red jacket he'd had on when she had seen him outside the school but his face was full of annoyance. 'Get off it,' he added, pointing an angry finger towards Jessica.

She stood up straight, the man only a few feet from her. 'Are you Simon Hill?'

He stopped, taking a half-step backwards, all of a sudden confused. 'Who are you?' he asked.

'I'm from Greater Manchester CID and you are under arrest.'

Jessica could tell Izzy was trying not to smile. 'Go on,' she said. 'You can laugh, everyone else has.'

The constable's lips crinkled upwards into a grin. 'So all in all, you didn't have the best of times in the north-east?'

Jessica was sitting in the Longsight canteen picking at a sausage. She rarely risked eating at work, having been warned off the food early into her career by Jason when he was a sergeant. He was very much in her bad books at that exact moment and Jessica's dining choice was a fairly pitiful act of rebellion. 'You could say that. At least we got something of a result from it all.'

'Let's hear it, then.'

'Haven't you already heard the story from everyone around the station?'

Jessica was still annoyed at how quickly Reynolds's version of events had spread.

'Yeah, but I want to hear yours.' Izzy picked up her mug of tea and took a gulp before shuffling forward in her chair. Jessica thought it was as if the constable was settling herself down for story time. She finished off the sausage and pushed the plate away, wondering if she would regret eating the station's food later in the day.

'All right, fine. What do you want to hear first?'

'Definitely the falling over.'

Jessica shook her head slightly. 'It was basically just

157

that. I saw Simon Hill, went running across the road, slid on some icy-frosty stuff and fell onto the pavement.' She held her palms up for the other woman to see. Diamond did purse her lips into an 'ooh' shape but her eyes told a different story of hilarity.

'It's way funnier when Jason tells it,' she said. 'Is it true there were kids laughing?'

'Yes, little bastards.'

'Jason reckons he's going to contact someone up there to see if there's camera footage anywhere.'

'There better not be.'

Izzy was clearly trying to hold it together, flicking her red hair over the back of her ears. 'All right, so what happened when you did catch up with that Hill bloke?'

'I was in the process of arresting him when this kid came out of the house and said, "Dad". I knew then we were in the shite. The child I'd seen him bundling into the back seat of the car was his own. It took some getting out of him but when he realised there could be much more serious charges to face, he came clean about having two lives. Not only is he married to Paula down here, he's got another wife with children up there.'

'So the lorry-driver thing is all just an act?'

'Sort of. He does it part-time which allowed him to tell both women he was off on business. He could get away with spending a couple of weeks at a time with one wife, then disappear back to the other.'

'Christ, that sounds like hard work.'

'I know. All that and he'll be charged with polygamy at some point in the next week. I don't know what is worse –

that, or having to admit what he's been doing to both of his wives. They'll chop his boll . . . bits off.' Jessica toned down her language as a few uniformed officers walked by. It wasn't something she'd usually care about but, with the story of her falling over flying around the station, she was trying to keep a low profile.

'How long has he been doing all that?' Izzy asked.

'Fifteen years or so. When I spoke to Harry, he said there was something not quite right about the guy and I guess it was this.'

'Rather him than me. I find it exhausting just having one husband and . . .' The constable tailed off but held a hand just below her stomach.

'Are you telling people yet?' Jessica asked.

Izzy leant in, whispering, 'About my peanut baby? Soon.'

'At least I've not blabbed it yet. How's it all going?'

'Not too bad. We're just beginning to get things sorted. There's so much to think about. There's all the obvious stuff like a cot and that kind of thing but we need a child seat ready to take him from the hospital back to our house because you're not supposed to just carry them. I only found that out yesterday.'

'Did you see that story in the news about the woman who had a twelve-pound baby girl the other week?'

Izzy pulled a face. 'Why would you tell me that?'

Jessica held a hand up to concede she had said something stupid. 'Sorry, I wasn't thinking. I'm sure yours will be a normal size.' Before making things worse, she hastily tried to change the subject. 'What happened around here yesterday while I was up north being an idiot?'

'The chief super was in. He was upstairs for most of the day with Jack and Superintendent Aylesbury. Everyone was shitting themselves about looking smart and all that kind of stuff.'

Jessica knew DSI William Aylesbury from when he was a DCI at the station. He had been her boss but, since his promotion which meant he oversaw the wider area instead of just their station, she rarely saw him. Their relationship had been awkward at first but she had come to respect him before his elevation.

'Have you ever met the chief super properly?' Jessica asked.

'No, I didn't even see him yesterday. It was just what people were saying. You?'

'I've met him a couple of times. There was some function thing last year. I'm always worried when senior people know my name.'

Izzy grinned. 'He knows who you are?'

'Yeah, the DSI probably told him because they'd worked together but it's like being at school. The headmaster only knows who you are if you're a really good student, or really naughty. I'm definitely not one of the really good ones, so I dread to think what he's heard.'

'I wonder if he's heard about you falling over?'

'If he has, I'm going to start my own internal investigation into information leaks.'

Izzy laughed again. 'What time did you get back?'

'About one in the morning, then back in first thing today for a meeting. From what was said, things will pretty much carry on as normal for us. Orders will be coming from on high through the DCI though.'

'So what's going on at the moment?'

Jessica leant closer to her colleague, lowering her voice. She wasn't uncomfortable telling the constable information but didn't want to be overheard just in case. 'Basically, not much. There's no sign of Lloyd. Nothing's come back from the students at the school, the CCTV cameras didn't see anything and the traffic cameras are still being viewed, although no one's really expecting much from those. The dig at the woods is crawling along because of the weather but they've not come across anything yet. They're looking for remains of Toby Whittaker but I'm not sure they'll find him. Meanwhile, the allotment lead, along with the hunt for the Glenn Harrison guy, has turned into a bit of a dead end. The most important thing is to find Isaac's murderer but that's going nowhere either. How have you been doing with that Ian Sturgess teacher guy?'

Izzy finished off the contents of her mug and put it on the table. 'I've not really had time. First we had people coming in to help with the workload, then they were taken away. I've been working on other things. All I know is that there's no one called "Ian Sturgess" who matches the age group we've been looking for. I can't find any teacher in the country called that either. It's like he vanished.'

'Just like Lloyd . . .'

Jessica spoke without really thinking. After the experience they'd had chasing one loose end with Simon Hill, it seemed unlikely her bosses would let her work on another. 'How busy are you at the moment?' she added.

Izzy smiled. 'About sixty per cent of my time is being taken up with telling people about you falling over. Other than that, I really am snowed under.'

'It's nice to know I have the support of my colleagues,' Jessica said sarcastically. 'Is there any chance you can keep hammering away at this Ian Sturgess guy when you get some time? Don't do anything that could get you in trouble but, if you find anything, let me know.'

'Do you think he's important?'

'I don't know, probably not. I think mobilising most of Sunderland's police force to find a guy guilty of polygamy has probably soured things a little when it comes to following these old leads. The word from this morning's meeting was to focus on finding Lloyd and we can come back to the rest.'

'Aren't we doing that anyway?'

'Yeah, but it's all about appearances. Kid goes missing and the press want pictures of police officers trawling through fields or walking the streets. It looks better than a load of people sat at desks . . .'

'. . . or falling on their arses,' Izzy interrupted.

'Yeah, or falling on their arses. Either way, it's all about looking good at the moment. We could do with people here to follow everything up but instead they're going around in circles hoping for the best. I think they're worried about news of that list of children getting out too. There wasn't much else we could do other than tell the parents to be vigilant – which we did – but if it gets leaked we had Lloyd's name before he was taken, everyone's in trouble.'

'What have they got you on?'

Jessica allowed herself to smile slightly. 'I'm sort of being allowed to do my own thing. As long as I stay broadly within the remit of looking for Lloyd, I've got a bit of freedom. It's all because the kidnap squad are also involved. Neither side wants to hand over jurisdiction to the other. They've got an officer staying with the mother while we're doing the legwork. Like most things, I think it's all about budgets. If we give way to them or the other way around, it could seem like we're passing on responsibility, meaning the other side needs more money. You know what it's like, everyone's really laid back until money comes into it, then they just scrabble for whatever they can get.'

'Have you met the kidnap person?'

'Yeah, she's called Esther. She's pretty sound. We've got each other's numbers. I don't think she's too arsed about office politics either.'

Izzy sighed and checked her watch. 'I'm going to head back. Are you okay?'

Jessica looked at her scuffed palms. Her hip had been stiff that morning but considering how hard she had hit the concrete, she was actually feeling all right. 'I'm fine, just a couple of grazes.'

'I meant, are *you* okay?'

Jessica knew her colleague was talking about her state of mind. They had become good friends and, although it wasn't something she would talk about, Izzy knew Jessica could become emotionally involved in cases.

'I've just . . .' Jessica paused to sigh. '. . . I've just never known a case with so many leads before. Usually if you had half of what we've got, we'd have someone charged in the cells and be moving on. Here, there's almost too much: Toby, Isaac, Lloyd, the woods, the allotment, the driver, "Glenn", Toby's clothes, Ian Sturgess, that list of names and so on. I've worked on cases with no leads where I've felt like I've got more idea what I'm doing.'

There wasn't much Izzy could add, other than offering a smile and a vague suggestion about meeting up after work one evening. Jessica knew the constable had enough on her plate considering the pregnancy, while her own problems weren't isolated to work either, with the tension she was feeling around Caroline. Altogether, she wasn't having a good time of it – and that was before she had fallen over in the street.

17

Lloyd Corless was beginning to think that watching whatever he wanted on television and playing limitless PlayStation games was actually pretty boring. The strange thing was that, if someone had said to him a few weeks ago he would be able to spend all his time watching and playing, he would have been pleased. Actually doing it was a very different matter. The truth was, he missed his mum and he missed Marcus. If they came through the hatch that led into the attic, he might even admit that to them.

The hatch was something of a mystery. He had tried to pull it up from the inside but couldn't get his fingers into the cracks around the wooden board that blocked the attic from whatever was below it. Once he had managed to squeeze two of his fingers underneath but it was really heavy, as if something was weighing it down to prevent it being pulled upwards.

A couple of times a day he would hear a metal ladder underneath being moved around. Usually it would be because food was arriving but, once or twice, it seemed like the person simply wanted to talk to him, asking if there was anything that would make him happier.

Lloyd couldn't think of anything other than to see his mum and Marcus but the person got angry whenever he said that, saying his mother was too ill in hospital to see him and that he would have to get used to it. He asked for his phone back but that wasn't going to happen, either.

He couldn't work out what was going on. As long as it didn't involve either his mum or Marcus, he was being offered anything he wanted. Lloyd had asked about his dad but the other person didn't really answer, then the hatch would be closed again and he would be left to play for as long as he wanted.

Lloyd did try to play but he could never really focus. Instead, he spent hours inspecting the room, wondering if there was another door or something he had missed. He was fascinated with the low parts of the ceiling he could reach. He had never touched a ceiling before as he was too short. He found himself walking in circles, running his hand along the full distance of the lower part of the roof. He also made his bed every day. It was something his mum kept on to him about when he was at home but he rarely listened. Without her, it was something he did almost to show that he could. If she did appear through the hatch one day, he wanted her to smile and be pleased with him, not angry because his bed was a mess.

The biggest thing he didn't like was having to use the toilet in the corner. There was nothing wrong with it specifically – it was just like the one they had at home – but it felt wrong to sit on it when the rest of the room was so normal, whether there was anyone else around or not.

Lloyd was in the middle of walking a lap of the room when he heard the now-familiar sound of the metal ladder clanging from underneath. The hatch lifted a small amount and Lloyd could see the person's eyes peering around the room looking for him. It was something that happened every time. Once, Lloyd had been standing quite close but he was told to go and sit on the bed before it would be opened any further. They locked eyes and Lloyd backed away towards the bed as the hatch opened fully and a plate of food was passed into the room.

'How are you today, Lloyd?' he was asked.

'I'm all right,' the boy mumbled quietly.

'Here's some food for you. Sausages, fried potatoes and beans.'

Lloyd had eaten baked beans a few days previously. They hadn't tasted quite right but, with nothing else on offer, he had finished them anyway.

'I'm just going to leave the plate here,' the person added. 'I'll be back later to pick everything up.'

Lloyd wasn't in the mood to give a proper answer, mumbling something as the person exited back through the hole, lowering the wooden cover in place. He moved quickly across the room and tried to get his fingers underneath it. He had seen some sort of hook on the wood and figured the person was hanging something heavy from it when they left, stopping him lifting it. He desperately tried to squeeze his fingers into the small gap but could not manage it.

Turning around, Lloyd looked at the plate of food as steam gently rose. He had figured out a day or so ago that the reason he was feeling so tired was because something was being added into either his food or his drink. He had seen a television programme once where a tiger's food had something added to it that made the animal go to sleep.

He had been left a large bottle of fizzy drink and some plastic cups a few days ago. If whatever was making him tired wasn't in that bottle, it was either in the ketchup he had eaten previously or the sauce that went with the baked beans. Lloyd didn't know what to do. He knew from school that you had to eat and drink so he didn't have much option. He tried to drink as little of the liquid as he could and left most of the baked beans, scraping off the sauce from the rest of his food. He was beginning to think his mother wasn't in hospital at all. Maybe the person who had taken him had done something to her? Maybe they had Marcus too? The only time he had seen the person unhappy was when he had made some noise by banging on the walls. Lloyd knew he had to get out but with the window so high and the hatch weighed down, it wouldn't be easy.

As he finished scraping sauce from the sausage and ate it, he thought that, if he could stop himself from feeling so tired all the time, he might be able to think of a way out.

18

Jessica stood solemnly, listening to the voice speaking from the front of the church. She wasn't taking in the words but whatever was being said sounded appropriately sincere. She was one of the officers representing the force at Isaac Hutchings's funeral. It had taken time for the body to be released due to the post mortem and further tests but with everything now complete and suffocation confirmed as the cause of death, the family were finally allowed some closure.

Kayla was standing at the front with her husband Mike and their daughter Jenny. It was the first time Jessica had seen Isaac's father. While Kayla had thanked the officers for coming, he had ignored them, refusing to shake hands. Jessica didn't blame him. Even outsiders could see they had achieved very little in trying to find who had taken and killed their son. Jessica watched Jenny cling onto her father throughout the ceremony, refusing to let him go. It was as if each was a comfort blanket for the other. Even from the very brief greeting at the start, it was clear there was a lot of tension between husband and wife. Jessica remembered Kayla telling her Mike blamed her for not collecting Isaac from school. She wondered if it would ever be reconciled.

The end of the ceremony was as awkward as the initial

greeting. Before everyone headed off for the wake, Kayla approached Jessica, Reynolds and Cole to thank them again for being there. Mike and Jenny were standing awkwardly, close to one of the cars that were carrying family members. He eyeballed the officers as if daring one of them to speak to him.

Sensing the unease, Kayla spoke quietly to Jessica in the churchyard. 'Don't worry about him,' she said. 'He's angry with everyone at the moment, me especially.'

'It's okay,' Jessica said.

'Are you any closer to . . . ?' Kayla didn't finish the question but she didn't have to.

Jessica shook her head without committing herself to anything specific. 'We're trying.'

'I saw on the news that someone else had gone missing. Have you . . . ?'

'Not yet.'

From the look on the woman's face, it seemed as if Kayla was closely following Lloyd Corless's disappearance. Jessica guessed she believed that finding Lloyd's abductor would be the key to Isaac's murder. She tried to offer a reassuring smile but false sincerity was something Jessica had never been good at. Kayla nodded and gripped Jessica's hand as she shook it. Her palms were still feeling raw from the fall a few days previously but she tried not to wince. Kayla's long black hair was clean and neatly tied back and she looked better than when Jessica had last seen her, although there were still heavy dark bags under her eyes, despite the concealer she had used.

'Can you do something for me?' Kayla asked.

'What?'

'Call if anything happens. If you find him or whatever, the other boy, can you let me know?'

'I'll try.'

Jessica didn't want to promise because if they did find Lloyd, whether he was alive or dead, there would be a lot of people who would need to be spoken to. Kayla seemed to accept what Jessica was saying.

'Okay, thank you. Are you coming to the hall?'

Jessica glanced across towards Mike, who was still staring at them. 'I'm not sure that's really for the best.'

Kayla looked behind her. 'You're probably right.' She stared directly into Jessica's eyes before turning and the look said more than her words could: 'I need to go, but please find whoever did this'.

As she walked away, Jessica looked to her colleagues. 'Are you off back to the station?' she asked. Jack nodded but didn't speak. Jessica had known him for years and he was looking older than ever, the stress of the past few days and lack of progress weighing on him heavily.

'We've got more meetings later this afternoon,' Reynolds said. 'Are you coming?'

'I think I'm going to visit Rachel Corless again and maybe Adrian too if you don't mind.'

The truth was Jessica wasn't enjoying the atmosphere at Longsight. To outward appearances, nothing had changed but everyone was feeling the pressure to make a breakthrough.

'Are you on to something?' Reynolds asked.

Jessica shook her head. 'I'm just going to check in.'

She hadn't told any of her colleagues but she had been text-messaging Esther each evening to swap accounts of what their respective departments had found out that day. There was very little but Jessica felt she probably knew as much as anyone given the tension between CID and the kidnap team. To the media they were presenting a united front but behind closed doors, they were blaming each other for not being able to find Lloyd. It was typical internal politics.

Jessica made her way back to where she had parked. The weather had been getting colder, the rain replaced by morning frosts and flimsy flurries of snow. None of it settled but each day seemed to be chillier than the one before.

As she sat in the driver's seat, Jessica took out her phone and called Esther. After making sure she was at Rachel's and not too busy, Jessica drove to the house. The giant Christmas tree and inflatable Santa across the road were still present and had been joined a few doors down by a huge snowman that looked as if it was made of polystyrene. Jessica shook her head and allowed herself a small grin, wondering how Esther had taken to the new oversized piece of tat.

She rang the doorbell and Esther answered. Before going inside, Jessica nodded across the road towards the snowman. 'I know,' Esther said with a wicked grin, stepping out of the house and pulling the door closed without locking it in place. Her hair was tied into a ponytail, and the suit had been replaced by a pair of jeans and woollen jumper. Because she was staying with Rachel as a permanent support figure, it made sense for her to dress more informally. 'Still cold out then?' Esther added, walking along the path with Jessica next to her.

'Bloody freezing. I was up in Sunderland the other day and it's worse up there.'

'I heard you fell over . . .' Esther turned, grinning.

'Who told you that?' Jessica was stunned the other woman knew.

'Oh, I have spies everywhere.'

'If we could channel all the energy that's spent gossiping about me into actual police work, we'd have wrapped this all up weeks ago.'

'Are you all right?' Esther asked.

'Fine. How's Rachel?'

Esther let out a small sigh. 'She's just . . . difficult to read. I think she's coming to the realisation Adrian isn't involved after all. She's been really calm because I think she was convinced Lloyd would be back any day and his dad would be in trouble. She was a bit upset last night and I think it's dawning on her that it's not going to happen like that.'

'Does she know anyone else who might be involved?'

The two women stopped at the end of the pathway. 'No, it's difficult to get much of anything out of her. Having her friend around helps but she can't be here all the time. She spends all day cleaning then watching TV in the evening. Then she keeps talking about getting the place ready for Christmas, as if everything's normal.'

'What about the other son?'

'Marcus? He spends a lot of time in his room. I had a

bit of a chat with him the other day but you've got to be careful talking to minors. I think he's coming to terms with it better than his mother. How's it going at your end?'

Jessica was perfectly happy to tell Esther the truth, knowing it wouldn't go any further. 'Shite. We've got nothing and, worse still, the papers know it. Everyone's assuming they're getting ready to lay into us. The chief super was around yesterday but it's not as if he can do much. He's putting loads more officers out onto the streets to make it look like we know what we're doing.'

'Sounds about right. Shall we go in? It's bloody freezing out here. I've got this jumper on but it's boiling in there. The heating's permanently on full. I'd hate to be paying those gas bills.'

'I was going to but it sounds like you've got enough going on. I think I'm going to nip up and see Adrian again. He might have some ideas now he knows we're not looking into him.'

'Have you formally ruled him out?'

Jessica blew into her hands to warm them. 'More or less. You know what it's like, you do as much digging as you can and, if you can't find anything, you just assume they've hidden it well. The official line is "not a suspect", the unofficial one is "keep looking". The even more unofficial one is that we don't have the officers to "keep looking" because they're all out on the streets.'

Esther turned. 'All right, let me know how you go.'

Jessica drove steadily up the motorway, not wanting to push her car too hard, and arriving just before sunset.

Adrian opened the door and invited her in. 'No one's been telling me anything,' he said and Jessica knew he had good reason to complain. While Esther had been sent to stay with Rachel, Lloyd's father had been left almost entirely out of the loop. The man offered her tea and Jessica waited in the kitchen with him while he made it. 'Can you tell me what's going on?' he asked.

'We're still looking for your son, Mr Corless,' Jessica said.

'Just call me Adrian. Are you having any luck?'

Telling the man the truth would be fairly unprofessional, so Jessica fudged the issue as best she could. 'We are following a few leads.'

'That sounds like classic police-speak. "Proceeding in a westerly direction" and all that crap. Have you at least moved on from trying to go after me?'

'You're not on our list of suspects.'

'That's one thing at least.'

Adrian poured boiling water from the kettle into two mugs and took two teabags from an open box on the counter top, dropping them in. 'I've been out driving each day,' he said. 'I know it's a waste of time but you just hope you'll spot something. Sometimes you see some kid with the same coat and your heart jumps until you get a bit closer and realise it's someone else. The worst thing is, I can't talk to anyone. Rach doesn't answer my calls and then you lot go to her, not me. He's my son too, y'know.'

There was a clear frustration but Jessica thought she would probably be far angrier than he was if the roles were reversed. She certainly wouldn't be making cups of tea.

'I know we asked you the other day but is there anyone you can think of who might want to harm Lloyd?' Jessica asked as sincerely as she could.

'I've been trying to think,' Adrian said, making eye contact. 'I've not just been sitting around and wondering – I've made lists. I thought about everyone over the years who I've fallen out with and so on. The thing is, apart from Rach and her family, I've not really pissed people off. I've worked when I've had a job and tried to find something when I've not. I don't owe anyone any money, I'm not in any gangs or anything and I hardly ever go out on the piss. Until I split with Rach, everything was simple.'

'Why did you break up?'

Adrian opened a small fridge and took out a pint of milk, pouring some into each mug before putting it away and offering one to Jessica. 'It was a build-up of things. Rach was happy when there was money coming in but when I lost my job, she couldn't accept it. When I couldn't get another one full-time and was relying on scraps from the job centre, she was furious. She thought I couldn't find a job because I didn't want one.'

He stopped to take a sip of his tea before waving Jessica towards the living room. He sat on one of the chairs at the dining table, Jessica taking another.

'Is that why you broke up with her?' Jessica asked.

'Sort of. I knew she was really materialistic when we were together. She always liked spending money on things but it was fine because we had the money to spend. Our wedding was ridiculous. It got to the point where I didn't even want to know how much she was spending because

I wouldn't sleep. Every time I brought it up, she'd go on about it being "her" big day. Never "ours", always "hers". I thought that once we got through that, it would change. Then Marcus and Lloyd came along and it was sort of better. She liked spending money on them. After I lost my job, she acted as if I'd failed her and the boys. She was used to a comfortable lifestyle and claiming benefits wasn't something she wanted to do. Then it was all her mum in her ear about how I was never good enough and all that. But we stayed together for the boys until I couldn't take it any longer. They were at an age where they were just about old enough to understand and I told her it was over. She'd been giving me all that abuse over the years but I still ended up being the bad guy because I was the one who split with her.'

Adrian tailed off, picking up his mug from the table. Jessica didn't think he was looking for sympathy but she felt sorry for him nonetheless. From everything he said, he certainly had been harshly treated. It was as if he sensed her thoughts. 'It's fine,' he added. 'I'm used to it all now. I don't want to bore you with my moaning, I'd rather you were out there looking.'

As he spoke Jessica heard the front door opening and a woman's voice calling out, 'Ade?'

'Shit, that's my mum,' Adrian said. 'You should probably leave.' Jessica didn't have time to ask him why before a woman burst into the living room with two bags of shopping. She was short and overweight, with shoulder-length greying hair, and wearing a dress that looked more like a curtain than an item of clothing.

'Are you coming to help me or not?' she demanded before noticing Jessica. 'Who are you?'

'This is DS Daniel, she's—' Before Adrian could finish speaking, his mother cut him off.

'And you let *her* in *here*?' She turned from Adrian and looked at Jessica, her eyes dark and wide with anger. She didn't look that much older than her son and Jessica guessed she was a teenager when she'd had him. 'Why aren't you out there looking for my grandson instead of harassing my son? Why would he kidnap his own child? It's that bitch wife of his you should be going after.'

Jessica stood, knowing it was time to go. The woman wasn't ready to stop as she continued shouting. 'Yes, go on, get out. And don't come back until you've got my grandson with you.'

As she left the house, Jessica could hear Adrian trying to calm his mother. She wasn't under an obligation to leave but seeing as the man wasn't under suspicion and she had only dropped around to reassure herself, Jessica knew there was no point in causing a scene. She walked along the pathway, passing a car which had the doors open and shopping bags on the seat, thinking it seemed about right that Adrian's mother did his shopping for him.

With everything that had happened over the past few days, Jessica was at a loss of what to do next. She unlocked her car and sat in the driver's seat fiddling with her phone, scrolling up and down the list of contacts, sometimes focusing on one and trying to remember the last time she had spoken to the person. As the list of names fizzed across the screen, one in particular settled in the centre.

She stared at it, her heart beating quicker as she remembered what he meant to her. She didn't know if it was fate or something she had done subconsciously but Jessica didn't think twice before pressing the call button next to Adam Compton's name.

19

Of all the things Jessica regretted in her life, the way she had treated Adam Compton was top of the list. They had gone out for a while and got on really well. She was his first proper girlfriend and he was one of the few people she could spend significant amounts of time with without wanting to cause them great harm.

A few years ago one of her friends had died but instead of using Adam as a shoulder to cry on, she had ignored him for weeks. If that wasn't bad enough, she then took advantage of his emotional attachment to her, asking him to do something illegal on her behalf. He had not got into any trouble but anything between them had been lost and aside from an unanswered text message she had sent him, they'd had no contact since.

As the phone rang, Jessica wondered if he had changed his number. Perhaps he'd kept the same number but was refusing to answer because her name had appeared on his screen? Jessica took her mobile away from her ear ready to press the button to end the call when she heard a voice. 'Hello?'

'Adam?'

'Yes.'

'It's Jessica.'

'I know.'

There was an awkward silence as Jessica considered what to say. She had thought about making this call many times in the past but Adam made her promise never to contact him again. She was breaking that and didn't know why.

'I . . . How are you?' she stammered.

There was another pause and she was about to ask if he was still there when Adam answered. 'Why are you calling me, Jess?'

She felt a shiver go down her spine from the way he had said her name. It had taken her long enough to convince him to call her 'Jess' instead of 'Jessica'. From nowhere there was a lump in her throat. She tried to speak but the words were stuck. She struggled to ask the question but swallowed hard before forcing the words out. 'Can we meet?'

There was another pause, longer this time, but she could hear Adam breathing. Eventually he responded. 'Where?'

'The bar where we first went out? Next to the cinema in the centre?'

His reply was instant. 'When?'

'Now?'

'Okay.'

Jessica took the phone away from her ear and saw the screen go black. She stared at it for a few moments, transfixed by the scrapes on the casing. It was as if someone else had made the call and arranged the meeting. She had no idea why she had called him, let alone planned to meet. And why had she said she would meet him now, when she was supposed to be working on the case?

Adrian's mother snapped her back to reality as Jessica saw a flash of movement ahead and peered up to see the woman standing next to the car with the open doors, pointing her finger angrily in Jessica's direction.

Jessica started the engine and pulled away, before stopping a few hundred metres down the street. With the speed and awkwardness of everything, she had arranged to meet Adam right away despite being in Chorley and having a rush-hour motorway to negotiate. She picked her phone up from the passenger seat and sent him a text message apologising and saying she was in Lancashire for work but that she would get there as soon as possible.

Jessica found being stuck in traffic jams frustrating enough at the best of times but when she actually had somewhere she wanted to be, it was excruciating. As the traffic crawled along the carriageway, she stayed as close to the bumper of the car in front as she possibly could, making sure no one could cut in front of her but then, when she wanted to change lanes, angrily berated anyone who wouldn't slow down and let her in. She was fully aware her behaviour was irrational and inconsistent but she couldn't care less.

The only amount of pleasure she took from the drive was when she was sitting in non-moving traffic and saw a man in the car in the next lane playing air-drums on his steering wheel. She couldn't hear whatever music he was listening to but when he spotted her watching him, he sheepishly looked away and stopped waving his arms.

With liberal use of her car horn, a questionable interpretation of the laws regarding traffic lights, at least three petrified cyclists, and a lot of swearing, Jessica eventually parked in a space not far from the bar specifically marked for 'permit holders only'. She figured that if anyone did clamp her car, she would show them her police identification and throw a few baseless threats around.

Taking extra care on the paths which were beginning to frost over, Jessica walked the short distance and spotted Adam straight away. He still had shoulder-length black hair, neatly tucked away from his face. He had let his stubble grow out and was sporting a dark clipped beard. He looked up as she entered, catching her gaze. His large brown eyes were darker than she remembered but he looked smart in a pair of jeans, T-shirt and black blazer. He didn't exactly smile but he didn't look angry or upset either. As she strolled towards him, Jessica became self-conscious about the black suit she was wearing. She had gone straight from the funeral to Rachel and then Adrian's house without changing. She tried to think of something clever to say but the best she could manage was a rather weak, 'Do you want a drink?'

Adam pointed to the cappuccino in front of him. 'I'm okay.'

Jessica tried to smile as she offered another feeble reply. 'I'll be right back.'

She went to the bar and ordered herself a soft drink, conscious of the fact she was driving. The bar wasn't very busy, with a couple of sofas occupied, while some of the stools in the front window had people on them. After being served, she returned to sit opposite Adam at the table. There were only two seats but the setting was more cosy than cramped. She could feel him watching her as she placed her drink carefully on the table.

When she was in the chair, Jessica looked up to meet his eyes. 'Hi.'

There was a half-smile on his face. 'Hi.'

She held out her hand for him to shake. 'I'm Jessica – but prefer to be called Jess by people I like.'

He shook her hand. 'Hi, Jess, I'm Adam.'

Jessica continued to meet his eyes. 'I'm sorry about this suit and everything, I've come from a funeral.'

Adam's face broke into a bigger grin. 'I figured it was either that or you'd become a grandma since I last knew you.'

Jessica laughed. 'Oi, sod off, Mr "I look like a rock star with my long hair, retro T-shirt, designer stubble and jacket".'

Adam laughed and finally broke eye contact. 'It's good to see you.'

From giggling, Jessica felt the lump in her throat again. She blinked quickly to avoid any tears seeping out. 'I'm so sorry. *Please* forgive me.'

The words hung in the air. She couldn't have added anything else even if she'd wanted to as she fought to stop herself from tearing up. Adam watched her. There was a long pause but it wasn't uncomfortable. Instead they looked at each other and she told him with her eyes how sorry she was. He didn't have to say anything verbally because his eyes replied, 'Let's forget it and start again.'

From nearly crying, Jessica burst out laughing. 'Don't turn around now otherwise it'll be obvious but give it a few seconds, then look at the guy who just sat down on that stool in the window behind you.' Adam grinned, before dropping a napkin to the side of his chair, bending down to pick it up and looking directly behind him.

He turned back around and started laughing too. 'What is he wearing on his head?'

'I think it's a cross between a tea cosy and a glove. It's made of wool but it's got those finger bits pointing upwards and it fits around his head.'

'Why would you go out in public like that?' Adam asked, smiling.

Jessica giggled. 'I don't know, why would you go out in public with black bum fluff stuck to your chin?'

Adam fingered his beard. 'Oi, you're one to talk, what's with the grazes?'

She looked at her hands. 'I fell over a kerb because it was frosty. I think you're the only person in the city who doesn't already know.'

There was another pause as they eyed each other. 'I've been thinking about you,' Adam said suddenly, blurting it out without thinking.

Jessica watched him but he didn't try to take it back. 'How come?'

'Lots of reasons, Grandma, she died three months ago—' Adam was still speaking but Jessica interrupted.

'Pat? Oh God, I'm so sorry.' The woman had brought him up as his parents both died when he was young. Despite being in his early thirties, Adam shared a house with her.

'It's okay, she didn't suffer,' Adam replied reassuringly.

'She was ill for a while so in the end it was no surprise. She kept saying I should call you. I never told her what happened but she'd mention it at least once every couple of weeks. She really took to you. She'd just casually drop it into conversation like, "I wonder what that Jessica is up to nowadays?" and so on.'

Jessica couldn't help but smile, though she felt awful about the time that had gone by. 'She was pretty cool.'

Adam smiled. He seemed sad but not emotional. 'You're privileged, you know what she was like around other people – no social graces and all. The fact she actually liked someone was different in itself. About a year ago, I'd taken her to this cafe in the city. There was a girl about twenty or so in there who had tattoos all the way up her arm. Nan started going on wondering why people would spoil their bodies and so on. I was trying to keep her quiet and change the subject but she was having none of it. She was talking really loudly and just went, "I don't get it", before starting all over again. In the end the poor girl left.'

'What were the tattoos like?'

'Oh, they were bloody awful but you don't say that, do you? Especially not to a stranger.'

Jessica laughed. Even though she didn't know the woman that well, she had seen just how little tact Adam's grandmother had. It wasn't necessarily deliberate but the woman had been at the age where she had spent a life of biting her tongue and couldn't be bothered any longer.

'I'm sorry I couldn't be there at the end,' Jessica said.

Adam shrugged an acknowledgement. 'How's everything with you?'

'Same as ever, really. Cases with no leads, bosses who don't appreciate me, not enough money, too many takeaways, car falling apart.'

Adam was laughing. 'Look at the state of us, we're both in our thirties.'

It was something consistently in Jessica's thoughts. 'The problem with being thirty-odd is that you still feel eighteen,' she said. 'To anyone else, you're that sensible – or not – thirty-something who has got a proper job and responsibilities and so on but, in your head, you're still just a crazy eighteen-year-old ready to take on the world.'

Adam was nodding in agreement. 'There was this new woman who started at work the other week. It was the week after her fortieth birthday. I caught myself looking at her and thinking, "Oh, she's only a few years older than me", then I thought, "*Bloody hell, she's only a few years older than me*". It's scary.'

'You're telling me. There's this woman I work with, Izzy. She's brilliant but she's like a proper adult. We're about the same age but she's married with a house and savings and a kid on the way. Meanwhile, I'm still slobbing around and living off takeaway curries. Do you remember Dave? We went to that pub quiz that time?'

'The spiky-haired guy?'

'Yeah, him. Even he's got a proper girlfriend and is settling down now. I just can't get over being halfway between thirty and forty. When you're a kid, you look at your parents and teachers and just assume they know what it's like to be an adult. You think that when you get there, it'll just come together. But it doesn't, well, it hasn't for me anyway. Sometimes I feel like I'm still trying it on when I order a beer, as if I'm trying to get served when I'm underage.'

'Growing up is shit.'

'Yeah, it is. I was talking to Izzy a few days ago and she was telling me about having to buy a car seat before she has the baby so she can take it home from the hospital and I was thinking, "What age have you got to be before you start thinking sensibly like that?"'

'You're not thinking of having a baby, are you?'

'No, I . . .' Jessica tailed off. A thought had occurred to her and she was trying to run through the day's events in her mind.

'Jess?'

'Sorry, no . . . I'm not after a baby. I just . . . thought of something.'

'Something important?'

'I don't know.' Jessica finished her drink in one final gulp. Because of the lump she'd had in her throat and the dryness in her mouth, she'd been sipping it throughout the conversation. 'Look, I'm really sorry but I'm going to have to go. I think it is important. I'm not trying to run away.'

Adam met her eyes and smiled. 'It's okay.'

'Can we do something again?'

'Definitely.'

'I'll call you, or message you or something – soon. I've got loads going on at work but I don't want you to think I'm ignoring you . . . again.'

Jessica stared into his eyes, imploring him to believe

her. The crinkles around his mouth as he smiled told her that he did. 'Whenever you're free.'

Adam stood and she followed his lead. He held his arms out and she stepped close, allowing him to hug her. She had held back the tears for the entire evening but Jessica was suddenly engulfed by them. Responding immediately, Adam pulled her closer, cupping the back of her head and allowing her to cry on his shoulder. Any display of affection, let alone crying in public, would usually have been something Jessica avoided at all costs. But in a small bar in the middle of the city she had lived in for ten years, she knew she was experiencing the most intimate moment of her life.

20

After saying goodbye to Adam, Jessica phoned DCI Cole. With all the tension regarding who was in charge, it wasn't a time to start doing things on her own. The chief inspector listened to her theory, acknowledged it could be something important, then said he would meet her at the station.

The pair worked together in near silence, doing tasks that would usually be assigned to people more junior. Given how fragile she felt after her encounter with Adam, it was exactly what Jessica needed to make her switch on again. Before they could act, it was essential they made sure their facts were correct. The more they checked and re-checked the information they had, the bigger the buzz Jessica felt building inside. By the time they were as certain as they could be that she might be right, it was almost midnight and the chief inspector felt it was too late in the day to act decisively and, more importantly, safely. Officers were dispatched to keep watch overnight while everything was put in place so they could move in the morning.

Jessica had another largely sleepless night – but this time it wasn't due to Caroline or her own insecurities. She felt excited at what the next morning might bring, the butterflies she had felt as Adam held her still lingering too.

By the time she arrived at the station the next morning,

everything was in place. The officers who had been on watch overnight hadn't reported anything untoward which meant that if Jessica was right, Lloyd Corless could be back with his mother within hours.

Desperate for a result, Cole said the chief superintendent had agreed to Jessica being able to do things her way, which was something that surprised the pair of them.

With a team of officers within a few hundred metres, Jessica knocked on Sharon Corless's front door. One of the first things she had checked the previous evening was all the background information on Adrian's mother. When no one answered, she banged loudly again. One of the officers who had been watching the property the previous night insisted he had seen the woman inside and no one had left. Just as Jessica was about to turn around, the door opened a small crack and she could see the mouth and eyes of the woman who had shouted at her the previous day. Before Jessica could speak, the door was opened a little further.

'What are you doing here?' Sharon demanded angrily, her eyes as ferocious as the previous day.

'I'd like to ask you a few questions about your missing grandson,' Jessica said as politely as she could.

'What do you want to know?'

'Can I come in?'

'Why?'

'Because it's cold out here and it would probably be best if we do this inside.' Jessica kept a level tone as the woman stared at her. Lloyd Corless's grandmother looked as if she was weighing up what to do before pulling the door open for Jessica to step through.

Jessica had already run through with both Cole and Reynolds what she was going to say, assuming she was allowed inside. She allowed herself to be led through to a pristinely clean kitchen. Light spilled through the window, gleaming off the white worktops. There were two stools at a high table and Jessica sat on one, although the other woman didn't follow, standing with her arms crossed. Her outfit was marginally better than the curtain-like dress she'd had on the previous day but she was still wearing a shapeless black blouse that looked enormous.

'What do you want then?' Sharon asked. Her tone wasn't angry, more impatient.

'Just a bit of a chat. I was wondering how you get on with your grandchildren?'

'Fine.'

'Adrian is your only child, yes? So Lloyd and Marcus are your only grandchildren?'

Sharon narrowed her eyes, glaring at Jessica, who already knew the answers before asking the questions. 'That's right,' the woman said after a short pause.

'And how often do you see them?'

'Maybe once a month? I visit them at my son's house.'

'How do you feel about that?'

Sharon was clearly trying to play along with Jessica's questions while also keeping a temper that seemed close to boiling point. Her voice was beginning to tremble. 'Why are you asking?'

'No particular reason, it's just a question. Is there a problem?'

'No, it's just . . . what do you expect me to say? Of course I'd like to see them more.'

'When was the last time you saw Marcus?'

The woman hesitated for a moment, thinking. 'Three weeks ago at the weekend, we all went shopping for Christmas presents.'

'What about Lloyd?'

'At the same time.'

Jessica kept her voice as calm as possible. 'What type of things do you usually do when you see them? Do you go to Adrian's house or do you have the children on your own?'

Sharon hesitated. 'Adrian will usually either bring them here or he'll take us all somewhere.'

'You don't take Marcus and Lloyd anywhere on your own?'

'Definitely not.' The woman stared at Jessica, who knew Sharon thought she had given the best answer to suit her cause when, in fact, it was the worst one she could have offered.

'And you've not seen Lloyd since that time you went shopping?' Jessica asked.

'No, of course not.'

'Are you sure?'

Sharon's anger suddenly boiled over. Jessica had seen the bottom of the woman's nostrils begin to flare as the conversation had gone on. 'How dare you,' she shouted, taking a step forward. Jessica didn't flinch, remaining on the kitchen stool as the other woman stood over her. 'What are you trying to say?' She stared at Jessica, eyes wide with fury.

'Do we *really* have to do this?'

'Do what? I want you out. Now.'

Jessica didn't move. 'Yesterday when I was at your son's house, you more or less chased me outside. Your car door was wide open because of the shopping but there was something else in there too.' Sharon stared back at Jessica. Her body language was defiant but her eyes, full of rage moments before, told a different story. She started to say something but couldn't get the words out properly.

'Why do you need a child's booster seat in your car, Mrs Corless?' Jessica asked.

The woman stumbled over her words for a moment but seemed determined to keep an upper hand she didn't have. 'Why wouldn't I?'

'You said you don't take the boys out on your own and your son did the driving or brought them to you. If that's the case, why would you need a booster seat?'

'I . . . I have them sometimes.'

'Really? You told me you didn't.'

'Not often, just every now and then.' The woman was talking quickly, her words blending together.

'So you only have the boys "every now and then" but you keep a booster seat permanently in your front seat just in case?'

'Yes, so what?'

'Where do the boys sit when you have them on their own?'

'What?'

Jessica knew she was right. 'When you have them "every now and then", where do the two boys sit in your car?'

'I don't know, in the back. One in the front, I guess.'

'Who sits in the front?'

Sharon stared hard at Jessica but reached out to put a hand on the worktop. 'I . . . Why does this matter?'

Jessica tried to calm the speed of her words. 'If they both sit in the back, you wouldn't have a booster seat in the front. If Marcus was in the front, he wouldn't need one because he's old enough and tall enough to sit on his own without one. So why does Lloyd get preference to sit in the front?'

'Just . . . because . . .'

'So the youngest brother gets to sit in the front every time and there's never any arguments between them? Because that doesn't sound like how eleven- and thirteen-year-old boys might act to me.'

Sharon weighed up Jessica's words, knowing she didn't have an answer. She replied in the way Jessica expected her to. 'Out. I want you to leave. I know my rights, you can't be in here without a warrant unless I invite you in. I'm uninviting you. I want you out. Now.'

The woman put a hand on the top of Jessica's arm and motioned as if to pull her out of the seat. Jessica stood voluntarily but held firm.

'Are you really sure you want to do this?' she asked.

Sharon continued to pull on Jessica's arm but with less force. 'Do what? Leave now.'

Jessica sighed. 'It's not just about the seat. We know you don't have any other children or grandchildren. We know you don't have any other properties or anything else in your name. And we know – I know – you have Lloyd

195

somewhere here. We can either do this the easy way and you tell me where you have him, or I can go outside and tell my colleagues at the bottom of the road to come along with the warrant we already have. We can do it whichever way you choose but it's up to you. One way will look a lot worse when it gets to court.'

Sharon stopped tugging on Jessica's arm. Her head was tilted to the side and she met the sergeant's eyes. 'Fine. Have a look for yourself. He's not here.'

As her son had done days before, she held her arms wide to tell Jessica she had nothing to hide.

For the first time since the previous night, Jessica felt a nervous twinge. She had been in control of the conversation until that point but Sharon's steady stare suddenly put doubt into her mind. What if she was wrong? Was there something she had missed? Jessica tried to appear confident as she walked through from the kitchen into the living room with Sharon just behind her. The atmosphere had certainly changed and she could feel the woman hovering. Jessica didn't have to do much exploration in the room to know there was no one there, not unless there was a hidden basement under the carpet. The rest of the ground floor was similarly inauspicious, everything tidily organised and offering nothing of interest. Sharon followed her around but said nothing.

Jessica knew she could ask the team waiting outside to enter at any moment. She wasn't bluffing when she told the woman they had a warrant. But if she was wrong, it would look terrible for everyone involved, especially her. Jessica walked steadily up the carpeted stairs studying the photos on the walls above a bookshelf which had been built into the wall. The books were largely romance novels and even from skimming the spines, Jessica could see they were in alphabetical order.

At the top of the stairs was a door immediately on her left, another in front and two to her right. Sharon was hovering halfway up, watching. Jessica entered to her left but it was a bathroom, while the door in front led into a library of sorts, with hundreds, if not thousands of books arranged neatly along the walls. She tried to weigh up the dimensions of the house, wondering if there could be space for an extra room or large cupboard but everything appeared correct.

The first of the doors to her right opened into a bedroom that Jessica thought was likely Sharon's own. There was a king-size bed neatly made with a clean white duvet on top. Jessica almost felt embarrassed for doing it but she crouched and looked under the bed but could see nothing. She checked the walk-in wardrobe but, aside from a dubious taste in clothes, there was nothing untoward. Jessica was beginning to get a sinking feeling in her stomach as she approached the final door. It was wedged open and without going inside, she could see that it was relatively clear. A single bed was pushed towards a back wall, a portable television was on a chest of drawers opposite. There was a cream-coloured carpet that Jessica felt strangely drawn to because of how bright it made the room look. The day was clear but cold and sunlight beamed through the window, illuminating the area. Jessica looked from the doorway, peering from one corner to the other, but couldn't see anything out of place.

As she turned to look away, defeated, Jessica's gaze fell upon an object on the floor holding the door open. It was a solid-looking dark weight, the type she'd used at school when they were learning about measurements. In her mind, Jessica was transported back to being young, holding the weights in her hand and thinking how heavy they were before balancing them on the scales as her teacher spoke about kilograms and pounds. She had half-turned towards the stairs but stopped to stare at the weight. Something about it didn't seem quite right. The rest of the house was completely uncluttered with all the doors closed. For some reason, not only was this door open but there was an item on the floor.

Jessica stepped back towards the room, crouching to pick the weight up.

The door didn't swing shut.

She could hear Sharon shuffling on the stairs. Jessica remembered a time when they had gone on a school trip to a local castle. One of her teachers had tried to measure how deep the moat was by tying a similar weight to a string. As the children sat in a circle and watched, the teacher had slowly lowered the object into the moat before offering a quick 'oops' and pulling out the string with no weight attached. Jessica still remembered the embarrassed look on the teacher's face as she realised the piece of school property was in the process of sinking to the bottom.

Jessica knelt and cupped the weight in her hand, bobbing it up and down to feel how heavy it was. She glanced around the room before noticing a hatch on the ceiling, a round hook in the centre. She stood, still holding the weight, and walked over to the bed. The covers were hanging over the side, touching the floor but she pulled them back and reached underneath. As her hands gripped the cool metal of what was undoubtedly a ladder, Jessica knew she was right.

She pulled it out with a clang and looked up to see Sharon standing in the doorway. Any defiance in her face was gone as the two locked eyes. 'Why did you do it?' Jessica asked.

Sharon spoke quietly. 'I just wanted to see him.'

21

The change in the atmosphere around the station in the days since Lloyd Corless had been found was remarkable. No one thought Sharon had anything to do with the other disappearances and the fact Lloyd's name had been on the list found in the allotment shed seemed to be a coincidence. The senior members were delighted the boy had been found alive and well – and the subsequent media coverage was very positive. Jessica thought a lot of the internal relief was because they had somehow managed to keep news of the list's existence in-house.

From her point of view, Jessica was still frustrated because they had only solved one mystery which it now seemed wasn't even connected to the wider one they were supposed to be looking into. Plenty of people around the station were happy to offer her a 'well done' and give the proverbial pat on the back but she didn't share their enthusiasm, instead retreating to her office.

Meanwhile, everything was being hampered by the weather. At least when it had been wet, they could get on and do things. As the winter freeze had taken hold, the ground where they'd discovered Toby Whittaker's clothes was becoming almost impossible to work on. They were no closer to finding the identity of the driver either.

Jessica was sitting at her desk when there was a knock

on the door and Izzy entered. Jessica welcomed the constable in, who sat on the corner of DS Cornish's empty desk.

'Are you all right?' Izzy asked.

'Not too bad.'

'Something else has happened, hasn't it?'

'What, with the case?'

'No, it's more than that. I can tell by the way you have been smiling to yourself the last few days when you think no one's around.'

'It's just because we found Lloyd.'

The constable laughed. 'There's a man involved, isn't there?'

Jessica tried to keep a straight face but cracked within a second, laughing out loud in a way she knew really wasn't like her. 'Maybe.'

Izzy started to laugh too. 'My detecting skills are really coming along. Who is it?'

'No one you'd know.' Jessica was trying to be overly evasive but she didn't want to talk too much about Adam either.

Izzy nodded and spoke with a big smile. 'Like that then, is it?'

'How's the peanut?'

'Getting bigger. I think I'll start to tell people next week.'

'Peanut's a good name. You should think about using it. Pretty for a girl, solid enough for a lad. I'll let you have it for free.'

'I'm not that mean. Anyway, you seem to be at the top of everyone's Christmas card list at the moment.'

Jessica shrugged. 'This was the simple part. We still don't know who killed Isaac Hutchings. Everything's going so slowly. I've been tidying up the stuff with Sharon Corless. She's pleaded guilty but says her son was nothing to do with the abduction. The super isn't convinced but we don't have anything to prove differently.'

'How's Lloyd?'

'I spoke to Esther from the kidnap team earlier. She said that when Rachel and Lloyd were reunited, the son seemed all right and the brother was pleased. But rather than being overjoyed, Rachel was apparently really angry, saying Adrian would never see his kids again and all that. Her mate was trying to calm her down but she wasn't having any of it. To be honest, there's something not quite right with them all. The grandmother was giving some sort of drug to Lloyd to make him stay quiet and not cause trouble. When I found him, he was asleep, even though it wasn't that early. She let me look around the house but I think that was because she knew her grandson was out like a light and wouldn't make any noise. She came quietly in the end but it's all a bit odd.'

'How did she manage to take him without anyone noticing?'

'We're not really sure but, if you know the area, you could figure it out. The cameras only covered the school gates so if she parked away from them, she was unlikely to be seen. There are so many kids getting into so many cars on roads outside schools, who would really notice someone going voluntarily?'

'I guess. And a result's a result.'

Diamond was trying to be cheery but Jessica wasn't particularly in the mood. While things were moving slowly, she wanted to get away from the office to spend the evening with Adam. For the past few nights, with Caroline still staying at hers, she had been stopping at Adam's house. Caroline had sensed something wasn't quite right and sent Jessica a text message saying she had a new flat lined up but wouldn't be able to move in until the new year. Jessica told her friend not to worry and that she could stay for as long as she wanted. In truth, she was practically living with Adam in any case, even though they had only been back together for less than a week. They had slotted straight back into the way they had been, as if nothing had happened in between.

Jessica's ambivalence seemed to spur the constable into action. 'I do have one thing for you. Your teacher guy, I might have found out who he is.'

'Ian Sturgess?'

'Sort of. I stumbled across a "Benjamin Ian Sturgess". "Ian" is the guy's middle name. He's more or less the right age and lives fairly locally. If he taught using his middle name, he could be the right person – and it would explain why we didn't find him before because we were searching for the wrong name.'

Jessica stared at her colleague. It wasn't the first time she had spotted a piece of information everyone else had missed.

'Have you told anyone else?'

'Not yet, it could still be the wrong person. I've been busy too.'

Izzy reached across and handed over a sheaf of papers that had details of the man she had found. Jessica skimmed through the pages. She knew roughly where the area was.

'Do you want to come for a drive?'

'Sorry, Jason's got me following some things up. He says that digital artist's impression of the driver is finally due today. It's cost them tens of thousands, apparently. Something to do with "3D digital remodelling" according to Jason. It's no wonder it took so long. Dave's probably free.'

'Yeah, but he's so loved up he'll be talking about learning to play the guitar or something stupid.'

'He did say he was writing a song.'

'Oh for . . . you're joking?'

Izzy laughed. 'I am actually. He's not been too bad with the whole Chloe thing this week.'

'If he starts talking about marriage or anything like that, I'm emigrating. I can't take a world where Dave Rowlands gets married before I do.'

The constable smiled and cupped an area just under her stomach in her hands. 'I didn't think you went for the whole marriage and babies thing? That is unless . . .'

Izzy had a small grin on her face as she looked at Jessica, who glared back in a silent but friendly warning. Jessica took another look at the top paper, ignoring the insinuation. 'I'm going to go talk to this Benjamin Sturgess and see if he's our man. Keep me up to date if anything happens around here and if that image arrives, send a copy to my phone.'

*

Rowlands drove out to the address with Jessica in the passenger seat, trying and failing to wind him up. Since his relationship with Chloe had become serious, he seemed utterly unflappable.

Already thinking ahead, Jessica noted the Sturgess house wasn't very close to the area where Daisy Peters lived. She still had her own theory that the person who stole her car must have been local to know Daisy's movements.

As they arrived, Jessica saw straight away there was a car parked on Benjamin Sturgess's driveway. It was similar to the one that had been crashed, relatively new, dark in colour and powerful. Jessica knocked on the front door and rang the doorbell but there was no answer. The main curtains in the front window were open but netting prevented her from seeing much. Despite the car, it didn't appear as if anyone was in. There was no gate preventing access so both officers walked through to the rear of the property where there was a small unkempt lawn and patchy grass. Jessica tried the side door but it was locked. Peering through the kitchen window revealed nothing except for the fact Mr Sturgess had the usual array of white goods.

The two detectives shrugged at each other. It was mid-afternoon so if the man did have a job, he could be at work, even though most people wouldn't leave a car on the drive.

Jessica pointed to the neighbouring house. 'You go knock on that door,' she said to her colleague. 'I'll take the one on the other side. If we don't get any luck we'll go over the road. Just ask if they know the guy who lives next door and if they've seen him recently.'

Jessica walked to the adjacent house and pressed the doorbell. It sounded a loud old-fashioned 'ding-dong' and was soon answered by a woman who looked as if she had long since retired. She was short with grey curly hair and looked quizzically at Jessica. 'I don't buy anything,' she muttered.

She had already started to close the door, so Jessica spoke quickly to say she was a police officer and took out her identification. After closely examining it, the woman introduced herself as Sue.

'Is this about those people at number thirteen?' she asked.

'What people at number thirteen?'

'I phoned you because of all the people they keep having over.'

Jessica looked at the woman with her eyebrows raised. 'I'm sorry, I don't know what you're talking about.'

Sue leant in. 'I read about it in one of my magazines. I think they're *sex* people.' She spoke the word 'sex' quietly, as if embarrassed, although she was clearly relishing telling the story. Of all the doors she could have knocked on, Jessica realised she had stumbled across the local busy-body. She wanted to steer the conversation around to the woman's next door neighbour but she couldn't get a word in.

'They have all these cars parked up and down the road a couple of times a week,' the woman continued. 'They park in front of everyone's house. The other week, someone parked outside mine at ten o'clock at night. I was watching from my top window and this couple got out. You should have seen what she was wearing.'

Against her better judgement, Jessica asked the question she knew she shouldn't. 'What was she wearing?'

Sue shook her head in mock indignation. 'I did phone the police that night so you should know. She had these big boot things on. It was outrageous.'

'Right, um . . .'

Seemingly oblivious to Jessica's lack of enthusiasm, Sue was gleefully continuing her tale. 'She and her husband, well I assume it was her husband, they walked over the road to number thirteen.' She pointed behind Jessica, who looked around to see Dave crossing the road. 'Anyway, I stayed up and watched all these couples parking up and they all went to the same house. They didn't start leaving until one in the morning. Can you believe that?'

Jessica tried to make an interested noise but knew anything she said would be largely irrelevant as Sue kept speaking. 'It's been going on for weeks now. All these couples coming and going. It's not right.'

'Okay, well, I'll look into the report but, from what you've said, I'm not sure it sounds like any offence has actually been committed.'

'No offence? What do you mean?'

Jessica couldn't tell if the woman was actually shocked or feigning it. 'It does sound like it's just a couple who have had friends around late at night. As long as they weren't making a noise or causing a disturbance, I'm not sure there's an awful lot we can actually do.'

Sue stared at Jessica as if unable to take in what she had been told. 'Well, I never. And you're a police officer?'

Jessica couldn't be bothered explaining the nuances of what her role actually was. She pointed towards Benjamin Sturgess's house. 'I was wondering if you know much about your neighbour.'

Sue still seemed annoyed but her eyes lit up at being invited to gossip. 'Benjamin? Ooh yes, he's a very nice man. He painted my skirting boards for me.'

Jessica struggled not to laugh because of the obscure nature of the statement. She wondered if she would ever reach an age where painting skirting boards became a concern. 'Have you seen him recently?'

'Ooh, I can't think . . .' As the woman paused and looked to the skies, Jessica thought it would be her luck if the one thing the local busybody couldn't remember was the only thing she actually needed to know. Just as Jessica thought she had lost five minutes of her life she would never be able to get back, Sue finally answered. 'I don't think I have, come to think of it. I don't remember seeing him at all in the past week or so.'

'Do you know if he usually leaves his car at home during the day?'

'I don't know. He does some writing but I think he does that from home.'

'Does he have a wife or a—'

Jessica didn't finish the sentence before the woman joyously interrupted. 'He used to. I think they're divorced, or separated. She doesn't live there any more.'

'I don't suppose you have a contact address or phone

number, do you?' Jessica hadn't expected anything but, to her surprise, the woman turned.

'I think I do.' She walked a few steps to a small desk just inside the front door and rummaged in a drawer, taking out a small hardback book and quickly flicking through the pages. She flipped the book around and handed it to Jessica. 'Here, it's Deborah. I think Benjamin gave it to me in case of an emergency.'

Jessica took the book and read the details, which had been written in neat spidery writing that she couldn't decipher. 'Can you read it back to me?' she asked.

Sue recited the address and phone number, which Jessica typed into her own mobile.

After she had finished reading, Sue nodded towards Jessica's phone. 'Don't even get me started on those things. All these kids today, talking on them all the time.'

Jessica wouldn't have dared to start the woman off again but didn't have much choice. She started taking small steps backwards but Sue seemed unperturbed.

'I'm sorry, I really have to go,' Jessica said as the woman muttered something about 'not being like this in my day'.

Jessica turned and called across the road to Rowlands. Once she was back in his car, she called the number. The woman who answered confirmed her name was Deborah and that her ex-husband was Benjamin Sturgess, who had once been a teacher that went by the name 'Ian'. She was at home and said it was fine for them to visit.

At hearing that, Jessica could feel the butterflies in her stomach, knowing they had found the right person. It wasn't a long journey but Dave spent most of his time laughing at Jessica's description of Sue. He didn't even seem that interested in the apparent sex parties that were occurring on the street, which was perhaps the biggest indication to Jessica that her colleague was growing up.

After knocking on the woman's door, Benjamin's former wife introduced herself as 'Deborah Sturgess' and invited them in. Jessica would have guessed the woman to be somewhere in her late forties but her eyes were bright and youthful. She had greying hair that had been bleached blonde. It came down to her shoulders but had been tied into a ponytail. There was little point in wasting time so, after being offered seats in the living room, Jessica confirmed the details about who the woman's husband was and where he lived. It was clear they were talking about the man that had years ago been vaguely linked to Toby Whittaker's disappearance.

'When was the last time you saw your ex-husband?' Jessica asked.

The woman shook her head, speaking confidently. 'Maybe a month? We divorced six years ago but are on okay terms. We see each other a few times a year, not often.' Jessica wondered why the woman had kept her ex-husband's last name but it wasn't really appropriate to ask.

'Have you had any contact at all since then, perhaps by phone?'

'Not really. I've got a key for his house and go around sometimes when he's away to open and close the curtains, that kind of thing. That's not very often though.'

'Does he work away? We're trying to get hold of him but neighbours say they haven't seen him recently.'

'He works at home. He became a writer a few years ago after giving up teaching. That's why he used his other name. You mentioned it on the phone. He's always been known as "Ian" for the whole time I've known him. When he started writing, he went back to using his first name.'

'I don't suppose you know of some other way to contact him? We could do with speaking to him.'

'Is it something serious?'

Jessica didn't know the best answer to give, so offered the one the woman wanted to hear. 'No.'

Deborah stood and started looking around. 'Like I said, I've got a key for his house. He has one for here too. It's here somewhere – it really isn't like him to go missing. I'll try his mobile first.'

At first she fumbled with her own mobile but after muttering something about being out of credit, Deborah walked across to a desk phone on a table at the back of the living room. She read a number from a list pinned to the wall and typed it in but looked up a few seconds later. 'He's not answering. I'll have a look for the keys and we can go over. I hope he's okay.'

She had almost left the room, when Jessica's phone buzzed to say a message had arrived. She glanced at it and then turned to the other woman.

'Mrs Sturgess. Could you look at this for me?' Jessica flipped her phone around to show her the photo of the digital artist's impression of the dead driver. Jessica could see Deborah nodding, a confused look on her face.

'Yes, that's Ian, is he okay?'

22

Rowlands went to speak but stopped himself, while Jessica didn't know what to say. They had not only found out the identity of their driver – but because Benjamin Sturgess was included in the Toby Whittaker file, they had discovered a direct link to Isaac Hutchings. As with everything else, it threw up yet more questions. Jessica and Dave hadn't even looked at each other, let alone spoken, but the look on their faces must have said it all. 'Is something wrong?' Deborah asked.

Jessica still wanted the woman to let them into her former husband's house. Now he was dead and the prime suspect for Isaac's abduction and murder, they would be able to get access to his property anyway – but the formalities and legal hoops would take longer than she wanted to wait. Not only that but if Benjamin had abducted Toby Whittaker fourteen years ago, Deborah would have been married to him at the time. She might well be the only witness to whatever had occurred in the past – or she could be involved. The time would come to let her in on what they knew but, for now, Jessica needed the woman's help.

Thinking quickly and hoping Rowlands followed her lead, Jessica pocketed her phone. 'No problem. We just need to find him.'

Deborah looked from Jessica to Rowlands before turning around and starting to hunt for the keys again. While her back was turned, the two detectives locked eyes and had a silent conversation where Jessica told her colleague she knew what they were doing wasn't exactly by the book but he should trust her. Their non-verbal sparring was interrupted as Deborah turned around holding a key ring with two keys attached. Deborah said she wanted to take her own vehicle, so the three of them walked out of the house, only to be met by a man in his twenties walking down the driveway towards them. He appeared slightly confused as he saw the two officers but turned to Deborah, offering a cheery, 'All right?'

Deborah finished locking the house before turning to face him properly. 'I'm on my way out, dear. Come back later if you want.'

He nodded an acknowledgement before asking the question Jessica dreaded. 'Is everything okay?'

Whether on purpose, she quickly allayed any problems. 'No, it's fine, nothing serious. I'll be back later if you need me.'

The man said goodbye before turning and walking back to a car parked on the road. Before Jessica could walk away, Deborah added quietly, 'That's Stephen, he's a friend of the family. Best not get him involved.'

Jessica wondered if the woman knew things weren't quite right.

Throughout the journey to Benjamin Sturgess's house, Jessica wondered how it could possibly be that Benjamin, or Ian, or whatever he was calling himself, could have been involved in both the Toby Whittaker disappearance and now Isaac's fourteen years apart. From what Harry said, Toby had a close relationship with his teacher, which was the only tenuous link to that first case. Fourteen years on, that now-former teacher had been driving a car with a kidnapped dead child in the back.

The return drive to Benjamin Sturgess's house took longer than it had the other way, traffic beginning to back up during the late afternoon and a frost already starting to settle as the sun went down. They parked on the road outside the house and Jessica could feel Sue watching them from the window next door. She didn't dare look just in case the woman took it as a hint to come and get involved. She knew a larger search team would return to the property at some point in the near future but, for now, she wanted to get a feel of the person she had spent the past few weeks struggling to find.

Deborah unlocked the door and it was clear no one had been around for a while because of a pile of mail on the mat. Deborah stepped inside, collecting the letters before holding the door open for the two officers. She didn't speak and Jessica knew she must now know something wasn't quite right. Deborah sat on the stairs just inside the door and started to flick through the post as they walked past her into the living room.

Despite the length of time she had been in the job, every now and then Jessica caught herself thinking like a civilian. As she walked into Benjamin's main room, an irrational feeling overtook her as she expected to find something that would ensure everything made sense. Maybe there would be a confession note or some obvious trace of either Toby or Isaac, or both? As it was, everything seemed normal. There was a flatscreen television on a cabinet, a sensible sandy-coloured carpet, regular cream walls, a leather sofa of the type which could be found in houses all around the country. Everything, including the photos on the wall, was just normal, normal, normal.

Jessica closed the living-room door behind her, leaving Deborah on the stairs as she and Rowlands strolled around the room. Her colleague spoke quietly. 'It's so . . .'

Jessica didn't let him finish the sentence. 'I know.' She didn't know what she expected to find from someone who may well have kept a secret for fourteen years.

On a side table midway inside the room, Jessica saw a wallet. She thought about how much easier things would have been if the man had picked it up on his way out those weeks ago. Had he forgotten it, or left it behind on purpose? She skimmed through its contents. Benjamin's driving licence sat in a clear section at the front, with notes and receipts. Jessica checked each one just in case but, aside from a liking for fast food – and a bizarre obsession with keeping the receipts – there was nothing untoward. She returned the wallet to the table and continued to look around.

Rowlands was checking a bookshelf at the back of the room where another door opened into a kitchen. Jessica pushed it shut as her colleague started to speak quietly. 'What's going on?' he asked. 'What are we even looking for?'

'I don't know. You know what the search teams are like, they'll tear this place apart, but sometimes, they're so focused on the bigger picture of bodies under the patio and so on, they miss the little things. Look for anything that might connect him to the stolen car he was in, or the allotments. It's got to link together somehow.'

'If I find a spade in the shed does that count?'

'No.'

Jessica had largely told the truth. She knew from experience things could get missed but if they stumbled across something then all the better.

Leaving Rowlands in the living room, Jessica walked into the kitchen. There were plenty of new-looking appliances but nothing she wouldn't have expected. A second door from the kitchen looped back into the hallway and Jessica went through, finding Deborah still sitting on the stairs. She had placed the letters in two piles on the floor and, as Jessica entered, answered the question the detective hadn't asked. 'That one is junk, the other one is proper mail.'

'I want to go upstairs for a bit if that's okay?' Jessica said, although she wasn't really asking.

Deborah shuffled the mail out of the way. 'Do you know how he is?'

'I . . .' Jessica stumbled but knew the time had come. Deborah was looking at her and she could see from the woman's face she already knew the answer. 'I'm afraid he's dead, Mrs Sturgess.' It was pretty brutal but Jessica had reached the point where she couldn't continue to stall.

Deborah nodded gently, waving her hand towards the mail. She looked more resigned than shocked. 'I knew something would be wrong when I saw all that. Even when we lived together, he would always pick up the post straight away and go through it. If we ever went on holiday, it would be the first thing he did when we got back, even above unpacking. Since we split, he's never gone away without letting me know. Sometimes it would only be a few nights when he was off signing books. I think I probably knew something was wrong the moment you told me he'd gone missing.'

Jessica looked down at Deborah, wondering what her former husband was like. She had only seen him as a contorted body in the wake of a car crash but the woman in front of her actually knew him. She didn't seem overly upset but they had been divorced for six years. Jessica blurted out the question without thinking. 'Why did you keep your husband's name, Mrs Sturgess?'

Deborah stared back. 'Are you married?'

Jessica shook her head. 'No.'

'If you ever had been, you'd know how hard it is to get your name changed in the first place. You send forms off to banks, insurance companies, employers, the tax office, all sorts of people. Everyone needs to see the original marriage licence too, not just a copy. Believe me, if you ever change your name and go through that hassle, changing it back and going through it all again isn't going to be high on your list of priorities.'

Deborah smiled slightly as she finished speaking before adding gently, 'We didn't break up on bad terms, everything just came to a natural end. Maybe if we'd had a bad break I would have been more interested in going back to my maiden name.'

Not for the first time in the past few weeks, Jessica wondered how many other 'normal' things simply passed her by. She had never really thought about it but just assumed that, once you were married, things such as changing your name were all done for you.

Deborah shuffled to one side of the stairs. 'You go look around. I hope you find what you're looking for.'

Jessica felt an obligation to make sure the woman was all right but wasn't sure there was much else she could say. She stepped over the pile of letters and walked slowly up the stairs, careful not to miss a thing. At the top was a varnished wooden landing, Jessica's footsteps echoing loudly as she walked across it. The upper level felt a degree or two cooler than downstairs. A few weeks had passed since she found Benjamin Sturgess in the front of that crashed car and the weather had certainly turned. Most people would now have their central-heating systems turned on during the day but this property had been empty for that time. Somehow the downstairs had kept a degree of warmth but Jessica pulled her jacket tighter around her as she struggled not to shiver.

She could feel a slight breeze and followed it to her left where a door stood ajar. It led into a bathroom where she saw a small window above the bath open a crack. Instinctively Jessica went to close it but stopped herself, wondering if, as implausible as it seemed, it could somehow prove crucial when the full search team came in. She closed the door behind her, walking back onto the wooden floor, conscious that each step she took could be heard downstairs. She was about to open another door when Rowlands called her. She went quickly down the stairs, into the living room. Rowlands was on the sofa holding two mobile phones.

'Where were they?' Jessica asked.

Rowlands crouched and pointed towards a small gap between the sofa and the side table where Jessica had found the wallet. 'There are plug sockets down here. They were on the floor charging.'

'Where's Deborah?'

Rowlands shrugged. 'I've not seen her.' He handed one of the devices to Jessica. 'What shall we do? Call the forensics team? They'll want to look at these.'

Jessica took the phone from him. It looked a few years old, with a sliding front panel and none of the fresh innovations many of the new gadgets had. 'So do I,' she said, pushing the front upwards so she could access the keys.

Rowlands was holding a far newer model than the one Jessica had taken. She knew a few people who had two mobile phones; one was usually for work, the other was personal. She wondered why a writer would need two. When she was younger and worked in uniform, one of the constables had two phones. The first was the one everyone he knew had the number for, be it his girlfriend, colleagues, parents or friends. The second had a pre-pay SIM card in it and he only gave out the number to women he met while he was out.

Jessica weighed the object in her hand. She suspected any second number probably wasn't used for giving out to women but wondered if the reason for Benjamin Sturgess having two phones was because of a similar type of duplicity.

She tried to find a call history but using an unfamiliar phone proved harder than she thought. It had taken her weeks to get used to her own and its various functions. After accidentally muting the device, then taking a photograph of the floor, Jessica found the contacts list but the italicised message made her even more convinced that she was on to something.

'No contacts found'.

She found the call history similarly empty and there were no text messages in the inbox. Jessica was about to put the phone down when she noticed there was a 'sent messages' folder towards the bottom of a long list of options. She felt her stomach jump slightly as two messages appeared on the screen. Both were to the same number, the date matching the day Isaac Hutchings went missing.

Jessica held her breath as she pressed the button to display the earliest one: 'Got him'.

The second was even more chilling: 'Will wait til its dark then meet you at the shed'.

Jessica slid the face down on the phone and put it on the side table before turning and dashing into the hallway. The two piles of mail were still on the floor and she picked up the smaller one. The top letter was a glossy pamphlet addressed to 'Ian Sturgess', a similar one underneath was for 'Ben Sturgess'. Jessica flicked from one to the other quickly before reaching a letter addressed to another person she had spent the past few weeks struggling to find. The shiny leaflet was clearly some sort of junk mail but the name on the front was printed in tidy black characters.

'Glenn Harrison'.

23

Still holding the letter, Jessica made for the kitchen. As Deborah hadn't gone upstairs or into the living room, it was the only place she could be. She found the other woman sitting on a stool staring out into the garden. Most of the light had gone and the only illumination was from the neighbouring houses. 'Deborah?'

The woman turned; her eyes were red but she wasn't crying. 'Sorry, I—'

'Who's Glenn Harrison?'

Deborah shook her head slightly, wiping one of her eyes. 'Who?'

Jessica held up the letter and pointed to the name. 'Glenn Harrison. This letter was for him, you put it in a pile with the other junk mail.'

Deborah blinked furiously. 'Oh yes. It's a bit of an odd story. When we first moved into our old house when we were married, we kept getting mail for this "Glenn Harrison" person. We assumed he lived there before us but there was no forwarding address and the house was sold at auction. We kept loads for about a year but ended up throwing them all away eventually. What we started to do was that whenever we had to sign up for something where you knew you'd end up getting junk mail or phone calls, we gave the name "Glenn Harrison". That way, if we got a letter for him, we knew it could go in the bin. We'd have all these companies calling up wanting to talk to "Mr Harrison". It was only for stupid things, not bills or anything like that.'

'Why would he still be getting letters here?'

Deborah shrugged. 'I don't know. When we divorced, we sold the place and got separate mortgages. I guess Ian did a similar thing with the name and his new address? I've picked up one or two in the past when I've been looking after his house. It's like that all the time now with junk mail and phone calls, especially if you do anything online. I do these survey things on the Internet for a bit of extra money but they're all for "Glenda Harrison". It was just a little joke we had between us.'

Jessica nodded. 'Can you wait here for a bit? I have to make a call.' Without waiting for Deborah to ask anything else, she walked through to the living room, closing the door before handing Rowlands the letter and pointing to the name.

His open mouth said it all. 'Wow.'

'Did you find anything on the other phone?'

'I didn't really look.'

Jessica nodded. 'Call the station. We're going to have to get people here to search the rest of the house plus experts to take the phones away and any laptop he might have. Someone's going to have to take Deborah in too, if only to question her about her husband.'

The constable realised the implication. 'Where are you going?'

'To the allotment.'

'Didn't they already check it over?'

'I want to see it again for myself. There was a text message about it. I think Benjamin was working with someone and they took Isaac to the shed. Make sure forensics take that phone. We need to get the number traced.'

The constable looked back at Jessica nodding, then it dawned on him. 'But we came in my car . . .' He tailed off as Jessica raised her eyebrows expectantly. 'Seriously? But you're a dreadful driver,' he pointed out.

'I am not. That's a myth, largely spread by you.'

'You're really going to take my car?'

'Look at it this way, if you get it back in one piece, you haven't lost anything. If I crash it then you were right all along. Either way, you win.'

Rowlands reached into his pockets. 'I win if you crash my car?'

'Yes.'

Jessica held her hand out and the constable placed his car keys in it. She pocketed them.

'Cheers, Dave. Is there a torch in your car?'

'In the boot. I started keeping one in there after we went to the allotment the last time and it was getting dark. Why?'

'Why do you think? Because it's dark.' Rowlands groaned. Jessica was about to leave before she turned back. 'Don't tell anyone where I've gone until they get here. I want a head-start.'

It took Jessica some time to finish sliding the seat forward and adjusting the mirrors before she could leave but she took extra care driving across the city back to the allotment. She was hampered because the levers for the windscreen wipers and indicators were on the opposite side in her vehicle. Each time she tried to indicate, she sent the wipers flying across the window at full speed, then tried to correct things while steering at the same time. Other than that and the annoyance of the roaring exhaust her colleague had purposefully had fitted at some point, the rest of the journey was quite smooth, even though she heard on the radio that part of the M60 had been closed, with traffic standing still on the opposite side of the road as she drove along Stockport Road.

Jessica had to go via the station first to collect the key for the allotment shed but she knew anyone important would already be on the way to Benjamin Sturgess's house so there would be no one around to question her.

Jessica remembered the route to the allotments from the previous time, parking outside the metal gate. She walked to the back of the vehicle and fumbled in the dark, using the light from her phone as she struggled to unlock the boot. It took a while before she realised the handle she had to pull to open it was actually what she'd assumed was simply the manufacturer's logo. Jessica was relieved to see the torch Dave mentioned was something suitable: heavy with a wide white beam which lit up the entirety of the boot.

She locked the car and swung around to face the gate. It wasn't that high but the beam from the torch showed a strong-looking padlock fastened to one side. Jessica climbed the gate and landed with a splash on the other side. She could feel water flowing over the top of her shoes into her socks and winced as she shone the light down to see her foot had gone straight through the top of a lightly iced patch of water into a brownish puddle. Jessica stepped steadily out of the water but the squelching sound made her cringe a second time as she walked slowly along the edge of the plots towards where she knew number sixty-one was.

She could feel a breeze blowing sideways across the open land and, having not expected to spend the final part of the day somewhere like this, she could feel her teeth chattering in the cold December air. Even as a rational adult, Jessica struggled not to think of what was in the dark while she walked. The combination of the wind, the temperature, the night and the noises that came with it felt creepy in a way she knew it shouldn't. She could feel her sodden sock sliding forward in her shoe with every step but tried to ignore it as she reached the turn where she knew the path led to plot sixty-one.

Jessica had not been back to the allotment since finding the list. After that, a handful of officers had investigated the site and she could see the plot of land next to the shed had been thoroughly excavated. Mounds of dirt were placed at the side, crystallised by the frost. She headed straight to the shed, taking the key she had signed out of the evidence store and putting it into the lock. Jessica had seen the reports of the team finding nothing of interest at the site. There was certainly nothing buried in the immediate area, while, exactly as Izzy had pointed out at the time, the interior was strangely empty.

Jessica unlocked the door and stepped inside, closing it behind her. It wasn't that much warmer on the inside but the wooden walls offered some protection from the wind. She shone the light slowly from side to side, not knowing what to expect. The text message had told her Benjamin had communicated with someone about this place on the same day Isaac went missing, leaving her to wonder if there was something obvious they had all missed. Apart from some dried muddy footprints, the shed looked much the same as it had before. The table and decrepit chair were in the same place but the gas canister and stove had been taken, presumably by the officers who searched the place.

Jessica re-examined the desk where she had found the list but it was empty. Foam was still coming out of the rips in the chair and she pushed her hands into the material to see if it contained anything further. More foam squeezed out of the sides but there was nothing else. Jessica thought about the wording of the text message.

'Will wait til its dark then meet you at the shed'.

Could it have referred to a different shed? She knew Benjamin was the same Ian Sturgess who Harry had been told had a close relationship with Toby Whittaker. He also used the name Glenn Harrison, meaning the cases of both missing boys could be connected to the place where she was standing. Surely this was the place he meant?

Her thoughts were interrupted by her phone ringing. Jessica took it out of her pocket and saw Cole's name on the display. As soon as she had made the decision to visit Benjamin Sturgess's house without calling in, she knew there would come a time when someone would want to shout at her. As good as her relationship was with her colleagues, there was always the odd occasion where she knew she had overstepped the boundaries. She had spent the past few hours allowing herself to be driven by her own determination to know what was going on, as opposed to the commitment she knew she should be showing to the job.

Aside from the torch, the illuminated phone screen was the only source of light in the room. Jessica watched Cole's name flash on and off before finally staying off. She pocketed the device and closed her eyes, listening to the wind buffeting the outside of the building.

Jessica opened her eyelids as the chill went through her. She put the torch down in the corner of the room and peered around, wondering what she was missing. If this was where Isaac had been brought, surely someone would have heard him? He could have been drugged but unless he was either watched the entire time, or restrained in some other way, there would have been too great a chance of him being discovered. The allotment wasn't quite a metropolitan hub of people but there was a steady enough stream to notice if something was different – or hear somebody either calling out or struggling. Jessica thought that if you were going to kidnap a child and keep him somewhere, there would be so many better options than here. In a city that had been built and developed over centuries, there were all sorts of hideaways where people could disappear.

On the other hand, Benjamin, Ian, Glenn or whatever

he was called not only had access to this shed, but there was also a list of names with Isaac's at the top.

Jessica started to pace, knowing the text message referred to where she was. At some point Ben had met someone else in this place on the night Isaac was taken.

For a moment the howl of the wind died down and Jessica noticed something – a slight difference in the sound of her footsteps. She retreated to the corner of the room, then walked to the opposite side, hearing the noise again. She thought about the previous time she had been there, when both Rowlands and Izzy had been present and how the other officers searching the area would have been in pairs at the very least. The wooden boards creaked as she stood on them but, towards the centre, the tone changed.

She sunk to her knees and began to tap the floor with her knuckles, remembering how she thought Rowlands was wasting his time doing something similar to the walls but now wishing he had been more thorough. As she switched to using her palm, Jessica could feel how there was a slight difference to the surface. She crawled across the floor, picking up the torch and returning to where she had been sitting, slowly running the light from side to side along the cracks between the boards, looking for something she had failed to see before. Eventually her eyes focused on a patch of wood she had already scanned twice. Now that she really concentrated, she realised that what appeared to be a regular grain on one of the boards was actually a thin gap. Jessica pushed a fingernail into it and slowly ran it along the length until she reached a corner. She continued to trace the outline until she reached another corner and, finally, the whole of her finger slid into the gap between boards. Jessica pushed the fingers from both hands into the thin area and pulled upwards. With almost no effort at all, a hatch popped up out of the floor. Jessica gasped and cursed herself, wondering how she had missed it the first time.

The underside of the wood had thick, shaggy light blue carpet attached which Jessica couldn't help running her hands through as she placed it upside down on the floor. She reached across for the torch and shone it into the area underneath. The opening was around a metre square but the space below was far larger. The first thing she noticed was more carpet. The whole of the floor underneath was covered with the same fabric as the underside of the hatch. The hidden room was very nearly as wide as the shed. She guessed it was around a metre and a half deep – not as tall as she was but high enough if you were going to keep an eleven-year-old child inside. As she shone the torch into the corners of the space, Jessica could see carpet attached to the walls too. She put the torch down and reached into the room with her hand, running it along the ceiling to feel more carpet. From what she could see, the entire area was covered. It would definitely keep whoever was inside warm but Jessica assumed it would give it a degree of soundproofing too.

She lay flat on her front and again shone the torch inside. There was no blood or any other sign of a struggle. If Isaac had been killed in the room below, considering the colour and texture of the carpet, it would have been almost impossible to clean. It seemed unlikely it could have been replaced without someone noticing although, at some point, it had clearly been installed without attracting undue attention. Jessica hauled herself up, sitting with her legs dangling into the gap.

As she took her phone out of her pocket, she wondered if Toby Whittaker had been brought to this place all those years ago. She flicked her fingers across the screen and pressed the button to show her list of missed calls. Cole might be unhappy with the way she had gone about things in the past day but he certainly wouldn't be able to accuse her of not making progress.

24

Jessica's telling-off hadn't been as bad as she anticipated. The first reason was that Cole had never been one to shout, swear or get upset, the second that everyone was too busy following up her leads. She was sitting in the chief inspector's office with Reynolds, Cornish, and, surprisingly to her, Rowlands, fully expecting a dressing down but instead had simply been told to follow procedure in future. While Cole gave her the most minor of reprimands, she could sense Rowlands looking at her, wondering how she apparently got away with it every time. The truth was that running headlong into situations had got her into problems in the past and she was fully aware she hadn't learned her lesson. Like a naughty schoolchild, she almost craved a punishment.

Instead, Cole moved quickly on from the brief admonishment to bringing everyone up to date with what had happened. He looked at his watch before pushing back into his chair and rubbing his eyes. 'Thanks for coming back,' he began. 'It's been one of those days and I know we're all supposed to be off tomorrow. I've been talking to Superintendent Aylesbury and he's delighted things are moving. It's just . . . unfortunate it happens to be Saturday tomorrow and then Christmas Eve the day after.'

Until that morning, Jessica had lost track of the date. She was aware of the decorations and cheesy music in the newsagent's and off-licence near her flat but had been so caught up with the case and Adam that the last week or so seemed to have passed her by. She had arrived late at Adam's house the previous evening and it was only that morning when he asked her what she wanted to do for Christmas that she realised it was just days away. Caroline sent her a text message to ask something similar and it hit her that not only had she made no plans, but that very little would happen on the case for the next week or so. It wasn't that she wanted to stop working on the investigation, simply that everyone else would. It was difficult to talk to people or request information when so many companies and organisations were closed for two weeks. It was like trying to work on a Sunday. Whether she wanted to get on with things or not, it made very little difference over a weekend because no one else was at work.

Around the station, Christmas was the time uniformed officers made their money and grumbled their way through a fortnight. It was full of domestic violence incidents, with family members getting drunk and fighting with each other before waking up in a cell on Boxing Day wondering what had happened. One by one the drunks filed into the station over the festive period and then, when the courts reopened, one by one they were sent packing again. For most, spending Christmas behind bars was deemed punishment enough.

Luckily for Jessica, unless there was an active element of a case to be worked on, many members of CID were given a certain leeway over their hours during the holiday season.

Put on the spot that morning, Jessica announced to Adam what she wanted to do for Christmas. It was fair to say he wasn't delighted at the prospect but he agreed, as had Caroline. She spent the whole day trying to catch a moment with Dave to see if he was up for it but had barely seen him until this moment. Izzy said she would have loved to be involved with Jessica's idea but already had plans.

Her mind was drifting when she was brought back by Cole. 'Jess?'

'Sir.'

'Do you want to go first?'

'Yeah, sorry.' Jessica turned in her seat to address the other officers. 'I've spent the day in the freezing cold watching a bunch of officers stare into a hole and ask, "Is that carpet?". Essentially we discovered a secret room of sorts underneath the allotment shed where we found the list of children's names. Everything has been stripped out and sent to the labs and, from what I overheard, there are a couple of officers in for a right bollocking for not finding the room in the first place. There's not much else to say really.'

Cole nodded his head towards Cornish, who uncrossed her legs and leant forward. 'I've been at Benjamin Sturgess's house. All the electronic items were taken away but because of the hidden room under the allotment shed, people have been tearing the rest of the house apart too. I've not had much to do with that but, so far, nothing has shown up.'

Her tone of voice made it clear she wasn't impressed at being taken from whatever she was working on to go and watch a house being destroyed. Ordinarily, a CID member wouldn't be needed or sometimes even welcome at a scene such as that but, given the complete failure to find the hidden room under the shed, Cole had called Jessica that morning to say the chief superintendent was on the warpath and wanted people 'with half a brain cell between them' to oversee the day's main activities. Because she and fellow sergeant Cornish had been out all day, Rowlands had been left looking for a paper trail along with Izzy.

Cole ignored the sergeant's tone and looked at Rowlands. 'David?'

As far as Jessica was aware, the constable had never sat in on a senior team briefing. She knew him pretty well and heard a twinge of hesitation in his voice. 'We've been trying to find out as much as we can about "Benjamin Sturgess", "Ian Sturgess" and "Glenn Harrison". It now seems they are all the same person and we know Ian gave up teaching around twelve years ago. He and his wife sold their house around six years back. That was where our trail ended until yesterday. We've been trying to fill in the blanks but, so far, there's not been anything to find. Benjamin Sturgess has a couple of books out but neither of them seem to be big sellers. We'll keep looking but it seems like he's lived a very normal life, albeit under his original name, as opposed to his middle name. Aside from finding them in a car together and the map, obviously, we haven't got anything to connect him to Isaac Hutchings and, apart from the fact he used to teach Toby Whittaker, we're struggling there too.'

Jessica winked at him to let the constable know he had done all right. Cole turned to the final person in the room. 'Jason?'

Reynolds let out a large sigh. 'I've spent the day interviewing Benjamin Sturgess's former wife, Deborah. They are divorced but still have some sort of relationship.'

'What was she like?' Jessica interrupted. She'd wanted to do the interview but hadn't argued with the chief inspector when he had given her instructions that morning.

The inspector tilted his head to one side. 'Hard to read; sad without being upset, confident without being aggressive. She didn't seem particularly evasive. She says they just drifted apart in their marriage. I asked her about the relationship with her husband but everything she said seemed as you would expect.'

'Did you ask about Toby Whittaker?' Jessica asked.

'Yes, we talked about all sorts. It was one of those awkward ones where you're not interviewing a suspect but, at the same time, you have to be careful how much you give away because they could become one at some point. She's now aware of what we think her husband did but I didn't ask too much because I would have had to reveal everything we knew. As for Toby, she says she hadn't heard of him.'

'What did she say about the shed?' Jessica asked, wondering if anyone else had any questions or just her.

'Not much. She reckoned her husband kept an allotment patch. Apparently his father did and he inherited the whole gardening thing. She says she had never been there, it was just something he did a few nights a week.'

It sounded plausible to Jessica. If Adam ever announced

he was a gardener in his free time, she would certainly have no interest in helping.

There was a small silence before Cole spoke. 'She was cautioned but not arrested and has been let out. We've got no reason to assume she had anything to do with any of this. The phones DS Daniel found at Sturgess's house have gone off to forensics and they've taken a computer too. As for results, they told us the number that was texted from the phone is unregistered so we don't know who the messages went to. Everything else has been deleted but they're working on it. I've been told not to expect anything any time soon. I spoke to the head guy over there but, to cut a long story short, he says they have to pay their staff double for working over the Christmas period. With budgets the way they are, they're shutting down for the best part of a week for anything except time-sensitive work. I spoke to DSI Aylesbury but he didn't want to get involved so I don't think we'll be getting much until at least next week, if not the new year.'

Adam worked for the forensics department, albeit not the electronics section. Jessica already knew he was off work until the middle of the following week. There was another pause as Cole scanned the room. 'Do we think this is it? Benjamin Sturgess kidnapped Isaac Hutchings, killed him, then got caught while he was dumping the body? We might be able to connect him to Toby Whittaker's disappearance and presumed murder because of the map – although we wouldn't be able to prove much as we haven't found a body. People above me seem keen to get this done and dusted.'

236

Jessica could hear the uncertainty in his voice. With the pressure he was under from his superiors, there must be a strong incentive to get everything tidied away nicely in time for Christmas. She could sense that he wasn't quite convinced.

'This is nonsense,' Jessica said. She could feel everyone's eyes on her as the words spilled out. 'Sorry, but it is. From the text messages, it's clear there's at least one other person involved. Benjamin messaged someone to say they should meet at the "shed". If nothing else, we've got to find out who that is.'

There was silence for a few moments before Cole replied. 'The forensics team will be looking into that but, for now—'

Jessica didn't let him finish. '"For now" what? We're going to tell the media we've got our man so everyone can let their kids out to play again? What about the map? Benjamin was driving but didn't know where he was going. If it was just him who had done all of this on his own, he would know. What about the stolen car? This is a guy in his fifties. Are we saying he hooked Daisy Peters's keys out of her house and drove away? He doesn't live anywhere near her but somehow he knew she lived alone? Where did he get the information for that list of kids we found? He's not a teacher any longer but he knew their names and addresses. He must have got that from some-where.'

There was a longer silence where no one dared say any-thing. Cole was staring at Jessica and she could see in his eyes that he didn't want to be there. 'What do you suggest we do?' he asked quietly.

'We find out who he was working with.'

'There's nothing to stop us doing that. Forensics are looking into things but we can't do anything else until those results come back. It's just been *suggested* to me that if we release the information about Benjamin Sturgess to the media tonight or tomorrow . . .'

He didn't finish the sentence but he didn't have to. Jessica knew what he was implying. If the information was released it would give the public a nice impression of them to savour over Christmas. Meanwhile, they could continue looking for whoever the second person might be. If they found out, great. If not, they already had a man to pin everything on – a dead person who wouldn't be able to refute anything.

'Are you going to go along with this?' Jessica asked, more aggressively than she meant to.

Cole spoke quietly but determinedly. 'It's not really up to me.'

'In the press conference, are we at least going to tell the media we are still looking for a second person?'

Cole said nothing but she could tell by looking at him that the answer was 'No'. It wasn't as if they were appealing for witnesses because, so far, all they had to go on was an unregistered phone number a text message had been sent to. Without anything specific to take to the public, it seemed someone higher up in the force had decided they would host a triumphant media event and conveniently ignore the secondary evidence.

Jessica met the chief inspector's eyes. She had known him for around a decade in total and been something close to a friend for some of those years. 'At least tell people the investigation isn't closed,' she said with a softer tone.

'It's not my call.'

'But you'll be there. You can say what you want.'

He spoke quietly but emphatically. 'No.'

'But—' Jessica couldn't finish before Cole spoke over her.

'We're finished here. Everyone go home and have a good Christmas.'

'Sir, I . . .'

The chief inspector suddenly rose to his feet, sending his chair clattering into the wall behind him. Jessica had rarely seen him angry but his eyes were wide and glaring straight at her. 'Don't even think about talking about this externally.'

It was the most threatening thing Jessica had ever heard him say and utterly out of character. She knew he was referring to a journalist friend of hers, warning her not to leak the information. 'I wasn't going to—'

'Out. Now. Everyone.'

For a second or two, nobody moved, stunned by the venom in the man's usually calm voice. Everyone stood at the same time and moved quickly towards the door. Nobody spoke as they headed down the stairs in unison towards the ground floor but together the four officers walked to the office Jessica shared with Cornish, even though she hadn't asked them to.

Once inside, Reynolds closed the door. 'Just be careful,'

he said firmly, looking directly at Jessica, who was sitting on the corner of her desk.

'I was just saying what we were all thinking. Or should have been thinking.' Jessica was feeling defensive but also a little shaken. She had never known Cole become so angry, whether as chief inspector or in his old DI role.

'Yes, but there are right ways to do things,' Reynolds went on. 'Don't forget he's getting it from all sides.' Jessica shrugged, feeling uncomfortable. 'Are you okay?' he added.

'Fine.'

The inspector weighed her up for a moment before responding. 'Right, I'm heading off. Have a good Christmas and . . . don't do anything *stupid*.' Jessica knew he was also referring to leaking information. Louise didn't add anything except for a 'Merry Christmas' and left the room, leaving Rowlands and Jessica alone.

The two officers stared at each other before Dave finally cracked and burst out laughing. 'That was hilarious,' he said in between sniggers. 'It was like being in church or assembly at school and you're just holding it in, desperately trying not to laugh.'

Jessica tried to remain serious but her friend's laughter was infectious and she couldn't help smiling. 'I'm glad you find it funny.'

'Oh, it was. For a moment I thought he'd actually swear. Everyone's always going on about how calm he is. Imagine if he'd actually told you to f-off or whatever.'

'Do you remember that shit game you lot started playing a while back?' Jessica asked.

'The "trying to get the DCI to swear" game? Of course. It was my idea.'

'No one managed it then?'

'No, but I got close. I found this news article online about some agricultural argument thing in Somerset. The headline was, "Forking Hell". I tried to get him to read it out loud but he wasn't having it.'

'In other words, you forked up.'

It was such a bad pun that neither of them could resist laughing.

'That was pathetic,' Rowlands concluded when he had composed himself.

Jessica couldn't deny that. 'Are you busy on Christmas Eve?' she asked.

He screwed his face up. 'I don't know. I'm probably going to be buying everyone's presents.'

'Seriously? I thought you'd finally grown up?'

'Just joking. Chloe and me are spending the day together.'

'Do you fancy coming to mine?'

'What for?'

'I'm cooking everyone Christmas Dinner a day early.'

Rowlands snorted. 'No, seriously, what for?'

Jessica refused to take the bait. 'Seriously. I'm cooking everyone dinner. Me, my mate Caroline, my boyfriend Adam, Hugo, plus you and Chloe if you're up for it.'

Dave must have realised Jessica wasn't joking as he stopped smiling. 'Hugo's going?'

'Yes.'

'You're seeing that Adam dude again?'

'Yes.'

'*You're* cooking?'

'Yes!' Jessica almost shouted the final response.

'But you don't cook. The last time I was round, you burned a frozen pizza then ended up getting everyone to chip in for a takeaway.'

'So what?'

'Well, what are we having?'

'A Christmas dinner. Roast potatoes, Yorkshire pudding, peas, carrots, parsnips, turkey, gravy. You know, a Christmas dinner.'

Dave stared back at her clearly not knowing what to say before finally stumbling over a reply. 'I don't eat peas.'

'Who doesn't eat peas?'

'I don't. They're all green and little and just *pea-y*.'

'Whatever. I'll leave them off your plate. Are you coming?'

The constable didn't seem to know how to respond, finally throwing his hands up. 'Fine. I'll check with Chloe but it should be all right. We'll be there.'

'Brilliant. Three o'clock.'

'Fine. There's no way I'm going to miss this. I'll make sure I've got the numbers "nine" and "nine" typed into my phone, then the minute you set the kitchen on fire, I'll press the other "nine". Let's just hope the fire brigade aren't on another call.'

25

The exchange with Rowlands calmed Jessica to such a degree that she wasn't fuming by the time she arrived at Adam's house to pick him up. She parked on the road outside and phoned him because she didn't fancy getting out of the vehicle to ring the doorbell. He laughed at her laziness but soon emerged from the house carrying a small overnight bag across his shoulder and a suit hanger in his hand, which he put on the back seat, then sat in the front.

'What's with the suit?' Jessica asked, pulling away.

'I figured if we're staying at yours tonight and you're cooking for Christmas tomorrow, it'd be nice to dress a bit smartly.'

'Is this to guilt me into wearing a dress?'

Adam laughed. 'You're so suspicious all the time.'

'It comes with the job.'

He chuckled again. 'What's the plan?'

'We've got to go to the supermarket to get some bits for tomorrow. I called Caz earlier and she doesn't mind sleeping on the sofa tonight. We're going to clear all the furniture to one side tomorrow, then pull the dining table out from the kitchen and eat in the living room.'

'And you're really cooking?'

Jessica sounded as indignant as she could. 'Yes. Why

does no one believe me? Caroline thought I was joking too.'

'Maybe it's because you don't cook?'

'I do.'

'Pot noodles, beans on toast and heating up a poppadom to go with a takeaway curry isn't cooking.'

'What is it then?'

'Heating food. You don't cook, you heat.'

'Well, thanks for your confidence.'

Jessica didn't particularly feel aggrieved and was aware her friends had a point. She had no idea why she'd decided to do something completely out of the ordinary for her. Since getting back together with Adam, she had made a pact of sorts with herself to stop being so stuck in her ways. The thought of cooking a large meal for herself and five of her closest friends was terrifying but she resolved to go with it.

The supermarket was heaving with people who seemingly had a similar idea to Jessica about buying food before Christmas Eve. Children were running in all directions and stressed adults heaving overflowing trolleys of alcohol and food up and down the aisles. Jessica could feel herself becoming frustrated by the lack of room to manoeuvre – and because a wheel on the back of the trolley she had chosen didn't seem to face the same direction as the other three. Adam said he was happy to push but that would have felt too much like giving in, so she continued to fight against it, tolerating his gentle amusement.

After finding most of what they needed, Jessica was left looking for one final item. She stopped one of the female workers walking past. 'Do you know where the flour is?' she asked.

'Flowers? We sell bunches in the front, right where you walk in.' The woman took two steps to walk away but Jessica managed to reply in time.

'Not "flowers", "flour", as in the stuff you make cakes with.'

The worker spun around. 'Oh right, "flour".' She pointed towards an aisle Jessica had already checked twice. 'It's that one, aisle twenty.'

'I already looked there.'

'It's about three-quarters of the way down the aisle at the bottom.' The person went to walk off but Jessica again stopped her.

'Can you show me?'

'Er yeah, I . . . okay.' The woman started heading quickly past Jessica in the direction she had indicated.

Jessica struggled to rotate the trolley, finally managing to turn it just in time to see the woman entering the aisle.

'Are you all right?' Adam asked.

Without looking at him, Jessica knew he had a smug grin on his face. She ignored him, walking as briskly as she could before sliding to a stop and skidding around the corner into aisle twenty herself. She was looking forward to the over-confident supermarket worker being proven wrong but felt her heart sink as she saw the woman pointing at a spot on the shelf she had definitely gone past twice.

As Jessica approached, the worker was still pointing and sounded particularly cocky. 'It's just there, see. Aisle twenty.'

'Thanks very much,' Jessica replied through gritted teeth. The worker walked away and Adam crouched down to pick up a bag of flour.

'Plain or self-raising?' he asked.

'It wouldn't surprise me if the flour wasn't here at all but that smug bitch just grabbed a few off the shelves somewhere else to make us look stupid,' Jessica said. 'We walked up and down here twice.'

Adam grinned up at her, repeating his question.

'I don't know, what's the difference?' Jessica asked.

'One raises, the other doesn't.'

'All right, smart-arse. Which one should I use?'

'You're the chef.'

'Fine. Get both and I'll use half of each.'

Adam stood and put one of each type of flour in the trolley. 'Are we done?'

'Yes, if I spend any longer in here, I might just murder someone. Preferably one of those little shits who keep running up and down.'

Jessica did her best to wheel the trolley to the end of the aisle. As far as she could see, each checkout counter had at least two people in line. 'We'll use the self-service ones at the bottom,' she said to no one in particular, shunting the cart in and out of the queuing people until she reached the tills that allowed people to scan their own shopping.

'Do you want me to scan?' Adam asked.

'No, I'm fine.'

Jessica was determined to retain some degree of control and started to swipe items, as Adam helped put them in bags. As they neared the end, she reached the alcohol they had bought. She scanned the bottle of vodka and a message appeared on the screen warning she had to be over eighteen. Adam placed the bottle in a bag but it wouldn't let her process any more items. Jessica looked up to see a red light whirring above her head and a spotty-faced young man hurrying towards her. The closer he got, the younger he appeared until Jessica concluded he was definitely no older than thirteen or fourteen.

'Is everything okay?' he asked in a high-pitched voice.

'Just this vodka,' Jessica said. 'It's checking our age.'

The man looked her up and down. 'Have you got ID?'

Jessica squinted at him, wondering if he was playing with her. 'ID?'

'Yes, to prove your age.'

'Are you joking?'

'Er, no, we require ID.' The worker pointed to a sign above the counter which mentioned something about having to look over twenty-one to buy alcohol.

'Do you think I look under twenty-one?' Jessica asked.

'I, er . . . we require ID,' the man repeated.

'I don't have ID. I'm thirty-four, for crying out loud. I've not been asked for ID since I was about fifteen.'

'I understand that, Madam, but . . .'

'Am I on camera or something? Is this going to be on TV?' Jessica knew some people who might feel flattered at being asked to prove their age but she certainly wasn't one of them. She knew there was no way she looked under eighteen, it was just this pre-pubescent was trying to make life difficult for her.

Adam spoke up. 'I've got ID if it helps, here.' He reached forward to show the man his driving licence but the worker shook his head.

'Sorry, I can't accept that because you could be buying it for her,' he replied, nodding towards Jessica, his face utterly serious.

'This is ridiculous,' Jessica said. 'Seriously, how old are you? Thirteen? Fourteen?'

'Ma'am, I . . .'

'Stop calling me that. Can I speak to your manager?' Jessica could see someone else in line behind them listening to the conversation.

'I'm sorry, the manager is currently busy. You could wait but it might be a while. He'll only tell you what I already have anyway.'

Jessica was weighing up the best way to tell the man exactly what she thought of him before Adam interrupted. 'It's okay, we'll just take the food.'

Despite stopping at an off-licence close to her house, Jessica was still angry when she arrived home, much to Adam and Caroline's amusement. 'You should take it as a compliment,' Caroline said but Jessica was having none of it.

Desperate not to completely mess things up, Jessica got up early the next morning and made a list of everything she had to do. Caroline had given her a cook book as a birthday present, no doubt wanting to give her a nudge in the right direction. She hadn't thought she would ever use it but now it would come in handy. She wrote down everything she was going to make, noted how long everything should take, then worked backwards so she knew what she would have to cook first. Essentially, everyone was right when they said she didn't cook but she figured that was largely because she had never tried. As she read the method for making Yorkshire pudding, she thought it couldn't be *that* hard.

That afternoon, Adam and Caroline rearranged the living room as Jessica continued to refuse any offers of help. Despite an accident opening one of the bags of flour which resulted in one of the walls ending up with a fairly heavy dusting, Jessica thought she was doing a fairly good job – particularly judging by the smells coming from the cooker.

Hugo was the first person to arrive. Caroline answered the door and Jessica heard her welcoming him in. She hadn't seen him in a few weeks, since her friend had moved in. His real name was Francis and he was a part-time magician, although he didn't seem to do anything else the rest of his time. He had helped her through a bad spell emotionally and always cheered her up when they met. He was an old university friend of Dave.

Jessica was at the oven when the door opened and Hugo stepped in. She glanced towards him, quickly doing a double-take. He was wearing a full suit with canvas trainers that didn't match and, most bizarrely, a top hat. Despite the smartness of the suit, he still made it look scruffy. 'What *are* you wearing?' she asked.

Hugo shrugged dismissively as she had seen him do so many times before. 'Dunno. I thought it best to dress up.'

'What's with the hat?'

Hugo took it off, twirling it impressively in his hand before putting it back on his head and shrugging again. 'I've been trying a new look for the act.' His long dark hair had grown a little since the last time Jessica had seen him and was now below his shoulders. He had tied it back into a half-ponytail, so some of it was still loose.

'You're so weird,' Jessica said affectionately, stepping away to give him a hug. 'Is this all part of some big trick you've got planned?' she asked, nodding towards the hat.

When it was just the two of them, he acted relatively normally but whenever there were a few more people around, Hugo would pull off some sort of illusion. He shrugged again, although that seemed to be his standard response to most things.

'Do you want some help?' he asked.

'Did *they* tell you to ask that?'

'Who?'

'Adam and Caroline?'

'No, you just look . . .'

'Right, you can go join them in the living room. Out.' Jessica shooed her friend away and closed the door again, checking the clock above it to see how long she had left. It was a few minutes to three and she was aiming to have everything ready for half past. As she put a tray of York-shire puddings she hoped would rise into the oven, the doorbell rang again and she heard Dave's and Chloe's voices from the hallway.

The constable was also in a suit and Chloe had a short

black dress on. 'Why has everyone dressed up?' Jessica asked in annoyance.

'I thought it was some official sit-down dinner thing and thought I'd make an effort,' Rowlands protested. 'If I'd known you were going to be slumming around in trackie bottoms, I wouldn't have bothered.'

Jessica looked down at the trousers she was wearing and realised the flour that had exploded had stuck to the cooking oil she'd dripped on herself earlier and created a crusty mess. She knew she was going to have to change.

Ignoring Dave, she turned to Chloe. The woman had short blonde hair with an incredibly toned physique that made Jessica think the woman probably *could* kick her arse if she so desired. Chloe was smiling awkwardly. 'Are you okay, Chloe?' Jessica asked.

'Fine, thanks.'

'What about me?' Rowlands asked.

'You're always fine. Now sod off and leave me alone.'

'Burnt anything yet?'

'Only *your* food, pea-boy.'

Chloe laughed. 'I keep telling him it's weird not to like peas.' Dave quickly shuffled his girlfriend out of the kitchen, perhaps suspecting the women were going to gang up on him.

When it was time to dish up the food, Jessica called Caroline in to help her get everything onto the plates while she went to her room and quickly changed. She thought about putting on the pair of jeans she always wore at the weekend but, given all three men were wearing suits, while Chloe had a short dress on and Caroline had made something of an effort too, she opted to go with the flow. Jessica opened her wardrobe and shunted ninety per cent of the items to one side before picking a blue dress from a hanger. She hadn't worn it for as long as she could remember. The hem came to just above her knee and it was the shortest piece of clothing she could remember wearing since the days when Caroline was a university student and they used to go out together. She was pleased it still fitted and untied her hair before dashing bare-footed back to the kitchen.

'Wow,' Caroline said as Jessica entered.

'Yeah, sod off, it's just a dress.'

'All right, aren't you touchy?' Caroline was clearly teasing. She was wearing a similar dress in red but had put an apron over the top of it while she scooped the food onto the plates. 'You've done a good job with this here,' she added. 'Potatoes a little burnt but all good apart from that.'

'I like them burnt.'

'Fair enough. They're ready to go through.'

Jessica carried the first plate into the living room. The table was set up with some placemats Caroline had found and she had also bought Christmas crackers. The chairs were a mixture of ones that folded and the regular ones from in the kitchen. Because of that, everyone was at slightly different heights. As she came into the room, Jessica saw Adam smiling at her but Rowlands exhaled loudly. 'Holy shit, you look like a girl.'

Jessica put the plate down in front of him, then slapped him on the back of the head before leaving and returning with another plate which she gave to Hugo.

When they were all sitting at the table with a plate in front of them, there was an uneasy silence with everyone waiting for someone else to start. 'It *looks* good,' Dave said.

Jessica picked up her fork and thrust it into one of the potatoes. 'Fine, I'll go first,' she said, stuffing the entire thing into her mouth. Once it was clear she wasn't going to collapse, the rest of her guests began to eat too. 'You could have started,' Jessica whispered to Adam.

He squeezed her thigh under the table. 'You look nice,' he replied, ignoring her. 'I've never seen you in a dress.'

'Seriously?' Adam shook his head as he removed his hand and started cutting into a Yorkshire pudding. Jessica realised that they saw each other almost exclusively after work when she still had her suit on. When they went out, she usually wore jeans – not just for him but because she always did.

Her thoughts were interrupted by Rowlands opposite her speaking far too loudly. 'What the hell is that?' He was pointing with his fork towards something on his plate. Everyone turned to look and Chloe stuck her fingers in and picked it up. For a few moments, Jessica thought she had done something wrong, before realising the other woman was holding a single pea. 'It was hidden under the turkey,' Rowlands protested.

'Sorry,' Caroline said. 'I tried to make sure there weren't any on yours. Jess said you didn't want any.'

'Ugh, it touched other things,' Rowlands added, a disgusted look on his face.

'It's just a pea,' Chloe said, putting it in her mouth. 'It won't hurt you.'

'How old are you?' Jessica asked mockingly. Rowlands nervously poked the rest of his food with the fork, checking underneath for any other hidden vegetables.

Jessica was pleased everyone seemed to enjoy the meal. Afterwards, Hugo insisted on doing the washing-up, while Adam and Dave helped out, even though the latter was reluctant. As the three women moved the table out of the way and started to rearrange the furniture, Caroline stopped to hug her friend. 'That was really good, well done.'

'Cheers.'

'I'm sorry for being a burden these past few weeks.'

'It's all right, don't worry, you're not. I've just got lots going on.'

As Jessica and Caroline carried the folded-down table into the corner, Chloe spoke. 'Can I ask you something?'

'Me?' Jessica asked.

The woman was standing in the centre of the room curling a strand of hair around her finger and letting it go again. 'Yeah. It's just . . . we've met a couple of times now and I know you're mates with Dave but you're always so, erm, friendly . . . I was just wondering if you've ever, erm . . . you know? Sorry . . .'

Chloe was clearly nervous about asking but it seemed to be something she'd had on her mind for a while. Jessica looked at Caroline then back at Chloe before bursting out laughing. It took her a little while before she could compose herself enough to answer. 'Sorry, I didn't mean to laugh but, oh God . . .' Jessica went across and hugged the other woman. 'Have you got a brother?' she asked as she released her.

'One older, one younger.'

'How do you feel about the younger one?'

'I don't know . . . he's just my brother.'

'Exactly. I don't have any brothers or sisters but Dave's just *there* for me to annoy. Believe me, nothing like that has ever happened between us.'

Chloe seemed relieved. 'Oh right, it's just that you're always fighting. I thought it was like at school where the boys only torment the girls they secretly fancy.'

Jessica didn't know the best way to respond, eventually opting for: 'Believe me when I say this in the nicest possible way, he's all yours.'

Chloe broke into a smile. 'Sorry . . . I just wanted to ask . . .'

When the men had finished cleaning up, the six of them sat around the living room chatting about their own memories of Christmases gone by. Jessica was sitting on Adam's lap with an arm around his neck, happy with any conversation that didn't involve work. Hugo was amusing them with a series of card tricks and had finally taken off the top hat.

'Hugo,' Jessica shouted, as the wine she'd had with the meal began to take hold. 'How long have you known Dave?'

Hugo was sitting cross-legged on the floor, shuffling a deck of cards one-handed by spinning and tossing them into the air. 'I dunno, since uni. Maybe nine or ten years?'

'Do you have any dirt?'

Hugo wasn't looking at her but was instead in his own world, playing with the cards. She had seen him in this mood frequently, where he would be fully engaged in a conversation but to anyone not immediately involved, it would seem as if he was oblivious to what was going on around him.

'What do you mean?' he asked.

'Steady,' Rowlands warned as Chloe, who was sitting next to him on the sofa, giggled.

'Yeah, come on, dish the dirt,' Chloe said with a hiccup.

'Shall I tell them about the business cards, Dave?' Hugo said, putting the cards down and picking up his top hat again.

The response was instant. 'No.'

'Oh, go on,' Jessica said. 'You've got to now.' Chloe joined in with the encouragement while Dave was equally adamant.

'Don't you dare,' he warned.

'Let's put it to a vote,' Jessica said. 'All in favour of hearing about the business cards, put your hands up.' She and Chloe thrust their arms in the air instantly while she opened her eyes widely and stared at Adam. 'If you don't put one of your hands up, you'll be needing it to perform other duties this weekend that I certainly won't be involved with.' Adam made his apologies, smiling, then half-raised his arm. Caroline was beginning to fall asleep as she rested her head on the corner of the sofa. 'Caz?' Jessica said to no response.

'Three-all,' Dave declared with a smug tone. 'That's not a majority.'

'Come on, Hugo, get that hand up,' Jessica urged.

It seemed as if he hadn't heard her as he spun the hat on one finger before, finally, he stopped and lifted his arm into the air, turning to Rowlands with a grin. 'Sorry, mate.'

Jessica slurred a cheer and knew she'd had too much to drink.

'When we were back at uni,' Hugo continued, 'we had this careers conference thing where some guy came in to talk to us about the future. It was all about how best we could present ourselves to employers and so on.'

'Stop—' Rowlands interrupted before Chloe dug him in the ribs.

Hugo didn't stop. 'Afterwards Dave went down to the train station. There was this booth there where you could put your details in and it would print off business cards for you. When he was done, Dave brought this pack of about five hundred back and showed us all. It had his name at the top with his phone number and one word at the bottom.' He paused for dramatic effect before revealing the moniker Rowlands had given himself. 'It just said one thing. David Rowlands: Trendsetter.'

As Hugo said the word, there was an explosion of laughter from both Jessica and Chloe. Jessica was already feeling tipsy and the laughing wasn't helping the room from stopping spinning. '*Trendsetter?*' she exclaimed loudly. 'What were you thinking?'

Rowlands looked indignantly at her. 'I don't know, it was just a word that stuck in my head. I thought employers would be impressed.'

'Yeah, I'm sure the local supermarket manager would

have been crying out for a "trendsetter" to stack shelves for him. What happened to the cards?'

'I don't know. I think I binned them all.'

Chloe was still laughing but at least making an effort to stifle it, which was more than Jessica had done.

'All right, all right,' Dave added, glaring at his girl-friend. 'Calm down, it's not that funny.' He turned to Hugo. 'What about you, anyway? You only took up magic to get a girlfriend.'

Hugo shrugged, continuing to play with his hat. Jessica was appreciating his humour more and more by the second. 'What about the speed dating?' Hugo asked.

'Oh, sod right off,' Rowlands said. 'Don't tell them that.'

Chloe composed herself enough to cross the room and sit next to Hugo. 'Go on, you can tell us.'

Dave leant back on the sofa, crossing his arms. 'Did you plan all this?' he asked Jessica accusingly.

'If I'd thought of this, do you think I would have waited so long?' Jessica replied. 'I'd have had Hugo round ages ago dishing the dirt.'

'Fine, just tell them,' Rowlands said, sinking further into the seat. Chloe gave a small squeal and crossed back to sit next to him, snuggling her head into his reluctant shoulder.

Hugo stopped playing with the hat, stretching himself out so he was lying flat on his back looking at the ceiling. 'When we were freshers, there was this speed-dating event in the first few weeks to help everyone get to know each other. Dave, me and a few other lads went along. There were about fifty or sixty people there and you got around a minute with each person before the buzzer went and you moved on. We'd only got to the second person when we heard this shouting and Dave was having an argument with some girl.'

Jessica looked across at Dave. 'You had a row with someone while speed-dating?'

He shrugged. 'Yeah, I dunno, something like that.'

'How can you fall out with a complete stranger in less than a minute?'

'She was going on about how "Return of the Jedi" is better than "The Empire Strikes Back".'

'Oh for f . . . So it wasn't even a proper argument, it was a geek argument?' Jessica said.

'Well, obviously it's not better,' Rowlands protested as Chloe hugged him tighter, a large grin on her face.

Caroline was the first to openly fall asleep, although she had been flagging for a while. Between them, they had drunk everything Jessica had bought, as well the bottles of wine brought by her guests. Finally Dave, Chloe and Hugo ordered a taxi. Caroline was asleep on the floor so Jessica and Adam helped her onto the sofa before covering her with two blankets. Jessica was feeling tipsy but not completely drunk. She led Adam out of the room holding his hand but as he shut the door behind them, he stopped and pulled her close to him, hugging her. 'Did you have a good day?' he whispered into her ear.

Jessica pulled his arms tighter around her, then turned so she could cuddle him properly. 'Yeah. It was great.'

'The food was good.'

Jessica didn't respond to his compliment but squeezed him tightly. 'Merry Christmas.'

Adam laughed slightly. 'Merry Christmas to you too.'

Jessica knew he couldn't see her because her head was snuggled under his chin but she closed her eyes anyway and took a deep breath. 'I love you,' she whispered loud enough for him to hear.

26

The police's press conference about Benjamin Sturgess had occurred just before Christmas. With little else going on and journalists generally being off work with the rest of the world, the story of Isaac Hutchings's kidnapper already being dead led the news agenda for four straight days. Jessica tried as best she could to avoid the coverage but she had either to endure it or watch no news at all. She tried to catch up with what was going on at least once a day, either on the television or through the Internet or, occasionally, by actually buying a newspaper.

Jessica had been to the station on Boxing Day and most of the rest of the week. Despite Adam being off work, she was determined to get something done before New Year. She visited the allotments but number sixty-one was roped off while a full excavation was being attempted. As with the woods where Toby Whittaker's clothes had been found, the freezing weather was making things difficult. Inside the shed, the floor had been pulled up to reveal the pit underneath, each piece of carpet sent off for analysis. With that gone, the hidden section seemed far less impressive and was simply a large muddy hole in the ground.

Jessica re-read the original documents relating to Toby Whittaker's disappearance twice to see if any of it made more sense now that they were pretty sure Benjamin

Sturgess was involved. When none of it did, she spent an hour pacing her office before deciding to go for a drive.

It had turned out even colder as Jessica pulled her car onto the side of the road fifty metres away from Deborah Sturgess's house. It was Wednesday afternoon, the sun was setting, and she didn't really know what she was hoping to achieve. She wrapped herself in a thick woollen coat and watched the woman's front door from a distance.

Reynolds had handled the questioning and, although she trusted him to do a good job, it annoyed her that she hadn't been present. She didn't know if she thought Benjamin's former wife was involved. She was certainly hard to read but perhaps it was just shock that her ex-husband had died and that a child's body had been found in his boot. She doubted Deborah had anything to do with Isaac's kidnapping and murder but there was still a question over whether Benjamin had been responsible for Toby's disappearance. They would have been married fourteen years ago, but then, if Benjamin did have his allotment patch and hidden pit, maybe he had been acting alone? The one thing she was certain of was that he hadn't acted by himself when it came to Isaac – he had arranged to meet someone at the shed. For now, other than Deborah, Jessica had no idea who that person could be.

As she was watching the front door, Jessica's phone rang. She scrabbled around for it in the well between the seats. The display showed a local number but it wasn't programmed into her phone so she didn't know who was calling. 'Hello?'

'Is that Detective Sergeant Daniel?' a male voice asked.

'Who's calling?'

'This is Kingsley James from the Bradford Park laboratories. I tried to contact someone at the Longsight station but whoever was working there gave me your number.'

'Okay . . .' Jessica was always suspicious when someone she didn't know rang her mobile.

The man didn't seem to notice the scepticism in her voice. 'I've got something you might be interested in. I've been in on my own today but I've got the phone I think you found in the Sturgess case.'

'Which one?'

'We examined the smartphone first but it was pretty clear there was nothing untoward with that one. It just seemed like one used for business. There were all sorts of messages on there but it didn't look like much had been deleted. I've been working on the other one.'

'Did you find any contacts?'

'Not contacts, no, but I did manage to get back into the call history that had been erased. We've traced a number for you. It's different from the one the text messages were sent to. Can I pass it on?'

'Hang on, let me get a pen.'

Jessica put the phone on the passenger seat and frantically searched in the glove box and door wells for a pad and pen. She used to keep at least one in the vehicle and could remember a time when she had lent one to her journalist friend in a supermarket car park. Back then he had complained it didn't work but now she couldn't find anything at all. Jessica looked over her shoulder but couldn't see anything in the back seat before she had an idea. She picked up the phone and opened the car door, walking around the rear of the vehicle.

'Okay, go ahead but read slowly,' she instructed. Kingsley read the number and Jessica scraped the digits one by one into the thin crust of frost which had started to form on her rear window. She thanked him for his help before hanging up and calling Reynolds with the number. She knew she should probably have contacted Cole but wasn't ready to engage with him quite yet. The inspector took the information and said he would start things moving.

Getting a number from the history was just the first part. The prefix made it clear the number belonged to a mobile, while they would know which operator the SIM card belonged to from the first five digits. Things became complicated if someone decided to keep an old number on a new phone. Even when they figured that out, if a phone number wasn't public knowledge in the telephone directory, they had to have a warrant approved to get the mobile network operator to release the details of the person the number belonged to. Sometimes that could all happen over the course of a morning, other times it would take weeks. In some cases, it would lead to another unregistered pre-pay SIM card that couldn't be traced.

Jessica had barely got back into her car when Reynolds returned her call. 'That was quick,' she said.

'Yeah, don't get your hopes up. It's just to say that the number definitely isn't publicly available, we're going to have to stick a request in. I'll get the paperwork moving tonight but you know what it's like at this time of year.'

Jessica returned to the station to find the forensics

worker had emailed her the rest of the details, including when the call from Benjamin Sturgess's second phone had been made and how long it had lasted. She cross-checked the dates with when Isaac Hutchings was reported missing and noted the call had been placed somewhere between three and four days before the boy had disappeared. The timing wasn't damning and proved very little but it was at least roughly in the time frame they would have expected.

Knowing there was little more she could do, Jessica phoned Adam. They had spent Christmas Day and Boxing Day with Caroline at Jessica's flat but were planning to sleep at Adam's for the rest of the week. 'On my way,' she said. 'Dinner better be on the table.'

Adam laughed. 'What do you want?'

'Just warm some of that turkey up with something. We've still got enough to get us through most of the next six months.'

As she drove back to Adam's house, Jessica couldn't stop herself from grinning. Many times over the past few years, her life had become dominated by things that were going on at work. She was still determined to find whoever was working with Benjamin Sturgess but, for the first time in a long while, Jessica was actually enjoying her life away from the station.

With another three-day weekend coming up, Jessica had largely expected things to drift into the new year before any details relating to the phone number were passed on. But in the middle of Friday morning, the information arrived. She was sitting in her office when Reynolds walked in with a pad of paper. 'I've got it,' he said.

'What?'

'The name and address of whoever Benjamin Sturgess called.'

'Anyone we know?'

'No, but there's one little snippet which should interest you – our guy's a teacher.'

Reynolds read out what details he had. Nathan Bairstow taught at a primary school on the outskirts of the city but, perhaps more importantly, his house was on the same estate as Daisy Peters's. From what they could tell, he was single and lived alone. The information answered at least two of the things Jessica had been trying to figure out. Firstly, he lived close enough to Daisy to have noticed her circumstances if he was looking and, secondly, his position might give him access to the details on the list they had found in Benjamin's allotment shed. Nothing had been proven yet but the fact Benjamin had contacted Nathan in the days leading up to Isaac's disappearance was an important breakthrough.

Jessica stood. 'When are we going?'

'Jack's sorting out a team to go with us.'

'Have we got a photo?'

'Nothing on file.'

'Do we know if he's in?'

'No idea. The information only came in ten minutes ago and I got one of the constables to sort the rest out. We've moved as quick as we can.'

Jessica made a humming noise. 'What was the DCI like?'

'Professional. You should apologise.'

It was good advice but Jessica wasn't ready to give in. 'I'm not sorry.'

'You should be. He's doing his best to protect us while taking a lot of stick from above.'

Jessica knew he was right but didn't want to admit it. 'Let's get going,' she said, ignoring his point.

The decision had been made to go in softly but with a large backup. Jessica and Reynolds would knock on the door and, as delicately as possible, arrest Nathan Bairstow and bring him to the station. A larger team of officers would be waiting at either end of his road in case he tried to run. The problem with mounting any kind of big operation was the amount of attention it would attract from regular members of the public. It could make things complicated for any number of reasons, from having civilians in the way, to – on certain notorious estates – giving the suspect a head-start. The area Nathan lived in was perfectly respectable and Jessica didn't envisage any problems there but, because so many people would be home from work in the week between Christmas and New Year, there was a much greater chance of unwanted attention.

Jessica and Reynolds travelled in his car, while the rest of the officers took unmarked vehicles. A secure van would be minutes away if it was required. The roads seemed to be full of families packed into cars stuffed full of bargains picked up in the sales. The traffic was worse than usual during rush hour, which left Jessica shuffling around restlessly in the passenger seat as the inspector drove.

Eventually, Reynolds parked his car a few doors down from the address they had for Nathan Bairstow. As the two officers sat waiting for confirmation that the rest of the team were in place, Jessica scanned the surroundings. Piles of slushy ice, snow and frost had been edged to the side of the road, with thin lines running along the centre of each carriageway, showing where cars had been moving over recent days.

Reynolds broke the silence. 'It's that one,' he said, pointing towards a red-brick semi-detached house to their left, but Jessica had already worked it out. There was a gold foil 'Merry Christmas' banner hanging in the window and a string of fairy lights switched off. Aside from that, the house was as plain as could be.

Jessica tried to work out the distance from where they were to Daisy Peters's house. The whole estate was a complex maze of one main road going through the middle, with a large number of streets funnelling from it. To drive from Nathan's house to Daisy's might take ten minutes simply because of having to weave in and out of parked cars. From where she was sitting, Jessica could see at least two pathways surrounded by overhanging branches that led from this section of the estate into another. If you had a good enough knowledge of where the various ginnels led, there was every chance you could navigate the complicated layout quickly and, more crucially, unnoticed.

The inspector's mobile phone rang. After the briefest of conversations, he put it back in his pocket. 'Let's go.'

Jessica opened the door and stepped over one of the piles of ice, making sure she was extra careful with her footing. Their footsteps crunched as they walked to the end of Nathan's pathway. Reynolds started to walk towards the door but Jessica stopped him.

'He's not in.'

The inspector turned around, looking puzzled. 'What?'

Jessica pointed to the driveway on the other side of a small patch of frost-covered grass. It had been shielded from their view while they were waiting in the car. 'Look at the drive,' she said. 'The edges have the same slush that's everywhere else but there's a clear patch where a car usually sits. You can see the tyre tracks across the pavement.'

The inspector looked where she was pointing and nodded. 'We'll try it anyway.' They approached the door and rang the doorbell. After a few seconds with no sign of any movement, Jessica approached the window, peering inside.

'The curtains are open,' she said. 'Either he's been around recently or someone's been coming in and doing it for him. What do you want to do, ask the neighbours?'

Reynolds started to walk away from the house and beckoned for Jessica to follow. 'Let's wait for a bit. It looks like he's been around today and there are so many people out shopping, he might have nipped out for an hour. He would have seen everything on the news about Benjamin Sturgess so if he was going to make a run for it, he'll already be gone.'

It sounded to Jessica like a relatively sensible plan, albeit one that would involve them sitting in a freezing-cold car.

She spent the next forty-five minutes half-watching the house, half-playing with her phone. Once again she and Reynolds had little to talk about, while the street was as quiet as could be. She was wrapped in Adam's coat trying to keep warm but Reynolds appeared oblivious to the conditions, wearing his regular suit and not even bothering with a pair of gloves.

Jessica was once again looking through her old text messages when she heard the sound of a car coming from behind them. She turned to see a small black vehicle passing them before it swung sideways across the road and the reverse lights came on as it eased back onto the driveway they were watching. Jessica touched the handle of the door but Reynolds spoke quickly to prevent her from opening it. 'Wait, let's just watch.'

She removed her hand and focused on the man getting out of the car a few metres ahead. He was wearing a pair of heavy boots with jeans and a puffy dark blue jacket which Jessica thought looked particularly warm and inviting. He was wearing a pair of gloves and a woollen hat which he pushed away from the top of his eyes as he reached into the back seat and removed two large carrier bags. 'Wait until his hands are full,' the inspector said, although Jessica had already thought the same thing. She sat waiting with one hand on the handle as the man put the bags on the floor and locked the vehicle before picking them up again and walking towards his front door. 'Now,' Reynolds said forcefully.

The two officers opened their doors in unison and Jessica again carefully stepped over the mound of slush. She walked quickly but steadily towards the man along the path, while Reynolds rounded his vehicle and slotted onto the pavement behind her. Their target got to his front door just a few moments before Jessica reached him. He spun around, surprised, as they scrunched their way up his pathway.

'Nathan Bairstow?' Jessica asked. He looked sideways, before focusing back on the officers. From the small wrinkles around his eyes, Jessica would have guessed he was somewhere in his forties.

'Who?' the man said.

'Are you Nathan Bairstow?' Jessica repeated.

He put the shopping bags on the floor next to the front door and pointed to the house on the other side of his. 'Wrong house.'

Jessica looked at Reynolds who had a puzzled look on his face. 'Nathan Bairstow lives next door?' the inspector asked.

'Yeah, sorry.' The man reached into his pocket and unlocked the front door, placing the two bags of shopping inside as the two officers looked awkwardly at each other.

'Who checked it?' Jessica asked.

'I don't know, one of the constables.' Reynolds began edging away from the door, clearly not wanting to be heard by the homeowner.

Jessica followed his lead. 'We should phone in,' she

said. The two detectives backed away to the pavement while the front door closed with a bang. The inspector took his phone out and started to press buttons as Jessica watched the house. Out of the corner of her eye she saw one of the downstairs curtains twitch. She took a few steps to the side and looked along the gap that led to the back garden. A waist-high metal gate separated the front from the rear and Jessica walked towards it, slowly at first, still watching the front window where she had seen the curtain twitch.

Her slow walk turned into a run as she heard the sound of a door banging. Reynolds's shouting behind her only confirmed what she already knew as she leapt the gate and ran into the back garden just in time to see a man disappearing over the top of a fence panel.

27

Jessica ran as fast as she could across the crusty half-frozen lawn towards the wooden panel she had seen the man climb over. She jumped and grabbed the top, heaving herself up with a grunt that reminded her quite how unfit she was feeling after a week of turkey and alcohol. Reynolds dashed into the garden and shouted 'He's Bairstow', as if straddling a six-foot fence panel in a stranger's garden was something Jessica did every day.

If she hadn't have been struggling for breath and trying to look below her to see which way Nathan had gone, Jessica would have replied with something withering and sarcastic. Instead she just about managed to exhale loudly before dropping down onto the other side, landing in an alleyway. She looked from one side to the other and saw a flash of dark blue running into another passageway far to her right. Cursing, Jessica turned and ran. The alley was covered in frost, overgrown branches flapping around her as she tried to dodge them. She skidded around the corner where Nathan had turned and saw the man running across a grassy area not too far ahead. Despite his head-start, Jessica could see he was struggling because of the size of his coat.

She tried to up her pace but her lungs were screaming out for air as Nathan glanced over his shoulder before veering off to his left. She kept moving as best she could but could feel a stitch developing in her abdomen. Despite the pain, she was slowly gaining on the man. Nathan's change of direction took him towards a children's play park where he stopped and stepped over a low red metal fence. He picked up pace as he ran across the soft black matting but Jessica hurdled the fence to gain a few more metres. From somewhere behind her, she could hear Reynolds's voice shouting but she drove forward, jumping the fence on the other side of the play park, taking her within ten metres of Nathan.

He had another look over his shoulder and Jessica could see the anguish on his face. The stitch was burning through her body as she dashed across the solid grass, before launching herself forward and crashing into the back of the man. She tried to wrap her arms around him but she bounced off the man's coat, falling painfully onto the back of his boots. She heard the crunch of her jaw before she felt the pain but Nathan's feet clipped together and he tumbled forward as she clung on to the bottom of his jeans and together they fell and rolled into a shallow ditch.

Jessica felt a thin layer of ice shatter as the pair fell the yard or so into the gap. She could feel mud and water sloshing around her as Nathan tried to get to his feet but she clung hard to his ankles, heaving herself up his body. She was seeing stars from the dual pain of the stitch and the ache from her jaw but held on, shoving the man into the dirt and reaching under his coat, pushing the base of her palm hard into the bottom of his spine. He screamed in agony as Jessica crawled on top of him, pushing her forearm across the back of his neck. She was careful not to apply too much pressure but he stopped wriggling. Jessica tried to keep her cool but found herself shouting at him, the adrenaline of the chase flowing through her.

Moments later, Reynolds arrived, out of breath and unable to speak, then three more officers raced into view just behind him. The inspector pointed them towards Jessica and she released her grip on Nathan, leaning backwards and sitting with a plop in what she knew was a shallow muddy stream. The officers shouted instructions at Nathan, who held up his hands open-palmed into the air, allowing two of the other officers to pull him out. He was lying face down on the floor having his hands cuffed when one of them reached towards Jessica and helped pull her back onto the grassed area. She could feel wet hair plastered to her face and a shiver went through her from the suit trousers stuck to the back of her thighs.

'Christ, you look a mess,' Reynolds said none too helpfully.

Scraping her hair behind her ears, Jessica tried cupping her chin, wincing as a sharp pain ran through her. 'Where were you?'

'Calling for help then trying to catch you. You're quicker than you look.'

'Thanks, you're slower than you look.' Jessica tried to smile but her jaw was hurting.

'I'll get one of these guys to drop you home,' Reynolds said.

'I want to do the interview,' Jessica protested, trying not to show how much pain she was in.

'I'll have to—' the inspector began to say but Jessica cut him off.

'I was the one who got kicked in the face. Just give me some time to go home and get changed.'

Two of the officers escorted Nathan, who wasn't struggling, to their car while Jessica went with another.

As they were walking, Nathan called across to her. 'I'm sorry about your face.'

Jessica wasn't used to fleeing suspects talking to her, let alone apologising. 'What?'

'About your chin, I didn't mean to kick you,' he added. Jessica glanced sideways at the man. His coat and jeans were covered in mud, his bobble hat skewed to one side, revealing short dark hair with touches of silver.

Noticing Jessica looking at him, Nathan tried to catch her eye but she turned away. It didn't stop him speaking loud enough for them all to hear. 'It's not what you think.'

A constable drove Jessica back to Adam's house. Her phone had been in her pocket as she landed in the ditch and wasn't responding when she tried to call him, so he was surprised as she walked through the door.

She squelched into the hallway and heard him call out, 'Hey, you're home'. Adam walked into the hallway, his arms wide to greet her before quickly withdrawing them. 'Whoa, what happened to you?'

'I fell in a ditch.'

Adam smiled but Jessica wasn't feeling in the mood to respond and she saw him straightening his face before saying, 'Why?'

'I didn't do it on purpose.' She felt herself wince as she spoke.

'Are you okay?'

'I got kicked in the face.'

'Ouch. So you've not had a good day then?'

'I'm not finished yet, I'm getting changed then going back.'

Adam smiled gently at her. 'Want a hug?'

'I'm all wet.'

'Never mind, I'll live.' Adam opened his arms again and pulled Jessica in close. She could feel her clammy clothes sticking to her and felt bad about getting Adam wet too, so released herself.

'This is weird,' Jessica said.

'What is?'

'I don't know . . . someone being nice to me. I don't like it.'

Adam laughed. 'Would you prefer if I kicked you in the face too?'

Jessica giggled but quickly stopped because of the pain in her jaw. 'I've got to go. I'll see you later.'

Even though she had taken time to change before heading back across the city from Adam's house in Salford to the Longsight station, Jessica was still stuck waiting for Nathan Bairstow to be brought up from the cells to be interviewed. Reynolds told her the suspect had been given clean clothes from a store that was kept on site. The replacement garments were effectively jogging bottoms and a sweatshirt and were usually handed out to the weekend drunks who were left in the cells to sleep off the alcohol but ended up losing control of their bladders or vomiting over themselves. It wasn't nice but it did leave some officers with cracking stories to tell at the Christmas party which, for whatever reason, had become a New Year's Eve celebration this year. When he was cleaned up, Nathan had been allowed to meet his solicitor, which was also taking some time.

Most of the rest of the CID team were either on leave or had left for the day. Jessica knew Cole was in his office upstairs but she hadn't gone to see him, leaving it to Reynolds to be the middle man. She was aware of not being the most patient person at the best of times but with her jaw stiffening up as the afternoon turned into evening – and a phone that wasn't working – she spent around an hour balling up pieces of paper and trying to throw them into the bin on the other side of her office.

Eventually, Reynolds knocked and entered. 'We're ready,' he said before noticing the large pile of paper next to the door. 'How old are you?' he added with a grin.

'All right, old man, calm down,' Jessica replied with a smile of her own. 'Just because you were outrun by a girl.'

They walked through the nearly deserted hallways towards the interview room where the inspector checked the recording equipment. Shortly afterwards there was a knock at the door and Nathan was led into the room by a man in a grey suit. Everyone sat as Reynolds ran through the formalities. As he spoke, Jessica took in Nathan's appearance. The wisps of grey hair she had seen as he was being escorted earlier were far more prominent under the white fluorescent light above them. He'd appeared youthful when she first saw him wearing a hat but his silver hair made him look his actual age. Before she had wasted an hour throwing paper balls into her bin, Jessica read the small amount of information they had on Nathan Bairstow and, among other things, she knew he was forty-six years old.

He refused to meet Jessica's gaze, instead staring at a spot on the table between them. When the inspector finished talking, Jessica went to start but Nathan interrupted. 'I just want to say I'm sorry for kicking you. It was an accident.'

Jessica didn't want to give him any kind of upper hand, so ignored him. 'How do you know Benjamin Sturgess?' she asked.

'*Ian* Sturgess?'

Jessica kept as straight a face as she could manage. 'Yes, Ian.'

'We taught together years ago.'

'*How* long ago?'

'I don't know, maybe thirteen or fourteen years?'

'Which? Thirteen or fourteen?'

Nathan seemed slightly distressed. He lifted his cuffed hands to scratch at his face. 'I don't know. I've been at St Jude's for six years, I was temping for two before that, then I did two years with Our Lady's. We were at the same school before that so some time between ten and fourteen years. I don't really know because he left.'

'Do you remember Toby Whittaker?'

'Toby? I . . . I know the name. Was he the boy who went missing?' Jessica stared at Nathan, waiting for him to meet her eyes. She didn't answer with her words, instead letting him see it in her face. 'I'm not sure what you think that has to do with me,' he added.

Jessica checked the sheet of paper in front of her and read out the phone number. 'Is that yours?' she asked.

Nathan nodded slightly. 'I think so. I don't really know it properly.'

'Let's make it easy then. Have you ever had a phone conversation with Ian Sturgess?'

'Yes, once or twice.'

Jessica read him the date and time of the call they had traced. 'Does that sound about right?'

'Yes.'

'So you're admitting you spoke to him?'

'Yes but it's not what you think.' Nathan's voice had a pleading tone.

'What am I thinking?' Jessica asked.

The man's solicitor motioned to step in but Nathan lifted his arms up. 'No, it's fine. I know what you're thinking because I saw on the news that Ian had been arrested but you were calling him Benjamin. I know it was something to do with that other kid going missing, Isaac. I saw it all and I knew I should have called you then . . .' He tailed off and sighed before continuing. 'I think I knew you would be coming for me at some point. I . . . I don't know why I ran. I'm sorry I kicked you.'

Jessica felt her jaw stiffen as he spoke. It was the third time he had apologised and she wasn't going to give him any satisfaction of acknowledging it. 'You've not answered my question.'

Nathan held his head in his hands, ruffling his fingers through his hair. 'You're thinking I had something to do with the kid going missing, or being . . . killed.'

'Did you?'

He spoke quietly. 'No.'

'So what were your cosy little phone chats about?'

'Nothing . . . I mean it was all theory. Well, I thought it was.'

Jessica continued to stare at Nathan, although he wasn't looking up from the table. 'What was?'

The man didn't say anything at first but took a deep breath before croaking out an answer. 'You won't believe me.'

Jessica sucked air through her teeth, keeping her mouth narrow and closed so she didn't have to feel the ache in her jaw. She didn't want to say anything that could sound sympathetic but, before she could answer, Nathan spoke again. 'Ask me something else.'

'I don't think you're in a position to make a demand like that.'

Nathan looked up and Jessica could see liquid running from his nose, dribbling over the top of his chin. In the couple of minutes he had been staring at the table, he seemed to have aged at least ten years. He wiped his nose on the sleeve of his sweatshirt. 'I know, I don't mean it like that, I just . . . Look, I'll answer. I'll tell you what we talked about but, please, just ask me the other stuff first.'

Jessica looked at Nathan's solicitor, who seemed slightly bemused, while Reynolds placed a hand briefly on her shoulder before removing it. Letting a suspect dictate what should and shouldn't be asked wasn't anything she would have comprehended doing but something felt right about the demand. After a pause, she began to speak again. 'What type of relationship do you have with Ian Sturgess?'

'None really. He contacted me through the Internet maybe a year or so ago. That was it.'

'Do you know someone called Daisy Peters?'

Nathan shook his head, slowly at first, then more vigorously. 'No.'

'Have you ever been to the allotments near to the reservoir at Gorton?'

'No, I don't even know where that is.'

Jessica asked him about the woods where they had found Toby Whittaker's clothes but he said he didn't know about that site either. 'Did you know who Isaac Hutchings was before you saw his name in the news?' she added.

'No.' Nathan was speaking even quieter.

One by one Jessica read him the other eight children's names they had found on the list in Benjamin's shed but he denied knowing any of them. They already knew none of them went to the school he currently taught at. After the final name, he seemed close to tears and again wiped his nose on his sleeve before apologising for doing so.

'Why did you run, Nathan?' Jessica asked.

Nathan closed his eyes and leant back in the chair. 'I don't really know, I just panicked. As soon as you came to the door and asked for me, I knew why you were there. I knew you would never believe what I said. I didn't really think. Have you ever done something really stupid when it seems like you're watching yourself? It's like you're in the sky screaming to yourself to stop doing the crazy thing you know you're doing but, by then, it's already too late. By the time I had started running and I knew you were following, I didn't know what to do. If I stopped, it would look bad, if I kept running, maybe I could have got away? I have no idea what I thought I'd do if I did get away. I left my wallet, phone and keys at the house.'

Jessica knew exactly what he was talking about. She'd had a moment similar to it while interviewing someone in this very room. There had been a few seconds where she had lost control and, by the time she knew what was going on, it was too late. She remembered an almost out-of-body experience of watching herself from the corner of the room, wondering what on earth she was doing. 'I accept your apology,' she said, almost without thinking. 'I believe you didn't mean to kick me.'

It was as if her acceptance turned a tap. Nathan began crying loudly but was trying to speak through the howls. Tears and snot ran down his face as he banged his bound fists on the table in what seemed to be an involuntary way. The words fell out of his mouth, a mixture of screams, sobs and coughs. 'Will you tell his mother that I'm sorry? Mrs Hutchings. Please tell her I'm sorry for killing her son.'

28

Jessica said nothing but it was as if a chill had descended on the room. Bairstow's solicitor remained completely still while his client bawled. Jessica took some tissues from the back of the room and handed them to Nathan but he was inconsolable. She looked to Reynolds, eyebrows raised. 'Shall we?' she asked.

The inspector started speaking into the tape recorder, saying the interview was concluded but Nathan began to shout over the top of them. 'No, no, I'm fine. Please, I'll tell you now. Don't leave it here, I'm not finished.'

The man's solicitor leant forward. 'Perhaps you could give us a few minutes in another room?' Jessica nodded and stood, banging on the door to get the waiting officer's attention. The constable and solicitor led Nathan out of the room but Jessica could still hear him crying in the hallway, even after the door was shut.

As the noise began to fade into the distance, Jessica turned to Reynolds. 'Wow.'

'Did he just confess?' the inspector asked, not seeming sure.

'I don't know. It sounded like it but it didn't seem quite right. Even if he did I doubt the tape got it properly.'

'I've never seen anything quite like that happen in an interview before.'

Jessica shrugged. 'I have that effect on men.'

Neither of them laughed, before Reynolds broke the short silence. 'We haven't discovered that much.'

'Only because I let him skip that question. We know that both he and Benjamin were teaching at the same school Toby Whittaker attended roughly at the time he went missing. We've got plenty with the phone call and confession. Well, sort of confession.'

'Does it feel right to you though?'

Jessica knew it didn't. There was something about Nathan's choice of words and the way he exploded with tears that wasn't what she might have expected. Lots of people cried in interviews but, for something as serious as this, suspects would usually be crying for themselves, not their victims. Remorse was something she rarely saw in the worst criminals, their only regret that they were caught. She didn't reply because she knew Reynolds could see the answer in her face.

Twenty minutes later, there was a knock at the door and a constable asked if they were ready to resume the interview. Shortly after, Nathan was sitting in the same seat as before. His face was red, the skin around his eyes was puffed out and looking sore.

'Are you okay, Nathan?' Jessica asked. The man nodded. 'I want you to clarify what you said to us before you left the room.' She spoke with a softer tone than she had in the first part of the interview. From the way the man's solicitor was holding himself, she could see something had changed.

Nathan took a deep breath and looked up to meet Jessica's eyes. 'I'm sorry. I've been holding onto this since I saw about Ian on the news. I *am* sorry about Isaac. It wasn't me who killed him but . . . I think it might be my fault.'

Nathan stumbled over his words slightly but, unlike earlier, the things he was saying seemed far more deliberate. Jessica wondered what the man's solicitor had said to him out of the room.

Nathan picked up a tissue from the table and blew his nose before continuing. 'Everything you know is correct. I knew him as Ian from school but you called him Benjamin and so did the news. He contacted me through the Internet about a year ago. It was one of these sites where teachers can register and get in contact with old colleagues. There are these forums where we all join and share war stories about bad students and the like. I'll give you my log-on if you like. Apart from a bit of swearing, there's nothing bad on there. Before then, I'd not had any contact with Ian since the time we taught together.'

'Were you friends back then?' Jessica asked.

The man shook his head. 'Not really, he was ten years older than me at least. I'm sure you have colleagues you're on decent terms with but, away from work, you'd never say a word to them.' Jessica felt uncomfortable, knowing Reynolds was one of those people.

Nathan took a deep breath and a sip from a plastic cup of water that was on the table. 'I knew him and he knew me but we were never friends.'

'So why did he contact you?'

'He said he was writing a book. I looked him up and he

had a few things published. He reckoned he was doing okay and said he'd never looked back since giving up teaching. He said he was doing research for his new book and wanted some advice. When we'd worked together, I'd been the IT teacher, so he knew I'd know about computers and technology. It all seemed normal.'

'What did he ask you about?'

Nathan sighed and looked at his solicitor before turning back towards Jessica. 'He said he was feeling a bit old and out of the loop. At first it was just simple computer things. He said he was writing about someone who stalked a victim via the Internet, then kidnapped them. I thought it was a pretty odd thing to be writing about if the author didn't know himself but I just thought I was helping. He would ask things like how to delete the history on an Internet browser. It was stupid and I think I wanted to show off, so I started telling him about proxies and how to hide your identity online and so on.'

'You gave him that information without him asking?'

'Yeah . . . I mean, as I said, I thought I was helping. To be honest, he didn't seem that interested.'

'I thought he contacted you for that information?' Jessica was feeling slightly confused by the conflicting details.

Nathan nodded quickly. 'Oh, he did, we would email back and forth. I've been thinking about it ever since I saw what he did on the news. I'm not sure he was ever curious about computers, I think that was just the start. He only really became interested when he began to ask about mobile phones.'

'What did you tell him?'

'Nothing, I don't really know that much. I think he thought that, because I'm good with computers, I would also be good with phones. I don't think he realised they are completely different things. He asked me about deleting browsing history on the Internet and so on – but then a few weeks later moved on to talking about clearing a call history or message history on a phone, so no one could trace you.'

'Did you tell him how?'

'I don't know how. I just said I'd read something about using those pay-as-you-go SIM cards because they can be registered in someone else's name. I told him basic things, like clearing your messages folder and so on. I thought it was just for his book.'

Jessica believed him and felt sure Reynolds would too. 'If he was more or less a stranger, why did you go out of your way to help him?'

Nathan leant back in his seat and looked at the ceiling, blinking quickly. 'Look at me,' he said, opening his palms. 'I'm in my forties, I'm single, I live on my own and I teach in a primary school. Being a twenty-something bloke and teaching young children would make people look at you strangely. Imagine how bad it is when you're forty-something. I thought I was helping him write a book. He said he'd give me a credit somewhere and I felt useful. I know it sounds pathetic but . . .' The man tailed off without finishing the sentence.

Jessica let him compose himself before asking the next question. 'What else did you tell him?'

Nathan shook his head and seemed close to tears and Jessica knew the worst was yet to come. 'He started to talk about the plot. He asked the best way to keep information securely. I think he thought things were safer on a computer. I told him the safest way to keep information was to not store it anywhere except your head, that you should only talk about things in person. I told him that any file saved on a computer can never really be deleted without physically destroying the hard drive. I don't think he really understood so I made it clearer. I said that, if you absolutely had to keep details of something, the best thing to do was pretend the last fifty years haven't happened. Write it down manually, keep it somewhere safe and, when you were done with it, burn it.'

Jessica felt a tingle at the base of her spine. She thought of the list of children's names she had found. It had been handwritten, kept somewhere unconnected to Benjamin himself and, from what Nathan was saying, would have been burned.

'Did you ever pass on the details of any students?' she asked, thinking of the names.

Nathan blinked and shook his head. 'What? No. Why would I do that?'

'He never asked you for names and addresses of children?'

'No, never. I don't really have access to that anyway and, even if I did, I'd never pass it on.'

Jessica nodded. She believed him again but, if her instincts were right and he was telling the truth, they still had no idea where Benjamin had got the information from.

'Did you keep the emails?' she asked.

Nathan rubbed his eyes with the palms of his hands before stopping to stare at the table. His solicitor had been silent since re-entering the room but he leant forward and spoke. 'My client tells me he deleted everything but is happy to do everything he possibly can to retrieve them.'

'When did you delete them?' Jessica asked, staring at Nathan and ignoring his solicitor. Neither of them answered, so she repeated her question, harsher the second time.

Jessica could sense a nervousness from the solicitor and there were tears in Nathan's eyes when he looked up from the table. 'Christmas Day,' he said quietly.

Jessica struggled to control the anger in her voice. 'After you'd seen on the news that we were looking for information?'

Nathan didn't look up from the table. 'Yes.'

'Why?'

'Because . . . I knew how it would look. I knew that if he hadn't deleted everything at his end, you might find your way back to me. I wasn't really thinking. I saw him on the news and panicked.'

'Why should we believe you about what was in the emails?'

Nathan finally met Jessica's eyes, pleading with her. 'Because it's true. Honestly, it is. I'll help them get everything back, I've still got the hard drive.' Jessica knew there was no way that would be allowed to happen. His computer would be seized and any examination would be done by their experts. As she thought that over, she realised he still hadn't answered the one question he had been arrested for.

'Why did Benjamin Sturgess call you?'

'I know you won't believe me but I'm not really sure. He hadn't contacted me for around six weeks or so but he emailed out of the blue asking for my phone number. I gave it to him and he phoned straight away. It was the only time I talked to him since we worked at the school.'

'What did he want?'

'He was talking about cars. It sounded like there was someone with him and he was asking how computers in cars work. I didn't know what he was on about but he kept saying how he'd read that modern cars were all locked by computers. I think he meant the electronics and so on but, to be honest, I wouldn't have a clue anyway.'

'Why didn't he email you?'

'I don't know, it sounded like he was in a hurry. I assumed he was just stuck with a chapter or something.'

'And there was someone with him?'

'I think so. I didn't hear a voice but I got the impression someone was telling him what to ask because he was stumbling over the words as if they were unfamiliar.'

Jessica immediately recognised the significance. Assuming Nathan was telling the truth – and she believed he was – it sounded as if Benjamin and whoever the accomplice was were trying to figure out the best way to steal a car. In the old days, a brick through a window, a screwdriver and jamming two wires together would do the trick. With modern vehicles, it was much more complex than that and pretty hard to steal a car without a key. If they had been unable to get information from their 'computer expert', that might well have been the point where they decided to take a different track which led to someone hooking Daisy Peters's car keys out of her house. Jessica wasn't overly pleased to admit it but a lot of his story not only added up – but helped fill in some of the blanks they had.

Reynolds asked Nathan where he was on the night Isaac Hutchings disappeared.

'I'm not sure,' the man replied. 'I keep everything on the calendar app on my phone. You took it away when I was brought in.'

Jessica looked at Reynolds. 'Has it gone yet?' She was asking if the phone had been taken to their forensics lab to be looked at.

The inspector shook his head and then looked at Nathan's legal representative. 'Are you happy for us to bring it into the room?' The solicitor asked Nathan and they agreed. The inspector left and returned a few minutes later with Nathan's phone in a small plastic bag. Again he addressed the man in the suit. 'I have no idea what I'm doing with these things and for reasons that should be pretty clear, there's no way we can let your client touch this. Are you happy for my colleague to open this bag?' Nathan nodded and his solicitor agreed.

Jessica took the bag and opened it. The rigmarole was slightly over the top and, legally speaking, not necessarily something they had to do but it certainly eliminated any future doubt over whether evidence had been tampered with.

Jessica switched the phone on and there was an agonising wait before the main screen appeared. She turned it around so Nathan and his solicitor could see what she was doing, as the suspect talked her through which buttons to press. Jessica soon reached the calendar and scrolled up to the date Isaac went missing. Two words were typed on the screen and she knew Nathan was telling the truth.

'Parents evening'.

After showing a relieved Nathan what he had been up to, the phone was switched off and re-bagged. Once reminded of that date, Nathan had a good recollection of how the day had gone. As school was finishing – the time Isaac was snatched from the other side of the city – Nathan had stayed behind to set up the classroom for the evening. He then went out for a pub meal with three of his colleagues before returning to the school. He said he stayed behind after the parents had left with a couple of other teachers to tidy up. His alibi would be checked but Jessica knew it would be verified.

With nothing else to ask, Nathan was taken back to the cells, leaving Jessica and Reynolds alone in the interview room.

'Do you believe him?' Jessica asked.

'Unfortunately.'

'Me too. We should still do him for deleting those emails. Perverting the course or something. He confessed to it, so it's a piece of piss for CPS, just the way they like it.'

'You know what's going to happen, don't you?' Reynolds asked, refusing to meet her eye. 'They're going to want this finished. Benjamin's done for the kidnap and murder, Nathan's done for either perverting or assisting, whatever they think they can get him for. That'll be it.'

'But who stole Daisy's car?'

'They'll say it was Benjamin. It's not like he can deny it. We don't have any prints from her house to say differently.'

'What about the texts he sent, telling someone to meet him at the shed that night? What about the list of kids' names? Where would he have got that from?'

Reynolds shrugged. 'Unless forensics get something concrete from his phone, trust me, this will be the end of it. The chief super and everyone else high up want this out of the way before anyone realises quite how badly we ballsed it up.'

Jessica could not think of a reply because she knew he was right.

29

Jessica cradled the empty pint glass in her hand and tried to ignore the music blaring around her. She was sitting in a booth in the pub closest to the station with Adam on one side and Izzy on the other.

'Are you all right?' Izzy asked.

'Yeah, it's just this whole New Year celebration thing.'

'What about it?'

Jessica was not in a mood for holding back. 'It's just . . . New Year's Eve is for twats basically. Whichever way you want to dress it up, it's for twats.'

Izzy laughed. 'At least you can drink,' she said, pointing towards her small glass of lemonade. 'Anyway, what's wrong with it? I always quite like New Year's Eve.'

Jessica stood as Rowlands returned to the booth with Chloe and a tray full of drinks. He put them on the table and everyone shuffled around to let the pair sit down. 'What's going on?' he asked.

'Jess is moaning about New Year,' Izzy said.

'Shall I add it to the list?' the other constable replied, which led to them both collapsing into giggles.

Jessica glanced from one to the other. 'What list?'

Diamond and Rowlands looked sideways at each other, then started laughing again. Diamond eventually answered. 'Every time you go off on a rant about something, we write it down. It's sort of a "Things Jess doesn't like" list. It's quite extensive.' Jessica looked around the table to see everyone, including Adam and Chloe, laughing.

'What's on this "list"?' she asked indignantly.

Izzy didn't even need to think before replying. 'Er, Christmas decorations went on the other week. Then there's Christmas music, radio phone-ins, charity collectors, carol singers, the rain, the snow, the frost, the wind, roundabouts, traffic lights, Dave's hair, supermarkets, taxi drivers, bus drivers, people who don't like wine, kids, teenagers, people who own dogs, people who own cats, dogs, cats, Londoners, and now New Year.'

'And that's just this month,' Rowlands added in between laughs.

'This is an outrageous abuse of my privacy,' Jessica said, but no one was listening; instead they were giggling at her expense. When she thought about it, she could clearly remember complaining about all of the items on the list but that wasn't the point.

'What's wrong with New Year?' Adam asked when the group settled down.

Jessica didn't need much thought. 'It's so forced. All these knobheads banging on about "What are you doing for New Year" all the time and then, when it's the actual night, everyone expects you to be out partying and having a good time. If you're not in the mood then you're a spoilsport. Then it's all about the countdown and "Auld Lang Syne". Seriously, I don't think I've ever met anyone who knows more than the first two lines of the stupid song. Even when that's all over, you have these morons and their stupid resolutions. I don't get it. If you want to stop smoking, just stop. If you want to eat less, just do it. But oh no, you have to tell the world you're bloody doing it, just because the year's changed and then, by February, you're back eating like a pig again. It's bollocks.'

Jessica's rant had spilled out almost as if it was one long word with barely a pause for breath. She looked up to see her friends staring at her and then couldn't stop herself from laughing either. Her jaw was still aching. 'All right, I do moan a lot,' she admitted as Adam put an arm around her.

'It is true about "Auld Lang Syne",' Izzy said. 'I just la-la-la my way through it after the first two lines.'

Jessica smiled and pointed. 'See, it's not just me.'

'It is mainly,' Rowlands said.

'Come off it,' Jessica said. 'Surely you've got to admit this is the worst Christmas party ever. Firstly, it's being held at New Year; second, it's in the pub around the corner from work and third, the music is older than I am.'

It was a set of complaints none of them could take issue with.

Jessica looked at Izzy. 'When did you tell everyone anyway?' she asked. 'I must have missed it.'

Izzy smiled. 'I didn't want the whole big announcement thing just because I'm pregnant. I told Dave and he blabbed it around everyone else. Perfect really.'

'Hey, it wasn't like that,' Rowlands protested.

'It was,' Izzy assured the table.

The New Year's celebration, however poor, was at least succeeding in taking Jessica's mind away from the other things going on. Everything had panned out in almost the exact way Reynolds had said it would. Nathan Bairstow was out on bail but would almost certainly be charged with something. Meanwhile, the case, while not officially closed, had been moved to one side. The few officers who were working over the festive period were being moved onto other things and, once the rest of CID returned after New Year, it was pretty clear the ones who had been investigating Benjamin Sturgess would be put on something else. They wouldn't quite have the full amount of evidence they needed but, with the suspect already dead, they had enough. There certainly wouldn't be a queue of lawyers desperate to dispute the evidence they had. Jessica was confident there was someone else involved but no one, least of all her, had a clue who that could be. Because the case around Isaac Hutchings was all but closed, the one surrounding Toby Whittaker's disappearance also looked likely to be stopped. The dig at the woods had taken lots of time and resources and, apart from a wide selection of carrier bags, they had uncovered very little. Although Nathan Bairstow had worked at the same school Toby attended many years ago, no one thought he had anything to do with the disappearance. Quietly, it would just be forgotten about again.

As she was lost in her thoughts, the music went silent and Jessica heard the sound of the television, volume raised, crackling through the speakers. Everyone stood and looked towards the screen as Big Ben appeared and the countdown began. Jessica joined in half-heartedly before the cheering began. Adam didn't seem bothered by her lack of interest and kissed her before pulling her in close. She could feel the vibration on her ear lobe as he whispered 'Happy New Year' softly. Jessica didn't reply but hugged him tight. She knew she was a hypocrite after everything she had said but, as the first line of 'Auld Lang Syne' began, she made a silent resolution that, no matter what, she wasn't going to mess things up with him again.

30

Jessica wasn't enjoying her first week back after New Year. A case which involved a string of street robberies over the Christmas period had been dumped on her while everyone seemed to have conveniently forgotten that somewhere out there Benjamin Sturgess had an accomplice.

She was sitting in the station's canteen picking at a plate of chips when Rowlands dragged a chair across to sit opposite her. 'Are you okay?' he asked.

'Yeah, I just can't get this Sturgess guy out of my mind.'

'Izzy told me you asked her to look into some things quietly. She's not been able to get away to see you but she says she hasn't found anything.'

'Me neither. I just wanted to re-check the guy's past. See who he used to be friends with, that kind of thing. I've been trying to look into Deborah too.'

'The wife?'

'Yeah, what did you think of her?'

Rowlands shrugged before taking a chip from Jessica's plate and biting it in half. 'I dunno really. Hard to read.'

It was exactly how Reynolds had described Deborah Sturgess after interviewing her and Jessica would have used the same expression too. 'I've not found anything,' she admitted. 'I checked her and her husband, the marriage, the divorce, all of it. They're just so *normal*. If he hadn't crashed that car we would never have found any of this.'

'Why would he wait so long?' Rowlands asked.

'How do you mean?'

'We're assuming it was him who kidnapped and killed Toby. If that was the type of thing that got him off, why would he wait fourteen years to do it again?'

'Iz was looking into that a few weeks ago because I thought the same. We couldn't find anything to connect him to any other disappearances from the past few years. Honestly, I don't know.'

'There wasn't anything to connect him to Isaac though, was there?'

Jessica nodded reluctantly. 'I guess . . . I just . . . how could he go undetected for so long if he was taking other kids during that time? I don't understand why you would kidnap a child just to kill them.'

Dave stole another chip. 'Who knows why half these nutters do what they do.'

Jessica winced. 'It's more than that. Think about the cases we examine and the motives people have. These aren't the first children to be snatched, but there's always a reason, even if it's only in the perpetrators' own twisted heads. There are sickos who do it for sexual pleasure – but Isaac wasn't abused in that way. Maybe you do get off on killing – but why would it be specifically a child? There would be so many easier targets. Look at all the people who live on the streets, or even those who walk home on their own after dark. If killing people excited you, wouldn't you be more likely to choose a different situation?'

Rowlands held up his hands open-palmed. 'I don't know. Maybe he liked killing kids? Perhaps it was a challenge to get away unseen?'

'I thought of that but it still doesn't really make sense. Think of the list we found. Why write their names and addresses down? Why that order? Isaac was at the top, so was he planning to kill all nine but do it from the first name to the last? If you just got off on killing children, why would you bother with all that formality? You'd do your homework, watch the schools and check what time everyone left and so on, then you'd strike. Even if you had access to those details – and we're pretty sure Sturgess didn't – then why would you go through all that effort?'

'And the map too.'

Jessica nodded. 'Exactly. I've been banging on about that ever since we found it. You only need a map if you don't know where you're going. Even if it was Sturgess who was responsible for Toby Whittaker's disappearance all those years ago, he didn't know where the clothes had been left. If he did, he would have just gone there.'

'So do you think his ex-wife was in on it?' The constable didn't sound convinced by his own question.

'I don't know, maybe. I'm not convinced she told us everything. She gave us just enough to wrap things up neatly from her point of view. She's not a suspect but she didn't really dish the dirt on her husband either. It's just very . . . *tidy*.'

Rowlands nodded and Jessica could see his mind working. 'Have you told the DCI all this?'

'Sort of. I spoke to Jason but I don't think it's up to

either of them. From the outside we look successful. It's only us who know how shit we've done.'

Rowlands gave her a weak smile. 'It's good that you care, Jess.' She looked back at him and thought about how much he had grown up over the past couple of years, then realised she had too. He must have been able to tell she was feeling uncomfortable because he quickly spoke again. 'Is there anything else?'

Jessica sighed. 'Not much. Results have started dribbling in on everything that was recovered. Forensics say there are traces of Isaac on the carpet from the shed but we expected that. No blood though, curiously. Adam's working on it, so he's already told me – even though it isn't official. The search team didn't find anything at Sturgess's house other than the computer and phones. All the emails he sent to Nathan Bairstow were recovered, so we know he was telling the truth.'

'Is he going to be charged anyway?'

'I'm not sure, it's with the CPS, but probably. We have the evidence and a confession. Forensics reckon there's nothing else they can recover from the phones while the number those two texts were sent to is apparently untraceable. Whoever had that SIM card hasn't used it since we found out about the number.'

Rowlands finished the final half of the chip he was holding before reaching for another but Jessica batted his hand away. 'They probably ditched it after whatever they were planning came off,' the constable added.

'Exactly. Either way, that's about all we're getting. With Deborah's statement about Benjamin using the name Glenn

Harrison, the allotment key being found on Sturgess's body and Nathan's statement – plus the emails they recovered – that's it done.'

'Did Jack tell you to stop working on it?'

'Not as such, they've just given me loads of work to try to ensure I don't have time to do any more.' Jessica picked up the final chip and held it out. Rowlands took it from her, swallowing it in one.

'Thanks,' he said with a mouth full of potato.

'I don't know how Chloe puts up with you.'

Rowlands grinned. 'Have you been back to see the parents?'

'I spoke to the liaison officer who was with Kayla, Isaac's mum. She's doing okay, just a bit shaken by the way everything came out. Our lot wanted to get it across the news over Christmas to make them look good, but they didn't bother to think of her feelings. I spoke to Esther from the kidnap team a couple of days ago. She checked in with Rachel, Marcus and Lloyd Corless and reckons they're about as back to normal as they're going to get, considering how dysfunctional they all seem.'

'What about Toby's mother?'

'Lucy? I don't know. The poor woman's been forgotten in all this. I might visit her just to make sure she's all right.'

'I heard you didn't get on too well last time.'

Jessica raised her eyebrows. 'That wasn't really her fault. We spent fourteen years not finding her son, then rocked up and said, "Here's his football shirt". I'd be pissed off too. Someone should at least let her know what's been going on.'

'Do you need me to make something up about where you've gone?'

'No, sod that. If I get any grief I'll just go to the papers. Bollocks to the lot of them.'

31

Jessica called Lucy Martin and asked if she could visit. Toby's mother didn't seem too pleased but didn't object either. She was on her own when Jessica arrived, but appeared better than on the previous occasion they'd met. She'd tied her long black hair up in a neat ponytail and was wearing a long red jumper with tight jeans. Jessica remembered her husband, Neil, telling her how December was a bad time emotionally for his wife. Lucy seemed to have more of a healthy glow to her as she let Jessica into the house.

Jessica wondered if she had misjudged Lucy's mood during the phone call because, as the woman showed her into the living room and offered to make tea, she seemed perfectly comfortable. She brought in two mugs and then settled on the sofa across from Jessica, tucking her feet underneath her. 'Neil will be home in about an hour. He picks the girls up after school,' she said. Before Jessica could reply, she added: 'I'm sorry about last time.'

'How do you mean?'

'When you were here before and I was a bit off-hand. I know everything that happened back then isn't your fault.'

Jessica waved her hand. 'It's fine, don't worry.'

'Why are you here?' Jessica realised she didn't really

have a reason. Lucy must have read it in her face because she added: 'I saw all the stuff on the news about that man being responsible for the other boy. I guess I wondered if . . .'

'I came to make sure you were all right. I didn't know how everything on the news might have affected you over Christmas.'

Lucy smiled slightly. 'Did Neil talk to you last time?'

'No, I . . .'

'It's fine if he did. Whatever he said was probably true, I'm not that good when the evenings draw in. Then Christmas comes along. I try to keep it together for Olivia and Tasha but it's hard.'

Jessica was struggling to know what to say but Lucy seemed happy to talk. 'Did I tell you that City shirt you found was Toby's last-ever Christmas present?'

'No.'

'Dean, his dad, was always a big football fan but Toby wasn't really interested for the first few years. I think it was just one of those things that when he got to a certain age he wanted to be like his dad. I still remember Dean's face when Toby came down to breakfast one morning and asked for the City shirt. It was as if Dean himself was getting the present.'

'I've never been into football myself.'

'Ha! Me neither. I think you pretty much expect it when you have boys.' Lucy took a sip of her tea. 'Do you have kids?'

'No, no . . . I'd never cope. I can barely look after myself.'

Lucy laughed. 'I used to think like that. It's just one of those things. Before you know it you're in the swing and it's as if you knew what you were doing all along. You get the odd moments but, most of the time, you just trust your instincts.'

Jessica wasn't so convinced she had those motherly instincts. 'What are the girls like?' she asked.

'They're great but it's different from having boys. Everyone says they're going to be a nightmare when they become teenagers together.'

'Isn't that the same for boys and girls?'

'I don't know, maybe. I'm just going by what other people say. My other daughter, Annabel, wasn't great as a teen but that was understandable with what happened to Toby, and then me and Dean separating. It's no wonder she won't speak to me.'

There wasn't much Jessica could add, as she didn't know the woman well enough to offer anything other than general condolence. It did seem as if Lucy was getting a lot of things off her chest that she had been coping with over a long period of time.

'I invited Annabel up for Christmas,' the woman continued. 'I always do but she didn't respond. I don't even know if she's got children of her own or anything.'

'Did you tell her or Dean that we'd found Toby's clothes?'

Lucy untied her hair and let it fall around her shoulders. As she spoke, she re-tied it into a tighter ponytail. 'I told Dean. He was going to come up but I told him there wasn't much point until you found . . . something.'

'We did look,' Jessica assured her.

'I know, I'm not saying you didn't, it's just . . . I've been waiting all this time for someone to come around and say you've found Toby. I don't know when I stopped thinking he'd be alive but I always expected something. When you came around that first time, I thought that was it, you'd found his body or something else and I'd be able to let it go.'

'I'm sorry.'

'No, don't be, it's not your fault.' Lucy stood and picked up her mug. 'Do you want another?'

'No, I'm fine.'

Lucy left Jessica alone in the living room. While she was gone, the detective stood, examining the photos on the wall. Most of them were of Olivia and Natasha, who looked strikingly similar to each other. There were a couple of just Lucy and Neil in various poses where they seemed happy. Jessica remembered her brief suspicion about Neil himself. He was certainly someone who gained from everything that happened but she hadn't followed it up other than a brief look into his background.

When she was trying to think of a motive, it was the one question she'd kept returning to. There was apparently no sexual motivation and there weren't too many people around who killed for the sake of killing. With that in mind, it left her stuck with the same question: assuming he was responsible for both, what did Benjamin Sturgess gain from taking Toby and Isaac?

'That was taken in Marbella,' Lucy said from behind Jessica, who hadn't heard her re-enter the room. She turned to face the woman, then looked back at the wall. The photo was of Lucy and Neil sitting together, each raising a glass of wine to the camera. 'We left the girls with Neil's parents and went away for a week,' Lucy explained. 'I didn't want to go because we had never left them before but he talked me into it. We had a good time but I was always worrying about everything being all right at home.'

Lucy sat on the sofa again, wrapping her legs underneath her as Jessica returned to her seat. 'Did the man on the news take my son too?' Lucy asked. Her eyes were fixed on Jessica, who felt compelled to answer.

'I don't know.'

'Are you just saying that?'

'No, I really don't know. We can't question him because he died in a car crash.'

Lucy nodded but didn't stop looking at her. 'Do *you* think it was him?'

Jessica paused, thinking of how she should answer. 'I'm not sure I should say.'

'Why are you here, then?' Lucy hadn't raised her voice but there was definitely a harsher tone to her words. Jessica knew she had a point. Deep down it was why she had come – because she wanted to tell someone what was going on.

'I could get into trouble if I tell you things I shouldn't.'

'I won't tell anyone.'

The two women were still watching each other and Jessica looked into Lucy's eyes before making the decision. She knew it was not procedure but felt that Lucy deserved an answer. She took a deep breath. 'I don't know if Benjamin Sturgess kidnapped and killed your son but I think he probably did. There's no way we'll be able to prove it and I'm not sure you'll ever get justice. I can only say I'm sorry.'

Lucy was cradling her mug of tea, interlocking her fingers through the handle and holding it close to her chest. She nodded slowly, taking in the words. 'Why do you think it's him?'

'He taught at your son's school. I read all of the paperwork from the time and, although his name was mentioned, there was absolutely nothing to properly connect him to Toby's disappearance. The team back then did everything they could.'

'Why did he take the child this time?'

'I don't know. I'm not sure we ever will.'

'Did he . . . touch him? Isaac?'

'No.'

Jessica wondered how long the woman had wanted to know the answer to that question with regard to her own child. Lucy nodded the slightest of acknowledgements.

Before either of them could say anything else, they were interrupted by the sound of the front door opening. Jessica heard young girls' voices from the hallway before the children from the photographs came skipping into the room. The younger of the two, Natasha, stopped for a moment when she saw Jessica before stepping shyly towards her mother, sitting next to her on the sofa, and hiding her face behind Lucy's shoulders. Olivia was a little bolder but also sat next to her mum.

Neil walked into the room behind them. When he saw

Jessica, he raised his hand in a half-wave. 'Hi . . .' It was as if he realised mid-sentence what her appearance might mean. His expression changed, with his eyes widening. 'Oh . . .' Jessica shook her head slightly to answer his un-asked question, while not letting on to the children that there was anything wrong. Neil was halfway through a word in reply but stopped himself and turned towards his family on the sofa. 'Have you told your mum what you got up to today, Olivia?'

Jessica couldn't stop herself from smiling as Lucy grinned widely. 'What have you done today, dear?'

Olivia reached into her bag and pulled out a sketch-book, opening it to show her mother something she had drawn.

'What was that?' Jessica asked, suddenly curious. Olivia smiled and turned the book around to show a drawing of a house with a row of people outside. The figures had over-sized heads and no shoulders but made Jessica smile.

The young girl could barely contain her excitement as she pointed from one character to the next. 'That's Mummy, that's Daddy, that's Tasha and this is me.'

'Wow, that's really good,' Jessica said but it wasn't the drawing she had been asking about, it was what Lucy had said. She paused for a moment, considering the previous few seconds, then stood. 'I've got to go now.'

Lucy stood too and escorted her out to the front door. 'Thanks for coming,' she said. 'Is it all right if I tell Neil everything you told me? He won't tell anyone.'

'Yeah, it's okay.'

Unexpectedly, Lucy held out her arms and hugged

Jessica, who didn't know how to react. Before she could feel too uncomfortable, the other woman released her.

Jessica walked out into the chilly winter afternoon wondering if Lucy had just solved their case without knowing it.

32

Jessica drove back to Longsight going over what she thought she knew. It was one thing to have a theory but she needed a way to prove it – without involving Cole or Reynolds. Apart from the odd word in passing, she had not spoken to the chief inspector since their argument before Christmas and didn't want to risk being shot down until she had some evidence. If she talked to Reynolds, it would simply put him in a difficult situation.

By the time she arrived at the station, the sun had almost set, even though it was barely four o'clock. Jessica parked on the road outside the main gates and phoned Dave. She asked him to make whatever excuse he had to in order to get out, then come and join her.

As he sat next to her complaining how cold it was, Jessica told him everything. There were still gaps in her theory but she indicated who she thought the accomplice was, and another person she believed was indirectly involved, a stranger she had never properly met whose help they would need, and why she had to break the law to prove it all.

'I don't mind if you go back inside and forget we ever had this conversation,' Jessica said. 'I know it's not fair to ask you to help me but I can't ask Izzy because of the baby and I can't take it higher.'

Rowlands didn't hesitate in his reply. 'Let's do it.'

Jessica knew it would take at least a couple of days to put everything in place. Before she could do anything, she realised she had one other responsibility to fulfil. That evening, she cuddled up to Adam on the sofa at his house and told him everything that had happened over the past few weeks. Then she told him what her plan was. Like DC Rowlands before him, Adam listened to everything she had to say before replying. 'Is it dangerous?'

'Maybe.'

'Can I help?'

'No.'

'Are you going to get into trouble?'

'Probably.'

Adam held her tight and kissed the top of her head. 'I love you.'

'So you should.'

The next part of the plan involved checking the facts. Jessica had already read everything they had in the files but sometimes mistakes could be made. She and Rowlands avoided Izzy, who was clearly suspicious of what they were up to, and went through every piece of information they had access to. None of it offered enough evidence to prove that Jessica was correct – but it didn't disprove her theory either.

With the easy jobs out of the way, Jessica again asked Rowlands if he wanted to change his mind before they went any further. Secretly she was almost willing him to say he did but, if anything, he seemed more determined than before to help her out.

On a cold January night just before three in the morning, Dave and Jessica got out of the constable's car and walked the few hundred metres through the deserted estate until they reached the front of Benjamin Sturgess's abandoned house. The official police search had been completed before Christmas but the place was now empty, secured by the officers.

Jessica was wearing a pair of old gym trainers to avoid making a crunching noise on the frost that surrounded the property. Without speaking, they moved around the side of the house, stopping by the side door. She crouched and gently pushed the cat-flap she had noticed on their previous visit. It had been locked from the inside but that was what she expected.

'Are you ready?' Jessica whispered.

Reynolds nodded. 'Just don't crash my car.'

Jessica could barely see his features in the gloom. The street lights were too far away, the only illumination coming from the bright white moon above them. She touched him on the arm. 'If anything happens, just run.'

She spun and walked quickly back towards the car. After readjusting the seat and mirrors, she drove slowly and carefully until she was outside the house next door to Sturgess's. She left the engine idling with the handbrake on and checked her phone before taking a deep breath and then she pressed her foot down on the accelerator, increasing the rev count to the maximum. The enhanced exhaust which so annoyed her roared into life as Jessica kept her foot on the pedal, watching the clock on her phone count twenty seconds. As soon as time was up, Jessica removed her foot from the accelerator, put the car in first and eased the vehicle away as steadily as she could. She had done her homework, memorising the layout of the estate and drove in a loop, parking it two streets away, before walking as quickly as she could back to the side of Sturgess's house.

As soon as she arrived, she could see in the moonlight that Rowlands had been successful. She walked around to the rear of the house where he was pressed against the wall. 'Dave?' she whispered.

'Jess.'

'Good job.' Quietly they walked back to the side door where the cat-flap had been kicked through, taking most of the plastic panelling with it. 'I take it no one saw you?'

'Didn't hear a soul. Like you said, anyone up and about would have only heard the car anyway.'

Jessica reached into her pockets and took out a pair of woollen gloves. 'I'll be five minutes. Call my phone if there's a problem. It's on silent but I'll see the light. Just call and ring off.'

She crouched and reached through the gap in the door. Not only had Rowlands kicked the cat-flap through but parts of the white plastic had broken too. It was a tight squeeze but, because of the flexibility in the plastic around where the flap had been, Jessica hauled herself into the kitchen of Benjamin Sturgess's house.

If she had asked, there was a chance she might have been given the key to the property the police were currently holding. Despite that, Jessica knew there would be a problem if DCI Cole stuck to his guns and refused. This way, if she was careful, the break-in would be blamed on an opportunist. If she had asked to be allowed into the house and been denied, it would have looked incredibly suspicious if someone had then smashed their way in shortly afterwards.

Jessica crept through the property, not bothering to use the light from her phone until she reached the living room. She remembered how she felt when she had been in here the last time. She'd had an almost overwhelming sense of how normal everything seemed. It was only when Lucy spoke to her daughter that Jessica realised the house was anything but regular. Hidden in plain sight was something that she, Rowlands and all the search teams couldn't have failed to see – except they didn't know what they were looking at.

Switching on the light from her phone, Jessica entered the living room. The space was a mess, carpet torn up and shoved to one side, furniture piled at one end. Jessica tiptoed across the room to the far wall where she used the light to check the photos hanging on the wall. It was the fourth one she checked that made her stomach lurch. She had spent the last few days wondering if what she thought she had seen was true but, with the evidence in front of her, she was almost disappointed. Jessica hoped she had made a mistake but it was now clear she was right.

She turned her phone around and took a photo of the picture that could only have been left hanging by someone who knew they had got away with everything. The flash went off, illuminating the room for a moment.

As she was about to put her mobile in her pocket, the light on the screen flashed Dave's name before a second screen appeared to say she had a missed call.

Someone was outside.

33

Jessica could hear voices outside the front door. She dashed to the front window and opened a gap in the net curtain narrow enough to peek through. A uniformed police officer was standing at the door looking at his watch. A few metres behind him on the road she could see a marked police car parked with the passenger door wide open and another officer sitting in the driver's seat.

She swore under her breath as she let the curtain fall back into place. Jessica didn't know if someone had heard Rowlands kicking through the cat-flap or if her distraction had been too overt and persuaded someone to call the police. She wondered if the officer outside knew the significance of the property, or if they had just responded to a standard call. Jessica froze, holding her breath until the loud bang on the front door shook her into action. If it was simply a complaint from a neighbour relating to the revving car, the officer wouldn't be knocking. She walked quickly into the hallway and moved silently up the stairs into the front bedroom.

The search team hadn't made anywhere near as much mess upstairs and, aside from the open drawers and cupboards, everything else seemed normal. She walked towards the window, opening the curtain a crack. There was still an officer sitting in the car, the one below was out of sight. Jessica sat on the floor under the window and took out her phone. Rowlands's name was still on the front screen from the missed call. Just in case he hadn't put his phone on silent, Jessica typed out a text message to him.

'Where r u? U on silent?'

She pressed her back hard into the wall as the sound of the officer knocking on the front door echoed through the house. She knew that as soon as he walked around to the side, he would see the smashed back door and the game would be up. Her phone flashed once with Rowlands's name. She pressed the button to answer the call. 'Dave, where are you?' she whispered.

Dave spoke quietly making it difficult to hear but Jessica pushed the phone hard into her ear. 'In the back under one of those plastic sheets the search team left.'

'An officer is at the front door.'

'Shit. I saw the car pull up. I didn't know if they were just here because they had received a complaint. Are you stuck inside?'

'I'm upstairs. There's one in the car, one at the front. I don't think they've noticed the side door yet.'

'How are you going to get out?'

'I don't know. You?'

'No idea.'

Jessica sighed. 'All right. Look, I'll think of something. When the opportunity comes, just make sure you run.'

She hung up and leant her head back against the wall. For a second or two she felt defeated but a third bang on the door brought her back to reality. There was no way the officer would knock a fourth time, which meant his next point of call would be the side door.

Jessica stood and looked around the room. On top of a dressing table was a statue of what looked like a small monkey. Jessica walked across and picked it up, weighing it in her hand. She didn't know what it was made of but it was certainly heavy. Pocketing it, she walked back to the window and peeped through a gap in the curtains. The second officer had switched the car's engine off and was standing next to it. He began walking towards the house as Jessica heard the other officer's voice booming through the house, shouting that whoever was inside should come out. She guessed he was shouting through the cat-flap but he wouldn't necessarily know the person who had broken in was still inside.

With the second officer disappearing out of view, Jessica tried to open the window but it wouldn't budge. There was a small keyhole in the frame and she looked around the sill just in case but there was nothing there. She dashed across the hallway as quietly as she could into the second front bedroom while the officer downstairs continued to shout. She flung the curtains open and tried the window. At first it stuck in the frame but she gave it a sharp shove, relief surging through her as it stiffly gave way.

Jessica leant out and looked below to see if either of the officers were there. With no one in sight, she had to take the chance they were by the back door. Lowering herself feet first out of the window, she gritted her teeth and closed her eyes as she held tightly onto the frame before letting herself drop.

Only too aware her body had taken a battering in recent weeks, she offered a silent prayer as she landed on both feet without any surges of pain shooting through her. Jessica almost gave a squeal of delight as she ran to the hedge that was furthest from the passage leading to the back of the house, edging along until she was on the road. She glanced at Sue's house, wondering if she had been the person who had called the police. Everything was still and Jessica quickly scanned the other houses to make sure no one was looking, then reached into her pocket and took out the monkey statue. She took a deep breath and made a promise to whichever god might be listening that she would definitely join a gym if he or she allowed her not to get a stitch this time around. Her silent prayer complete, Jessica arched back and hurled the statue into the rear windscreen of the parked police car.

Things seemed to move in slow motion as the glass cracked with a loud crunch. Jessica turned and ran in the opposite direction, deliberately heading past the passage-way where she knew the officers would be able to see her. She heard a shout from behind but knew she would have at least a thirty-metre head-start on whoever was chasing her. She thought of the uniformed officers at Longsight, knowing there were plenty she would definitely fancy her chances against in a race and hoped that whoever was now after her came from a similar mould.

Although she had memorised the layout of the estate so carefully, converting that into three dimensions while running as fast as she could in her old gym shoes was a different matter. Grabbing a lamppost, she used it to swing herself around and headed into a ginnel she felt certain would lead to a second passageway that would hopefully bring her out next to Rowlands's car. She hoped he had used her distraction to get himself off the property but there wasn't much else she could do.

She was starting to tire as she hurled herself into the second alley, risking a look over her shoulder but there was no one there and she couldn't hear footsteps. Instead of slowing, she upped her pace, sprinting for the car while reaching into her pocket for the key. As her fingers closed around the fob, remote central locking seemed like the greatest invention ever. Without breaking stride, she pressed the button and saw the vehicle's indicator lights flash twice. Jessica grabbed the handle, opened it and hurled herself onto the back seat.

She lay in the foot well barely breathing and not daring to move. It seemed like hours but it was definitely still dark when there was a tap on the window. For a moment, Jessica froze, expecting to look up and see one of the officers peering in. Instead, it was a weary-looking Dave offering a thin smile as their eyes met. She sat up and pressed the button to unlock the door again, allowing him to slide into the driver's seat.

'I didn't know you had such short legs,' Rowlands said, shunting the seat backwards while Jessica climbed into the front and passed him the keys.

'They were long enough to outrun those two,' Jessica said. 'You got out all right, then?'

'As soon as I heard that crash, I looked out and they were running off towards the road. I watched them around the corner of the house. One of them went after you, the other got on the radio. As soon as he was facing the other way I legged it. Nice job on the car window by the way.'

'Thanks, it felt ridiculously good to be honest.'

'Did you get what you needed?'

'Yeah.'

'So you were right about everything?'

'I think so.'

After seeing the photo, Jessica was as confident as she could be that she was correct. Things had not gone according to plan but at least neither she nor Rowlands was in trouble. In the list of things she had to do, getting access to the picture was the third toughest, so it was hard for her not to feel too relieved as there was so much more to do.

The next night's task wasn't as hard but it did need a degree of setting up. Jessica arranged to meet Dave at the allotments at two in the morning but she arrived half an hour early. She jumped the fence and made her way across to plot sixty-one, trying to avoid the muddiest parts in order to not leave any clear footprints, just in case. The moon was particularly bright, making the whole area of land clearly visible, except for where the hedges cast their shadows.

The outside of the plot looked the same as before, with mounds of dirt from the excavation. She approached the door and lifted a set of bolt cutters, squeezing hard and eventually slicing through the thick metal of the padlock.

Jessica's dad had been keen on DIY when she was younger and always told her it was worth spending a bit more to get the best-quality tools. She had taken that on board at the hardware store earlier that day, buying the most expensive set of cutters, hoping the outcome would be this easy.

Unlike the outside, the interior of the shed was a total contrast to how it had been. The floorboards in the middle of the room had been torn up, exposing the pit underneath, the table and chair removed. Jessica had tried to think of a better place than this for her final confrontation but something about this cramped room seemed right.

Rowlands soon arrived with the items they needed and together they fixed the shed as best they could. It was never going to look as it did before but at least they managed to sort out a solid floor with a combination of the wood Rowlands had brought and the broken floorboards which had been shunted into a corner.

As they left the shed before sunrise, Jessica put on a new padlock and handed Rowlands one of the keys.

Her penultimate task didn't involve breaking the law but it did call for her to be at her persuasive best. She visited Lucy Martin at a time when she knew the woman would be on her own and asked for Annabel's contact details on trust alone. The woman was reluctant to pass on the information, especially as Jessica insisted she couldn't tell her why she needed it. Ultimately, as silly as it might have seemed to an outsider, the bond they had made over a mug of tea was enough to swing it.

Jessica phoned in sick the next day, taking the train to London to meet Lucy's estranged daughter. Annabel was an essential part of Jessica's plan, but the years apart from her mother and the bitterness she felt made her reluctant even to listen to Jessica's idea, let alone help. She kept repeating that she had a new life – she was twenty-seven with a career, a boyfriend and a flat. Everything that happened up north when she was a child felt as if it had occurred in a different lifetime.

Annabel's passion for making the most of the life she had created for herself made Jessica wonder if she was doing the right thing. As she watched the woman drink her cappuccino, she saw herself, albeit a little younger. Annabel was a person who had left home and gone to find out what a big city could hold. Jessica wondered whether finding out the truth was worth it, but then made a decision she knew she would have to live with for a long time.

Her recent activity involved her breaking and entering twice, committing a burglary and damaging public property. In the next few days she would have to lie and become a thief. As Jessica broke Annabel's heart by telling her that over half her life had been a lie, there was no doubt in her mind what the greatest crime from that list was.

34

Without Adam to listen to her, Jessica wasn't sure she would have been able to go through with everything. He met her off the late train at Piccadilly Station. 'Your chariot awaits,' he declared with a smile. Jessica immediately burst into tears and told him how she had destroyed a young woman's life. He didn't say very much, listening without judging.

After the conversation with Annabel, it was too late for Jessica to retreat from what she had set in motion. In a quiet moment at the station, she told Rowlands that everything was almost in place. She made the phone call to set up the final meeting and, after their shift was over, Jessica and Rowlands made their way to Deborah Sturgess's house.

The woman welcomed them in, seemingly unaffected by everything that had been in the news about her husband. Jessica noticed that her roots had recently been bleached so that she no longer appeared to be greying. Accepting the offer of a hot drink, they were left alone in the living room while she went off to the kitchen.

As soon as the door closed, Jessica sprung to her feet and stepped across to a side table. 'Can you see it?' she hissed.

Rowlands was looking from side to side but shook his head. 'No. Where do you keep yours?'

'In my pocket.'

'Yeah, but you're not really a girl, are you – she must have a bag or something.'

Jessica ignored the first half of the constable's remark. 'All right, I've got an idea. When she gets back, keep hold of your mug but only take the odd sip.'

Rowlands looked at her suspiciously. 'What are you going to do?' Jessica had no intention of answering but Deborah entered the room shortly after with three mugs of tea. She placed them on a table and then settled into a reclining seat facing them. Rowlands picked up his mug and took a small sip.

'How can I help you?' Deborah asked.

Jessica tried to sound as empathetic as she could. 'We're just here to make sure you're okay after . . . everything.'

Deborah nodded. 'Oh, right. Thanks for coming. It's been hard with the neighbours. Some of our old friends have been back in contact and said they couldn't believe it about what had happened. You think you know someone . . .'

Jessica didn't want it to sound like an interrogation. 'How long ago did you divorce?' she asked, already knowing the answer.

'Around six years.'

'It must be hard for you?'

Deborah was clearly revelling in the gentle questioning. She put her feet up on the seat, cradling her mug in the same way Rowlands was doing. 'I just can't understand why he would do something like that.'

Jessica slipped her hand into her pocket as she listened

to the woman's response. It was so guarded, so *perfect*, the words were barely worth paying attention to. In the brief silence after Deborah had finished speaking, a cheery pop song begun playing from somewhere outside the room. For a moment, the woman looked confused, then she hopped up, returning her mug to the table. 'Sorry, that's my phone,' she said, going quickly out to the hallway, returning moments later with a puzzled look on her face, holding the phone in the air. 'Um, it's you . . .' she said.

Jessica put her hand in her pocket and took out her phone, swiping her fingers across the screen with a puzzled look on her face. 'Sorry, I must have left it unlocked and called by accident. It's not the first time, I once called my mum fifteen times in an hour when I was in the cinema. She told me she would pick it up and hear a rustling noise, then she'd hang up but it would ring again two minutes later.'

Jessica kept hold of her phone as Deborah returned to the armchair, putting hers on the armrest. Jessica hadn't known if her number had been stored on the other woman's phone but it really didn't matter.

'I'm not great with technology either,' the woman said, pointing towards the phone. 'I'm not sure of half the things it can do.'

Jessica nodded enthusiastically. 'I'm like that too. I only found out mine could do this a few days ago.' She turned the phone around so the screen was facing Deborah and swiped her hand across the front wildly, swinging her elbow back and knocking into Rowlands's hand. The tea he was holding cascaded over the top of the mug, spilling into his lap. Dave yelped and jumped up, dripping more of the liquid onto the floor.

'I'm so sorry,' Jessica exclaimed but Deborah was already on her feet.

'Quick, quick, through here,' she said, beckoning the constable towards her as she rushed out.

With the room empty, Jessica reached across and snatched the woman's phone from the armrest. She pulled the back compartment off, forcing her nails into the small gap and taking the battery out to ensure it couldn't ring before putting everything in her other pocket.

Jessica walked through to the kitchen where she saw Deborah dabbing at Dave's crotch in a way that would have been hilarious, if what she had just done hadn't been so serious.

Jessica held her own phone in the air. 'We've got to go,' she said.

Deborah glanced up and nodded at Jessica. If she was suspicious, she did not show it. 'Are you going to be all right?' she asked the constable.

Dave grimaced. 'I'll be fine.'

Jessica raised the phone higher. 'Come on, they said it's urgent.' She turned to Deborah. 'I'm sorry, Mrs Sturgess, something's come up. We'll come back another time.' The woman nodded and led them back to the front door before saying goodbye.

Rowlands didn't say a word until they were back in his car with the doors closed. 'Did you get the phone?' he asked as he started the engine.

'Yes.'

'Couldn't you have thought of something better than that? You could have asked her to show you where the toilet was or something, then I could have grabbed it.'

'Sorry. That would probably have worked too.'

The constable indicated and pulled out onto the road. 'Why couldn't I spill tea in your lap, then grab the phone?'

'Because if either of us was going to be touched up by a middle-aged woman, I'd rather it was you.'

Dave laughed but Jessica could tell there was no real amusement in it. He changed his tone. 'Are we ready?' he asked seriously. Jessica took the pieces of Deborah's phone and put it back together, waiting for it to start up. When it arrived at the home screen, she pressed the button to bring up the contacts list.

'Yeah, we're ready,' she said, pointing at one name but knowing her colleague was watching the road.

'Isn't she going to realise you took her phone?'

'I don't know and I don't care. She'll probably think she's lost it somewhere first of all. By the time she's checked through the house and called it a few times, I'll have used it.'

'Tonight?'

'Tonight.'

Over the course of her life, Jessica had taught herself not to be nervous. It was a hard thing to describe to other people because apprehension was such a natural emotion. No one would have believed it now but as a twelve-year-old, she was a good athlete. She never practised but could run fast and beat other people with little effort at all. Her dad loved coming to school events and watching her win but, even though she knew she was the best runner, her nerves would become too much for her. She would eye her competitors and wonder what might happen if she tripped, or if one of them got a better start than she did.

Eventually she taught herself to lock the emotions away. Instead of thinking of what might go wrong, Jessica started every race not caring if anything went awry. Though she had grown out of sports, that ability to ignore any nerves was something that had stayed with her.

But now, as she sat in a fold-up chair in Benjamin's shed, she felt the type of anxiety building she had rarely experienced in over twenty years. In the course of her career, she had had amazing highs and the worst of lows. Nothing compared to the way she had made a mess of things with Adam the first time around and, as she stared at the patched-up floor, Jessica thought of him waiting at home for her. He was the man who pretty much forgave her anything and was quite happy to support her no matter what the consequences were. She wasn't sure she had forgiven herself for everything that happened with him initially but the fact he had smiled and said it was okay amazed her every morning she woke up next to him.

The night was cold and Jessica could see her breath drifting out of her mouth. She looked up at Annabel, who was sitting in a similar chair. 'Are you okay?' Jessica asked. Annabel said nothing but she could see plumes of air coming from the other woman's mouth too. 'I'm sorry,' Jessica added, knowing it meant nothing.

Both women looked up as they heard a gentle tapping

sound on the wood at the back of the shed. 'Be brave,' Jessica whispered as everything went silent again. She could hear footsteps outside, a mixture of crunching from the frost and squelching from the puddles that hadn't frozen over. Jessica found herself holding her breath as the door rattled and then opened. In the dark, a silhouette of a man stepped into the room.

'Hello?' he said.

Before he had finished speaking, the door banged into place with the sound of a padlock slotting into the bracket. The man spun around towards the door with a startled 'hey' as Jessica pressed the button to turn on the light they had rigged up. She found herself squinting as the bright white lamp illuminated the room and the man twisted to face her.

His eyes were wide with surprise as Jessica spoke. 'Hello, Toby.'

35

The man had gelled black hair with trimmed stubble on his chin. He had dressed for the weather, with a pair of heavy boots, jeans and a thick coat. He blinked rapidly, stunned by the light, and stared open-mouthed at Jessica, then noticed Annabel sitting to his right. 'What?' he said, barely able to get the words out.

'Do you want to sit down?' Jessica asked, pointing towards another fold-up chair resting against the wall. He turned around and tried to open the door. 'It's locked,' Jessica added. 'And people are outside so don't even bother. I think it's time for a chat.'

The man turned around and looked from Jessica to Annabel then back again. 'Who are you?' he asked.

Jessica snorted involuntarily. 'That's an odd question coming from you. I'm Detective Sergeant Jessica Daniel and this, as I'm sure you remember, is your sister. Don't worry about Deborah, she's fine. I just borrowed her phone to send you a text message.'

The man shook his head. 'I really think you've got the wrong person,' he said, reaching back towards the door. 'My name's Stephen.'

Jessica nodded. 'I know, we've met. Do you remember when I was leaving Deborah's house with a colleague, and you were walking down the drive?' The man nodded slowly. '"Friend of the family", that's what Deborah told us you were at the time.'

The man picked up on her words. 'That's right.'

'You're not, though, are you?'

'Why do you think that?' He was still standing close to the door, looking at Jessica.

'A hunch, a turn of phrase, a photograph. If you were just a friend, why would she call you "dear"? Why would there be pictures of you with both Benjamin and Deborah from when you were younger?'

It had been the way Lucy Martin called Olivia 'dear' that had made the connection for Jessica – it had been exactly how Deborah referred to the man on her driveway all those weeks ago. It was all in the tone of voice, an inflection of concern that didn't happen when you were speaking to a random person.

'What's wrong with that?' Stephen countered.

'Why would someone keep pictures of themselves posing with a teenager if it wasn't their own child?'

He stared back at Jessica defiantly.

'I didn't even notice it the first time I was at Benjamin's house,' she continued. 'Everything was so normal, pictures of an apparently happy family. It was the type of thing you wouldn't even notice but I checked the records. Benjamin and Deborah had a son named Stephen – but he died within a week of being born a few months before you went missing. One of your friendly teachers took you home one night and never gave you back. After everything had died down, they raised you as their own.'

Jessica paused for breath, trying to keep her emotions

in check. 'When I was a kid, all our neighbours knew who I was,' she continued. 'It was a bit of a pain because if I ever got up to anything, it would always get back to my parents. I guess it depends on the area. I checked the housing records and within six months of you disappearing, Benjamin and Deborah moved into a new house. I'm guessing their new neighbours would have assumed you were their son. If you happened to look a little like a boy who had been in the newspapers months earlier, then it was just a coincidence.'

Stephen was still staring at Jessica. 'Sit down or we're going to be here all night,' she added.

He turned around and picked up the chair, opening it out and placing it next to the door before sitting on it. Jessica didn't need him to confirm or deny it to know she was right. On the surface, it seemed so simple. For whatever reason, Benjamin and Deborah couldn't have children after Stephen died, so they simply took one. Whether it was a Stockholm Syndrome situation with the boy falling for his 'captors', or whether it was voluntary, Jessica didn't know. For whatever reason, Toby – or Stephen – had willingly been brought up by parents who weren't his. By moving to the opposite end of the city, possibly dyeing his hair or doing something else to change his appearance, with new, unfamiliar neighbours, they didn't have any awkward questions to answer about where he came from.

None of that answered what had happened with Isaac though.

The man sat forward, hunched and ready to move

quickly if necessary. 'If I'm not Stephen, then how come that's the name on my driving licence?'

That was one of the key things Jessica had struggled to figure out but she had stumbled across a possible answer on the Internet. She spoke firmly: 'If the real Stephen was registered at the hospital, Deborah and Benjamin could have applied for a birth certificate then. Given the speed things move, they might have received it in the post weeks after he had already died. Assuming they kept it in a drawer, it would have been easy enough for you to use it to register yourself for a driving licence, as well as anything else you needed to live a normal life under a name that isn't yours.'

He didn't say a word, locking eyes with Jessica in an uncomfortable silence.

Annabel interrupted their non-verbal sparring. 'Why didn't you come home?'

The man adjusted the way he was sitting and glanced towards Annabel, although Jessica could see he wasn't looking high enough to meet her eyes.

'Why?' she repeated.

He glared at the ground but Annabel leapt to her feet and ran across the room, launching herself into him. The echo of the chair crashing to the ground rang around the room as the two people collided. Jessica realised what was happening too slowly, jumping forward in an effort to pull Annabel away.

The man had been blindsided and knocked backwards with his coat and shirt ruffled up around his face. Annabel pointed towards him and spat out the word: 'Look.'

Jessica squinted at where she was indicating and saw a zigzag-shaped mark across the man's abdomen. As he picked himself up, Annabel returned to her seat. She made no attempt to hide the fury in her voice. 'Don't tell me you don't remember. I was only nine. We tied that rope to the tree on the edge of the park near our house. We were taking it in turns to run at it and swing across the stream. I'd got across but you came sprinting over and slipped. You got one hand on the rope then landed sideways in the water. *That* scar comes from the rock you hit when you landed.'

The man straightened his clothes but wouldn't look up from the floor. 'Just tell me your name,' Annabel shouted at him.

'Stephen,' he replied quietly.

'Oh, fuck you, Toby. Why didn't you come home?'

For a moment, Jessica thought the man was going to remain silent but then, finally, he spoke. 'Because I didn't want to.'

Toby's words hung in the air as he ran his hand through his now-dark hair. Jessica felt a mix of vindication for everything she had done, along with an almost over-whelming feeling of regret because, in some ways, she had hoped she was wrong. Nobody said anything but Toby had finally met his sister's stare.

'Why?' Annabel asked forcefully.

'I enjoyed being with Ian and Deb. They bought me things, they looked after me.'

'They *bought* you things? That's why you chose to stay with them? Did they take you or did you go willingly?'

Toby spoke quietly but firmly. 'None of your business.'

'Is that all you've got to say to me? We thought you were dead. Mum still thinks you're dead!' Annabel didn't sound upset, just angry. Jessica was already feeling guilty about what she had asked the woman to do and was wondering if she had gone too far.

'You don't understand,' Toby said dismissively.

'So make me.'

'I got bored. All the kids at school had everything I didn't, Mum and Dad argued all the time. You got the best things because you were older.'

'Are you joking? That's it? You were only ten.'

'Eleven.'

Annabel shook her head and kicked at the floor. 'You're disgusting.'

Jessica wondered how bad things could have been, but then she remembered Annabel had also left home and not returned. Lucy's account might well have put a rose-tinted view on what life was like with her and Dean. What Jessica did know is that there had to be something seriously wrong to make an eleven-year-old want to leave his birth parents and not go back. Everyone had moments as a child where they threatened to leave home and not return. To have actually gone through with it must have meant he either genuinely hated it there or, even at such a young age, he was materialistic enough to put gifts above everything else. She didn't know which category Toby fell into.

'You moved out too,' Toby said.

'How do you know that?'

'I looked you up on the Internet a few years ago. I saw

you'd moved and wondered if you were thinking like me. I was going to contact you but Dad convinced me not to.'

'"Dad?"'

Toby didn't reply to Annabel but looked towards Jessica. 'Can I go now?'

Jessica narrowed her eyes and stared at him. 'Did you ever live in this shed, Toby?'

'For a bit.'

'Do you know we found your old clothes? The football shirt and the rest.'

Toby smiled and shook his head mockingly. 'It was in the papers, I'm not an idiot. Who do you think buried them there? It was time to say goodbye to the old Toby for good and embrace Stephen.'

'Why those woods?'

The man shrugged. 'Why should I tell you?'

'Tell me,' Annabel shouted. 'I'm still your sister.'

For the first time, Jessica could see pangs of regret in Toby's face. He looked at the ground, as if embarrassed with himself. 'Did you miss me?' he asked quietly. There was no edge to his tone, it was a genuine question.

'Of course I did. I was your older sister.'

Toby nodded. 'I missed you too.'

'Why those woods, Toby?' Jessica asked again.

Toby didn't adjust his position and seemed to reply without thinking. 'I wanted to return them to that place where we used to play football. I hadn't been around there in years but, when I went back, there were all these factories. I found those woods by accident but it was quiet and no one was around. It just felt right, like coming full circle.'

'What about Isaac Hutchings?' she asked.

'What about him?' The response was instant and dismissive.

'Why did you take him?'

'Who says I did?' Toby turned to meet Jessica's gaze, his eyes defiant, daring her to give him a good reason to continue speaking.

'What do you usually call Deborah?' Jessica asked.

'Why?'

'Just answer the question.'

Toby smiled slightly, shaking his head as if pitying the question. 'I call her Mum, because she is.'

Jessica nodded. 'You've got two options now, Toby. Option one is you tell me everything, then I take you to the station and you repeat it all on tape.'

'Why would I do that?' Toby grinned and stood. 'You've got nothing on me. This is ridiculous, dragging my sister out because you think it'll make me confess.'

'You only listened to option one.'

'Fine, what's the second one?'

'Option two is I open that door and let you walk. Then I get in my car and drive straight to Deborah's house. I'll arrest her not only for your kidnap but for the kidnap and murder of Isaac Hutchings. Either way, I get a conviction and me and my colleagues look shit-fucking-hot. Personally, I don't care who goes down for it. It's your choice.'

It was as big a lie as Jessica could have told.

'How can you arrest her? You don't have anything on her.'

'Really? Well, for one, I sent you a text message using

342

Deborah's phone asking you to meet her at the shed. The fact you didn't question her knowledge of it tells me she knows all about this place. Admittedly that could never be used as evidence but it's a start. What could be used is all the little bits. How about I go find some of your old neighbours and ask them about little Stephen? How do you think that would go down in court along with the official records to show she never had a child? What about the photos at Benjamin's house with you, him and her? That's pretty damning. It might be circumstantial but how do you think a jury would view that in relation to Isaac's disappearance and everything that's already been in the media? I'm sure if we really looked into her alibi for that time Isaac was missing we might find a hole here or there. Do you want to take that risk?'

Toby stared at Jessica, eyes bulging with fury. 'It wasn't her.'

'Do you think a jury will believe that?' Jessica raised herself up from the seat and met the man's gaze, assuring him she was serious, even though she had no idea if she would be able to find anything like enough evidence.

'What do you want me to do?'

'I want you to sit down and tell me everything. Then I want you to go to the station and repeat it all.'

'What about Mum?'

'It's up to you. If you want to tell us your name is Stephen and conveniently forget the Toby stuff, I couldn't care less. I'm not helping you though so you'd better have your story straight. Somewhere along the line you must have sorted yourself out with an identity but I don't want to know. The deal is you tell us everything you did and, if no one asks any other questions about Deborah, then she's off the hook. If you drop her in it, then tough shit.'

Toby stared at Jessica before slumping to the floor, holding his legs to his chest. He looked across at Annabel, who had returned to the chair. 'I'm sorry,' he said.

The woman didn't reply.

'Are you sure you want to hear this?' Jessica asked, turning towards Annabel. The young woman nodded gently but didn't seem completely aware of where she was. Her eyes had drifted towards the ceiling and her skin had turned pale. 'Are you okay?' Jessica added.

'Yes.'

Jessica eyed her, wondering what she should do. Before she could say anything further, Toby began to talk. 'I just wanted something like I had with Mum and Dad.'

Jessica looked back from Annabel to Toby. He was cradling himself, rocking gently on the floor. 'What do you mean?'

'I wanted a child of my own. That's why I was done with the old "Toby". I put together this list. They were all children with brothers or sisters. They'd all been in trouble at school and so on.'

'Where did you get the information?'

'I do temping at the LEA office. It's all there.'

'The Local Education Authority?'

'Yeah, it's amazing what companies give you access to when you get a temporary pass. I did some work at the council offices last year and managed to search through the full council tax records for everyone.'

It was such a matter-of-fact statement that Jessica didn't doubt him. His tone was completely uncaring, as if talking to a friend in the pub. She knew the exact details of what he did and how he found that information could be sorted out at a later date. 'What did you do when you had the names?'

'I went and watched them. Some barely left their houses but others would go to the park or whatever. Eventually I came up with a list of lads who I thought might want a new dad . . . like I did.'

'You made a list of kids to take?' Annabel spat out the words, then stood, pacing at the other end of the shed. Toby didn't answer.

'So you decided on Isaac?' Jessica asked.

'I watched him walk home on his own a few times. Sometimes his mum would pick him up but not always.'

'And how did you take him?'

'It was easy enough to know his route because he always walked the same way. Once I figured out where the cameras were, it was just a case of getting him into the car when there was no one else around. It nearly happened a few weeks before but this other car pulled in behind me.'

The casual way he spoke terrified Jessica, as if he had no idea of the enormity of what he had done. 'And you brought him here?' she persisted.

'Yes.'

'Did Benjamin know?'

'He didn't know I was going to go through with it. I'd just talked about theory. I sent him a message that night to say we should meet here.'

Jessica didn't say it out loud but, if that was true, it meant the second phone they found at Benjamin's house belonged to Toby. With the emails Benjamin had sent to Nathan Bairstow about maintaining privacy, it now seemed obvious the unregistered SIM card belonged to him. That meant Benjamin hadn't sent the text message to say the snatch had happened; he had received it.

Trying to take it all in, Jessica attempted to speak calmly. 'Why did you kill him?' Toby began to rock even harder on the spot, tears streaming down his face. Annabel stopped pacing and moved across to stand next to Jessica. Together they looked down at him. Jessica couldn't feel any sympathy for the man but she wondered if his sister did. The only sound in the room was Toby's ever-increasing sobs. He tried to speak but it was impossible to make out what he was saying.

For the first time since he entered the room, Jessica began to feel cold. The adrenaline had been keeping her warm but now she felt nothing but disdain for the man crying at her feet. 'What did you do, Toby?' she asked, harsher the second time.

The man calmed himself slightly, the howls giving way to gentler sobs. 'He wanted to go home.'

'So you killed him?'

Toby nodded but the movement escalated into the whole of his body shaking almost uncontrollably. 'It wasn't violent, I didn't hurt him.'

Jessica could join the dots herself. Toby had snatched the boy, assuming he would want a new father in the way he himself had but when the inevitable rejection had come, he hadn't been able to cope. She already knew Isaac had been suffocated but didn't want to know the specifics. When Toby was at the station, someone else could interview him.

There was an anger burning inside her, a fury for poor Kayla Hutchings, for the child taken from her and a selfish regret for the laws Toby had made her break in the last few days.

'Did you steal Daisy Peters's car?'

Toby didn't reply so Jessica stepped forward and kicked him with as much force as she could manage. His head rocked backwards, bouncing off the door before cannoning forward again. He looked up at Jessica, lip snarled in rage. He placed his palms on the floor as if to pick himself up. 'Don't move,' Jessica said. 'You're going to sit there and answer all my questions without crying. Did you steal Daisy Peters's car?'

Toby seemed more shocked than hurt. The impact had achieved what it was meant to and he had stopped sobbing. Jessica had acted on impulse, not necessarily wanting to hurt him but, at the same, not caring if she did.

'I didn't know that was her name but yes, I took the car,' he admitted.

'How did you know to hook the keys out?'

'I live across the road. It's quite hard not to notice a pretty girl with a nice car.'

'You live across the road?' The fact she had stood just metres from his house was barely believable. Toby shrugged, a broken man.

'Why was Benjamin driving the car, not you?'

'It's not his fault.'

'I didn't ask that.'

'I asked him. He didn't know what I'd done but, after Isaac had . . . gone, after that, I couldn't go through with it. I asked if he'd help me move him.'

'Why bury him in the woods?'

'I don't know. I just knew about them because that's where I left the clothes. I knew it was quiet. I figured he wouldn't be found. I gave Dad a map.'

Jessica was appalled at the cowardice of the man slumped in front of her. Not only had he killed Isaac because of the boy's rejection, he didn't even have the guts to do anything with the body.

She didn't know if she felt sorry for Benjamin. Fourteen years ago, he had done something terrible. In this instance, he was trying to help out a son that wasn't his. The call to Nathan Bairstow must have been made in a panic because Toby had told him that Isaac was dead. There were still bits and pieces someone would have to get out of him but whoever interviewed him at the station, it wouldn't be her.

'Get up,' she commanded. Stung by her aggression, Toby climbed to his feet. He almost seemed to have shrunk in size since first walking into the room. 'We're going to drive you to the station now,' Jessica said. 'You're going to walk inside and you're going to confess to everything you've just told me. You're not going to mention the text message that brought you here and you're not going to mention this meeting. One word and I'll be around Deborah's house with a warrant. Is that clear?'

Toby nodded limply.

Jessica banged on the side of the shed, which was the signal for Rowlands to remove the padlock. She felt sorry for the poor guy, who had been waiting outside for the whole time, first hiding out of sight until Toby was in the room and then waiting by the door just in case.

Jessica reached out and touched Annabel on the shoulder. 'Do you want to say anything?' she asked the woman.

Annabel shook her head and looked away. 'They should bring back hanging,' she said with a tearful snarl.

36

After dropping Toby off at Longsight station and watching him walk in, Jessica drove Annabel back to Piccadilly Station.

'I'm so sorry,' Jessica said as she pulled up. 'I hope you understand why I needed you to be there. He never would have admitted anything without you.'

Annabel barely acknowledged her. 'Don't tell Mum who he really is,' she said, opening the car's door. 'She'd kill herself if she knew Toby walked out on her deliberately, then went on to murder someone else.' She stepped out of the car. 'I don't ever want to see or hear from you again.'

With that, she slammed the door and stalked off. Jessica didn't blame her.

As she was pulling away, Reynolds phoned to say someone had walked into the station and confessed to everything. Apparently he was a family friend of Benjamin Sturgess. Jessica tried to feign surprise but told him she wasn't interested in coming in to take the interview. If it sounded suspicious, she was past caring.

The atmosphere in the station the following day was unlike anything Jessica had ever experienced. No one could quite believe someone had confessed to a case they thought was already shut. Officers were frantically looking into Stephen's story but, rather than scepticism, there was an overwhelming sense of relief that everything was over. Jessica's threat seemed to have worked because there was no mention of Annabel, herself or the text message she had sent. The only missing piece of evidence was Deborah's mobile phone, which was currently sitting at the bottom of the reservoir next to the allotments.

Forty-eight hours later and everything was as close to over as it could be. Toby, or Stephen as everyone else knew him, had fully repeated everything he had told Jessica. She still wasn't speaking to Cole but had heard everyone from the chief superintendent downwards was delighted with the outcome.

Jessica wondered if anyone would put two and two together and realise Toby was Stephen, her biggest worry being Lucy recognising her son, but no contact came. Jessica didn't know if it was because the woman hadn't seen the coverage or, more likely, because a twenty-five-year-old man looked significantly different from an eleven-year-old boy.

On their next day off together, Adam took Jessica for a drive to Prestatyn. It was cold but the day looked gorgeous. The town held special memories for Jessica as it was there, while she had been out with Adam and his grandmother, where she had first begun to think she might be in love with him. The low sun shone across the beach onto the path they were walking along, the sky blazing blue overhead.

'Beautiful, isn't it?' Adam said, pointing out at the horizon and pulling Jessica towards a bench with his other hand. She didn't reply but rested her head on his shoulder as they sat together looking out across the sand. 'Are you going to be okay?' he asked.

'It's not very easy to forget everything I did.'

'How's Dave?'

'He seems all right but things are different between us. Izzy thought we'd had a falling out because we didn't take the piss out of each other for two days. I'm sure it'll be fine but, for now, every time I see him I know he's the person who helped make everything happen.'

'What about Iz?'

Jessica laughed. 'Still talking about being fat. I think she knows something isn't quite right with Dave and me but she's good at keeping things to herself.'

'And Caroline?'

'She's doing okay. She moved into her new flat yesterday and says the divorce is going to go through smoothly. I don't know how she got herself into that mess.'

'You didn't say she had moved out already.'

'That's because I like staying at yours.'

Adam laughed. 'And how are you?'

Jessica reached an arm around Adam's waist and pulled him tightly to her. 'I'm not sure I'll ever forgive myself for what I did to poor Annabel.'

Jessica gulped as Adam squeezed her a little too strongly, lifting her head from his shoulder and pulling him towards her, cradling his head. 'Why did you forgive me for walking out on you?' she asked.

Adam said nothing at first before gently responding, 'Because you asked me to.'

Jessica said nothing but gazed towards the horizon. She didn't really like the cold weather but sometimes the crisp days where the sun offered a wonderful bright light with no heat could be utterly enchanting.

She thought of being young, running through fields and getting muddy, wondering what it would be like if someone had separated her from her parents in the way Toby had been parted from his.

Jessica had felt close to tears every day since the night Annabel stepped out of her car and walked into the train station. A few years ago, she could have counted the number of times she had cried as an adult on one hand. She didn't know whether it was her age but, just recently, she was finding it harder to control her emotions.

Jessica released Adam's head, allowing him to sit up straight. As she started to stand, he motioned to move too but she pushed him down. Ever since he held her in the cafe and let her cry on his shoulder, she knew this moment would come. Jessica dropped to one knee, took Adam's hand and asked if he would marry her.

Afterword

One of the things I get asked a lot is where my ideas come from. Sometimes it might be an article I have read in the news, often not a big story but a small, hidden-away item which sparks my imagination.

I have a fairly set way of working in that I write most of the book in short form, usually a mix of bullet points and key sentences. After that, I write everything out 'properly'. I still go off at tangents and come up with what I think are better ideas along the way but I nearly always have that set framework to work with.

Think of the Children was a little different because I wrote the first chapter before I had anything else.

A few years ago I was driving home from work on a Saturday evening. It was early summer and still light, even though it was around 9p.m. A couple of miles away from where I live there is a roundabout which connects one dual carriageway to another. As you may expect, some drivers zip across at a speed that even Jessica might shy away from. Unfortunately, just after the roundabout is a turn which is easy enough to take if you are accelerating, but not so comfortable if you haven't slowed down in the first place.

As I drove, a vehicle three cars ahead of me sped across the roundabout and tried to take the turn. Instead, it spun 180 degrees and flew off the road, across a lay-by, and down an embankment. The taxi which was overtaking it (yes, really) kept going, as did the two cars directly behind.

I pulled into the lay-by and could feel my heart beating. It's one of those clichés that everything happens in slow motion but that's what it felt like. I knew the bank dropped steeply, before opening out onto a tight row of trees, so anything could have happened if the vehicle had hit those.

As I got out of my car, the first thing I noticed was a woman in a black cocktail dress and short coat walking up the embankment with her heels in one hand and a mobile phone in the other. Miraculously, the car had spun so perfectly that it was resting parallel to the road in between two trees, having hit neither of them.

'Are you okay?' I asked in what was perhaps one of the most obviously stupid questions ever. Her car had just spun off the road at speed and slid down a grass bank. She was hardly going to be jumping around in delight.

Her eyes were blank and she was blinking really quickly, not entirely aware of what had happened. She told me she had been listening to 'Robbie' a bit too loudly and got carried away. I assumed she meant 'Williams', though never clarified it. Perhaps she was really into an audio book being read by Robbie Coltrane? I asked if she was cold (she wasn't), then phoned the police while she waited. After I hung up, she turned to me and said she should call her husband.

I remember the conversation exactly:

Her (sounding shaky and slightly panicked): 'Hi, it's me. I've had an accident in the car . . .'

<Short pause while he replied>

Her: 'No, the car's fine . . .'

I was a little shaken myself, more by her than anything else, so it was only later that I realised her husband had asked about the car's welfare before he had checked hers.

That scene and the way I still see it in slow motion has stayed with me ever since and one morning I woke up with a really clear vision of a car crash which Jessica and Dave witness. The driver's identity was always unknown, although, in my first notes, the person in the boot was alive. Much of the rest of the story moved around in my head and through my notes but that first chapter is almost exactly as I wrote it.

This was an incident where nobody was hurt and no one else stopped. Instead, it was ten minutes of my life while I waited with a bare-footed stranger as the sun started to go down on a summer's evening. But that's where a lot of the purer scenes and ideas I have come from – a few seconds here and a few minutes there: people and life.

As for the book itself, there are a few people who have collectively helped get this into your hands. Firstly, Claire, who helped me with the initial drafts of the first Jessica book, *Locked In*, what seems like an age ago. Without her, that would have been a lot worse and the rest of the series would likely not exist. Secondly, Imogen who gave me a hand with the ebook exclusive *As If By Magic* (yes, that's a cheap plug).

The team at Pan Macmillan have been terrific in welcoming me into their family – and not just as that annoying cousin who turns up on Christmas Day getting on everyone's nerves. Thanks to Natasha, Jodie and Susan, plus Trisha in particular, for their help, guidance and good humour. I've spent years learning the hard way that sarcasm in emails rarely comes across but somehow none of them have taken anything I've written too literally. Well, yet.

Then there are the two women in my life.

My wife, Louise, and I have been together for ten years. We lived in a small flat with noisy neighbours and no money. We scrimped, we saved and we moaned about our jobs and neighbours (obviously) – but it is our relationship which enabled me to write these books. They have very little in common but, simply put, without Louise, there would be no Jessica.

The 'other woman' is my agent, Nicola. She read *Locked In* and approached me at a point where the rest of the publishing industry didn't know whether to poke me with a stick, or ignore me completely. Her help, faith, humour, and ability to ignore my complaining has been invaluable. She probably could have just emailed me though, as opposed to literally poking me with a stick.

Finally, I will thank my mum for forcing me to read as a kid. It's easy to plonk your annoyingly loud hyperactive son in front of a television to shut him up but it isn't so simple to invest time in him. I may have learned to read through Terrance Dicks's *Doctor Who* books and Stan Lee's comics but you still need someone to give you them in the first place – and then plonk you in front of the television and tell you to shut up.

Kerry Wilkinson

Readers' Questions & Answers

All of the questions below have been submitted by readers either on Jessica Daniel's Facebook page (http://facebook.com/JessicaDanielBooks) or through my mailing list (drop me a line at kerryawilkinson@gmail.com). Please be aware there are spoilers for the previous books included below, so read on with caution. I had lots of questions and unfortunately could not use them all.

Do you agree with everything your characters say and do or is it just for fictional purposes?
– Rod Sharp, Bromley
It is mainly for fictional purposes although some of the things that really annoy Jessica are things that get on my nerves too. Sometimes characters say or think things utterly opposite to my views. It's good trying to think about other people's opinions, even if you disagree with them.

What is your favourite part of the series?
– Rebecca Rogers, Liverpool
This is really harsh. It is when Jessica first breaks up so brutally with Adam in the pub in *Vigilante*, telling him to test the swab for her, even though he said it was that or their relationship. In my first notes, Jessica and Adam started going out but they were never meant to be the couple they became. As I wrote

their scenes together – especially the one in Adam's kitchen when he told her about how his parents died – they seemed so right for each other. But then I knew I had to break them up. I was devastated writing that but it really worked for the story and her text message to him gave me my ending too. So much of that grew organically the more I wrote.

Has your style of writing been modelled on anyone else's?
– Martin Nicholson, Ashbourne, Derbyshire
I read a lot of *Doctor Who* books growing up that were only 100–150 pages and skipped along pretty quickly from set piece to set piece without too much in the way of description, etc. That said, I don't really read enough to model myself on anyone. I don't get time! When I was writing the first two books, I was watching the complete *Lost* set and I was definitely thinking about long- and short-term plotting when planning the books. There are odds and ends littered throughout them that I've left myself to come back to if I want to and I always like writing towards cliff-hangers.

When you start writing a book, do you write a synopsis of the plot and characters, or do you just have a sudden brainstorm of an idea and start writing?
– Sheila Easson, East Yorkshire; Robert Van, Southport;
Gill Green, Bridgemere, Cheshire
In the early days, it was literally Post-it notes. I had them everywhere. Now, most of my initial notes are handwritten in a notebook. Then I type the book in short form. It is usually around 5,000 words and very bullet-pointy. Once that is done, I will start writing properly. Things always change because

I have better ideas, or the plot evolves as I write. Because I have that skeleton to work towards, I can usually work pretty quickly.

What gave you the idea to create a character like Jessica Daniel? Her manners, her style, her way of thinking . . . she is quite peculiar but she is really close to reality.

– Barbara Gomez, Madrid, Spain

Jessica is supposed to be 'normal' as I see it. Most people aren't super-confident and they aren't brilliant in social situations – but they have a public face. Jessica is confident to the point of being abrasive at times – but the truth is that she's filled with self-doubt. I try to show both sides because that's what we are all like. It's too easy to create caricatures, who are either unlucky in everything they do, or ultra-confident – good with the opposite sex, perfect at their jobs, and so on. People often create either the ideal person they'd like to be, or they pile all of the worst features they can think of into someone. Jessica has good and bad times, she's liked and disliked. That doesn't mean she always does 'normal' things – because sometimes she ends up in abnormal situations and she doesn't always make the sensible decision.

You managed to create a woman who is not just the typical fantasy image. How did you manage to conjure up such a character?

– Ellen Finlay, Northern Ireland; Kelly Kemp, Birmingham;
Terry Chisman, Hazelwood, Derbyshire

I think a lot of the differences between the sexes are things talked up by media and movies – men are from Mars, women from Venus, etc. But most people care about the same things. What do my friends and family think of me? Does my boyfriend/girlfriend/husband/wife love me as much as I love them? People don't want to be alone – they want a job, a career, or something that stimulates them and pays them reasonably well. They want to feel safe. They want time off. They want enough money to go out and entertain themselves once in a while. And so on. At our core, most of us share the same concerns about life. These things aren't exclusive to either gender but there is a lot of generalisation throughout society that men like X and women like Y.

Do you always know the end of the story when you start a book?
 – *Gail Thompson, Lowestoft, Sussex;*
   Charlotte Hughes, Birmingham

More or less. Sometimes I don't know the exact beats of a final showdown. For instance, with *The Woman in Black*, I knew the 'trick' and I knew I wanted to write something to prove Jessica had learned her lesson from *Locked In*. The swimming-pool scene became an idea as I moved further through writing it. *Think of the Children* was completely different because I had a very vivid picture of the shed in my mind and knew it was going to end there. A lot of it depends on how minutely I have plotted things. Sometimes I have the final chapter before the first chapter.

How do you come up with the different characters in your books? Are they based upon people in your life?
 – *Philip Beard, Staffordshire; Craig Pampling, Essex*

Not really. There will always be bits and pieces which you absorb through everyday life and end up in the stories. People think Garry is based upon me or someone I know because he's a journalist, but he's really not. That said, I used the double-R spelling because someone I know spells it that way. It was entirely so I could have Jessica make that one joke around a third of the way through *Locked In* where she says she doesn't trust anyone who can't spell his own name properly. Of course, now I'm stuck with it being spelled that way!

Who was your favourite or most memorable author growing up and why?
– Annie Glenn, St Helens
As above, I used to collect and read *Doctor Who* paperbacks – so Terrance Dicks. He wrote about eighty to ninety per cent of the books I read as a kid. But I read plenty of *Marvel* comics too, so Stan Lee has to be in there somewhere. The things they have in common are very strong central characters.

Are there ever any points in the writing process when you decide on a certain point but then later go back and change it thinking it would fit better?
– Mark Wright, Ash Vale, Surrey
Sometimes this happens during the plotting but I rarely change major things in the course of the actual writing. Often it will be lots of little changes, rather than anything big.

Is there anything you wish you could have changed about the characters or storylines before they became so popular?
– Daniel Clark, Shipton under Wychwood, Oxford

Not really because I thought about this quite a lot before I started. I tried to leave things as open as possible. So there is very little information about Jessica being at school and in her home town – and not much about earlier boyfriends. I have written hardly anything about what Jessica and Caroline did in south-east Asia. I tried to set up a lot of things I can come back to if and when I want.

Why are your books based in Manchester and why do you choose the specific locations?
– Dawn Meikle, Bebington, Wirral
Manchester is a fun place to play. It's huge and there is so much difference between the affluent areas to the south and west compared to some of the poorest areas in Western Europe. You just need a lot of ways to describe the rain.

Where do you get the ideas for the stories from for your books?
– Dean Field, Hanworth, Middlesex
Often throwaway lines here and there. Much of the premise of *Vigilante* was based on the final line in a newspaper article about people who didn't have national insurance numbers. Someone left a review saying it was unrealistic when it was the only true part!

Do you create Jessica first and then build up the story and the plot around her and her colleagues?
– Maureen Gornall, Garstang, Lancashire
Jessica's story is now plotted a long way ahead, although it wasn't at first. I could tell you more or less where she will be

in book eight. The individual plots of the books fit around that – but in a natural way. My best idea for a novel is still sitting on my pad because it doesn't yet suit the direction Jessica's life is going in. One day . . .

Did you wear trainers to your wedding?
– Suzanne Ryan, Frome, Somerset
A very quick bit of explanation here. I'm from Frome and, although I don't know Suzanne, we must know people in common. Anyway, yes, I did wear trainers to my wedding and the line where Jessica scolds Hugo for doing just that in *The Woman in Black* – 'What kind of idiot wears trainers to a wedding?' – is indeed a massive in-joke at my own expense.

COMING SOON

PLAYING WITH FIRE

Jessica Daniel Book 5

Seven years ago Martin Chadwick set fire to a building, not knowing a teenager was sleeping inside. With the media hyping the man's impending release from prison and the victim's father hinting at revenge, Detective Sergeant Jessica Daniel is given the task of keeping an eye on the former prisoner.

Graffitied threats are just the start of what seems to be an escalating campaign of intimidation as the apparently remorseful man is left fearing for his life. At first the culprit seems obvious – but with Martin's son connected to the death of a young girl, and a private investigator making a nuisance of himself, Jessica is caught squarely in the middle. Meanwhile, someone in her midst seems intent on burning everything to the ground . . .

This is Book 5 in the Jessica Daniel series, following on from *Locked In*, *Vigilante*, *The Woman in Black* and *Think of the Children*.

An extract follows here . . .

ISBN 978-1-4472-2341-2

Extract from Playing with Fire

Detective Sergeant Jessica Daniel glanced up from her plate to face the man sitting opposite. She put the metal fork on the table, loudly enough to ensure he knew she wanted his attention.

'So, Garry,' Jessica began. 'Who the hell is Sebastian Lowe?'

She watched Garry Ashford squirm. Despite the fact she had known the journalist for a few years, she knew he was still that little bit afraid of her.

Garry looked up from his breakfast, where a congealed fried egg yolk had blended into the leftover baked-bean juice. All that was left of his breakfast was a final piece of black pudding, which he was chewing on while swirling his hand in the air, as if pointing out to Jessica that he would answer when he had finished. She had purposely picked her moment to ask the question, so that he was at his most uncomfortable. Jessica fixed Garry with a steady stare, telling him with her eyes that she was waiting for the answer.

The journalist swallowed and started to speak before spluttering and gulping the final mouthful of tea from his mug.

'Sorry,' he coughed. 'I was just finishing off.' He smiled apologetically but Jessica didn't relax her glare. 'Sebastian's newish,' he went on. 'He's been working for me for around six months. I hired him but he's just been bumped up to senior news reporter.'

'When did you start hiring people?' Jessica replied, failing to hide her surprise.

'Since I was promoted to news editor.'

Jessica weighed up his response, not overly satisfied with it. 'What's he like? A bit of a troublemaker?'

Garry shook his head. 'Sebastian? No, he's a bit like I was. He gets by story to story, although he seems to come up with better stuff than I did.'

Jessica looked sideways at the man, flicking her long dark-blonde hair away from her face and wishing she had tied it back. When she had invited Garry for breakfast, she hadn't known if she wanted to play on the fact he was scared of her, or that she was pretty sure he still fancied her – despite apparently having a girlfriend. Torn between the two, she opted for a bit of both and left her hair down.

As they waited for their food to arrive in the cafe around the corner from his newspaper's office, Jessica hadn't said too much. She allowed the tension to build, watching him devour a full English and deciding she would definitely be going down the 'scare' route. She quickly finished her sausage sandwich, wondering if the large breakfast was a usual thing for him, or if he had ordered it because she was paying.

'Does he have better dress sense than you?' Jessica asked.

Garry peered down at his brown corduroy trousers, before realising what he was doing. In fairness, Jessica had to admit he was looking as smart as she had ever seen him. His previously long scruffy hair had been cut short and was tidily shaped, with the goatee on his chin looking as if it was there by design, as opposed to because he hadn't bothered to shave. His cord trousers were perhaps a little outdated but, for as long as she had known him, that seemed to be his style.

'Why do you want to know about Seb?' Garry asked, not taking the bait.

Jessica reached into the bag under her seat and scooped out a copy of the previous day's *Manchester Morning Herald*. She pushed a ketchup bottle to one side and unfolded the paper before turning it around so Garry could see the front page, pointing at Sebastian's byline on the lead story.

'Did you have anything to do with this?' she asked.

The headline read 'FLAMING HELL' with 'Killer Out This Month' underneath.

Garry must have known what was coming but he still fidgeted awkwardly. 'I didn't write the headline but I knew about Seb's story.'

Jessica pushed the paper away. 'Didn't anyone think about the implications? What if this guy gets hurt when they let him out of prison?'

The journalist sank into his seat and Jessica began to feel a little sorry for him. 'That's exactly what I said,' Garry insisted. 'I told my editor that. I told Seb that. I said we should be careful if we were going to run it.'

From her earlier dealings with Garry, Jessica knew he had a pretty good grasp of what was right and wrong. Or, more specifically, what she considered to be right or wrong. She wasn't as prejudiced against the media as some at the station but, as with all professions, she knew there were good guys and bad guys. Garry was one of the better ones. He had certainly helped her in the past, although she was loath to admit it – especially to him.

'I've been assigned to keep an eye on Martin when he comes out of prison,' Jessica said. 'It's not even our job but after this,' she pointed to the paper again, 'we don't have much choice.'

Garry looked a little apologetic, his eyes slightly wider than before. 'You have to admit it's a good story.'

Jessica knew it was and had made that exact point in the staff briefing the previous day. It was probably that which prompted Detective Chief Inspector Jack Cole to give her the job of escorting Martin Chadwick when he left prison in a few days' time. Unknown to Garry – she hoped – everything had been moved forward by a day in an attempt to avoid any further publicity.

'Where did Sebastian get the story from?' Jessica asked, fully aware Garry would never give her the answer. She was curious because the day of a prisoner's release wasn't the type of information that should have been freely available. All they had managed to come up with in the briefing was that the second subject of the article – who would have been told by the prison service that Martin was due to be released – had taken it to the media.

Garry shook his head. 'You know I won't tell you that.'

'Was it Anthony Thompson?' Jessica asked, hoping Garry's body language would give him away. As he had grown older, the man had clearly learned his lessons from dealing with her. He sat impassively, refusing to answer. 'Don't get me wrong,' Jessica added. 'I know Anthony might have every reason to want to hurt Martin – but flagging it up for the world to see isn't going to do anyone any good.'

Garry nodded slowly and Jessica could see he agreed with her, although the congealed egg yolk on his chin did detract slightly from the serious conversation she was trying to cultivate. She leant across the table and wiped the yellow liquid from Garry's face as he writhed away from her. 'You're not my mum,' he said with a smile.

Jessica grinned back, the atmosphere lost. 'Believe it or not, I didn't invite you to breakfast to simply bollock you. Whoever this Sebastian is should do his homework. There are mistakes in the piece and, although it's not my job to clean up after you, my boss and I thought it would be much better if we gave you some proper facts for next time.'

'On the record?'

Jessica shook her head. 'You give me your source and I'll give you something on the record.' Garry smiled back but didn't answer.

'Fine,' she said. 'Off the record it is. Have you got a pen?'

The journalist stacked his empty plate on top of Jessica's and moved them into the middle of the table, before fumbling in a shoulder bag hanging over the back of his chair and taking out a notepad and pen.

When it was clear he was ready, Jessica began. 'You got most of it right. Martin Chadwick is due out of prison but you know I can't confirm exactly when that's going to happen. Up until seven years ago, he was a bit of a pest with sporadic criminal offences, none of which was very serious. Then he set fire to a pub he thought was empty. Unfortunately, a twenty-one-year-old man named Alfie Thompson was sleeping inside.'

Garry was making notes, although Jessica hadn't yet told him anything he wouldn't already know. She paused to let him catch up, continuing when his pen scratched to a halt. 'Martin was so drunk, he was picked up sleeping on a bench less than a hundred yards away from the pub. The lighter and empty bottle of vodka he used to start the fire were still in his possession. He didn't exactly confess, largely because he said he couldn't remember doing it. With the CCTV footage and forensic evidence, he pleaded guilty to manslaughter and received his prison sentence.'

The journalist looked up from his pad. 'We know this . . .'

Jessica interrupted. 'What you don't know is that Martin had an eleven-year-old son who was taken into care when his father went into prison. He is now eighteen and, apparently, he's been in regular contact with his dad. I don't know much about his mother but the son is called Ryan. Although I've not met him yet, strictly unofficially we would rather you be careful of mentioning him. He doesn't have anything to do with this and I am only telling you because I know you will find it out at some point anyway.'

She let her words hang. Garry hadn't written down any of the last pieces of information. 'All I can do is ask,' he said.

Jessica nodded. 'Obviously you know about Anthony

Thompson. It was his son killed in the fire. I'm assuming he was your source about Martin's release because he was informed. We don't know that much about Anthony, except for what you printed.'

She picked the paper back up and began to read. '"There's no bringing back my Alfie but everyone has to pay for what they've done".'

She looked up to see Garry wince. 'I know it's ambiguous,' he said.

'Deliberately so?' Jessica asked. She fell silent as a waitress came close to their table and picked up the plates.

'Can I get you anything else?' she asked sweetly, although the twang of her local accent made it sound as if she was offering them a fight. The woman was somewhere in her early twenties, with bleached hair tied neatly in a bun on top of her head. Jessica watched Garry eye the waitress up and down, before stopping himself when he realised she was observing him.

Jessica giggled slightly, shaking her head. 'No thanks, just the bill.'

When the woman had moved away, she raised her eyebrows. 'Are you really a ladies' man now?'

Garry offered an apologetic 'No' but Jessica already knew he was far from the type. He might have wandering eyes, as did most men she knew, but the journalist lacked the social grace to be discreet.

Jessica lowered her voice. 'From what Anthony says, I don't know if he's referring to the jail sentence as Martin "paying" for what he's done, or if there's a veiled threat there.'

Garry spoke slowly and cautiously. 'I don't know. Sebastian did the interview. I know you can read it both ways. I said we should take it out.'

Jessica returned the paper to her bag. 'I don't think any of us want something stupid happening when Martin comes out. Whatever you think of the guy, or the punishment, he's done his time.'

Garry put down his pen and nervously wiped his chin with a napkin from the table.

'How are things anyway?' Jessica asked in a lighter tone.

He stopped dabbing his face and smiled. 'Are you actually being nice to me?'

Jessica grinned. 'Hey, I left my hair down for this impromptu bollocking. I'm not all bad.'

Garry shrugged. 'I'm doing okay. I've been promoted and I've moved in with my girlfriend.'

'Is she the blind one?'

The journalist snorted gently and shook his head. 'I thought you were being nice?'

'This is me being nice,' Jessica replied with a wink.

'What about you?' Garry asked. 'I heard you were loved-up, engaged and all that?'

Jessica tried not to fidget but couldn't stop herself. Instead of answering his question, she shunted her chair backwards and picked up her jacket, before crouching to retrieve her bag. 'I've gotta go,' she said.

Garry laughed. 'Thanks for the breakfast.'

'Judging by the amount you left on your chin and shirt, it certainly looked like you enjoyed it.' He glanced down at his clean shirt before looking back up at a smiling Jessica. 'Gotcha,' she said.

The journalist put his coat on while Jessica paid at the counter. As she turned, he looped his bag over his shoulder and stretched out his hand for her to shake. 'It was good seeing you again, Jess,' he said.

Jessica rolled her eyes but shook his hand anyway. 'Can you deliver a message for me?'

'What?'

'Tell this "Sebastian" that I will kick his arse if anything happens to Martin.'

extracts reading groups
competitions books new
discounts extracts extracts
competitions discounts
books new
extracts
events books events
extracts reading groups
new titles reading groups
interviews extracts
events extracts
discounts events
new books events interviews new books extracts
events new interviews new books extracts
discounts extracts discounts
www.panmacmillan.com
extracts events reading groups
competitions books extracts new books